Mick Herron is an award-winning novelist and author of the Jackson Lamb series. His work has won the CWA Gold Dagger for Best Crime Novel, the CWA Steel Dagger for Best Thriller and the Ellery Queen Readers Award, and has been nominated for the Macavity, Barry, Shamus and Theakstons Novel of the Year Awards.

Mick Herron was born in Newcastle upon Tyne, and now lives in Oxford.

Praise for Mick Herron

'The new king of the spy thriller'
Mail on Sunday

'Herron proves himself to be a master of wit, satire and surprise'
Daily Telegraph

'Herron is spy fiction's great humourist, mixing absurd situations with sparklingly funny dialogue and elegant, witty prose'
The Times

'The new spy master'
Evening Standard

Also by Mick Herron

Jackson Lamb thrillers

Slow Horses
Dead Lions
Real Tigers
Spook Street
London Rules
Joe Country

Zoë Boehm thrillers

Down Cemetery Road
The Last Voice You Hear
Why We Die
Smoke And Whispers

Nobody Walks
This Is What Happened
The Drop

RECONSTRUCTION

MICK
HERRON

JOHN MURRAY

First published in Great Britain in 2008 by Constable,
an imprint of Constable & Robinson Ltd

This paperback edition published in 2019 by John Murray (Publishers)
An Hachette UK company

1

A CIP catalogue record for this title is available from the British Library

Paperback ISBN 978-1-47364-708-4
eBook ISBN 978-1-47364-709-1

Typeset in Bembo 11/13.75 pt by
Palimpsest Book Production Limited, Falkirk, Stirlingshire

Printed and bound in Great Britain by Clays Ltd, Elcograf S.p.A.

John Murray policy is to use papers that are natural,
renewable and recyclable products and made from wood grown in
sustainable forests. The logging and manufacturing processes are expected to
conform to the environmental regulations of the country of origin.

John Murray (Publishers)
Carmelite House
50 Victoria Embankment
London EC4Y 0DZ

www.johnmurray.co.uk

For Anne, David, Paul, Peter and Martin
and for Mick, Tig, Emily, Tonya and Sarah
and for Sarah, Matthew, David, Thomas and Matthew
and for Pat, Cedric, Horace and Lewis

AUTHOR'S NOTE

South Oxford Nursery School, where key scenes of this novel take place, occupies a similar space to that filled by Grandpont Nursery School in the real world, but is an imaginary institution, as are its staff and pupils.

Part One

A.M.

I

IN CARTOONS, WHEN THE alarm rings, the cat, mouse, dog, what-ever, hauls a mallet from under the pillow and BAM! – cogs, levers and coils go everywhere; the clock face droops from its casing like a cuckoo on a spring . . . Morning is broken. In the real world, you simply reach a slow hand out and depress the button so the ringing stops. And for the moment it takes this to happen, you're held between two worlds: the dream life in which mallets are hidden under pillows by pyjama-clad animals, and the default waking mode in which you blink twice, remember who you are, and feel detail seep back into you the way light infiltrates the room – you're Louise Kennedy, you're thirty-two years old, and today is either the first day of the rest of your life or the last day of your old one, depending on how things work out. It's Tuesday, April 3rd. The weather's set for fair. Sunlight has already reached the bedspread, drawing upon it a range of shadow moun-tains whose outcrops and valleys exactly match the folds and ridges of the curtaintops. It's time to get up. It's time to get up.

Louise muffles a sigh, and pulls herself out of bed.

6:45.

This is where it begins.

And this, too, is where it begins; an hour earlier, and some five miles from Louise's bed: in a grey lay-by, shielded from the A40 by a row of gasping trees.

3

This stretch of the road, this time of the morning, most traffic is headed the other way; the first leg of the pilgrimage into London, hauling workers on to the motorway and firing them through the chalk cutting on the county border, where red kites ride the thermals overhead; then on past the redaubed stretch of graffiti (*Why do I still do this every day?*) to the stilted Westway and the congestion-charged canyons beyond. But George Trebor's on the homeward leg of the Lille–Birmingham run, and this lay-by is where he parked overnight; partly because the legislation won't let him ply his sixteen-wheeled trade twelve hours at a stretch; partly because there's a loo here; but mostly because the back of his cab's a fine and private place, unlike a two-up, two-down containing three teenage boys and a harassed wife. Which is maybe why he's overslept, and is still in the cab sorting out shaving gear when a car pulls off the road, passes his rig, and parks outside the brick toilet. There's another truck behind George's but nothing in front, so he has a clear view of the car, which is a dark blue BMW with two occupants, neither of whom emerges. They're both male. No clue as to what they're doing: checking a map, maybe. Drawing straws to see who takes the first leak.

That's when he sees the boy coming out of the toilet.

Most days, Louise played the radio softly during breakfast; the *Today* programme, or – if reality pressed too heavily on her – Radio 2. This morning, though, she opted for silence, or what passed for it in this stretch of South Oxford, where the early morning hum from the railside works plugged any gaps left by the Abingdon Road traffic. Her kitchen window looked out on a meadow – the Ham – beyond which lay the railway line, where Railtrack operated a pick-and-mix gravel concession, or that's what it looked like. Trucks and what the Darlings called digger lorries shunted to and fro around it from the early hours, their diesel-powered belching blunted by an eight-foot baffle without which – presumably – everything would have been much noisier. It was part of the background hum, and throbbed beneath the morning like the area's heartbeat. Louise was barely conscious of it; was utterly irony-free in choosing radio silence.

Besides, she wasn't at liberty to make noise these days.

The bedroom above the kitchen – there were two bedrooms in this almost comically narrow house, whose front door opened directly on to the living room – had, until lately, been the *other* bedroom; the one that wasn't Louise's. And now it had become her mother's bedroom instead; that *M* attaching to *other* to produce a wholly opposite shade, the way dawn changes to dusk, one letter at a time – down, mown, moon, moot, most, must, musk . . .

Above her head her mother slept, while Louise prepared breakfast in silence.

The boy saw the BMW and came to a halt, middle of the lay-by. George Trebor, watching for no special reason – except that's what you did, watch, when something was happening – had a plain view of this; enough to realise that already, even before he was fully aware of paying witness, his version had come askew from reality. Because this wasn't a boy, precisely. More like twenty – bum-fluffed rather than bearded, but beyond the point at which the mouth seems too big for the head; the nose too small for the face. He was dark-skinned, and looked, George thought, exhausted – like the next big wind would blow him away. He wore jeans and a dark green bomber jacket, and a rucksack hung from his left shoulder; he grasped its strap with his left hand, while his right was thrust into his pocket. No: it hung from his right shoulder, and all those details were reversed. George had trouble with left/right when applying them to someone facing him. Anyway, middle of the lay-by, halfway to the car, the young man stopped and dropped his head to one side, as if assessing the occupants. Working the rent, was George's appraisal. He himself had worked the roads long enough to be unshocked by the probability. Working the rent: but Jesus, kid, you really don't want to be getting into a car with two men. Any professional sex situation involving two on one: you'll be torn apart.

Maybe that's what the boy was thinking. Either way, he moved no closer to the car. Looked, in fact, kind of scared.

George wasn't even pretending he wasn't watching now, but it wasn't like anybody knew. Height of the cab, he might have been sitting in the royal box. The boy wasn't looking his way anyway; his eyes were fixed on the car, and his lips moving – saying what, George couldn't tell: might have been a price-tag; might have been a name.

The car door opened, and one of the men stepped out.

Elsewhere, alarm clocks weren't necessary.

Eliot Pedlar lay on his back, eyes open, and listened to family life unfolding along the corridor – his wife's happy murmur; his children's giggling – the way it did every morning. The children were awake by six – hell, six was a *good* day – and two seconds after their first stirring, Christine was out of bed and through the door; his last glimpse of her, the flash of a dimly remembered bottom under a solely functional nightie.

'The wheels on the bus—'
'go round and round round and—'
'round round and rou—'
'nd the wheels on the bus go—'
Round and round. Sometimes he couldn't tell where his sons' voices broke off; where his wife's began. As if, together, they formed a perfect circle, outside of which he was always hovering; going round and round, without ever breaking in.

The twins were nearly four; his wife almost exactly three

decades older. And he couldn't tell them apart? That wasn't cute so much as kind of disturbing.

It was 6:50. He had time for another ten minutes' sleep, but his chances of achieving it were zero.

Waking thoughts were supposed to be creative thoughts – the hinterland of dreams was where consciousness dipped into the myth kitty, and pulled out useful images. That was the theory, but actually he'd woken up drenched in the Memory again – the Memory being less of a series of mental pictures tied to emotions than an actual physical state he'd been imprisoned in for almost a week . . . His right hand reached for his cock. His eyes remained fixed on the ceiling. Chris bustled into the room. 'Are you still okay to do the boys this morning?'

Eliot eased both hands from under the duvet.

'Of course,' he said.

'You hadn't forgotten?'

'No,' he said. 'Of course not.'

Forgetting wasn't his problem, recently. Remembering was what was driving him crazy.

And then there was Judy . . .

There was a clock radio on Judy's bedside table, which was paid for. When she opened her eyes, it read 6:55. Waking – coming round to what the clock said – was the usual brutal infraction: a list to be ticked off – what the world owed Judy; what Judy owed the world. The equation always weighed heavy on her side of the maths. The world should know this by now, but feigned ignorance.

Judith Ainsworth turned the radio off, and dragged herself out of bed. The light creeping through the curtains pointed out her surroundings' imperfections, but then it always did.

I don't want to be a burden.

You're not a burden, Mum. I like having you here.

7

Don't let me stop you doing what you want to do.

You don't. Honest.

Have you thought about getting some nice ornaments for that mantelpiece? It's a bit bare.

(Louise lived in fear of returning home to find an unacceptable ceramic the new centrepiece of her living room: a thank-you gift it would be impossible to overthrow.)

I won't be with you longer than I have to be.

And how did Louise respond to that? Which meant what, anyway? That death was so imminent there was little point in Louise increasing the milk order? Or that her mother, Susan, would be heading home soon; the heart attack filed away under Unpleasantnesses We Don't Talk About, Thank You Very Much?

Louise buttered toast, and wondered whether not putting the radio on was because she didn't want to hear it, or because she didn't want to disturb her mother (*I don't mind you listening to the radio in the morning, dear. It doesn't wake me*). You were always ten years old when you were watching TV with your parents and a sex scene erupted. And you were always prone to the most painful guilts when your mother told you what she didn't mind: *Go on and rip my heart out, Louise. Trample it into the carpet. I don't mind. It's been attacked once already.*

She gave up on her toast. There were more important aspects to breakfast. Fishing the back door key from its hook, she let herself into the yard – twelve square feet of cracked, uneven paving, hemmed by a low wall bordering the Ham – and lit a cigarette; the first of her daily pair. Giving up had never been a problem for Louise; it was only the first and last of the day she had trouble forgoing. Those were the two she'd hung on to when she'd discarded the habit, along with her previous job, a lover, her London flat, cocaine bingeing, and the sense she'd somehow – it didn't have a name, this feeling; was simply a cloud that descended in the early hours – that she'd somehow fucked up everything, even if from the outside it had looked like she was fast-tracked to the glittering prizes. Not smoking between the bracketing pair was made easier by the fact that she rarely smoked in public. Secrecy (she preferred to consider it discretion) was something she'd had to learn anyway. Her lover, for instance, had been her married boss.

Who today, of all days, was likely to weigh heavy on her mind.

Resting a palm on the wall, Louise looked out across the meadow. Mist curled round the trees at its farthest edge, but it would be fine later – this was a simple rule: days you felt low were likely to shine, just to make you feel worse. Besides, this had been the pattern lately; mist giving way to bright warm weather.

She smoked her cigarette to its filter, and dabbed it out on a mossed-over patch of brick. One tiny coal survived its bludgeoning, until a gust of wind whipped it out of existence.

It was 7:14.

Memory plays tricks, everyone knows that: it shuffles the deck, charms the snake, hoists the rope into nowhere. It convinces you you know just where you were, what you were doing, then *whap*, the detail betrays you. Reconstruction is never simple. Two days from now, a grainy, after-the-event newspaper photo will show Jaime Segura wearing the jacket he's wearing now, and it's not a dark green bomber at all: it's brown, it's faux leather; it has long sleeves turned up at the cuffs, and drops to mid-thigh. George Trebor will look at that picture and wonder how much else of what he remembers actually happened, and how much was simply processed by a mind taught, like everyone else's, to join the dots. Nobody studies events every second that passes. Like speed cameras, we take one picture, then another; and allow the data gathered by experience to fill the gaps between.

And, like speed cameras, sometimes there's no film in the machine.

What George remembered was recorded later in newspapers and police reports, often in words quite similar to those he'd used in his various statements.

And what he saw was something like this.

The man who stepped out of the car's passenger door was a bulky character in a knee-length grey overcoat, with a haircut that made George Trebor think *Services* – short on top; razored to stubble at the back. He moved like a soldier, unbuttoning the overcoat as he did so. The boy's grip on his rucksack tightened at the man's approach. He spoke again – George had no chance of making out the words. If Overcoat Man replied, his answer was similarly lost . . . With every minute, the day took on weight: light and sound gathering in a kaleidoscope of detail. Traffic rumbled yards away: an Oxford-bound coach; a white van with *Budgie-hire* stencilled on its panels. A magpie clattered on to the toilet roof. The man, his back to George, tilted his head to one side, as if asking a question. And as the boy shrugged an answer – *dunno* – the rucksack's strap slipped down into his hand, from which he swung it in a wide loop to catch the man on the side of the head.

George had forgotten about shaving; forgotten about the miles that lay ahead – miles, anyway, that would have to be put on hold now. He didn't know that yet, but the next minute made it a certainty.

The man stumbled but didn't quite fall; he recovered before hitting the ground, propelling himself onward with one hand on the tarmac. Behind him the car door opened, and the second man emerged. Even without seeing his face, George could tell Man Two was not happy with this. The boy, meanwhile, had left the lay-by; had almost reached the point where the curve of the road would hide him from view. Another car belted past, hitting its horn as it did so, and the last George Trebor saw of the boy, he'd lost his balance and was hurling himself on to the verge. Man One wasn't far behind, coat flapping madly, but slipped on the dew-slick verge before reaching him. What happened next was horrible. Instead of falling inwards the way the boy had done, he fell into the road where the next car hit him full on; sort of sucked him under the front wheel, thought George, who'd never seen anything like this before. The noise, too, was outside his experience. Imagine a piglet being forced down a waste-disposal unit – a squeal, a slam, and a point at which organic sound stops and mechanical screeching takes over. Something flew high and wide into the air; part of the car or part of its victim, George couldn't tell. It fell to earth and vanished.

Man Two came to a halt at the lay-by's exit and flinched at the impact, as if experiencing it himself in a minor way. George, too, stopped breathing. George, in fact, closed his eyes at this point.

When he opened them again, he was looking at aftermath. The car that had hit the man had somehow stopped sideways, blocking both lanes this side of the dividing tract, its driver's door hanging open. Someone was being sick beside it. Man Two was crouched over the broken man, shouting into a phone. The body was largely hidden from George's view. Was it a body yet? As for the boy . . . George opened the cabin door, and climbed down into the lay-by. Behind the straggly hedgerow, a queue of cars was building up; would be a mile long before any kind of traffic control was established. He went to join Man Two, to see if he could help.

When he looked towards Oxford, the direction the boy had been heading, all George Trebor could see was the empty road.

News broadcasts aside, George never saw him again.

Judy had to be quiet getting up. She'd not been here a week before having that pointed out – not as a you-make-too-much-noise-in-the-mornings edict, but as part of a monologue about the selfishness of people who make too much noise in the mornings; a general if-the-cap-fits warning, which, taken the right way, could become an invitation to join a two-woman chorus decrying the behaviour of others. Judy understood such language. She spoke it herself. In a perverse way, it was something of a pleasure to know she'd found herself sharing a roof with a fellow expert.

It was sometimes necessary to form alliances, though it would be a mistake to take this as a sign of weakness.

In the bathroom she took care of the usual, then had a quick wash standing at the sink. A bath would have been nice, but the hot water system made a noise like anti-aircraft cover. This was a compromise, it was true – and compromises laid end to end were indistinguishable from surrender – but such things happened in enemy territory; you took time to check out the terrain, then drew a line in the sand you could defend. She rehearsed this silent theory to the face in the mirror, and the face in the mirror relayed it back.

(This face, for the record, was a round face; its eyes brown, its mouth a straight line. Judy was fifty-three. No; Judy was fifty-four. Her last birthday had snuck in under the wire; unnoticed, uncelebrated. And Judy smoked, and this was written in the lines round her eyes; the million squints that prove that songs come true: smoke gets in your eyes. Her hair looked painted on. Literally: her hair looked like it belonged on an Action Man doll; moulded close to her skull like a punishment, a scold's bridle. There was something else, too, in those brown eyes, in that linear mouth, which spoke not only of disappointment, but of a constant mission to avenge that disappointment. This would be why she held her head at an upward tilt in company: the better to spot an opportunity for scoring points. Anything taken from somebody else was added to what was hers, even if what was taken was only a moment's peace. She was owed a lot, and the debt was everyone's.)

Washed, dressed, she made her way downstairs.

'Boys—'

'Dad.'

'Daddy.'

'Boys, could you quieten down a bit? Daddy's trying to concentrate.'

7:36.

Eliot was in the car; the boys in their seats behind him. Strapping twins into car seats was an activity that, on a bad day, encompassed emotions traditionally associated with the classical definition of tragedy. On a good day, it wasn't much more complicated than juggling traffic bollards. Today was a good day. The boys went through phases when they seemed to achieve communication the far side of speech, and were too intent on developing this to create problems on a mundane level. 'Twins,' people said knowingly when Eliot or Chris mentioned such things – twins being one of those subjects on which everyone's an expert. Everyone bar Eliot, who often resisted the temptation to mention the Midwich Cuckoos when discussing the boys.

Today they were wrapped in a strange dialogue deeply meaningful to both, but incomprehensible to humans. It didn't require Eliot's involvement, but was a little noisy when he was trying to drive.

Usually, this was part of Chris's routine. Like almost everything involving the boys, she had full charge of it, and took his offers of help as an attempted putsch. Which caused conflict, but mostly only in Eliot's mind. He still keenly remembered the Chris he'd been married to until about four years ago; the Chris who reckoned that those peasant women who gave birth in the fields then carried on working had it right. She was a legal secretary: hardly field work, but the hours were long. But discovering that she was carrying twins had changed her attitude, as if something more fundamental than a simple mathematical substitution – two for one – had taken place, and overnight had gone from a breezy acceptance of impending change to a siege mentality; one in which all the world's workings had to be weighed and measured for their effect on this primary unit: Gordon + Timmy + Christine. Eliot being optional.

A burst of giggling from the back seat underlined another joke from which he'd been excluded.

This morning, Chris was paying a visit to her old office. Which would have been a more welcome development if it had been her idea, instead of something Eliot had badgered her into over what was probably weeks rather than the months it felt like. Returning to work had always been the plan, he'd reminded her, as if the Plan had been chiselled into the same rock the Ten Commandments were hewn from, and equally impervious to circumstance. Which, in this context, included the fact that it would be pleasant to have a second income again, given the doubling of their expenditure these past few years. But sometimes, when trying to introduce such subjects in a non-contentious way, he'd had the feeling he was attempting conversation with somebody who wasn't there any more; somebody who, tidally struck by the advent of children, had been, quite simply, washed away . . .

'Dad—'

'Daddy—'

'—Can it wait, boys?'

'We're building a *castle*.'

'A real one.'

'. . . That's nice.'

Which it was. If his sons were building a castle, it might as well be a real one. That way, whatever happened later in life, they'd always be able to look back and say *Well, at least we built a castle.*

But they'd returned to their republic of two. He tried to concentrate on driving; feeling, as he did so, the Memory hug him tighter, as if something he wore was shrinking round his shoulders – there was an ache involved in this; more pressure than you could define as comfortable. But it was good, too, to be held so close, and his heart beat faster as he dropped a gear.

Louise closed the door behind her as gently as she could; this, too, causing her guilt – that the *chunk* of the latch might wake her mother. But with the noise came a sense of release; she was out in the world again. Now that home territory had become shared, it was somewhere to escape from rather than a refuge from everywhere else. Walking up the road, she had the sense of her own footsteps receding – becoming a departing *tip-tap* – as if they were a measure of the distance between herself and her mother; bringing, of course, more guilt.

It wasn't a long journey. A matter of minutes. There wasn't much life on the street at this time; she was, naturally, ahead of the mothers delivering children to school; ditto those with nine-to-five jobs up in town, but behind milkmen and commuters, and never quite in synch with the dog walkers, who enjoyed a society all their own on the Ham. As a matter of course, though, she'd nod good morning to anyone whose path she crossed, sometimes wondering whether they recognised her, or knew where she was headed. Neighbourhoods held few secrets, she suspected. Which was not an especially welcome thought, given last week's Incident – an episode she was hoping to write off as an aberration, without seriously believing it would be without consequence.

At the time, she'd thought it involved just the pair of them, but of how much could you truly say that? Every connection plugged you into someone else's network. A neighbourhood was a web, with any thread plucked *here* reverberating *there*. Even in the big city, secrecy wasn't straightforward. Louise remembered visiting a mobile phone outlet more than a year ago, looking to upgrade her deal now her calls had gone through the roof. 'Has there been a change in your life lately?' the boy on the counter asked, leafing through her bills and seeing the same number again and again . . . She'd found herself blushing; had blushed since at the memory. What irked was the realisation that great chunks of private life – once the province of confidantes and therapists – were now open to teenagers with McJobs. Secrecy was a professional skill these days; amateurs were crying out to be discovered. Yup: the Incident would have consequences. The best she could hope for was, they wouldn't threaten her new career.

Speaking of which, she turned left at the corner, and the nursery school gates came into view.

By now, George Trebor's morning had caught up with Louise's – long spells of nothing happening had swallowed the time she'd taken to breakfast, smoke, and walk up the road. Not that entirely nothing had happened, of course – an ambulance had arrived, swiftly followed by two police cars, followed in turn by a third; traffic, meanwhile, was backing up as far as the motorway turn-off and probably beyond – but his participation had not been called upon. He couldn't leave, though. Leaving the scene of an accident might cost him his licence: they could get you that way. And Man Two, he was pretty sure, had noted his plate.

He'd tried talking to Man Two, once the ambulance arrived.

'Your friend – is he going to be okay?'

'Do I look like a doctor?'

'. . . He was still alive, though? I could see you were . . .'

George didn't want to say *kissing* him. But introducing the phrase *artificial resuscitation* into this sentence was suddenly beyond him.

Man Two said, 'Go and wait in your truck. They'll want to talk to you.'

Something about the look on his face drove George back to his lorry, where he leaned against the door, heartily wishing he'd not stopped to shave this morning. He watched the policemen approach Man Two; saw Man Two show them ID. Saw the glance they shared before one backed off and started talking into a radio.

And George understood that whatever he'd witnessed this morning, it was nothing to do with a rent boy running out of luck.

The kitchen didn't enjoy much light even on the sunny side of the year, so the overhead strip was needed, though its effect was like too much caffeine: if you stood long enough in the glow cast by tubular lighting, your blood would start to fizz. Children who grew in the shadow of pylons turned out to have leukaemia. But the alternative was to muddle in the half-light, so Judy pressed the switch, and there it was: the kitchen, drenched in unforgiving electricity. Smaller than she deserved. Small should equate with neat: rooms could be compact, tidy. But this small aspired to grubby. That was what Judy thought, looking at the kitchen. That its size was a badge of failure, and failure was streaked and grimy, and anyway she was a lodger, and strict prohibitions on certain cupboards and any shelf of the fridge bar the third applied. So there wasn't even pride of possession attached to the badge of failure. If these circumstances were anyone else's, they'd be funny.

The view from the window was equally cramped. It gave straight on to pavement, on the other side of which sat a blank wall made of the same brick from which the house and all its neighbours were built. This served as a rampart shielding these houses from the road, which was only partly residential – it was mostly car park and ice rink; plus a PO collection point, the College of Further Education, a garage, and a deadly night-club. This row of housing was the northward edge of a modern estate, the choicest properties of which enjoyed small, mossy patios facing the river and the meadow beyond. Which wasn't quite a rural idyll – a hotbed of dogging, apparently; certainly a jousting ground for winos and junkies, and nowhere to linger after dark – but on a misty morning, at least you could look out from the kitchen window of those houses and pretend beauty wasn't a stranger; you could admire geese on the meadow, and the occasional heron. But round this corner, it was beyond pretence. Your view was a brick wall, and that summed it up as far as Judy was concerned.

She drank a cup of tea and – after checking at the door for signs of Deirdre, her landlady – removed a Tupperware container from the fridge's third shelf, and from it took a clingfilm-wrapped chocolate eclair, which she unwrapped and ate hurriedly, standing up. No enjoyment bothered her face while she did so. It might have been a pleasure endured for someone else's sake; a ludicrous sexual demand, or a children's party game. Afterwards she rolled the clingfilm into a tight ball, and pushed it down a few layers into the swingbin. She couldn't swear that Deirdre examined her Tupperware while she was out – couldn't positively say Deirdre would swing the bin's lid to survey its most recent deposits – but Judy wasn't certain, if their roles were reversed, that she'd not be doing those things. And of course, Deirdre had all day to do them in. Deirdre didn't need to work. Deirdre was a woman of property.

That done, routine locked into place. Judy checked her necessaries: keys, purse, cigarettes, lighter. Shuffled slippers off and fastened shoes. Slipped into her anorak – a green number, long past best – and out the front door; headed right, negotiating the pair of overlapping railings (there must be a name for these) planted to confound cyclists, then pacing another fifty yards before turning right again, to make her way between flats and garages: a wasteland of cracked paving stones, litter, and the ever-present possibility of an encounter with a dog – one of those bullet-headed breeds familiar on such estates, whose owners don't so much like dogs as not like people. And all of this just part of Judy's everyday; nothing to comment on later, if there'd been anyone to listen. So far, this morning bleached into every other: a series of moments that would grow closer together as the day wore on; would blend until she couldn't tell one from the next; until – thankfully – it would be time to switch off again; turn out the lights, and hope for sleep. Which never lasted long enough, and always broke the moment you noticed it.

These weren't her thoughts, precisely, but she would have recognised and agreed with them if they'd been presented to her. But for the moment, having crossed the pedestrian bridge at Friars Wharf, she was walking down the street towards her place of work; chin tilted upright; bad thoughts painted on her face; cigarette jammed into a mouth that was a straight line, except for the downturn at the corners.

7:41.

Eliot glanced into the rear-view mirror for what he could see of his boys – heads together like a pair of squirrels – and caught sight of part of the upper left quadrant of his own face as he did so: one blue/grey eye sheltering under a dark eyebrow he should trim really, except only old people did that, didn't they? Or needed to, anyway; their eyebrows like GM hedges. His weren't that bad yet, but the operative word was *yet* . . . Face facts, the prevailing condition was 'yet'. Because Eliot was looking at forty; or rather, forty was looking at Eliot: suppressing a snigger, wiping a grin off its face. Forty wasn't in itself anything to worry about, but everything that followed it exercised his imagination. Forty sounded the starting pistol on hair-loss and paunch extension; it was the point at which – time would tell

– you discovered whether your penis was going to drop off, or develop its own mindset and acquire startling new inclinations. Schoolgirls, if you were unlucky; or, if you were *really* unlucky, schoolboys. All of which supposed, of course, that you weren't securely bedded down in a warm and loving relationship with wife or long-term sex-partner. Eliot, for his part, had Christine, who was beautiful and warm and loving, it was true, but for whom sex had slipped off the agenda the same time everything else had, with the exception of her children.

As this familiar complaint reared up, it was banished almost immediately by the Memory.

And then somebody – definitely one of his boys – said, 'Daddy, when we've built our castle, you can visit it.'

'Thank you.'

(He was touched, actually.)

'Will you bring cake?'

'Yes,' he said. 'I'll definitely bring cake. Can Mummy come too?'

'Mummy'll live there.'

'Oh.'

'With us.'

'Yes. With just us.'

'. . . Okay.'

A whole different memory threatened his composure now – a vague daydream he and Christine had concocted back in their summer of love; something about a chateau in the woods where they'd live alone forever – but swam out of reach before he'd taken a grip on it.

. . . So what else? Eliot was dark, lean, reasonably tall; had somewhat gaunt features which, when he was pursuing an idea with particular intensity – something he was prone to when alone – tended to cast themselves into shapes usually associated with melancholy; expressions which could earn him a 'Cheer up, mate, it might never happen' on the street. Which was fair comment, unless what you worried about was having fatuous platitudes flung at you by strangers, in which case it just had. Truth was, though, he was inclined to introspection, which usually took the form of self-grilling; a minute examination of where he was, and where he'd expected to be by now. The destination had grown hazy, but a hollowness he'd grown used to – it lived in the pit of his stomach – reminded him he'd had ambitions once, though it was no longer clear how he'd expected to achieve them. Or even what they'd been, beyond the unspecific *I-expect-I'll-be-successful* variety that went with having been top of the class at school, and never having had to struggle to get there. The gap between never having had to struggle and never making an effort, though, made itself felt around the forty mark. As for the others who'd been in the same class, he googled them occasionally, to confirm their continued obscurity, but worried that it was the names he'd completely forgotten that were lighting up the search engines. That was the nightmare. That it was the unconsidered, the unremembered, who were carving their initials on the world's windows, while he'd achieved nothing.

The twins shifted behind him, as if sensing this deep injustice.

Nearly there. Making a right after Folly Bridge – leaving the main road just before it descended into its constant chaos of roadworks – Eliot navigated a channel between two rows of tightly parked cars, thankfully reaching the end without anything coming the other way. As he turned left, Gordon, unless it was Timmy, gave a high-pitched squeal, and Timmy, unless it was Gordon, dissolved into giggles in reply.

'Boys, please. I'm driving,' he said.

This was funny enough that both laughed harder.

The Memory wrapped him again, the way bandages wrap a mummy . . .

He didn't notice, and wouldn't have given it a moment's

thought if he had, the squat, anorak-clad figure he drove past now, making its way down the road on his right; chin tilted upright; bad thoughts painted on its face; cigarette jammed into a mouth that was a straight line – Judy Ainsworth, who'd not long crossed the river herself, though she'd used the pedestrian bridge at Friars Wharf.

As Judy herself might have put it: Some drive. Others walk.

To wind the clock back a little: at 7:30 in the morning, this time of year, there's often mist hanging over the river as it cuts through Grandpont, South Oxford, though it's already in tatters by now; pulled to whispery ribbons by the encroaching day. I've lived here, time of writing, for fourteen years, but it's only the past four that I've been crossing the river at Friars Wharf at 7:30, heading for the London train; way long enough for routines to become established – routines do that without invitation, often only noticed when you break them. For eighteen months, I passed the same man every morning; after the first thirteen, we were nodding at each other. But the train timetable changed, and the four minutes' adjustment meant I never saw him again.

Other routines are the opposite of what the word usually means; they're once-in-a-while happenings, the equivalent of the comets that underline the universe's otherwise ordered existence. There's a woman I see occasionally – there's no rhyme or reason to her appearances, or none I'm privy to – and sometimes she'll cycle past me, and sometimes our paths cross because she's heading the other way, and whichever direction she's taking our eyes never meet, we never exchange smiles, we are strangers. But we share the same community, so if too much time passes without my seeing her, I wonder about her, and hope she's okay. Because that's how it works, even on the uptight suburban fringes – a neighbourhood is a web, with any thread plucked *here* reverberating *there*. So an actual local drama, with police aplenty, and junctions cordoned off with emergency bunting; with helicopters thrashing overhead, and armed-response officers yomping across the adventure playground, actual guns in states of readiness; with news crews baying behind hastily erected barriers – all of this, it had an effect on everyone in those streets. The effect varied depending on the character at issue – from stunned horror to secret glee – but no one was immune. Acts of violence, like acts of love, damage not only the participants but those around them.

This opening is a bit busy: bound to be, really – a number of characters to be introduced; a lot of events happening simultaneously. Arguably, not simultaneously enough – DS Bain won't be disturbed by a phone for another ninety minutes – but waking is the starting point of everyone's day; we're on different timelines, but we all experience the same grey nowhere in that space between sleep and consciousness. So, allowing for the odd bit of slippage, all of the following is happening at roughly the same moment: Louise approaches the nursery gates, still thinking about the significance of today's date, as Eliot drives his boys past the squat unhappy figure of Judith Ainsworth, and George Trebor – who, like me, won't be appearing in this story again – watches Bad Sam Chapman, whom he only knows as Man Two, search one hundred yards of roadside verge for the Heckler & Koch that went flying after the car hit Neil Ashton. He's assisted in this by police officers, but it's clearly a waste of time. They're not going to find it. And the time they're wasting is being swallowed up elsewhere, because it's at least an hour since the accident, and Jaime Segura could be anywhere, and the odds are good the missing gun is with him . . . Sam Chapman has long since admitted this to himself, but is uncharacteristically reluctant to act on it, as if a response would somehow confirm the event. He's currently thinking a lot of things, but the most accurate summation would be *fuck fuck fuck fucking fuck*.

And as for Segura himself . . . Later they'll go over the map with pairs of compasses; there'll be fakes in jeans and brown faux-leather jackets, whose rucksacks' contents match exactly what was found in Jaime Segura's, making their way from lay-by to nursery by whatever route seems fastest. Some will take the backstreets; others will plug on down the main road for far longer than consistent with nobody having seen Segura doing that; some'll even hop on buses, though no bus driver will lay claim to picking him up – the fact is, nobody knows how Jaime Segura did what he did, which was disappear on one side of the city and reappear on the other an hour later. Not in itself an especially mystifying achievement, granted, but few who've managed it have had 'them' on their case. Because 'they' are the shadowy experts with access to hi-tech gimcrackery; able to blow up grainy stills from CCTVs and produce positive ID from pixellated fuzz, or watch screens aglow with thermal imagery, and trace a target as it edges past a blast furnace. Reconstruction is their business, but Jaime Segura slipped their digital leash.

Eliot's further down the road now; Judy, wrapped in her daily mist of complaint, is closer to work too. DS Bain twitches a little in sleep – 'Target acquired.' *Steady* – and freezes in readiness, while miles away Ben Whistler is hurtling down the Central Line, trying not to study too obviously the legs of the woman opposite, but allowing the richness of the image they suggest to colour the mental picture he's forming of his possible future.

Bad Sam Chapman gives up all hope of finding the missing gun, and says something to the seven-years' copper next to him of such mordant foulness that the copper blanches.

And Louise reaches the nursery gates at about the same moment I board a train – only six minutes late that morning – and leave these events behind; to be uncovered, embroidered, and faithlessly reconstructed over the year that follows.

The gates were five foot high or so; good chunky black iron things with sensible weight to them, though they opened smoothly enough once the lock was dealt with – this being a keypad arrangement, because the days when you could clap a padlock to something and assume people understood it was meant to keep them out were long gone. Louise had been taught the key code by Claire: Claire treating the ritual as on a par with handing over St Peter's keys. Crispin had been barely less uptight about the network passwords in Louise's previous job, which was so patently Louise's previous life that that was how she generally termed it. Crispin had been her lover. Vice-Control, European Investments, DeJohn Franklin Moers. V-C/EurInvs, DFM. Much about her previous life had been abbreviated, including, in the long run, that life itself.

7:52. Louise wasn't always first to arrive – Claire, who was the nursery head (abbreviated to *Miss*), was often there before her – but procedure demanded the gate remained secured until 8:45, when the children were allowed in. The preceding time was for clean-up and organisation, the former technically being Judith Ainsworth's remit, though Louise's take on Judy's cleaning abilities was that if she got much worse, she could be classified disabled. She'd said as much to Claire, but Claire had shaken her head disapprovingly. Louise knew Judy's husband had walked out a year or so ago, and okay, that was sad, but hardly unprecedented and not remotely surprising. And Louise didn't see why it meant she had to put up with substandard cleaning.

This morning, as it happened, Claire would be late, because she had a dental appointment. Louise, once she'd let herself into the nursery grounds, would be their only occupant.

The building facing her sat low on the ground. Essentially diamond-shaped, it had wings jutting out on two sides – on paper, it looked like a first draft of a cartoon character – and was built of light-coloured brick, with red roof and window frames, and a plaque over the door spelling out *South Oxford Nursery School*, though you'd have had to be pretty wayward not to have picked up on the clues already. The surfacing around

25

the main building was of the soft, spongy variety used in play-grounds, and arranged in swirly red-green patterns which from overhead might have looked like a miscoloured sunflower device. Round the rear a wide porch arrangement sheltered a wooden picnic table and some haphazardly stacked chairs, and along the northside wall was a row of plastic storage bins, holding the overflow from nursery cupboards: outdoor toys, mostly – bats and balls; buckets and spades; skittles and skipping ropes. Where the spongy surfacing ended, a sloped and hillocky grassed area took over, punctuated by a number of small flower beds holding the sturdier type of bush – the kind intended to with-stand bats and balls and skittles, and games of hide and seek, and other less organised activities. Bisecting this was another set of railings, the gate in which was secured with a Yale, and behind this was a second building; more of a hut, really, and this was Louise's domain. The annexe, it was usually called; translated by the Darlings' infant tongues into the Palace, which suited Louise fine.

A hand dropped on her shoulder, and she yelped in fright. Turning, she saw the last person she wanted to see.

Dreams come in different sizes, most of them smaller than others. This one is very small indeed. It is of a man framed in a window; he's walking up and down, angry about something – he appears to be shouting – and though no others are visible, it's apparent he's not alone in the room. He's carrying something in one hand, but whatever it is can't be seen from this angle, at least two storeys higher, and the width of a street distant. The man's face is red, his eyes bulge; he wears a sleeveless T-shirt which could do with a rinse, and the veins in his arms pulse crossly. But he keeps slipping out of frame, into that part of the room where anything could be happening. The rest of the house is in darkness; only this one window lit . . . So this is the size of the dream: it's one small piece of activity beamed on to a flat expanse of plain brick, as if the whole house is simply a wall with a single window, through which, half the time, the angry man isn't even visible. Half the time, the window's merely a hole from which light pours.

A trickle of sweat drops from an eyebrow, and for a moment the window puddles into blurry nothingness. And then the eye blinks, and focus returns, and the window is there again, and the man appears behind it for the sixteenth time since counting began, pausing dead centre of the crosshairs.

Somebody's voice – impossible to say whose – says for the sixteenth time, 'Target acquired.'

Steady, a voice in the ear repeats.

(Sometimes, it seems as if the dream will repeat this loop forever – 'Target acquired.' *Steady*.)

The man dips out of shot again, but the crosshairs remain; a circular adornment to the shape of the window frame, as if a passing architect had sketched out an embellishment.

And at last things interrupt.

The room, already lit, is lit further; something flashes, and there's an almost simultaneous noise – a crack; something breaking, something broken. And the voice in the ear crackles into furious life: *Shots fired shots fired*, and as well as being an announcement that something has happened, it's a signal that other things should occur too now; that the waiting part of the dream is over, and the doing part must begin.

The man in the dirty vest appears once more, and the thing in his hand acquires definition as he turns to the window, looks directly through it – enraged – and brings the object level with his chest, pointing it outwards, out of the dream, into the night.

'Target acquired.'

. . . *Take him? Break him? Wake him?* The reply isn't entirely clear.

But the finger squeezes anyway, in accordance with years of training: this finger has been taught in gyms and galleries and out in the open air, where targets have swung in complicated, restless patterns, which have never been enough to save them in the end.

The window shatters. And the man's head . . . What happens to the man's head remains obscure, because at that precise moment something shrill and insistent rips the picture apart as if it were an unsatisfactory sketch, leaving only tatters and fragments. The wall, the shattered window: everything disappears, to be replaced by a view of duvet, through which 9-a.m.-type light is soaking.

As with almost every other occasion on which this has happened, it is a dream; one from which Detective Sergeant B. J. Bain emerges as if from a dripping, smoking, shit-bespattered, bat-infested tunnel.

But the phone is still ringing.

2

'Jesus!'
   'Sorry—'
'You *scared* me!'
'I'm sorry—'

She'd turned and stepped back, when he'd touched her shoulder, the image flashing through her mind one of violence; not violence directed specifically against herself, but against who and where she was. No one who worked in a nursery could fail to have these moments: unguarded slices of nightmare, in which playgrounds were targets for lone men with grudges and indecipherable pathology. But it was a different nightmare taking shape here; one best called *consequences*. Where Memory and Incident collided, scattering shards that needed collecting before anyone turned up to gawp.

'I'm sorry,' he said again.

And he was: you could say that for Eliot. When he was sorry, it was spelt out in capitals, all over his face.

'. . . It's not eight yet,' she said.

(This was something she'd noticed of herself and others: a tendency to remark on the time when trying to grasp a situation.)

'I wanted to see you.'

'But *here*?'

'I've got the boys. They're in the car.'

Oh, fucking great, she thought.

'Louise—'

'It's the middle of the street,' she said. 'Broad daylight.'

'There's no one around.'

'It's my place of work. I work here, Eliot. You can't just turn up like this. We don't open for another hour—'

'That's why I thought we could talk—'

'What about, the boys?'

'They're in the car. They can't hear—'

'Oh, for God's sake!'

Her back to the gate, she surveyed the scene behind him; the junction where the riverbound road bisected the street the nursery was on. A car rolled in then out of view, and any moment now one of a hundred pedestrians – dog walkers, newspaper boys, joggers, winos – would spring out of nowhere and recognise the nursery lady having a tête-à-tête with a dad. Information that could circuit a neighbourhood twice in less time than it took to jump to a conclusion. 'You can't leave them in the car, Eliot. They're boys, not dogs.'

'I thought it would be more private—'

'Eliot. Eliot? This is not private. This is where I work. Now take the boys somewhere else. We open at quarter to nine, you should know that.'

'We have to talk about this, Louise,' he said.

Why? Because you just said so? But she couldn't deliver that reply; it was neither fair nor honest. Because they did have to talk about it; otherwise it would hover over both of them, with the deadly potential of the not-yet-mentioned.

'Okay,' she said. 'Yes. But not here. And not now.'

'So—'

'Call me,' she said. Then remembered that that was off-limits; that her home phone was potentially in enemy hands. 'Not at home – look, come back when we're open. I'll give you my mobile number.'

30

Fifty yards behind Eliot's back, a dumpy anoraked figure turned the corner and headed towards them. Louise's heart sank.

'Now *go*,' she hissed, or tried to. It came out a hoarse whisper; one she had to retract immediately: 'No, wait. Ask me something.'

'. . . Ask you what?'

'*Anything*. How the twins are doing, or when half-term is, or—'

'Oh. There's someone coming. How are the boys doing?'

'Just fine,' she said, her voice hitting a slightly higher pitch. 'They mix well with the other children, which isn't always the way with twins – there can be a tendency to become a republic of two, if you know what I mean.'

'Yes, sometimes it's like they speak their own language.'

'Well, so long as they're socialising, you don't have to worry about that – oh, good morning, Judy.'

'Morning.'

'Anyway, as I was saying, we don't actually open doors until 8:45, so—'

'Not to worry. I'll take them on to the recreation ground for a spin.'

Spin – he wondered why he'd said that as soon as it left his mouth.

8:45 or not, Judy was opening doors now, four swift jabs on the keypad – a diagonal downward slash, left to right, then another figure, obscured by her hand.

Louise saw Eliot notice, deliberately or not, and frowned.

Judy pushed the gate open, and marched in, towards the main building.

Eliot said, voice low: 'Does she clean up after the kids, or cook them and eat them?'

'Keep a close eye on the boys, if you're going on the rec ground. It's early, yet.' She followed Judy through the gate, making sure the lock had secured behind her, but didn't look back until she'd reached the nursery door, and Eliot had left by then.

Some mistakes you keep on making. A year ago, she thought, I'd have been at my desk half an hour by now: telephone soldered to my head; mind locked into the international money market (except that part wondering when Crispin would stick his head round the door: *Ms Kennedy? Do you have a minute?*). On my third Americano. The aromas of spoilt milk and plasticine definitely absent; the artwork tending towards Rothko and Kandinsky rather than the homage to BritArt four-year-olds produce. But pulsing underneath these new surroundings was the same old heartbeat; the one that reminded her – *lub-dub* – that she'd done it again: slept with someone she shouldn't have.

But let's not deal with that right now. Let's postpone introspection until there's a glass of wine in hand, and some work behind us.

'Judy?'

They were in the nursery vestibule. Judy had her back to Louise, and was hanging her anorak in the store cupboard where the props of her trade were quartered: squeezy bottles and pump-action canisters; mops and dusters; dustpans and brushes; bleach and disinfectants. If she got half an hour's use out of this lot in the average week, thought Louise, she was keeping things clean Louise hadn't encountered yet. And she wasn't listening, either. Or deliberately ignoring her. 'Judy?'

'What?'

'When you're opening the gate, try not to let anybody see the number, please. It's not good security.'

'Don't you trust him?'

'That's not the point. The system's meant to preserve security. Nobody's supposed to know the number.'

Judy flashed her a look, face predictably set to offended spite.

'I'm not used to being spoken to like this by junior staff.' Her voice rose in volume and pitch: that too was predictable. 'Mrs. Christopher wouldn't—'

'Claire will be late this morning. But when she gets here, I'm sure she'll be only too happy to listen to your latest grievance.'

She left Judy standing, closing her mind for the moment to the obvious: that there were any number of tactical errors there, from *latest grievance* to the interruption. But it was impossible to occupy space near Judy Ainsworth without causing offence; Judy always gave the impression that, last time you'd met, you'd attacked her with a broom-handle, and while you might have forgotten this, she wasn't about to. Besides, there came a point in any woman's morning when she'd spent too long biting her tongue. 'Junior staff,' anyway, was a joke: Judy'd not worked here herself much more than a year. And the fraction of that spent doing actual work was significantly shorter.

The office was just off the vestibule. Louise shut the door behind her, removed her jacket, and tried to summon up what the day held – there was a chart on the desk, with activities marked in half-hour blocks, but until she could hold a day in her head without paperwork, she'd still feel a beginner. Claire seemed to carry the whole week with no mental effort, including any variations the three of them agreed on a Monday morning, always supposing bright ideas had sparked over the weekend: the three being herself, Claire and Dave, the other nursery assistant. Dave was younger than Louise, but had been doing this longer; he was a nice guy, quiet, helpful, and had a great way with the Darlings, who worshipped him. One or two of the yummy mummies found his presence reassuring too, though that wasn't an area Louise was in any hurry to discuss with him.

Speaking of which, while she remembered, she wrote her mobile number on a Post-it for Eliot. More shades of the same old mistake, but this hand was already dealt. She just hoped Eliot had the sense to work out that this was Part 1 of how to say goodbye, and not an invite to continue the conversation.

Eliot, meanwhile, had unloaded the kids and taken them on to the recreation ground. This had the advantage of retroactively validating the reason he'd given Chris for coming out so early in the first place, but felt like defeat anyway – in his mental rehearsal, the encounter with Louise had resembled one of the sparkier scenes from *The Philadelphia Story*, with her matching his every quip. In real life, he'd had the knowledge of impending grief. He hadn't had much practice, but even he knew when the Conversation was coming. It's one of those moments that's familiar the first time.

Eliot—

Sorry. I'm sorry. It was stupid to come, I shouldn't have—

(Unequivocal surrender. The first line of defence.)

No, you shouldn't. Look, I've been thinking—

And that, right there, was the Conversation; it made little difference now whether they had it or not. She'd been thinking, and that was the kiss of death. What he had to do now was head her off before the words were spoken; before they could weevil into his head and haunt him for weeks, or possibly years.

It's not eight yet, she'd said. She wouldn't have cared what time it was if she'd been planning to match his quips. Actually, what little they'd said to each other hadn't stuck. He might be misremembering. But it had ended with *Call me*, he was certain of that. Which simply meant the Conversation had been postponed, didn't it, unless it meant something else.

Jesus, Eliot. Face facts.

There followed one of those sudden brain-drenching moments when he became aware that he had charge of his children, and they weren't actually in his field of vision – *Fucking hell* was how this expressed itself, quickly followed by *She'll kill*

34

me – and then there they were again, chasing each other round the nearby basketball hoop. Over the far side of the field a man was walking a dog, but neither were anything to worry about: the dog was on its last legs, and the man – whom Eliot had seen up close a time or two – had cheeks the colour of broken roses; the ever-after legacy of too many nights on the beer.

Keep a close eye on the boys on the rec ground. It's early, yet.

Some of the nightfolk might still be hanging around, she'd meant.

The recreation ground was bordered on all sides by ditch, tree or hedgerow, broken by a barrier – a padlocked pole on a hinge, blocking cars and quad bikes, with a bin for dog-waste next to it – in its south-east corner, opposite the nursery gates. A sturdy, six-foot fence marked off the nursery perimeter; between that and the rec ground was a footpath that ran to the railway line. As for the rec ground itself, it boasted an open-air basketball court and a couple of five-a-side football pitches, but not many years back had been a dusty grey nowhere; a former gasworks' site, whose soil, if not terminally ill, wasn't terribly well. Environmental redemption wasn't impossible, then, provided the target area was reasonably small. Kids from the local primary school, a short way up the road, played here in the summer months, and Eliot had rarely passed in the evening without the sounds of one ball game or another floating into the open sky. Even without a ball, there was space and grass enough to run around.

'You okay there, boys?'

'We're not boys, Daddy.'

'Daddy, we're lions.'

'Of course you are.'

He should be joining in, he knew that, but pretending to be a lion this early in the morning was beyond him.

'Rrarrrr?' said Gordon.

'Rrarrrr!' said Timmy.

'Rar,' Eliot replied.

They rushed him, and he put both arms out to scoop them up, and when they hit, it was with a force beyond their combined weights; was one of those heart-slapping moments like when you stand on a low bridge while an express train thunders underneath, or turn a corner into heavy wind. There never seemed much time for this kind of malarkey lately, or if there was it was always Christine at its centre, so Eliot's heart-slap went well beyond the physical thump . . . With one arm wrapped round each, he commenced tickling, and the twins dropped to the ground, this form of assault always having immediate effect – basically, you could put them on their knees at a distance if you threatened to tickle them loudly enough. Pretty soon he had a son clutching each thigh; their small but very very phys-ical bodies shaking with fun and laughter while he growled nonsensical noises over their heads, rubbing his nose into each of their scalps in turn, while biting large but make-believe chunks out of them. For as long as it lasted the Memory was banished and he was simply Eliot Pedlar: not a great father, but he answered to Daddy. Then, in between biting one boy and starting on the other, he looked up and saw the figure with the gun slipping through the hedge. He blinked and it was gone, but it had been there, maybe fifty yards away. The gun had been real.

Eliot stopped, the tickling game turned to one of statues.

'—Boys . . .'

'Dah—dah—dah—'

'—Daddy! You're *ticklin* us.'

'Boys, stop a moment.'

'*No!* Don't stop!'

'Don't stop, Daddy—'

But he pulled his arms away, letting Gordon slip to the ground with a bump while Timmy, who had a knack for maintaining balance, hit his feet and stayed upright.

'What did you see?'

'Hush a moment.'

'What did you see, Daddy?'

Eliot reached into his inside pocket at the exact same moment he received a mental picture of his mobile, nestling in the plastic well beneath the dash of his car.

'Daddy, tell us what you *seed*!'

He wasn't sure any more what he'd seed. Certainty was fading with every passing moment. A gun? There was no shortage of local horror stories, but guns were pushing it. Guns were more an East Oxford thing.

'Was it a man?'

'Did you see him?' Eliot asked, before he could stop himself. Gordon's face curled into a frightened guilty mask. 'Who?'

'Who did Gordy see, Daddy?'

'I *didn't*!'

'Daddy, who did Gordy see?'

'Hush, now.' Eliot hoisted Gordon into his arms, while Timmy clutched his leg, and began snuffling too. 'There wasn't anyone. Nobody saw anyone.'

Except he had . . . He'd seen somebody holding a gun, and even if it turned out it was just a mobile phone, it had looked damn like a gun a minute ago.

Small fingers nipped his leg. 'Timmy's scared.' It was Timmy telling him this; the third person being a temporary refuge from Timmyhood. Both boys practised the technique.

'Let's go back to the car,' Eliot suggested.

He'd parked on the curve of the road just yards from the nursery gates, and the three of them had walked up the same road and over the drainage ditch to the rec ground, crossing by the troll bridge. No troll had waylaid them; trolls, Eliot had promised, didn't wake early, and always hid from daddies; trolls were even scareder of daddies than they were of billy goats. But when he turned that way now Timmy gripped tighter, while Gordy – already wrapped round him like a bandage –

began vibrating in his arms, and Eliot knew that one false moment in the morning had woken the troll, and there was no way they were using that bridge again.

Keep a close eye on the boys on the rec ground. It's early, yet . . .

There was space here to kick a ball, and grass enough to run around on, but it wasn't any kind of idyll. It was true that to the south of the nursery lay another meadow, the Ham – a flood plain – and that between nursery and railway line was an adventure playground, containing a vaguely military array of wooden constructs for climbing over or tumbling out of; true, too, that the curved suburban road the nursery looked on to didn't see much traffic outside of the school run, and that every so often, from a cool blue summer sky, hot-air balloons would drift down to land in the long grass on the meadow, like a Cadbury's advert come to life. But it was equally true that the nature park to the rec ground's north – a rarely mown strip of land hugging the river – was a haven not only for rabbits and foxes, but for outdoor sex addicts and drug abusers; the former huddling in the bushy clumps and among the strangled copses, scrawling semi-literate invitations on the stanchions of the bridge across the Isis, while the latter congregated round the wooden sculpture – four fingers and a thumb pushing out of the earth – to scatter hypodermics and scorched roaches, and trample scrunched-up balls of silver foil and glassine envelopes into the mud. It was true, too, that when mist clung low to the ground in the early hours, the occasional junkie would miss his footing stumbling for a piss, and fetch up in the river. And then a small battalion of emergency officers would congregate in Day-Glo coveralls, and pull bicycles and fridges from the water, until they got lucky, and gathered him in.

Put another way, Eliot thought, not all trolls lived under bridges. And not all of them were frightened of daddies.

And maybe some of them carried guns.

★

Louise, emerging from the office into the entrance hall, couldn't see Judy anywhere, but right that moment someone passed along the lane outside, or didn't pass so much as sneak – that was her impression. A man, half crouching. He'd disappeared before she'd registered more, like what colour he was, or how he was dressed – sports gear would have been a clue. She crossed to the window, but saw nobody on the lane. Vague figures huddling on the rec ground, figures she could just make out through the trees, would be Eliot and his boys. Nobody lurking, though. Probably a jogger.

Which was why sports gear would have been a clue. The lane was a favoured route for joggers; it hopped over the railway track via an iron bridge, then dropped into one of the college sports grounds. But it was also much used by the local winos, who'd gather on the nearby junction on their way from nowhere in particular to anywhere else, and while Louise neither felt threatened by them nor subscribed to the belief that they lowered property prices, she was aware that they worried the kids, and wasn't happy about them hanging round in the lane. Nobody could wander into the grounds – the keypad on the gate saw to that – and the fences might as well have been mountain ranges to your average chubby wino. Still. She'd better check one of the skinny ones wasn't trying to squeeze through the mesh: she was, after all, in charge.

She did a quick tour of the main nursery, though they always left things battle-ready the day before. Nothing looked out of place except Judy, who should have been mopping the kitchen area but wasn't. Louise gritted teeth. Judy was a trial, Claire occasionally admitted. Louise was starting to feel she was a sentence. If it was just the lack of work, she'd see the funny side; even DFM had had passengers, though they'd generally had the decency to be promoted to board level before really kicking back. But Judy radiated hostility, and it was hard not to respond in kind; hard not to feel there was little about her worth knowing better, starting with her appearance. Because it was as if, Louise sometimes thought – and felt guilty about thinking, but when did that stop anyone – it was as if there was a list somewhere of colours Judy really shouldn't wear, attached to clothes Judy shouldn't go within a mile of, all topped off with a haircut Judy should desperately avoid, and out of what was possibly lack of self-awareness, but might just have been anger, Judy had decided to go for all these things at once, every day. Who was anybody else to tell her what to wear, what to look like? An attitude there was a lot to be said for when it went hand in hand with *joie de vivre*, but the rest of the time it made you cross the road in fear.

But fuck. The woman had a problem, but being the woman was no doubt a bigger one, and Louise had more to worry about. She checked the window locks were secure – something the insurance policy demanded – then went to open the annexe, which was where the first-term children spent their days: Louise's Darlings. This was behind another set of railings, a safeguard against the kids wandering into the car park during outdoor play, but the gate in this one had a straightforward lock. Which had already been opened, and left unsecured, and while this wasn't a major offence, it irritated Louise: Judy hadn't finished in the nursery, or even started there. There was an order to the morning, for God's sake . . . She locked it behind her.

And then, while she remembered, she walked down to the fence adjoining the lane, and peered along it, without seeing anyone. A while back, in the wash of some horror that had happened elsewhere, Claire had floated the idea of an incident book, a journal for jotting down stuff that might need remembering later, once it became important – after it had passed, in other words, from peculiar irrelevance to corroborating evidence. But the days were busy, and the idea hadn't taken shape; besides, what would Louise have written? That somebody had walked past, looking like they didn't want to be seen? She shook her head; one of those silly but not ineffectual gestures for banishing unwanted thoughts. Twenty minutes from now, she'd be passing Eliot her phone number on a Post-it, hoping no one would notice. Shadowy figures would be less a worry than a welcome distraction. She turned back to the annexe. Time to get the day in gear. And an important point to bear in mind would be to stop using expressions like *but fuck*, or even *for God's sake*: even mentally. The first time one of the Darlings headbutted a nipple, then repeated whatever Louise said in response, was likely to be the last. Claire was a sweet woman, but pure iron where the children were concerned. You couldn't run a nursery any other way.

She headed for the annexe, and had almost reached it when a noise behind her made her turn.

He'd got the boys as far as the corner, Gordon still wrapped round him and gaining pounds every moment; Timmy trotting by his side, but with one fist wrapped round Eliot's trouser leg, which didn't help either. At the barrier, he stopped –

'What's the matter, Daddy?' Timmy immediately asked.

– but the only figure in sight was the dog-walking alcoholic on the far side of the field.

'Nothing, Timmy.'

'But what were you lookin at?'

'Look*ing*. Nothing. I wasn't look*ing* at anything.'

'But you were starin over there –'

'Star*ing*. And no I wasn't, I was glancing. Gordy, are you sure you can't walk?'

'. . . Yes.'

'But Daddy's getting tired, and it's not far—'

'Was it that man you were lookin for?'

'. . . Which man, Timmy?'

'The man who was there before.'

'Before when?'

'What man?'

'Nobody, Gordy . . . Which man, Timmy?'

'Why are we goin to the car, Daddy?'

'Daddy has to make a phone call. Which man, Timmy? Did you see a man?'

'. . . I *thoughted* I did.'

'Not thoughted, Timmy. Thought. Gordon, you're going to have to walk. You're hurting Daddy's back.'

'*No!*'

'You can hold my hand. It's only a little way. It's *all right*, Gordy. There's nothing wrong, Daddy's here.'

'He was over there.'

Eliot lowered Gordon to the ground, and looked the way Timmy was pointing: towards the railway line. There was no one to be seen. But the lane twisted before meeting the tracks, and whoever it was could have turned a corner, or dropped into the ditch either side, though why would he want to do that? Unless he'd been carrying a gun, of course; carrying a gun might be reason to hide . . . Though not from a man with two little boys. Both of whom were frightened now, and gun or not – it had probably been a mobile phone – Eliot had reason enough to call the police: you couldn't be too careful. He glanced at his watch. It was ten past eight.

'Is nursy open yet?' Timmy asked.

'Nur*sery*. Not yet. Soon. We just have to go back to the car for a moment . . .'

A boy's hand in each of his own, he steered them round the barrier, making sure Timmy didn't get anywhere near the dogshit bin – Eliot had a terrible memory associated with that dogshit bin: you couldn't take your eyes off a child for a moment – and on to the lane by the nursery gates, where he'd spoken to Louise twenty minutes ago. Twenty minutes seemed a lifetime. Down the lane's far end a train rattled past; a reminder that things happened elsewhere. What happened here was a man stepped into their path and said, 'The gates?' He was dark-skinned, dark-haired; young and chocolate-eyed, with stubble that looked glued on, the way eighties pop stars' did. He wore a brown leather jacket. He had a gun in his hand. He said, 'The gates?' again.

Gordy shrieked, and flung himself around Eliot's left leg while Timmy wordlessly, breathlessly, grabbed his right, though Eliot didn't fall – instinctively, he wrapped an arm round each child, recoiling as far as he could without actually stepping back; tried to make himself a shield, a wall, anything bullets bounced off. And already his mind was splitting sideways, as if he were twinning too; one half saying *This isn't happening this doesn't happen this is an ordinary Tuesday in South Oxford* while the other informed him, coldly, clinically – with something almost satisfied in its tone – that this was real and this was true, and this man held a gun.

'Please. You will open the gates.'

'Don't hurt my children,' Eliot said.

'You will open the gates, yes?'

He wasn't aiming his gun at Eliot – he held it loosely by his side, as if it were a pint of milk or a banana or . . . or something else, anyway, and both seemed to grow wise to this at the same moment, because no sooner had Eliot allowed the fact to take shape than the man – the boy – looked at the instrument in his hand, and a change swept over him, as if he'd put on new knowledge, which was power. Now he raised the gun, and now he was pointing it at Eliot.

'You will open the gates, yes.'

Power turned questions into statements.

Eliot said, 'Please, we were just passing, don't hurt my—'

'The gates. You will open them.'

'Please—'

He couldn't look down. His boys were clinging to him, one

leg apiece, and his world had shrunk to this small bubble, just big enough for the five of them: himself, his children, this stranger, that gun – but he couldn't look down; couldn't tear his eyes from what might blow his world apart to what made it worth living in.

'The gates.'

The gates. It was only now the word penetrated – the Gun wanted him to open *the gates*. The gates were the nursery gates, and were securely locked; there was a keypad security system, and the number wasn't given out to parents, so what made the Gun think he knew how to open them? Though he did, of course – he'd been watching the cleaning woman's hand as she punched the numbers with her stubby finger, and could still see the pattern she'd made: *four swift jabs on the keypad – a diagonal downward slash, left to right, then another figure, obscured by her hand* . . .

'What do you want?' he asked, and the words came out a whisper.

'Open the gates.'

Timmy said, 'Daddy—'

'Hush, Timmy. Everything's all right.'

'Gordy wants Mummy,' Gordon said.

'Everything's all right,' Eliot said again. He was amazed his voice sounded so steady – amazed he hadn't burst into tears, actually.

Cued, primed, ready, Gordy started to cry.

'Please. I do not want to hurt you.'

But even as the boy spoke the words, the gun twitched in his hand, as if to underline that it wasn't the boy in control of getting what he wanted.

'Gordon—'

Timmy was tugging wordlessly at his trouser leg – soon, very soon, the high-pitched keening would begin.

'Timmy—'

'The gates.'

Eliot said, 'Don't,' because he couldn't keep the word in.

The boy raised the gun level with Eliot's face. His expression was a mask; an otherworld disguise behind which Eliot's future hid – all he'd ever miss of love and laughter; of beauty, food and sex; the whole mishmash squandered in less than a second by this pretty zombie with a trigger . . . And then the gun twitched again; not to release the gram of lead that would reshape Eliot's world, but just to indicate where they were, these famous gates under discussion. Three yards or so from where they stood.

Gordy had quietened, but only because he was aching for breath, and Timmy was vibrating at a pitch possibly audible to neighbourhood dogs. Manoeuvring them to the gates was like learning how to walk with kitchen chairs roped to his legs. The keypad waited: twelve hostile plastic buttons in four rows of three: 1–9, 0, #, *. He wondered momentarily what * was for, then decided there were more important things at stake. 'I don't know the whole number,' he began, but let the remainder fade unspoken. He suspected there was a language issue here, even beyond the obvious – that one of them spoke Gun, and the other didn't. He suspected that explanations of numerical security systems, even if delivered at a level of coherence currently beyond him, wouldn't meet with sympathetic under-standing. He suspected there was a bottom line, which was that he opened the gates. Anything below that line, he didn't want to know about, ever.

Eliot released Timmy's hand, though Timmy didn't want to release his . . . Hush now, he said, or maybe only imagined he said. Timmy whimpered, and Eliot squeezed his shoulders briefly, then brought his hand up to the keypad.

A diagonal downward slash, left to right . . .

He keyed 1, 5, 9.

Then another figure, obscured by her hand . . .

He had no idea what happened if you hit the wrong key. If it worked like an ATM you got three goes, though he couldn't remember that ever happening to him . . . And in lieu of swallowing your card, what happened here, exactly? An alarm sounded? Overhead, or in the local police station? Which wasn't far – was five minutes' walk – but might as well be the other side of Oxford if he pissed off the Gun . . .

Who was looking at him, waiting.

'Is open, yes?'

'Not yet,' Eliot said.

The cleaning woman's hand had lifted again after punching the 9, he was sure of that. Trying to recapture the moment he shut his eyes, but all that came to mind was the long dark barrel of the Gun. He reopened them in a hurry, and stabbed the 2.

When the right code was entered, a green light flashed on the keypad, and the gate's lock released.

That didn't happen.

He pushed the gate anyway, and felt only unforgiving resistance.

Across the nursery compound, beyond the second set of railings – over towards the annexe – somebody moved.

She wasn't sure what made her turn. It wasn't the children's squalling – too much her daily background to ring alarm bells – and it wasn't Eliot pushing the gate, because she'd turned in time to see that. Maybe it had been his finger hitting the keypad: not a sound she'd expect to carry. But more critically, not a sound she'd been expecting at all: neither Claire nor Dave would be here for a while. So that was it, then; a quiet noise that shouldn't be happening made its way across the morning, and reached Louise before she reached the annexe.

Eliot was pushing the gate. His children were wrapped round

him, one leg each, and a man she'd never seen before was holding a toy gun at his head – why would he want to do that?

The sky blackened for half a moment, and broke clean open the next.

The man jabbed at Eliot with the gun that wasn't a toy, and Eliot stabbed the keypad again; puncturing numbers that would unlock the gate . . . Louise felt her legs give as tomorrow's headlines unfolded: a man with a gun on nursery grounds – the fact that no children were here yet was a detail. He could shoot them all, and wait for the kids to show . . . He could do any number of things, but he had to get through the gate first.

Her legs were given back to her, and she ran.

The gate didn't lock if you punched the wrong number in, or it would have fused shut long ago: you couldn't persuade the children it wasn't a game, though the keypad was technically out of their reach. So no bells would ring, either here or with the local police, and as far as Louise knew, you could keep entering numbers forever until you hit the right combo . . . And Eliot knew the number, didn't he? He'd watched Judy open the gate earlier, so he'd be through any second. Unless Louise got there first, and locked the gate from the inside.

But the first gate she reached was the internal one that she'd locked behind her just moments ago, in that version of the world in which guns did not appear. And the key was – the key was where it always was: in the right-hand pocket of her jeans; a pocket which refused to cooperate as she tried to jam her hand into it and pull her keyring out. An everyday action, not to be attempted under exam conditions. Less than a hundred yards away, Eliot was attacking the keypad again: either he didn't remember the code, or his finger was shaking on account of the gun at his temple. Or he was deliberately getting it wrong. Would a man do that, with a gun to his head, his children at his side? Louise didn't know; all she knew was her keyring wouldn't come free of her pocket, and she swore again, and then it did, but snagged a loose thread on the way out, and she had to tug until the thread broke, and punched her own breast when it did . . . She dropped the keys. Eliot looked towards her, his face a desperate mask. The man with the gun looked too. It occurred to her that he could shoot her through the railings before she reached them. She picked the keys up anyway. Something else had just become clear to her, as it maybe already had to Eliot; that there were situations in which bravery ceased to have relevance – when your fate was no longer in your hands, you did what was needed. He might shoot her before she locked him out. But if she didn't lock him out he could shoot her anyway, and then he'd be inside, and the children would be arriving soon.

On her third, or possibly fourth, attempt, the key fitted the lock. Tumblers fell, springs tightened, the lock did the opposite of what it was built to do. The gate swung open, and Louise all but fell into the outer part of the compound just as Eliot took a fifth crack at getting the numbers right.

A diagonal downward slash, left to right . . .
    He keyed 1, 5, 9.
Then another figure, obscured by her hand . . .
    He'd tried 2, tried 3, tried 4. There was method here, and he was reluctant to abandon it, but the Gun had become more assertive, had begun grinding into his temple, and it was difficult not to respond to this increased pressure in the standard manner: forget order, and do something random instead. He hit 8, and pushed the gate. Nothing happened. Except that his children wrapped themselves more tightly round his thighs, and the image that invaded him – of his blood and brain spraying their infant faces – had all the force of premonition.
    'Open the gate? Yes?'
    'I'm trying, right?'
    Across the compound, Louise was coming through the other

gate, the one that divided the nursery grounds. Except she'd dropped the keys, and was having to scrabble around for them . . . This was what it did, fear: it turned you into a butter-fingered dolt – except, however scared Louise was, she was heading this way. Hoping to what – prevent their entry? And if that happened, what would the Gun do? The blood and brain image recurred, followed swiftly by another: of the Gun trained on Gordy, on Timmy . . .

He keyed 1, 5, 9.

The Gun might shoot them all anyway, but something could happen between now and then to prevent it. Keep trying.

Without taking his eyes off Louise, Eliot hit another button: never knew which.

And pushed the gate.

This is what happens in dreams.

In dreams, things of vital importance reveal themselves. Life is full of vital importances, but rarely do they manifest as buttons that need pressing, or doors at the far end of corridors, that have to be reached at all costs . . . And in dreams, the buttons turn into carrots or coat hangers, and remain unpressed; and the corridors elongate (of course), and the doors are forever unreached.

In dreams legs turn to lead, and the floor sucks at the feet. The ability to move forward decreases in exact proportion to the need to do so.

In real life, exactly the same thing happens.

Louise dropped the keys as the gate swung open; flung them to the ground, as if the force of the action would propel her forwards. But her legs wouldn't move properly; her muscles wanted to relax – wanted to flop her on to the ground, as if she were one of those little finger puppets on a box, held upright by the tension in its strings. When a thumb is applied to the base, the puppet collapses in a tangle of joints . . . The taste of old pennies filled her mouth. Ahead of her, Eliot was pushing at numbers again, as if this was all he would ever do.

. . . *Run* . . .

And she did. It was like breaking free of gravity; a sudden loosening. No distance at all to the outer gate – she'd be there in less than a moment.

Her heels on the path tattooed the morning; drilled through every other noise – the passing car heading up the road; the gravel shifters over the meadow. Eliot looked up again. So did the man with the gun. Then Eliot's expression changed from fear to something unreadable, as if he'd just slipped over the edge of one large event and landed in another. Without looking back at the keypad, he jabbed it with a forefinger. A green light blinked on Louise's side of the gate about half a second before she got there. And the boy with the gun raised it, and aimed at her through the railings.

Eliot's elbow twitched, and the gun was pointing elsewhere – up at the blue nowhere. It didn't go off.

And Louise slammed into the gate, fumbling for the lock mechanism; a matter of flipping the latch across, sealing this danger outside.

But her thumbs were butter. It was dreamland again, where simple tasks subdivide into previously unencountered complication, and limbs and joints you'd once enjoyed control of become strangers. She'd never locked this gate from the inside; never had occasion to. Had been shown how, but the memory was swallowed by the situation: the gun behind the railings which might be pointing anywhere; the way Eliot leaned his weight into the gate just as her fingers discovered how to work the catch . . . For a moment, everything was happening the way it ought to on waking: that emergence into a reality if not ideal, then at least bargained for. And then the weight on the gate was too much for her, and that happy ending slipped from her reach . . . The gun was at Eliot's head, she distantly registered. That noise she'd been hearing was English, filtered through a mouth born to other languages. *Push. Push or I shoot your boy.* He would shoot the boy. The fact that he hadn't specified which was a detail you could hardly blame Eliot for: besides, Louise was beyond blaming now – the gate, so immovable seconds ago, was swinging into her, and the latch she'd just triggered was slamming a bolt into thin air, an inch or so from its socket. She felt gravity taking over again. The ground reached out and took her.

Push. Push or I shoot your boy . . .

He hadn't known how he might react to guns – forced to answer a questionnaire on the subject, his pen, like any man's, would have hovered over the box marked *Hero*, but he had too much self-knowledge to tick it. Yet seconds ago, Eliot had angled an elbow into a gunman's arm to throw him off his aim.

Push or I shoot your boy.

And then he'd pushed the gate, to open it, like he was told.

All this time, his boys had been hugging his thighs, tugging him different ways: left right; up down – he wanted to hunker and shield them with his body; rise up and smite whoever'd do them harm. But when the threat had been made, it had been his head the gun was pointing at, so what did that say? Whatever it was, for the moment it went unspoken: the gate was opening; Louise was falling to the path. And Eliot was tumbling through the gate, Timmy and Gordon attached to him like small moons, dragged onwards by his movement, and all three of them still unshot – though that, too, remained in the balance, because the Gun was coming with them, one hand on Eliot's collar, shoving him forwards so he tripped over Louise's prone form, taking the boys down with him.

Another nursery accident. How many little bodies had this path seen, sprawled and screaming? But don't think about that;

check, instead, that the boys are okay – that this is just the usual tumble, with no bones broken. And then look, for one brief moment, into Louise's eyes, which are inches from yours, and share the horror. There are five of you here; six, if you count the weapon. But for an instant only two of you count. If you're to come through this alive, you need each other.

Eliot blinked. Louise's gaze left him; turned, instead, to the Gun.

The boys clutched him again, and he felt himself dragged down.

She'd never been this close to a gun – stupid: *nobody* had ever been this close to a gun; nobody with a normal life, and ordinary aspirations. Eliot's boys were crying, but that seemed a long way distant; much closer was the gun itself, which was this side of the railings now. While Louise gazed into its mouth, the boy holding it – the only one among them on his feet – closed the gate. That, at least, was normal; everything else had rattled free of its holdings, scattering reality around her like spring rain.

He was brown-eyed, black-haired – this a curly mess; tucked behind his ears, and dropping below his jacket collar – and his toffee-coloured skin was smooth as milk. Under other circumstances, Louise would have wanted to touch his cheek. Even holding a gun, he looked nineteen; clean-shaven, he'd have got away with it. But his stubble was grown-up stubble; his eyes weren't simply exhausted, they were adult-exhausted – he had seen stuff, been places. And all this, he was bringing with him into her nursery.

'You're the lady?' he asked.

'. . . What?'

'We go inside now.'

'Who are you?'

'We go inside.'

The gun twitched in his hand.

Eliot was trying to lever himself up, keeping one arm folded round each of his boys. Not so long ago – less than twenty minutes – the biggest problem in Louise's world was the Incident, and the undiscovered ways in which it might come back to haunt her. Now this: thanks, Eliot.

No. That wasn't fair.

'Now. Please.'

She stood, unsteady as a baby giraffe. Then reached down to help Timmy, unless it was Gordon. But whichever twin it was pulled away, and buried deeper into what it could find of its father.

The gunman looked at the boys, at Eliot, at Louise.

'Eliot,' she said.

His face was assuming that spaced-out, lost-in-Toyland expression the Darlings slipped into when they'd reached their limits.

'*Eliot!*'

He snapped out of it.

'You've got to get the boys moving.'

'Yes . . .'

He stood, scooped his boys up; set one of them – Timmy – upright, and grasped his hand. Gordon, he clutched under one arm, like an awkward parcel. Gordon's legs stuck straight out behind Eliot, but only because his knee joints worked; his arms dangled down like broken branches. Eliot didn't seem to notice. The parcel might have been one he was collecting for somebody else.

Timmy said, 'Timmy wants to go home.'

'Hush now. Soon.'

The gunman said, 'We go inside.' He wasn't pointing the gun at anyone in particular, but the fact that he was holding it spoke for itself.

Behind him, the light on the gate had gone out. When it was locked, Louise knew, the red light shone unblinking; right

53

now, anyone who knew the code could get through it . . . Dave would be here soon. It would be a really good idea if she could lock the gate.

'Inside.'

She began to move, leading the way. Her legs belonged to some other woman, who'd had something of a night; her limbs felt misappropriated. Where she was heading was where she'd come from: the gate in the second set of railings separating the annexe from the nursery proper.

'Wait. Where you go?'

She didn't answer.

'Stop!'

She stopped.

Behind her Eliot was breathing heavily. Below that, the twins' lungs were working overdrive, and Louise flashed on the memory of holding a frightened hamster; its heartbeat pounding in overdrive, too urgently for such a tiny beast. She remembered knowing that if she just stood holding it – presenting no threat other than her enormous size and power – the animal would have no alternative but to die of fear. So after a while, she'd put it down.

'Where do you go?'

She turned. 'You wanted to go inside.'

'There.' He pointed at the main nursery building, but – and this might have been her imagination – a question mark quavered after the word. What she had to do was force it into the open.

'It's locked. I don't have the key.'

His eyebrows tightened.

'Key.' She mimed an action: finger and thumb, a twisting wrist. 'I know key.'

'Well, I don't have it. Only the teacher has the key.'

'You are not teacher?'

'She's not here yet.'

'She is the lady?'

Eliot said, 'Are you looking for Claire? Claire Christopher?'

Said it with a mixture of incredulity and something like relief: there was a reason this was happening, and it was nothing to do with him or his children.

Louise spat fire at him, using only her eyes. 'She's not here yet,' she repeated.

'We need to go inside,' the Gun said.

Going inside meant putting walls round the situation. It was containment, but it meant containing herself, and the twins, and Eliot, with it.

There was little choice involved. But what little there was, she'd grab while she could.

'Then we have to go in there,' she said, pointing towards the annexe. And started moving again, to show she meant it.

She sensed rather than saw what happened behind her: the men and the boys frozen for a moment; the larger pair by uncertainty; the smaller by being locked in orbit round the uncertain. And there was an invisible thread connecting Louise to the four of them, and the further she got, the tauter it stretched . . . If it broke now, something awful would happen; and with that thought she slowed, stopped, just a few feet short of the gate that hung open in front of her, just this side of the thread's breaking point. Behind her the boy said something: words she didn't catch. And then came footsteps, and they were following her – she reached the gate, went through it, and a moment later all five were the other side of those railings, and the boy was shutting the gate behind them. But it remained unlocked, the keys on the other side – somewhere in the grass, where Louise had flung them on her way through.

'We go inside.'

(That was how it was when you had a gun. Whatever

55

happened was your idea. Though Louise was just as happy to let him take the credit.)

Timmy said, 'This's the palace.'

'Hush, Timmy.'

'Wha' did Timmy say?'

'Gordon—'

'Wha' did Timmy say, Daddy?'

'Hush.'

Louise pushed open the door of the annexe – the palace – and went in, followed by Eliot/Timmy/Gordon all in one mass; then the Gun, following so close he was part of the community.

The room was long and narrow; lengthwise, it ran adjacent to the footpath heading to the railway line. The wall on that side had no windows, and so had become an art gallery by default – primary-coloured splodges and potato shapes triumphantly labelled Mummy and Daddy; some Miss Kennedys too, as well as a Queen. The absence of windows was to prevent lookers-in. The days when watching infants' innocent pursuits was an innocent pursuit were long gone.

Against the narrow wall at the adventure park end of the annexe was a stainless steel sink and draining board, above which, out of reach of hurtable hands, hung a water boiler, from which a hot water tap descended on a swivel. There was a door either side of this fixture: one leading to a toilet; the other to an office which doubled as a sickroom, and was the space in which emergencies were dealt with. Windows punctuated the other long wall – to Louise's left as she entered – and these served as natural dividers; the space between the second and third being the soft play area where mats were piled, and a circular plastic-mesh playpen sequestered a menagerie of squashy gonks and ungendered mannequins. At the far end, a waist-high arrangement of hooks was known as Cloakroom Corner. Between the first and second window, on a wobbly plastic table, sat a hamster cage. The floor below it was scattered now with its usual morning libations: lengths of straw and flakes of cereal; balls of hamster shit. This confection always struck Louise as a curiously tidy mess, being arranged as an outward-flowing spray with a razor-sharp edge, dictated by the tabletop two feet above. As for the hamster itself, by popular poll it was called Trixie, though had only been two votes short of being Wayne Rooney. Allotting a name by ballot was a useful way of introducing the concept of democracy to the under fours, and the hamster was itself a means of broaching the possibility of death, in a gentle, not terribly important way. Though not so unimportant Louise had confessed it when, arriving on Trixie's third day, she'd found the beast had turned its toes up: one frantic dash to the pet shop later, and a very similar hamster was in residence. ('She's grown a new spot!' an observant child had exclaimed. 'So she has!' said Louise.)

The metal shutters over the windows meant the day had made few inroads yet, though through the skylight a grey imitation of April filtered down on everything. The smells were of children, hamster, paint, glue, the toilet, yesterday's lunch, and hand cream.

Into none of this was supposed to wander a man with a gun.

The door that shut behind them sounded, to Louise's ears, like a shot.

3

THE WAY SAM CHAPMAN saw it, three things happened in life:

1. You did your job faultlessly and didn't get thanked, or
2. you fucked up and were
3. dumped on from a great height.

Chapman was hovering around the two-and-a-bit mark; waiting for the other shoe to drop. The thing was, not to let anyone know he was doing just that. There was always a chance he could clean up before the Office released the Dogs. The fact that he was Head Dog was an irony not bringing him great pleasure.

Meanwhile, he was being kept waiting. This was in the police station, foot of St Aldate's, Oxford, within whose walls Bad Sam Chapman was halfway between nasty smell and suspect device, as if his appearance could only trigger catastrophe. Policemen don't like spooks. That was okay. Chapman didn't like policemen.

Edgy, tense, Chapman was a short, dark, sharp-featured man, so in an ideal world would have resembled Al Pacino. But where Pacino's terrier intensity and brooding surliness added up to sexual magnetism, in Sam Chapman the same combination produced a dangerous sulk. Besides, his features weren't arranged like Pacino's — instead, he resembled an ageing football hooligan in a suit. Late forties; a number two cut not quite eradicating the grey; brown eyes deep enough that getting to the bottom of them was no simple matter – an ex-wife could have glossed on this. Currently, he was sitting in a plastic bucket seat that doubtless figured on an Amnesty International to-do list, facing a noticeboard whose posters reminded onlookers that they'd recently been mugged, burgled, assaulted or had their bike nicked, though anyone close enough to read probably remembered that's why they were here. And, every time he closed his eyes he was back in the lay-by, watching a big car making a mess of Neil Ashton. He'd been folded like a piece of damp laundry when Chapman reached him. The gun was nowhere – you had to assume Segura had taken it.

It was likely Ashton had a girlfriend somewhere – possibly even a mother – and either or both would be receiving grim phone calls about now. Which was sad, but when you scraped away the sentiment Neil Ashton had displayed a gun on a *collect and comfort*, then compounded the error by losing it. He'd better hope he died on the operating table, because if he ever walked upright again, Sam Chapman would break him in two and kick the halves in different directions.

Blessed are the unforgiving, for they shall come out even. That was the lost frigging beatitude as far as Bad Sam Chapman was concerned. As for the meek: we'll make them give it back.

A police officer, not a day over seventeen, appeared in the doorway and beckoned him to follow. Beckoned – not invited. But house rules were in play, so Chapman rose and went with her: down a corridor, through a safety door, up a stairwell, through another door – a labyrinth to disorient suspects. He wasn't a suspect, of course; a fact it would be wise to keep in mind, given God only knew how today would pan out. In Bad Sam's experience, what started badly soon got worse.

The last door boasted a plastic strip reading *Superintendent Malcolm Fredericks*. The officer knocked, an 'Enter' was barked, the door was opened, the officer retreated, and Chapman was inside, looking at Superintendent Malcolm Fredericks, who didn't rise, offer his hand, or invite Chapman to sit. Instead he said, 'I presume you have ID?'

Wordlessly, Chapman showed him a card he could have run up in a stationer's half an hour previously. But there were rings you had to jump through when you'd fucked up. Like tumbling down a snake in the game: once you'd thrown a bad number, you were at the mercy of the board.

'It would have been courteous to let us know you were running an operation in the area.'

'It wasn't exactly an operation.'

'Wasn't it? And what was it, then? Exactly?'

'We were picking up a witness.'

'Well, what a splendid job you made of it. In my line of work, we'd call that an arrest. And when it's planned in advance, we'd describe it as an operation.'

'It wasn't an arrest,' Sam Chapman said.

'But you were armed.'

'No.'

'Your companion was armed.'

'I hadn't been aware of that.'

'You hadn't been aware of that.'

It was a technique Chapman used himself: repeat the last thing said in a tone somewhere between incredulity and sarcasm. *Exactly how stupid would I have to be to believe that?* And Malcolm Fredericks didn't look stupid: he had one of those open, intelligent faces Chapman just naturally wanted to give bad news to.

'What exactly was this witness a witness to?'

'I can't tell you that.'

'Do you know, that's the answer I was expecting?'

Chapman shrugged.

'The gun was lost,' Fredericks said.

Chapman nodded.

'And now could be anywhere.'

'It's pretty clear who has it.'

'And is he dangerous?'

Well, he has a fucking gun, Chapman thought. Join the dots. But what he said was what he'd practised saying, sitting in that plastic chair: 'I suspect his intention will be to disappear. Head underground.'

Fredericks said, 'Let's cut to the chase. We're talking about terrorism, is that right?'

'I can't answer that.'

'Your fuck-up has put an armed terrorist on the streets of my city. No, let's get this straight. Your fuck-up has armed a terrorist and put him on the streets of my city.'

'I imagine he'll leave your city as soon as possible.'

'Well, what a relief. But forgive me if I don't base the official response to this on what you might imagine.' He did something with his hands: rearranged some biros, or perhaps shifted a small piece of desk furniture from one side of his blotter to the other. Physical punctuation; the prelude to a new mode of discourse. He was about to deliver instruction. 'I'll need a description. I expect it to be a good one.'

Chapman showed his palms, fingers wide. 'I didn't get much of a look, I'm afraid.'

Fredericks stared long enough that a lesser man would have confessed.

A police car left the station a couple of storeys below, siren wailing. Traffic stopped to let it out; it zipped round a corner; everything returned to normal.

Fredericks said, 'I thought you people kept files on your targets.'

'Witnesses.'

'You're coming very close to crossing a line you don't want to cross.'

Chapman said, 'It was Ashton's call. I was along to observe.'

'He was new to the job?'

'I'm not sure he's in the past tense yet. But either way, no, he's not.'

'So what are you, his line manager?'

Chapman said, 'We're all slaves to procedure, aren't we?'

Fredericks picked up a pencil – he actually had a pencil on his desk. Chapman wondered what he used it for. He rolled it briefly between finger and thumb as if it were a cigar, then put it back. He might have liked to snap it, but had too much control. That was how you climbed the ladder in the Force these days. A big reason Sam Chapman was glad he'd never worn the uniform.

'We've got a lorry driver,' Fredericks said at last, 'who saw the whole thing.'

Chapman didn't answer. It wasn't, after all, a question.

'When we find this man of yours,' Fredericks went on, 'I'm going to have a long talk with him. Personally.'

Chapman said, 'Now, there we have a line that *you* don't want to cross.'

Fredericks looked at him long and hard, and the spook looked right back through him – Fredericks was nothing more than an interruption of his view of an office wall. Chapman's eyes had a vacancy Fredericks hadn't often seen. The time that came to mind was a years-old event: an arrest he'd made, his first summer on the Job. The eyes belonged to a sanitation engineer; a binman as was. And the blood on his shirt had belonged to his family, whom he'd just murdered for, as he explained to PC Malcolm Fredericks, 'a very good reason'.

When more than enough time had passed, Chapman said, 'When he turns up, I'll be informed immediately. Don't question him. Don't release him into anyone else's custody.'

'Who the hell do you think you are?'

Chapman nodded towards the window. 'Remember those

streets? Walking the beat?' He stood. 'I'm the man who'll have you back doing that if you even think about interfering with my job.' He produced a card and tossed it on to Fredericks' desk. It showed a mobile number; nothing else. 'Immediately. Got that?' Then he left.

Out on those streets he'd mentioned, Sam Chapman took a deep breath: petrol fumes, mostly. They didn't mention that in the tourist guides. Crossing at the lights, he headed up to the city centre. Cup of coffee: first place he came to. He hadn't been offered any at the copshop; the whole encounter had not been wisely handled. But he'd never been good with uniforms. And besides, the thing about making enemies was, they worked harder to fuck you up. Jaime Segura wouldn't be on the streets long. Fredericks would have him collared, just to show who ran this place.

And then Fredericks would hand him over, because one thing a ranking officer wouldn't risk was his status.

The grey morning was breaking up; shafts of sunlight slicing through cloudmass to pick out local landmarks – a tower here, a spire there; a DIY superstore over to the west. Might turn out a good one, but you couldn't base judgements on passing interludes. The day so far had been full of deceptive appearances. The op, for instance, had been a collect and comfort, or that's how it would appear on the books.

But Jaime Segura had never been meant to survive it.

So far, she'd been operating on remote. That part of Louise Kennedy that had made her run towards the Gun instead of away wasn't a part she was in daily contact with, though she could recognise it as a survival instinct, appearances to the contrary notwithstanding – if she'd reached that gate first, she wouldn't be in this room now. The chances of leaving which didn't look pretty. Guns and schools didn't mix.

63

And there were other parts of her, too; parts which hadn't done anything brave lately, not even to save herself – one was curled into a ball in the darkest room her consciousness could find, waiting until this was over. Another part was blaming her mother – there was a good solid reason for this; an unbreakable link in a chain of logic she couldn't lay a hand on right now – and another still was blaming Eliot, whose undeniable guilt was scribbled all over the fact of his presence. She hadn't blamed the boys, though their turn might yet come. And curiously, she wasn't blaming the gunman, either – the gunman was a given right now; above criticism, because he was what everything else was about.

All of which might have her screaming any moment but she had to take a grip because nobody else was going to, that was clear . . .

Five of them, then. Thrust into this room built for twenty: one had a gun, another had two boys, and only she had a voice it seemed, because nobody else was saying anything, though the boys were whimpering in a peculiarly syncopated way. She had to speak because whatever made the silence collapse, she didn't want it to be the Gun.

Emotion triggers emotion. *Keep calm.* There was a formula for this; you took control—

'Who are you? What do you want?'

he had a gun he had a gun he had a gun

'You're the lady?'

he had a gun

'I'm – who are you, what do you want, this is a *nursery school* –'

And she bit her tongue: don't tell him *that*. As if, by not mentioning its purpose, she could disguise the school's reality, and thereby neutralise his intent. You didn't carry a gun into a nursery for fun. If they could all pretend it was a barracks, a Territorial Army hangout, somewhere this might pass for a practical joke . . .

He said, 'The lady is the teacher, yes?'

Louise said, 'I don't know which lady you mean.'

Eliot caught her eye but said nothing.

The gunman looked around. He stood between them and the door, and seemed to become aware of this as he took in the surroundings: with his weapon, he waved them further inside, reducing – Louise supposed – the chances they might rush him . . . yeah, right. Maybe Eliot could pick up a twin and throw it. Draw his fire. Eliot, who was hobbled by his boys; they clung to his legs like a pair of clown's trousers as he shuffled backwards past the hamster cage, whose occupant chose that moment to push her snout through the bars – please don't shoot Trixie. The chances of a second successful substitution were not good. Perhaps Trixie caught Louise's thought wave, or perhaps gun recognition was filtering down the food chain; either way, she retreated into her straw castle without even a token spin on her wheel as they all edged past to the soft-play area, a more optimistic setting for an armed siege. If that's what this was.

Against a rising red panic, Louise tried to mentally clamp down: she was on home territory; these were familiar surroundings. There must be a way of establishing control, because that's what she did here every day – the Darlings weren't armed, of course, or not so far, but a battle or two of nerves had occurred, and she hadn't lost hers yet. There was an overlap between what was happening now and what ought to be, and she knew – because this was the golden rule: in teaching, in business, in sport, in love – that whoever took charge in the first few moments stood the best chance of coming first. Every other cell in her body was screaming at her to give up, lie down, take shelter, but the moment she did that it was over. She had to do what she could before events took control, and the natural momentum of catastrophe splashed the four of them across the furnishings.

She looked at him. He had the gun, but he wasn't only a Gun; before he'd picked that weapon up he'd been a boy, and she doubted she'd have noticed him – there was beauty here, true, but it was the beauty of youth, and it had been a while since that was of anything but theoretical interest to Louise. He wasn't looking back – was taking in the surroundings: the exits; the windows – but the intensity of her gaze must have registered, because his eyes were suddenly on her, and they weren't just deep and brown, they were bottomless. It was like staring down a well. Her first reaction was to pull back in case she dropped, but that would be to let the situation slide . . . She spoke instead. 'My name's Louise.'

He didn't reply.

'Louise Kennedy. I'm the nursery assistant. Second in command.' *Second in command?* Words were like that – they escaped without warning; attached themselves vaguely to the meaning you'd intended, then burst into the open air. This could be a nightmare at dinner parties. Here and now, though, it wasn't likely there'd be arguments about nomenclature. He still didn't reply.

'And this is Eliot Pedlar. He's one of our parents. And these are his boys, Timothy and Gordon. Timmy and Gordy. They're twins.'

Twins and terrified, but quiet now – one each side of Eliot; Timmy clutching his right knee, Gordy his left. Eliot had an arm round each; was trying to divide his attention three ways – two parts for his boys; the third for the gun.

'They're nearly four years old.'

Become a person. Wasn't that the mantra? She'd read an article; an interview with a woman who'd disarmed a multiple killer after he'd taken her hostage. She *became a person*, a risk-control expert had concluded – odd phrase; as if the process involved effort. But the point was, she made it difficult for him to treat her as an object . . . She'd managed this with God on her side, Louise recalled – well, Louise was going to have to cope without God. Any God that fell for a conversion under these circumstances wasn't as omniscient as She ought to be.

'Maybe you should tell us what you want. Maybe if we talked about this, we'd find . . .' Find what? Find a useful noun: answers, resolution, peace. 'Maybe we'd find a way out of this. Nobody has to get hurt.' And again came that clunking feeling, as if she were putting ideas in his head.

Absurd. He'd crashed into her nursery, gun in hand. The idea of causing harm was not new to him.

'Are you going to tell us your name?'

That way you'll be a person too.

'Or tell us what you want?'

Or show us what's under your jacket? A Semtex bandolier; a jury-rigged belt of plastic explosives?

There was sudden clarity in the image that reached Louise then; of how this was going to look later, all over the world. Views of the school she'd elected as a refuge from personal strife would be beamed into homes in Paris, Sydney, Houston; less a sanctuary than an object of pity and terror, with a scrolling text updating channel-hoppers as to what they'd missed so far. In Wimbledon, Crispin would watch, and just for a moment his eyebrows would knit – *Oxford? Wasn't that where that girl ended up – what was her name again?* 'Oh, nothing, darling. Just wool-gathering.' His eyebrows proved that.

'Please . . . ?'

'You're the lady?'

'I don't know,' she said honestly. 'I don't know which lady you mean. Who are you looking for?'

He released a snort of air through his nostrils, making a bullish, frustrated noise that recalled one of her Darlings: a sweet troublemaker; happy as Christmas, right up to the moment things stopped going his way. Then there'd be tears, and broken bits to sweep up; cross words and necessary admonishments. If any of that happened now, the broken bits might be a bit more difficult to tidy away.

'Please?' she said.

In the back of her mind, the clock was ticking . . . Dave would arrive. The gate would be opened. Parents and children would flock in, some of them coming through the door behind the Gun: he would turn in alarm, his hand would clench, the trigger would squeeze . . .

And then came a sudden calm, as if the world wound down for a second – she'd heard of such moments; moments of crisis in which time slowed so you could appreciate its subtler workings. She was looking into his eyes, and there might have been understanding there; a nanosecond in which the bigger picture asserted itself, teaching him that whatever twisted motive had propelled him here was wrong; that he shouldn't do what he planned on doing . . . Whatever that was. Anything might happen.

He opened his mouth to speak.

Please, she thought, in a sudden access of desperate clarity – *please don't ask if I'm the fucking lady again . . .*

Something collapsed.

He fired the gun.

The trouble with Louise Kennedy was –

(The trouble with Judy Ainsworth was; too many of her thoughts began *The trouble with somebody else . . .*) –

The trouble with Louise Kennedy was, she was too big for her boots. Hardly been here a year, and acting like she was in charge the moment Claire wasn't about.

I'm sure she'll only be too happy to listen to your latest grievance.

Judy had a routine, same as everyone had a routine. The difference between this routine and the one she'd once had was, this one was imposed on her by other people. A checklist had been drawn up for her – not for her, even; the checklist had already existed when she took the position – and what she was supposed to do was, well, check it off. Do this, then do that. This is the order you do it in.

Which, right there, was life in a nutshell. You did one thing, then moved on to the next. Except you didn't always – you hardly ever – got to say when you wanted one thing to stop and the next to start.

What had happened to Judy was precisely that: one thing had stopped, then everything else had started. She hadn't been ready. Still wasn't. And while it would never have been true to call her a happy woman, she had the trick, in common with the rest of humanity, of painting a different picture when the canvas demanded. Looking back on how life used to be she saw a picture of content, in which even Derek had been a welcome fixture. There'd been a wedding photo on the mantelpiece of the home she'd thought they owned. She'd burned it after finding out about the other woman; burning being the appropriate response, given everything that came after.

First one thing, then the next. That was the order things always happened.

So this morning, after Ms Up-Herself Kennedy's *only too happy to listen to your latest grievance*, Judy had mentally torn her checklist up: if Loubloodyise didn't like it, she could complain to Claire; then we'd see which way the wind blew. Claire was a fair woman, with the sense to know that bad luck visited everyone, even those who didn't deserve it. She'd sense the injustice in Kennedy playing high and mighty just because her name appeared on a staff register while others were reduced to mopping and dusting.

He had been in construction. Derek had built things. That, too, was an injustice, when you considered the wreckage he'd left in his wake.

So anyway, where was she? Adjusting the checklist was where; she'd do things in her own order, especially if that meant keeping clear of Louise Kennedy in the meantime – she didn't trust herself, Judy didn't, not to give her a piece of her mind; and Louise needn't think Judy hadn't noticed that little spectacle by the school gates. The pair of them having a nice little chat: don't tell Judy there was nothing going on. Something else Claire was fair and commonsensical about. She wouldn't be putting up with any of that nonsense from the staff, no matter what high-powered job in the City they'd come from.

Run from, you wanted Judy's opinion. Who surrendered money like that to come and teach in a nursery school? Guilty secrets hid everywhere, and you weren't telling her Louise Kennedy didn't have a peach.

So where Judy was was in the annexe, where she wasn't supposed to be until after she'd done the kitchen in the main building (which was how it worked on the checklist: kitchen, toilets, cloakroom – tick tick tick – then the floors). And what she'd been doing was examining Louise Kennedy's desk, in the tiny office up the far end; the office the same size as the toilet it shared an adjoining wall with. It wasn't as if she expected to find anything revealing – sly cats like Kennedy don't leave secrets in the open – but that was no good reason not to look. But the desk had been bare. Just registration sheets, a few pages scrawled with indecipherable jottings, and bits and pieces of desk-junk: paperclips rubbers pens pencils, like that. A small collection of pencil-top gonks and gremlins; an occupational hazard of working with children – the things they thought were precious, they sometimes gave away. Even Judy had something: a one-inch plastic bear, moulded to look like it wore a leather jacket and sunglasses. It had come from a cornflake packet: did the child not think Judy realized that? She didn't even know why she'd kept it, but it sat, anyway, on the table in the corner of her room. But no secrets here. The drawers just held supplies: elastic-banded bundles of crayons and felt-tips; old Christmas cards, ready to be cut up for next year's decorations. Judy skimmed a few, but they were donated; none addressed to Louise herself. Too sly for that . . .

Someone entered the annexe.

No: some people entered the annexe. More than one. It was too early for parents and children; too early for Dave too – he was another: timed his arrival to get here with the mothers, though Judy thought that was him being clever; there was something light-of-tread about Dave . . . It must be Kennedy, with company. They didn't know Judy was here, and she was about to open the door – just march out: this was part of her job, cleaning the office – but stopped. There was a man out there. Judy didn't know who, but then Judy didn't know the parents; it wasn't like they formed a queue to meet the woman who cleaned up their kids' mess. But whoever it was, Judy wanted to hear about it, so instead of opening the door she leaned against it, ear to the wood, her right hand holding the door tight shut, the way an expert eavesdropper might.

Who are you? What do you want?

You're the lady?

I'm – who are you, what do you want, this is a nursery school—

It had the quality of a TV show that had been going on some time, and wasn't the one she'd been expecting; as if Judy had switched channels in search of a romantic comedy – because what was funnier than romance – and found instead a brutal moment from a soap opera, in which familiar surroundings became the backdrop to the latest issue: rape, domestic violence, terrorism . . .

My name's Louise Kennedy. I'm the nursery assistant. Second in command. And this is Eliot Pedlar. And these are his boys.

Something was wrong. The words fitted an ordinary context – an inspection; a model parent rolled out, with appropriate children – but when that happened there was preparation involved; extra polishing required. And Kennedy's voice wasn't normal. In place of that confident tone – the one that said she was doing you a favour, just breathing your air — something wavered, and nearly broke.

Judy pressed closer to the door.

Maybe you should tell us what it is you want . . . Nobody has to get hurt . . .

Judy snatched her hand from the handle: what was going on? There was danger behind this door, and if she'd kept to the checklist, she'd be out of its reach — yards and walls away, with iron railings between her and whatever Louise had brought into this nursery.

I don't know which lady you mean. Who is it you're looking for?

One moment Judy was by the door, ear to the wood — *You're the lady?* — and the next she was falling through it, because her grip on the handle had slipped, or her knee gave way — it was hard to tell the precise order of events; the exact thing that happened that preceded the next thing happening . . . And it barely mattered, in the long run. Whatever: she lost her balance. Gravity took control.

She fell through the door.

And somebody shot her.

That moment Louise had noticed — the one in which time slowed, allowing insight into the inner workings of stuff — didn't stretch far; serious confusion followed the gunshot, and Louise's main concern was whether or not she was hurt. It was as if a curtain had fallen between one event and the next: she'd been watching the boy, but couldn't work out whether the gun had been pointing at her when he fired — if she'd been shot it would hurt, yes? But she suspected, from having read a regrettable number of thrillers, that when you were shot, the hurt came later — as if bullet-pain were a subtle social slight; the sting registering afterwards, on your way out of the room.

But Louise wasn't leaving the room, and it wasn't her he'd shot at . . .

All of this, of course, took no time; noise was still bouncing off the walls, looking for an escape route, and there was screaming from various sources, herself among them. The boy, though, was silent. Only a tremble at his lips betrayed emotion. His eyes were still black depths, fixed on a point behind Louise's back – the point from which another noise was issuing, she realized at last; a screaming that wasn't herself, or the boys, or Eliot . . . She turned.

It was Judy.

Something collapsed, she'd thought, a second before the gun had gone off, and Judy was what it had been: Judy had collapsed through the door into the office, and in falling on to this larger stage had drawn fire from its principal player. She looked like baggage was Louise's unkind thought, and then her second reaction took over, which was that Judy wasn't shot at all – only one bullet had been fired, and above the door frame where she now crouched a small round hole had been punched. It was leaking plaster dust, a tiny cloud of it dancing around its circumference. Judy's screaming diminished all at once, as if she'd come through an inverse of Louise's journey moments ago, and had worked out, from the absence of pain, that she wasn't in fact dead.

And just like that, the noise all ceased.

The boy with the gun looked at Louise. 'I did not shoot her.'

'I know.'

'She is not shot.'

Before this could turn into a grammar lesson, Louise knelt by Judy's fallen form. Judy's eyes were open, but right that moment she wasn't seeing anything – they were dark holes; broken windows in an empty house.

'Judy?'

Then the usual human light filtered to the surface, and Judy's eyes were hurt, frightened, hateful, confused, shocked . . .

Timmy looked up at his father. 'Is that lady dead?'

'Hush.'

Louise said, 'Nobody's dead. The gun went off, that's all. Nobody's hurt.'

'But—'

'Hush.'

Judy moaned something unintelligible, then licked her lips, leaving a faint white sheen on them. Louise suppressed a shudder.

'Wha—'

'You're okay.'

'Bitch,' Judy said, quite clearly.

'Stand away.' The gunman again. 'Stand away from her.'

Louise did as she was told. Judy was no more hurt than a sudden tumble causes.

'Get up now.'

Judy looked at him murderously, but with more fear than contempt in the mix. 'What's going on?'

'You will get up.'

She did. There was a crazy, graceless stagger in her movements, and her attention was now focused on Louise. 'What's going on?' she said again. 'This is you, isn't it?'

Oh, for God's sake . . .

Louise faced the gunman. 'What do you want?' she said.

'Your phones,' he said. 'Your mobile telephones.'

This wasn't the answer she'd been expecting.

'Now! On the floor. Put your mobile phones on the floor.'

'I don't have one,' she told him.

'Yes! Put it on the floor!'

'I mean, I've got one, but not with me. It's in the other office.'

Do you want me to go and fetch it? A giggle threatened to erupt.

'You others. Your phones.'

Eliot said, 'Mine's . . . it's in my car. I don't have it with me.'

'You?'

This was to Judy. She was shaking her head too.

'The boys?'

'Well, of course not, they're children.'

'Children have such things.'

'They're *three*,' Eliot said.

Three adults, two children, and not a mobile between them. Hold the press. Louise wondered why he'd wanted them, and the unwanted answer popped up immediately: he didn't want them; he wanted them not to have them. So they couldn't use them. Couldn't call for help.

Why was he here? What did he want?

'Against the wall. All of you go there.'

'Why?'

'Just go. All of you. Where I can see you.'

Gordy started to cry: a heartbreaking, end-of-his-tether sob.

His father scooped him up one-armed; gathered Timmy closer with the other. 'Come on. It's okay. It's going to be all right.'

Why tell them that? How can you know? Louise remembered the weeks following the suicide bombings in London, and the countless accounts of the near misses everyone had suffered: the Tube just missed; the change in routine; the five minutes that had made all the difference. And underneath that, the untouchable certainty that terrorism happened to other people . . . But here it was, a happening fact: real, live, now. And she did not know that it was going to turn out all right. It was possible that it wouldn't.

Judy said, 'You brought him here, didn't you?'

'Judy—'

'And he's going to kill us all!'

'Shut up!' It made it worse that she'd just had such thoughts herself. She dropped her voice. 'Think about the boys.'

Eliot said, 'Both of you be quiet.' He spoke to the gunman. 'What do you want? Do you seriously think any good can come of this?'

'Against the wall. Please.'

The windowless wall, he meant. Louise reached it without consciously covering any ground – were those the last steps she'd ever take? He couldn't just shoot them, could he? But that was what terrorists did: they perpetrated pointless acts of violence, whose victims were never more than counters on a board game. It was only afterwards that they'd be listed in newspapers, alongside inappropriate smiling photographs. While it was happening, they were less than human; their only purpose, to prove someone else's point.

Become a person . . .

She said, 'You haven't told us your name yet.'

Judy stared at her as if she were insane. If Louise could have killed Judy with a look, she'd have done so; though admittedly, that might have been self-defeating. She risked a glance at her watch, and it told her time had passed; that it was 8:40; that any moment she'd hear the nursery gates opening as Dave arrived, followed by parents and hordes of tinies . . . She'd been wondering how things could get worse, and there was her answer. There could be more children – more unwitting counters – and this gunman could panic, and start picking them off.

He said, 'It is not important.'

'It is to me. I've told you my name, I've told you all our names. Oh, except Judy's. This is Judy Ainsworth. She's our cleaner.'

'You *fucking cow* . . .'

He said, 'Please. Against the wall.'

'You're not going to shoot us, are you?'

'I hope not to shoot anyone.'

He *hoped* . . .

'I just want order.'

And now Timmy began to cry.

'Make the boy stop.'

Eliot flashed him a parent's look as he crouched so Timmy could lean into him. With Gordon already wrapped round him, he was starting to look like a game of hide and seek. 'I'll try. But he's only small, and he's not used to having guns pointed—'

'Eliot,' Louise said. There'd been a creeping inflection in his voice: climbing towards hysteria. A tone children's ears were quick to pick up, the way dogs heard the higher registers. 'Let me take him.'

Timmy didn't want to go – when the familiar world was collapsing into threat and loud noises, his father's arms were the safest place to be. But his father only had two arms, and Gordon wasn't surrendering either.

'Timmy? It's okay, Timmy. Come with me for now. Nothing's going to happen. We'll just sit quietly, and everything'll be sorted out in no time.'

Amazing what you could say when you needed to. There was always a lie handy when the alternative was unthinkable.

Timmy, slowly, tearfully, crossed a yard of floor and fell into her, sobbing.

Hoisting him into her arms, Louise heard the first of the morning's cars arriving.

A small but not insignificant gaggle was waiting when Dave Osborne arrived: three mothers, seven children – part of the local boxing and coxing: mums transporting kids plus chums in exchange for an about-turn next week. All on foot so far, though there was a car pulling up, and a small bike heading down the road in a slow, wobbly way with a not-much-less-wobbly big bike behind it, cycling slowly being a skill that eluded many adults. His own machine, a gleaming 25-speed top-whack RoadBuster, would probably move backwards if he wanted it to, but right now he was allowing it to glide gracefully to a halt even as he lifted his right leg over its frame to touch earth; feeling like a world-class showjumper, though he'd never sat on a horse in his life. Didn't matter. Three or four of those watching thought him capable of riding anything he wanted. One or two probably wished it was them.

He was good with names: Bryony, Carrie, Jane, Mishka.

He could do the children too, no sweat.

'Morning, ladies. Morning, kids.'

'What time you call this?'

'You know how long we've been here?'

This friendly chorus of complaint was his daily welcome.

'Twenty-four seconds, max. I missed the lights at Donnington Bridge by a gnat's whisker.'

Bryony and Jane were blonde, or passing; Carrie and Mishka dark. Average age: call it thirty-four. Did it matter what he planned to do with these statistics? He didn't plan to do anything – he just loved being among the women, that was all; there was a secret knowledge in their easy friendship, a secret he shared with every one of them: that each, solely and alone, was the woman he thought about when the others were absent. Not true of every last mother in the nursery, of course – this kind of fun got dangerous when the desperate or cynical joined in – but the point was, he loved his job. Some mornings, it was like a front-row ticket to *Desperate Housewives*.

It helped he liked children, too.

It was the kids he turned to as he hoisted his featherweight bike on to one shoulder and made for the gate. 'Now, which of you can remember the number?'

Ali, Amy, Caspar, Julius, Lawrence and Piers produced a communal giggle; Wanda a 'We don't knoooooooowww, silly.'

'Don't call David silly,' Bryony warned.

'But he *is* silly, we don't know the number.'

'Nobody knows the number,' Caspar said.

'Looks like we're stuck then,' Dave said cheerfully. 'Unless I can . . . Let me see.'

Bike still balanced on one shoulder, he took a supporting hand away – favourite trick for the little ones, this – and pinched the bridge of his nose while squeezing his eyes shut. Deep thought. More giggles from the tinies and indulgent smiles from the yummies. 'Who's got a favourite number?'

'Ninety-nine.'

'A million.'

'A hundred and eleventy.'

'Four,' said Amy shyly. 'That's my next birthday.'

'Well, let's try four, shall we?'

Opening his eyes, Dave resisted the temptation to wink at any of the mothers – even Carrie – covered the keypad with one hand, and tapped in the code with the other. 'Four,' he said. 'What do you know?' The green light flashed, and he pushed the gate open.

'That wasn't four!'

'It added up to four,' he said.

'Thank you,' Amy whispered.

He let them trot in, and left the gate open: it was 8:45. Louise would be here, along with Broody Judy; the latter in the annexe by now, and Lou – he had to remember never to call her that – probably in the office. U-locking his bike to the railings, he stood looking down the road another moment. Those cyclists were almost here now, and a nearby car was being unloaded. The school run mostly meant the combustion engine. Dave tried not to be a pain about this, but had his opinions. Come to think of it, he recognized that car up the way – the red one with a sloping bonnet: Christine. Mother of twin boys. She must have arrived early. The boys – Timmy and Gordon – were generally keen on staking their claim to the day. They must be kicking a ball on the rec ground, and lost track of time. They'd be here soon.

His bike firmly attached to the railing, he followed the mothers and children inside.

There was a mural on one of the walls in the main building, painted by the children; it showed all the known planets in the solar system, but what Louise most liked it for was a comment by Amy, a shy little girl. 'Everything's in the right place,' she'd confided, and it was clear from her smile that this satisfied a major demand of her own universe.

Not much was in its right place now. There was a man with a gun where he shouldn't be, and there were people in the nursery grounds – she could hear the hum of incoming life. The gate leading to the annexe was open; the keys lying on the grass where she'd flung them. Someone would be coming this way soon: Dave, a parent, children. A situation teetering on the edge of violent calamity was about to get worse. She didn't know what could be done about this.

Her back to the windowless wall, Louise could see the door through which the children would come; could already picture the carnage as the gunman opened fire. It would not last long – he appeared to have only the one weapon. Louise knew nothing about guns, beyond the brutal fact of their existence, but understood that, technically, the damage he could do was limited to the number of bullets it held. That merely accounted for physical damage, of course. The wider hurt would spread outwards; it would scar those who hadn't yet heard of South Oxford Nursery School, and become one of those dates etched on the public consciousness, like 9/11 or 7/7. In a strange way, freedom came with this knowledge. The time was past for worrying about the complications of her life. Where she was now put her beyond the trivial; or rather, redefined as trivial what she'd previously considered problems.

'Now what?' she heard herself say. Her voice was strained

and peculiar, as if it were a recording. 'We're where you wanted us. Now what?'

He didn't look like he knew now what – looked as if he were the one under duress. 'Where is everybody else?' he said at last.

'People are coming. I can hear them.'

'They will come in here?'

'Only when the security guard lets them,' Louise said. 'We have a security guard. Didn't you see the signs?'

(A generic warning placard: *Guards with dogs patrol this site.*)

He said, 'I don't believe you.'

'When he finds the outer gate open – the one we came through? The gate in the railings? When he finds it hanging open, he'll call the police. That's standard procedure.'

'That is not how things work here.'

'The police respond very quickly. The station's just a quarter of a mile away.'

In this, at least, she was not lying.

'The police will come, I know this. But they will not enter here, in case I shoot you.'

Timmy stiffened at *shoot*; she felt his panic-tremor in her bones. But she had to keep her own voice steady; had to fight the contagion, before it overwhelmed them all. 'And what then? What is it you *want*?'

He said something – a name? Whistler – and the door behind him opened.

Carrie Mannion had charge of three that morning; her own pair – Caspar and Piers – and little Amy, her friend Fi's daughter. They alternated weeks shuffling the pack into school, and as far as Carrie was concerned, she got the best of the deal, because Caspar and Piers, being boys, outnumbered Amy six to one. Amy was perhaps the sweetest child Carrie knew, in a not especially crowded field. Boys were mostly who she contended with. Her own were magnificent, obviously, but their friends – if evidence didn't exist that the occasional boy grew up into Dave Osborne, there'd be little call for them.

There was a level on which she pretended to believe that; another on which she knew it for a joke; and a third on which – well, Dave was one of those men put on earth to worry husbands. Pretending not to notice him was ignoring a rule of nature.

Caspar had trotted into the main building; Piers, her youngest, had scampered off; was rooting around in the grass. He'd probably found a worms' nest. 'Don't get dirty, darling. We're hardly here yet.'

Amy was holding her hand – little girls: the sweet things they did that made adults happy. And would cause them no end of worry and grief, a decade down the line.

'Where's Miss Kennedy?' she asked.

'I don't know, Amy.'

'She's *usually* by the big doors. She *usually* says hello.'

The big doors were those into the main building – this was how smaller universes were arranged. You started at home, and next came the Palace; after that, you were through the Big Doors. One by one, the mysteries of growing up revealed themselves in their two-dimensional glory. Until you were left half wishing you could start again; half relieved the process was over.

'Piers?'

'I'm *coming*, Mummy!'

As if it were a completely unreasonable request, to expect him to get up off his knees on the damp grass.

'I expect she's in the annexe already,' Carrie continued.

'The Palace,' Amy said shyly, as if revealing an important secret.

'The Palace.'

Which was a deeply uninspiring building, in fact – looked

82

exactly what it was: a temporary erection which, for reasons of economy, had endured. A recent coat of paint – eggshell white; green borders – lifted it out of the eyesore bracket, but a palace? You had to be a child.

The door was shut but not, she assumed, locked – Louise Kennedy must be inside; she'd evidently arrived, as the main nursery was open, and she wasn't anywhere else in evidence. As Carrie reached for the door handle, Piers barrelled up: 'Mummy, look!'

'Where did you get those, darling?'

'They were over there. On the grass.'

'They're *keys*,' Amy explained.

'They look like nursery keys,' Carrie said. She held out a hand, and Piers dropped them importantly into it. A bunch of five: one quite large – probably for the gate. The keyring was a friendly black and white cow. 'I expect they're Ms Kennedy's.'

'*I* found them,' Piers reminded her.

'Then you'd better give them to her.' She returned them to her son, and reached for the door handle again. Turned it, and stepped into a nightmare.

He said something – a name? Whistler – and the door behind him opened, and he turned. Louise was sure he was going to shoot.

Little Amy Slater tumbled in, the exact Amy Louise had been thinking about not two minutes ago. *Everything's in the right place,* she'd said, looking at the mural of the solar system. Blonde curls, blue eyes, shy voice: it was impossible not to look at her without expecting her to lisp. And here she was, falling into the room, while the Gun turned to welcome her.

And immediately after came Carrie Mannion, whom Louise didn't know well, but had marked down as someone she'd like to.

The next few seconds were chaos.

★

83

Eliot's instincts were to reach for his children – Gordy was already wrapped round him, but he stretched out a hand for Timmy and pulled him from Louise even as Louise moved forward. The thug had turned when the little girl burst through the door; had pointed the gun at her, though had raised his arm when he saw the height of the threat. But levelled his aim again when the woman followed: one of the mothers, a brunette, quite striking in a sharp-featured way – where did that thought come from, a moment like this? Timmy was in his arms now, or his free arm anyway, and Gordy had contrived to make himself even smaller, a tightening process which involved squeezing Eliot's thigh to the point where he'd have keeled over, any other circumstance, but managed to stay upright long enough to see Louise launch herself into the gunman's back – and Eliot tightened too, and tried to make himself a shelter for his children, one in which, whatever happened outside it, would keep them safe from harm, safe from harm . . .

Sometimes a door is more than just a door; sometimes the distance between one side and the other is greater than expected. Narnia springs to mind. But wasn't what Carrie encountered, stepping into the annexe on Amy's heels; instead of an alien landscape of snow and streetlamps and Turkish delight, she found the totally familiar, utterly perverted – found the annexe, the kids' palace, with its carefully cordoned sections and fully representative art on the walls; with its foam mats piled in one corner, and various islands of primary-coloured equipment marking out boundaries, invaded by a man so obviously not a parent . . .

The man held a gun in his hand, and he pointed it first at Amy, then at Carrie herself.

What passed through her mind, in less time than it would take to utter, was: her children, her husband, Amy, herself. Her children were not in the room; her husband was on his way to work. As for Amy – Amy had come to a dead halt: frozen by a sight out of synch with anything she'd yet known – she was too young for entertainment in which this happened; for serious exposure to the news. Which was how it ought to be. But somewhere deep inside Carrie, the bitter knowledge clunked into place that she'd always expected something like this, that life would have a serious kick in the teeth waiting. Thoughts like a photograph: a frozen moment. And then all she was aware of was the gun pointing at her, and underneath that, but swiftly reaching the surface, that Piers was behind her; that soon he would be coming through that door.

And then came movement and noise, and Carrie lost track of immediate events.

What Amy thought mostly happened below comprehension, and would best be captured by a list of words, the kind Miss Kennedy sometimes asked them for – so a picnic, say, would be *grass river blanket sandwiches swans lemonade*, though there were other words she'd never say out loud, like *daddy farted*, because he had, at a picnic. None of the grown-ups noticed; they just carried on like it never happened. And what were the words here? She loved the annexe; the annexe was *the Palace*; the annexe was *painting soft-play stories sunlight*. The annexe was *Miss Kennedy*. And now suddenly the annexe was *man stranger pointing frightened* . . . The annexe was still *Miss Kennedy*, but Miss Kennedy didn't look her usual self, and why was everybody up against the wall? Amy started to scream.

As for Judy, what else would Judy think? She was thinking *Why me?* Just half an hour ago, crossing the bridge, she'd stopped to cough – a serious hack; not the ordinary morning interruption. She should have called in sick. Instead, she was caught up in horror, and you couldn't tell her this wasn't *Miss Kennedy's* fault, there'd never been guns in the nursery before . . . She'd been dragged from the office and made to stand against a wall – *dragged* was how she remembered it; how she'd tell it if the opportunity arose. And now things were getting worse, because the gunman had turned as a child burst in, followed by her mother, and in that same moment Louise Kennedy leaped at him, even though he held the gun – even though anything could happen, and probably would, and to stop any of it happening to her, Judy Ainsworth closed her eyes and willed herself safe at home.

In that moment—

There was a thought Louise had never voiced, because it seemed cruel. But in the wake of 9/11, she'd thought that the heroism of the passengers in the third plane – those who'd fought their captors, preventing increased carnage on the ground; *let's roll* – had been, if not easy, at least simple. Their survival was not in question; they'd been doomed from the moment the terrorists had taken control. And they knew this; reports of planes hitting the towers had reached them. So their choice was straightforward: they could suffer death meekly, or do what they could to prevent it visiting others. Any danger from the airjackers' box-cutters was temporary. Gravity already had it in for them: death in the air was just jumping the gun.

In that moment, if any thought was running through her head, that was it.

But it was more likely that pure instinct propelled her. As Eliot grabbed Timmy, Louise pushed herself from the wall: there was no real aim to her onslaught, just a desperate need to change the direction of events; particularly the one in which bullets flew and Carrie Mannion dissolved in red mist . . . Amy's scream split the air. Louise hit the man in the small of the back and he went down, gun or not. Which didn't go off – didn't go flying, either; it would have been fine to see the gun go skittling out of his reach, but he kept a firm grasp on it as he hit the floor, and he was no sooner down than he was trying to get up again. Louise, her own bones jarred by the collision, was half on top of him, half on the floor; she looked for the gun, didn't see it, then scrambled to her feet and sprang like a jack from its box for the door.

Watching, Eliot thought numbly: *What about us?* With a boy clamped to each leg, he had as much chance of making a break for the door as the door did of making one for him: *bitch*, he thought – but only with the lower part of his brain. The rest of him clenched in hope that she'd make it out before the gunman recovered his feet; it wasn't far, but there was no chance she could cover the distance faster than a speeding bullet . . .

And Judy thought *No*. And other words, as hopelessly out of order and incoherent as Amy's: *door cow run scared help wait gun* . . . She'd have run herself; been out into the big safe world before anyone noticed she was gone, except – except she couldn't move. Whatever was flowing through her veins wasn't blood; it was thicker, sluggish, and bound her where she stood the way heavy sap keeps trees from walking. With open eyes, open mouth, she watched Louise in motion. She made no sound. No words, anyway. A faint tortured expulsion of air, maybe. And Louise kept moving.

Carrie snapped out of limbo about a second after falling into it – Amy's scream had cut into the moment; the man with the gun was on the floor, and the teacher was on top of him, but scrambling to get up . . . What happened to the gun, she didn't know. All she knew was *Piers* – he was right behind her. She turned and there he was, rooted to the spot: eyes round, shocked to the core – what was Miss Kennedy doing on top of that man? He was still holding those keys . . . And then Carrie was moving, a barely willed sequence of actions which involved grabbing her son, dragging him through the door, and hoisting him into her arms as she ran for the gate, the *chink*

87

of the keyring on the path as Piers dropped it chiming exactly with the name *Amy* in her mind – Amy was in there. She'd left her friend's daughter in that room, where a man with a gun had been waiting.

Everything probably sped up or slowed down, Louise thought afterwards. That was what happened in crisis: time threw connniptions, and everything fitted a different framework, so what seemed to last minutes had been over in seconds, or possibly vice versa. Did that happen here? She didn't know. She was on her feet without thinking; looked for the weapon but he'd fallen on top of it, and no way was she getting involved in a hand-to-hand tussle for a gun . . . She sprang like a jack from its box just as Carrie Mannion grabbed her son and carted him backwards through the open door like a frightened sack of shopping. Louise thrust from her mind what lay behind her and seized Amy mid-scream – sound shut off as if a switch had been thrown. Everything had its place, and this wasn't Amy's; the child was light as a bag of feathers in her arms . . . Louise was expecting punctuation: the sudden slam of whatever a bullet would feel like, but it didn't come – she was out of the annexe a moment later; Carrie ahead of her, Piers in her arms, and the keys to the gate falling from Piers' hand and hitting the path at Louise's feet.

She scooped them up as smoothly as if she'd practised for this: a parent–child obstacle event for Open Day.

They reached the gate. Louise became conscious of others standing near the main nursery entrance, staring – she became conscious of noise again, but this wasn't Amy screaming, it was herself. *Run! Get out!* Or maybe *Gun! Fuck!* But more probably something beyond words' reach; the altogether more scary noises any beast makes when a bigger beast attacks. The keyring was clutched so tight, she could have had copies cut from the imprint on her palm.

And then realized they weren't alone this side of the railing; that a few of the bigger children were playing on the grass.

Carrie was through the gate now; running for the car park and the bigger world beyond. At her approach, panic rippled through those gathered there like wind through a field of corn. With no understanding of events, they found room for dire possibility: anything can happen these days. Everyone knows that. So they gathered those most precious to them, and ran for their cars and bicycles. Louise, past the gate, thrust Amy at the first adult she encountered who wasn't making for the hills. *Go. Call the police.* Maybe she imagined saying that. Then she turned, and ran back the way she'd come, to shoo the children playing on the annexe side of the railings into the outside world. Most fled like lambs at the wolf's approach. Some she had to bare her teeth at – a pair sat on the grass, playing something complicated involving plastic figures – *Leave them!* They wanted to collect their toys – *Fucking leave them!* Didn't matter about the language, so long as they fucking scattered . . . Louise was flapping like a demented scarecrow, but it was doing the trick. All she'd learned about giving children confidence, about assuring them she was a calm stable source of authority – all of it blown away in a mad rush of limbs and angry language, and every second her eyes were fixed on the door of the annexe, expecting the Gun to blast through it, and turn the remnants of the morning into an abattoir.

And then they were gone. It was as if she were the danger. They were gone through the gate, in search of their parents, and though that was the result she'd wanted, something faltered inside her, recognizing that however the day turned out, what they'd always remember was, she'd scared them . . . *Doesn't matter.* They'd live. She was alone now, with no sense of how much time had passed, and the keys were biting into her palm, but at least the children were gone, and some kind of alarm raised, even if it resembled panic. She walked towards the gate. In the car park, yards away, people she'd known for months transformed before her eyes into creatures from a mob; it was like one of those late-night movies, in which suburban normality decomposes to a zombie carnival – she was looking at people, but seeing teeth, wide eyes and fear. Parents were survival animals, focused only on moving their cubs out of danger. The details could be determined later. In days like these, you did not wait for the small print. You left the scene, and asked questions afterwards.

High overhead an aeroplane passed; its nervous passengers miles out of reach.

In Louise's hand, the keys still bit. She reached the gate, and checked behind her again – no children there. Apart from the two in the annexe.

Amy bobbed in and out of sight, her blonde head tucked into an adult shoulder hurrying off the premises. Carrie, too, was out on the street; Piers still under one arm. He was too big to be carried: his mother had no doubt told him that more than once. No doubt, too, Carrie would have hoisted a car if one had been resting on his body. With no time for anything, Louise found time to marvel at the strength women had when the world bared its teeth at their young.

There was noise, but nothing transcribable. Just the sound that drums beneath enormous events: a groundswell of human confusion and panic, half a beat out of synch with everything else.

And then came a face she recognised; the only one heading her way.

Dave Osborne reached the gate just as she slammed it shut. He stood in front of her – the iron railings between them – his young face twisted and clenched by unknown fears. But he'd come towards her anyway.

She slipped the key into the lock before he could speak;

turned it, then threw the keys high over his side, towards the car park, where the rattle of their landing was lost as the last of the nurserys-goers departed.

'He has a gun. Call the police,' she told him, very clearly.

And then she walked back into the annexe.

4

HE'D WATCHED ONCE, ON a Leicester Square screen, an action movie whose few interior scenes were set in a building that supposedly housed the kind of activities this one actually did: the set designer had gone for clean white corners and soundproofed glass walls, behind which boilersuited extras test-fired handguns, while pinstriped English roses delivered cut-glass commands to voice-activated computers. So he always suffered a twinge of disappointment arriving at work, where the walls were grimy and the computers deaf. Keying his security number into the touchpad by the door, Ben Whistler, as ever, wondered if his entrance/exit clearance was just a way of keeping track of his working hours – he was ten minutes late. This was not unusual . . . The roses in pinstripe he encountered were mostly on the Central Line. Office space was at a premium, and work-stations were cubicled, the way they were in call centres.

As the door closed, he caught a glimpse of the bookshop across the way. Ground floor: remaindered travel books, failed novels and poncy art books. Downstairs: floor-to-ceiling porn, with specialist items in cupboards, for those who knew to ask. The difference between the two operations was that the book-shop window spelt it out in neon-tubed lettering: *Private Bookshop Below*. Ben's building didn't have *Secret Service Above* plastered anywhere, but then that, in a nutshell, spelt the gap between 'private' and 'secret'.

The stairs were steep but the lift was temperamental, and the last time it had packed up the engineers had needed three hours to release its captives; significantly longer than it took Bruce Willis to clear a skyscraper of terrorists. So the stairs it was, but that was okay – city life didn't allow for much exercise, unless you counted trudging. He took them two at a time to the first landing, one by one thereafter, and met nobody until he'd reached the fourth floor, where another security keypad waited – the 8, he could never help noticing, more worn than the others, the way *e* tends to be on a keyboard. What would a code-breaker make of that? Probably think it a clue.

Coming out as he went in was Reggie someone or other. One of these years, Ben was going to have to make an effort with the Reggies of this world.

'There's a flap,' Reggie said.

But if this effort involved adopting World War II slang, it was never going to happen.

'What kind of . . . flap?'

'The flappy kind, basically. How many kinds are there? Nott wants you.'

'Me?'

Again . . . ?

'You're still Ben Whistler?'

'Was when I got up.'

'Then you, yes. But cheer up. Basically, they do quite a decent redundancy package.' Reggie grinned; always a mistake when one side of your mouth doesn't work. 'Do let a chap past.'

Probably every English organisation had a Reggie, Ben supposed – well, probably not garage forecourts, etc., but every branch of the Civil Service – but that somehow didn't mitigate his presence. Every encounter with the type, however brief, felt like a time-slip into films the Beeb used to show on Sunday afternoons: it didn't matter what the movie was, it was always raining outside, and rationing had just been repealed. Before Reggie disappeared down the stairs, Ben called, 'Where?'

'His offi—'

'This flap. Where is it?'

'Oxford.'

Oxford. Ben had never been to Oxford. He was a Loughborough man.

What the hell did Nott want?

So Ben Whistler, anyway: Ben Whistler looked like what you got when you thought about a rugby player, then fixed his teeth. Six two and broad in the shoulders with pale grey eyes and straw-coloured hair; a slightly crooked nose, which he'd never had the decency to break. 'That's just its normal shape' was a phrase he was called on to use more than most men. And he carried everywhere this air of untidiness, despite the suit, despite the tie; always looked – as one of the distinctly unroselike Queens of the Database once put it – like he'd just been dragged through a blonde backwards. A comment which had caused a momentary lull in conversation, as her fellow worker queens filed the image for private perusal later.

He was thirty-four, and if not quite an underachiever, hadn't set the world alight. The targets he'd had ten years ago remained just that: undiminished concentric circles that might as well have been nailed to a distant tree. It was handy he'd set different targets since.

As for Jonathan Nott, he wasn't head of department; he was head of the whole damn building. Which wasn't Vauxhall Cross, but still . . . Ben was fourth floor. Operations Director didn't visit the fourth floor much – the basic idea behind departments like Ben's being, they should run in such a way the Operations Director forgot they existed. The lift should skip the fourth floor altogether. Ben had rarely met Jonathan Nott, still less been wanted by him.

The fourth floor. He was here now, so went to his cubicle – the way he'd left it; a benign mess, delivering the impression that work was happening, but wasn't getting on top of him. He took his mobile from his pocket, and dared to turn it on at last, already inwardly flinching from the anticipated fallout from last night's misbehaviour – he'd got talking to a girl in a bar; talked to her so long, he'd stood his date up . . . And yep, here came the voicemail alerts. At the same moment, Ben saw the new Post-it attached to his monitor: *JN wants you – now (or sooner)*. He was a bit late for now. 'Sooner' would have demanded prior notice. Switching his mobile off, putting it down, he headed back to the stairwell, his heart pumping so much he didn't really need more exercise.

Last time he'd had this summons – two weeks previously – he'd been more or less expecting it, and Nott's first words were, 'Any idea where Weiss is?'

Three seconds into the room, this was. No *Whistler, sit down, cup of coffee?* Then Nott had glanced at his watch. He was mostly bald, and what hair still fringed his ears and the back of his head was shaved to stubble. Broad shoulders and eyes like pebbles, though not so friendly. Probably sixty, but Ben guessed he'd been that for a while, and would remain so for ditto. Some people had an ideal age and stuck to it. Ben was hoping his own was thirty-four . . . Miro Weiss. Ben had known this would be about Weiss – there was no other reason for Nott wanting to see him.

'None at all, sir.'

Firmly voiced; unfaltering gaze.

'The Dogs have already asked, right?'

(The Dogs were precisely that: the Service hounds. Their bark, rumour had it, was softer than their bite – and Ben, along with everybody else on the fourth floor, had endured the bark lately, which was harsh enough. Bad Sam Chapman had been prowling incessantly; now there was a bite you didn't want to know more about.)

'That's right, sir.'

'And nothing's occurred to you since.'

'If it had,' Ben said, 'I'd have—'

'Right, right, right. You'd have taken it to the Dogs.' Then Nott said: 'Sex, money, boredom.'

And leaned back in his chair.

Jonathan Nott: probably a Jonty. In some ideal future, in which all possible promotions had come to pass, Ben could see himself partnering Jonty on a croquet lawn – partnering him being the only way to win. Competing would involve fluffing shots and bollocking strategy, then being enthusiastic about being whupped: 'Well played, sir.' No need to stand on ceremony, Benjamin. Call me Jonty. Probably Jonty had a daughter or two: damn fine fillies, they'd be. Already he could see the old man wiping away a tear of undiluted joy when Ben asked permission to—

'The three great motivators.'

Sex, money and boredom, he meant.

'But I'm not sure boredom comes into play. You accountant types have a pretty high threshold of that, don't you?'

'So we're told, sir.'

'Wouldn't be accountants otherwise, hmm? Did you know him well?'

'Not too well, sir.'

'Gay, wasn't he?'

Past tense.

'I always assumed so,' Ben said carefully.

'Ever make a play for you?'

'Not overtly, sir.'

'Care to elaborate?'

Well of course he fucking wouldn't.

'If he ever made a pass, it was too subtle for me, sir. When a man asks if I'd like a drink after work, I generally assume he wants a drink after work.'

'And did you?'

'Occasionally. Never just the two of us.'

There was a pub on the corner – name a junction in Soho there wasn't – and Ben and Miro Weiss had indeed passed an evening or two there, with other colleagues; even Reggie once. There'd been a World Cup game on, and half the department was clustered round the big screen.

'I'll take your word for it. I'm sure the Dogs didn't.'

They hadn't. Dates, places; what was said, what was drunk. Every detail they could unearth, recorded.

'Well, he lived alone. I'm sure he got his end away now and then, but he was damn bloody careful about it. Rumours about some boy he might or might not have had, but even the Dogs haven't sniffed that one out. So for the moment, we've narrowed it down to the money.'

'Yes, sir.'

'Though mind you,' said Nott, 'the missing quarter of a billion pounds was a clue there.'

And that had more or less been that. Everyone on the fourth floor had been through something similar, and more than one had been granted the same pay-off line – hard not to imagine Jonty honing it between interviews; playing around with the stress until he had it just the way he liked it. Which was argu- ably abuse of power, but the Service had no strong tradition of employees' rights.

Meanwhile, *Oxford* was still floating through Ben's mind. Nothing he could remember linked him to Oxford.

Twenty past nine. He knocked, and went in. Jonathan Nott was leaning back in his chair, apparently chewing the inside of his mouth. Ben collected the tics and posturings of those above him.

As before, Nott jumped right in. 'Sam Chapman was in Oxford this morning.'

Ben said, 'I heard there's a flap, sir.'

'Sam Chapman was doing a C & C. How many of those do you suppose he's handled?'

Numbers being treacherous, slippery objects — Ben, an accountant, was wary of the little devils — he didn't hazard a guess. 'A lot, I should imagine. Sir.'

'Too many, it seems. He got careless.'

Ben had a sudden image of what carelessness might mean: blood on the pavement; hair coating the walls. *Collect and comfort* wasn't quite a euphemism; it meant bringing someone in gently. But when the someone didn't want to come, comfort could turn unkind.

And what did this have to do with him?

'What happened, sir?'

'It's not yet clear. Chapman's got a containment issue on his hands. We'll run the post-mortem later.'

'Figure of speech?'

'For the time being. Neil Ashton was hit by a car. A big car, apparently. Four-wheel drive.' Nott glazed slightly. Maybe car-porn was his thing. 'He might live. Stupid prick needn't think he's coming back to a job, though.'

Ben kept an unshocked face. In this line stuff happened, everyone knew that, but Ben's was a desk job; the worst it involved being a paper-cut, or a bawling out for jamming the shredder. Neil belonged to the Dogs, who were nearer the sharp end, but didn't usually get hit by cars . . . Ben had the sense of being underneath a wall, a major brick of which had just slipped loose. Any moment now, debris would rain.

Because Nott wasn't saying anything, and someone ought to, he said, 'What about the target?'

'Oh, the target. Yes. That's interesting.'

Seconds ticked past, while Ben was allowed to absorb the adjective.

'The *target* snaffled Ashton's gun and vamoosed. Now he's turned up in a nursery school in a suburb. He's got hostages, children among them, and he says he's going to start shooting soon. Unless you, Ben Whistler, go talk to him. Couldn't pop up there, could you?'

In the nursery, backs to the wall, they sat: Judy, Louise, Eliot, Timmy and Gordon. The man with the gun stood a few yards in front of them. The metal shutters were over the windows, and with just one overhead light on, it felt like mid-evening instead of 9:45 in the morning – *quarter to ten!* Louise couldn't believe so much had been crammed into such a short time; couldn't credit, either, that so little had happened since she'd walked back into the annexe, having cleared the immediate area of potential victims. She could have been on the other side of the gate by now. Instead she'd become part of this stasis; this short queue against the wall, waiting for God knew what.

Neither Eliot nor Judy had believed it when she'd walked back in.

That had been almost an hour ago. The intruder was off the ground by then; had recovered his gun, though not his composure. Sweat shone on his forehead, and something wild had broken his eyes, two parts fear and one part something Louise didn't recognise, though she felt its force when he spun towards her and pointed the gun. He spat something – Spanish. He was spitting Spanish. The gun looked ready to spit too; its barrel round as a cannon's, dark as a well.

Eliot shouted: 'No!'

'You—'

'Don't,' said Louise.

For a moment everything froze, while different realities

struggled to be born. In most of them the trigger was pulled, the world grew dark, and Louise ceased to be. In this one the boy released his breath, and lowered the gun. Louise's heart began again, though she hadn't noticed it stopping. Timmy raised his head from his father's leg, his face a blank mask awaiting its next expression. What that would be depended on the next outrage life delivered.

'You go against the wall,' the boy said at last. Then he backed away from them, and kicked the door shut. He looked at the lock.

'The keys aren't here,' Louise told him.

'You shut up now.'

Judy said, under her breath, 'You came back.'

'Yes.'

'Fool.'

'Thank you.'

'Be quiet.'

What next? Outside, the morning's noises followed their usual routine – cars heading up to the council car park, or down towards the main road – but that couldn't last, and without consciously knowing what she'd been waiting for, Louise felt something relax inside when she heard the first siren. The police station was less than five minutes away. That time had been crammed with activity elsewhere – with phone calls from Dave and others; with a rehearsed police reaction to news of firearms on school property; with a mad scramble for equipment and instructions, along with things she couldn't know about, such as the rude awakening of DS Bain – but for her, it had been filled with the slow realisation that this was where life had led her: that all her career decisions and emotional mistakes were nothing more than an elaborate joke, leading to this punchline: Louise Kennedy, trapped in the nursery she'd chosen to teach in, alongside a man she'd had an overwhelmingly stupid one-night stand with, his two terrified children, and a woman she couldn't stand and who, she was increasingly certain, had wet herself in the recent past. Oh yes, and a man with a gun.

It must have been nine o'clock when the Dalek spoke.

He'd read somewhere, a couple of years ago, that the mystery of how birds navigated had been solved. It seemed they used the road network: like an AA map, only actual size. How they'd managed before roads was presumably awaiting resolution; meanwhile, Ben could see their point. From the helicopter, the landscape was a thing of rolling wonder: interfolding shades of green across which cloud shadows tumbled; tripping over trees; skiing over reservoirs – beautiful, but useless if you needed to know where you were heading. But the roads that ribboned through it knew the way, and the helicopter's own shadow skated alongside the largest of them, zipping past cars as if it weren't simply moving faster, but on a different scale altogether. Oxford drew closer with every beat of the blades, and Ben didn't have to be a swallow to know that much.

The pilot said something: too used to being in one of these things to realise he was inaudible. Ben just nodded.

So how fast had this happened? Half an hour ago, it had been an ordinary morning: he'd turned up at work with the usual expectation of boredom, adulterated by that intestinal queasiness which had been present since Miro Weiss's last day. And now he was in a helicopter, which was a first, and ideally a last, as it wasn't helping the queasiness any. The chopper had collected him from the roof not five minutes after Nott dismissed him: those images of working among soundproofed glass walls and handgun galleries no longer seemed far-fetched. It was tempting to wonder who'd noticed, though not much impressed the local girls. But why him? Ben was a desk man; he shuffled numbers – big numbers, but still a far cry from being whisked away in an airborne blender. Sure, when he'd joined the Service, he'd had those Leicester Square pictures of foreign assignments and shiny gadgetry, but he'd been recruited for his accountancy degree. Five years later, his BlackBerry was state of the art as he got, and that was ex-display from Dixons.

And he couldn't help wishing this had happened next week, when he wouldn't be here. Ben had holiday booked. He was taking the road to Rio: margaritas, señoritas, *hasta la vista*s. All of which could still happen – bottom line was, he was Civil Service; they could take his life, but they'd never take his annual leave – but he recognised that this morning could throw his future out of whack. The helicopter wasn't just taking him from his desk. It was flying him into the world of the Dogs.

The pilot was tapping his arm now, pointing at the headset hanging off the dashboard. Ben hadn't realised his hands were clamped so tightly to his seat's metal frame; releasing himself, he detached the headset from its hook, and wrapped it round his head – odd how such a simple action felt so dangerous in a way-high electric mosquito, as if concentrating on anything other than keeping airborne might result in a sudden plummet. He'd developed a whole new relationship with the landscape: it was low enough that he could feel it zipping past, but he was high enough that any sudden encounter with it would be terminal. A helicopter was a collection of thousands of small interlocking parts, any one of which could go wrong at any moment. The same could be said of a washing machine, of course, but you never found yourself bombing above a motorway in one.

But the contraption, it turned out, relied on something other than his thought processes, because it remained on course as he fixed the earpiece into his left ear, his spare index finger into his right, and shouted, 'Okay.'

A voice told him, 'We have two names.'

This was Tina, queenliest of all the Queens of the Database – so much so her name seemed wrong: she should have been a Beatrice or a Caroline; something boasting royal precedence. In person she was tall, fiftyish, with stern ash-blonde hair. Over headphones she was equally precise and intimidating. Every syllable clearly defined. Every word knowing its place.

'Hostages?' he shouted. 'Or the hostage taker?'

'The former. Did you remember to pick up the BlackBerry?'

'. . . Yes.'

'Well, turn it on, there's a clue. You have email.'

He nodded, then realised what he was doing. 'Thanks.'

'There'll be more. Keep checking.'

'Yes.'

'Good luck, Benedict.'

Because she knew he was no Benjamin, of course. The Queens of the Database knew everything.

He plucked the earpiece free, and fumbled in the case at his feet for his BlackBerry. As he straightened, a wave of dizziness washed over him – vertigo, which could have its roots in many things (childhood traumas, insecurities; probably sexual confusion, too), but was most infallibly triggered by being really fucking high up. But best not to dwell on that, so he switched his gadget on, and in the comforting buzz its micro-screen emitted, felt connected to the ground once more.

The first of two unopened emails had the tag line *Kennedy*; even as he opened it, a third appeared. Deal with that in a moment. First up was Louise Ann Kennedy: b.1975, Chester. Educated there and Sheffield University (PPE), after which she'd done a PGCE at Oxford Brookes, then had a career rethink, and joined a City bank: DeJohn Franklin Moers, where she'd worked her way through several desks – company practice rather than low attention span: DFM didn't recruit just anybody. Probation over, Kennedy had settled in European Investments, where she'd remained seven years, the middle one in Zurich, and then abruptly quit. Evidently the City lifestyle and matching salary had turned out less attractive than a roomful of preschoolers in Oxford. At first glance less exciting too, but that was before a man with a gun wandered in.

All of this in brief, fact-heavy snatches. Given another half-hour, Tina would come up with a concrete explanation for Kennedy's downshift, but it wasn't hard to conjure a reason or two in the meantime. Sex and drugs, those fabulous standbys, filled the gaps in a lot of CVs, and Ben had spent enough evenings in the City to know what was happening when the kids went off to powder their noses. At thirty-two and single, maybe Louise Kennedy had had enough of the work hard–play hard carousel; maybe she remembered being happy doing her teacher training. It took guts to make such a change, and Ben, who planned alterations of his own in the near future, tipped an imaginary hat to her. He'd be meeting her soon, he supposed. And a sudden lurch in his stomach, nothing to do with altitude, prompted the whisper *if she's still alive*.

Too early for negative thinking, though. The day stretched ahead of him, as immediate and intricate as the landscape unfolding below. He could fuck things up quite handily himself, without dwelling on disasters occurring in his absence. And again he reminded himself: *This man asked for me by name.* Whatever he wanted, he was unlikely to start before Ben arrived.

The Dalek wasn't a real Dalek, though by this frayed stage, that wasn't beyond possibility. The voice was human; its electronic edge simply the tang the loudhailer bestowed.

Hello in the annexe. My name's Peter Faulks.

Wasn't this cosy?

Is everything all right in there?

Essentially, the voice – Peter Faulks – was speaking to the Gun, though it was clear that, for the moment at least, the Gun had no intention of replying.

We'd like you to come outside now.

Sounded all right to Louise.

Beside her, Judy moaned. Not in itself unusual, but in place of the usual aggrieved self-interest was the animal undertone a frightened weasel might betray.

Louise said, quietly: 'It's important we don't panic.'

'It's all right for you.'

This without logic or sense: in what possible way was it all right for—

'He's going to kill me.'

'He's not going to kill anybody.'

'They always do. And I'm the one he'll pick. It's obvious.'

'You'll frighten the children, Judy. Keep calm.'

'Why did you come back?'

'Because of the boys. I'm their teacher.'

Judy said, 'Their father's here.'

'. . . Keep calm. Say nothing.'

Can you hear me? I'd like some acknowledgement you can hear me.

She said – full voice: she was speaking to the Gun – 'You have to let them know you're here.'

'I know this.'

'You have to talk to them. Otherwise . . .'

Otherwise they'd come in anyway. With guns, because that's what happened these days – you fought fire with fire. It was an equation tested on the streets: bombs went off in Tube trains supposed terrorists were shot dead. The police wouldn't wait all day on the off chance this particular terrorist would wander out eventually.

I'm going to read a number. That's the number I'd like you to call. Are you ready? Here it is.

'Do you have a phone?' Louise asked him.

Peter Faulks's mechanised voice began reciting numbers. It was like hearing an electric till.

The boy shook his head.

'Tell him.'

. . . seven eight four . . .

He was holding a gun, and she was telling him what to do. Maybe she'd made the right decision: she was a teacher after all.

. . . nine three. Did you get that?

'I'll go and tell him.'

He looked at her.

'They have to know what's happening. Else they'll . . . they'll come in anyway. Do you understand what I'm saying?'

Eliot said, 'Lou—'

'Shut up.'

The boy barely glanced Eliot's way. He was staring directly at Louise; the gun dangling in his hand like an empty milk bottle.

If you got that, I'd like you to call the number now.

'I understand enough,' he said.

'Okay. If you—if we don't start communicating, if we don't start talking, bad things will happen.' Men with guns will enter. Bigger guns than his. If he understood English, he'd understand what she wasn't saying, too.

Did you hear that? If you don't have a phone, we'll supply one. But we need to know what you want. If we don't know that, we can't progress any further.

'. . . So what you do?'

He was asking her? But yes, he was asking her.

'I'll go outside, I'll fetch their phone. Then you can talk to them, tell them what you want.'

And what you're prepared to do if you don't get it.

He said, 'You are my . . . hostages. Hostages, yes?'

Jesus Christ.

'Yes,' she said. 'We're your hostages.'

'If you go out now, I have one less.'

She said, 'I've already been outside. I came back. Remember?'

'. . . Why you do that?'

Why had she done that? Because the boys were in her care. That was the answer she'd given Judy, but below it rippled things she couldn't put a name to: expiation of guilt? A desire to be at the centre of things? What was happening would put her name in newspapers the world over, and going back into the annexe when she could have walked away ensured those reports would show her in the finest light. She'd be a *heroine*; she'd be *brave*; the opposite of an unsung hero . . . She'd be on first-name terms with the tabloids. Was that why she'd come back? To be famous? To be *sung*?

'Because this is my nursery. Because there are children here. In my care. Which means I have to protect them.'

'You protect them from me.'

'Yes.'

She was pleased they'd established that much.

'I do not want to hurt anybody.'

That was good. That was very good. Though didn't do much to quell unease: if he meant no harm, why was he here with a gun?

We have to know everyone's all right in there. You do understand that, don't you?

'It is too much noise.'

In point of fact, she agreed – you'd have thought it comforting, knowing there were policemen outside, but the Dalek voice was disturbing; an intrusion on something that had started to feel private. Loud, unacknowledged instructions were not the way forward. That too was something she'd learned as a teacher. If Peter Faulks had anything useful to contribute, they'd all be better off if he could deliver it mildly, over a phone.

'I'll go outside. They'll give me a mobile. A mobile telephone. Then the noise will stop.'

It wasn't so very different to negotiating with an infant.

He said, 'If you do not come back, if you let them come in – I will use the gun.'

She was looking directly into his eyes when he said this. Nothing she saw there suggested he didn't mean what he said.

'I'll come back.'

'Yes.'

Judy said, 'I'll go.'

'No.'

'I'll come back I promise if you'll let her why won't you let me I'll come back just as much as she will—'

Louise slapped her.

Judy screamed; a sudden high-pitched squawk that cut off mid-breath as she covered her mouth with her hand. But the echo of the slap bounced around the annexe a second or two, and if that wasn't the first time a slap had been delivered here, Louise would have liked to know the details of the previous.

'Judy. Listen to me. We can all get through this, but you have to stop—'

'Bitch!'

'—behaving like—'

'*Bitch!*'

In the word was more venom than Louise would have believed possible. There was a man here pointing a gun who didn't radiate such hatred.

Eliot said, 'Judy, you're endangering my children.' The words would have sounded sensible and appropriate if not for the tremor that revealed his own boiling helplessness. 'Shut up or I'll . . .'

He'd, yes, he'd do something. Like what?

'Stop it. Everyone.'

And the boy, too, said, 'Be quiet, please. This is not good.'

I'm going to repeat that number now.

More than anything, at that moment, Louise did not want Peter Dalek-voice to repeat that number.

'I'm going outside,' she said. 'I'm going to fetch a telephone. And then I'll come back inside, and we can sort all this out.'

In the seconds that followed, the only sound was the low whimpering of one of the twins — Gordy, she'd bet. Was this also part of being a teacher? Not the immediate identification of the noise maker, but the insistence on taking charge, even in the face of ridiculous odds.

Then the boy said, 'Okay. You go now.'

She would go now.

Before — when she'd jumped him, hoping to grab the gun; managing, at any rate, to carry little Amy out of the danger zone — movement had come fluidly. The only comparison she could find was playing squash: she hadn't played squash in months, but that was the clearest sense memory she retained of fast-flowing, thought-free motion; where the body takes over from the mind, as if the desired result is hardwired into flesh. Now, she felt the way she imagined the morbidly obese must feel: her body pinning her to the wall, as if surrendering to a mightier gravity. Why *morbid* anyway — weren't the fat supposed to be jolly? Pulling herself from the wall was like tearing Velcro from its mate.

One of the twins released a long wail.

'Hush, darling': Eliot.

The damned numbers were reciting themselves again: the threes, the fours, the nines; presumably in the same order as before, but weirdly unfamiliar all the same.

The boy said nothing. Judy was breathing harshly: a smoker's ragged struggle.

The door handle met her hand: the tactile equivalent of one of those *familiar objects from an unusual angle* photographs.

Outside, the world was changed utterly.

Second email.

The Queens of the Database had been busy, and though Ben knew they did what they did digitally, barely leaving their cocoons without serious enticement (tickets to *Mamma Mia*;

happy hour at Gordon's), it was impossible not to picture them as custodians of a vast library, its shelves stacked cloud high; its holdings classified according to a system only understood by the precious. Inside its walls, knowledge multiplied and was fruitful, and every time somebody in the outer world used a piece of plastic, or hit the speed dial, or crossed a border, or had their loyalty card swiped, a new line was written on a page inside an expanding volume; and whenever an order was barked down the corridors where Ben worked, off went the Queens of the Database: scurrying up and down ladders; foraging through alphabets; scouring the fascinating collection for the titbits that meant the difference between understanding and bafflement.

All of which meant it was a bit of a let-down, this second email, because it didn't say much. Eliot Pedlar, thirty-six. Worked for a local publisher. Twin boys, Timothy and Gordon; both (obviously) three and a lot. Details to follow. But the very scantiness of the info told Ben this much: that Eliot Pedlar had no criminal record, had never served in the forces, never been a civil servant, never suspected of terrorist affiliation or sympathies . . . Ben wondered what a Venn diagram of those categories would look like. And at the same time felt a twinge of sympathy for Pedlar and Kennedy both; not just for the situation they'd found themselves in, but for the scrutiny they'd have to suffer as a result. Press, eventually, of course. But meanwhile Tina and the queens, because whoever had wandered into their lives with a gun had been on the run from Bad Sam Chapman, which made them Office business for the duration.

9:45. What time did nurseries open? – 9:00, probably; he wasn't an expert. Whatever, for matters to have come this far – for Ben's name to have whipped through the channels; for Ben himself to have been loaded on to a helicopter and shipped halfway to Oxford already – this must have started before the nursery doors opened, which prompted two immediate questions, though more might follow. What was the hostage taker after? Occupying a nursery was headline news, but lost impact if no children were involved. And how come Eliot Pedlar, local resident, was there so early? There might be an innocent explanation, but innocence was something Tina & Co. got round to eventually; not what they expected from the outset.

Office business for the duration . . . That was the kind of thing Ben had meant.

The third email, he now saw, was labelled *delete immediately*.

After reading it, Ben assumed. Not that it contained much of use: *C & C target was level-3 confidential. Chapman will advise.*

C & C: collect and comfort. Whoever Chapman had tried to pick up presumably hadn't been aware of the essentially non-harmful definition.

But then, non-harmful wasn't what Bad Sam Chapman radiated. Chapman had questioned him about Weiss, of course: he was Head Dog, and Weiss's disappearance was Big Trouble. Though even when big trouble wasn't involved, Chapman's bad-tempered intensity managed to suggest it might happen anyway. You saw him in a bar, you'd sit on the other side of the room. He wasn't necessarily about to start a fight, but if one happened to occur, you could bet he'd be involved.

So you were just colleagues?

Yes.

Nothing closer?

No.

You gay, Whistler?

Fuck off. But self-preservation had held Ben back: *fuck off* was exactly what Chapman wanted him to say. He'd peel an angry man like a banana.

Not as far as I know, he'd said. *But maybe I've just never met the right man.*

He didn't really think that – who did? And there was little chance Miro Weiss could have engineered a lifestyle-altering epiphany. Miro Weiss: the Mirror Man to some, though Ben didn't know how *that* started – Miro wasn't vain; had nothing to be vain about. Prematurely balding, with washed-out watery eyes, and a hunched physique that never seemed to relax, as if he'd constantly been guarding secrets. Miro was the type who might sit facing you through nine halts on the Underground, and the second he got off, you wouldn't remember his gender. And just now, sitting in this helicopter, the reason for Mirror Man struck Ben – Miro; mirror. No more than that. One of those connections you'd never admit to missing, because that would be tantamount to explaining how dim you were.

Sometimes, the obvious took a little longer.

Glad you're finding this funny, Whistler.

A missing quarter of a billion pounds had ruined a lot of senses of humour.

Neil Ashton had been there too, in lieu of a dictaphone, which Bad Sam would never have lowered himself to. Deniability was Bad Sam's lodestone. He probably regarded a birthday card as a breach of security.

. . . C & C target was level-3 confidential. Chapman will advise.

Yeah, right. Ben had level-1 clearance, which meant he had his own shredder, but his phone calls were monitored. Whatever had happened this morning, Chapman wasn't going to tell Ben about it, regardless.

There were a lot of things Chapman didn't talk about. A lot of bodies whose locations only he knew.

The helicopter dipped, and Ben's stomach with it. He turned to the pilot, who was pointing down. They'd reached Oxford. Those things below them – not far enough below for comfort, actually – would be the famous spires: from this perspective they looked less dreaming than sharp, carrying a not entirely academic promise of impalement. Ben's future was in the hands of this stranger beside him, whose features were obscured by goggles and headset, and while it was true that every plane or train ride you took, you placed your life in another's keeping, it wasn't often that you sat right next to him, able to observe that he hadn't shaved this morning, and that there was a smear of oil on his left wrist – man couldn't wash his hands: what did that say about his ability to land a helicopter? Nothing, it turned out. They scooted over the last of the big buildings, crossed the river, then descended on to what looked like a recreation ground. The road alongside it was cordoned off, and lined with police cars stationed at haphazard angles. As he watched, a big white lorry lumbered to a halt by a junction, and was flagged through by an officer. It was like watching a circus being set up, he thought. Send in the clowns.

Ben deleted the email, and turned his BlackBerry off.

Some days, it would be better if you'd stayed in bed.

No, there was a level deeper than that – some days it would be better if, the night before, you'd reached some previously unattainable plateau of drunkenness; a level at which you didn't simply sleep through the following day, but it didn't technically exist – it was a hole in your calendar, forever out of reach.

Superintendent Malcolm Fredericks, who'd been drunk on precisely three occasions in his life, and remembered each in embarrassing detail, was having one of those days now. He was well aware of the burgeoning gun culture – even Oxford had its violent underbelly. The handgun laws didn't mean they were impossible to get hold of: it just made them more expensive. So last thing he needed was some cack-handed spook handing a lethal weapon to a 'witness' . . . And witness to what, anyway? Nothing pissed a policeman off more than being told there were things he didn't need to know. A prick like Chapman would have ruined his day even without the gun. And the gun turning up in a nursery had a nightmare edge.

Especially today.

'How many have you got?'

'We have a full complement of AFOs.'

'I'm not talking about who's authorised to use firearms. I'm talking about marksmen. How many officers do you have who can take a target out from a distance? And who've been here before?'

Fredericks had suppressed a sigh. 'One.'

'Fucking hell.'

This had been four, no, five minutes ago: one of those phone conversations you didn't want to have. Chief constables swore like any other rank – better than most; they'd had more practice – and when this CC swore, the swearee tended to wind up on his grudge list.

'But we've got two more who've done most of the training, and—'

'Whose idea was it to send them on a course anyway?'

'I assumed it was yours, sir.'

Had he really said that?

No: he'd said, 'The instructions came from headquarters, sir. All distance marksmen with two-years'-plus experience to attend the refresher in Yorkshire. I've sent an alert out, but—'

But as of this moment, he had only one authorized firearms officer on-site who'd actually worked a hostage situation.

This was what was meant by economies of scale. Pack ninety per cent of the team off on one forty-eight-hour course: two days later, you had a team with all the boxes ticked on the latest Home Office questionnaire. Looked great on the paperwork.

What could happen in forty-eight hours?

'You've passed word to the Met?'

'I was about to, but—'

'And how would that make me look?'

Like a chief constable who couldn't control a firefight in his own backyard. Sir.

'With all respect, sir, we need—'

'Who's your scratch man?'

'DS Bain.'

'Bain's back on full duty, then.'

It wasn't a question, but could hardly be left to dangle.

'Yes.'

As of fifteen minutes ago.

'So no major effects from the last outing.'

Again, not a question. And that *outing* sounded like a picnic, which it hadn't been: DS Bain had shot a man, just as – the inquiry had determined – there was cause to believe he'd been about to turn a gun on his family. It had been an incredibly difficult kill: through a window. Then again, that's what Bain had been trained for.

'It was deemed an appropriate response,' he said.

'Not really the issue. Training and reality, don't you see?' Which was a question, but didn't require an answer. 'Doesn't matter how many bullseyes you drill on the range, when the target's flesh and blood, it has an effect on any normal person. Even an AFO.'

He said, 'I'm sure you're right. But there's been a lot of evaluation, a lot of psychometric testing—'

'A lot of trick cycling.'

'—all of which indicated that Bain is fit for duty.'

'Even if that duty might involve killing another man.'

'All of which indicated that Bain is fit for duty,' he repeated.

'Well, I hope to God you're right.'

That *you're* didn't escape him. A lot of evaluation, a lot of psychometric testing – but in the end, putting Bain in the shotgun seat was Fredericks' decision.

Didn't matter who'd signed the paper putting every other trained officer out of reach; didn't matter who'd just told him not to seek help from outside forces—

'Keep me informed. Minute by minute.'

'Sir.'

Five of those minutes had passed. Now Fredericks was at the scene, which at least had the decency to be close by the station, and DS Peter Faulks, qualified negotiator, was reciting numbers through a megaphone, trying to establish contact with whoever was inside. But Fredericks didn't believe in coincidences; there was statistical evidence somewhere that they never really happened. He might not know precisely who was inside the nursery, but he knew where the gun came from – a cack-handed spook.

If you don't have a phone, we'll supply one.

The area was locked down. From where he stood, just outside the main nursery gate – there was nobody left on the nursery grounds, barring hostages and gunman – he could see the door to the annexe, and the metal shutters over its windows. There were no windows on the footpath side; nor facing the adventure playground. Another set of railings, six foot high, cut the nursery grounds in half, and their gate was locked. The woman had locked it, before going back inside. Unlocking it, or going over the top, wouldn't take two seconds, but that was substantially longer than needed to squeeze a trigger. There was a skylight, but the roof was metal, so a silent approach impossible. A flash-bomb through a window wouldn't work, because of the shutters, and there was only one door, which was the same as the number of guns inside . . . The acceptable level of casualties here was zero. He hadn't needed to hear the Chief Constable not say this for the message to come through loud and clear.

He wondered why the woman had gone back inside, when she'd had the chance to escape. Hero or idiot? Was there a difference?

Or did she know the man involved?

Someone said, 'Sir?'

'What is it?'

'There's someone coming out.'

★

Every day she stepped through this door: how many times? A dozen, twenty. In the time she'd been here, she'd seen the view it presented in every season, and once – late afternoon, long after the kids had gone – had surprised a fox examining a stray scent. It had looked at her with obvious disdain, then taken one last breath of whatever intrigued it, and trotted off towards the railway line. There'd barely been an occasion since that she'd come through that door without a memory of the fox nudging her. Certainly, she'd never expected to see anything wilder.

But the world that met Louise this morning was one she'd never stepped into before.

It was the lack of children, for one thing – sure, this time of the morning, the children were all inside, but you were never in doubt of their presence. Children en masse exerted gravity, and their absence here tainted the air. To anyone but an expert, it would have registered simply as an unpindownable oddity: the colour blue, missing from a landscape oil. And there was more . . .

Beyond the nursery grounds were police cars: eleven, her mind suggested, though she didn't count them. And there'd be more she couldn't see. Several were blocking the road at the junction, and the various figures stationed around them were all looking her way. From being her place of work, the nursery had turned into a focal point: a crime scene in progress. Louise had never seen one from this perspective before. She'd always been on the safe side of a TV screen, or staring up from a cinema seat. Now police officers were clustered by the nursery gate, and might be elsewhere too: hiding round corners, or on the roof of the nursery – and what did they know, other than that a man with a gun was in the building behind her? They might suspect her of complicity. She'd suspect herself, in their shoes. She'd walked back in, when she could have walked away.

The Dalek spoke.

Miss Kennedy?

For some reason, she'd put a hand up to shield her eyes, though it wasn't so bright they needed protection.

Miss Kennedy? You are Miss Kennedy, aren't you?

So why had she walked back in – what answer would they accept?

She said, 'Yes. Yes, I am.'

Miss Kennedy, would you come out now, please?

She said, 'We need a phone. You promised us a phone.'

Would you come a little closer, please?

She wished she could – last thing she wanted was to go back into the annexe. But events had come too far for her to walk away. *If you do not come back, if you let them come in – I will use the gun.* She'd seen no reason to disbelieve his words. There'd been truth in his eyes. The dizzying image struck her of that perfect circle, the hole in the plaster where his bullet had struck. Dust had issued from the wound. What shape would his bullets make in flesh? Whatever: dust wouldn't be the issue.

'You promised us a phone,' she repeated. Even to her own ears, her voice sounded disconnected.

Miss Kennedy, would you raise your arms to shoulder level, please?

They thought she had a gun.

But they couldn't be that stupid. What would she be doing with a gun? She said, 'A phone. We need a phone inside. So you can talk to him.' She stayed exactly where she was, two yards outside the door. 'If I don't go back, he'll use the gun.'

One of the men at the gate raised a hand; the man with the megaphone – she assumed that's what it was; it looked no bigger than a mobile – lowered it and listened to what he had to say. Peter Faulks, that's what the Dalek was called. And he knew her name; all of these gathered men did. A kind of fame, she supposed.

Her legs felt wobbly, like a newborn giraffe's. All of this – the accumulated cars; the anxious policemen; the doubtless imminent cameras – were part of her story now, because that's what this was, her story, and to have sidelined herself at the earliest opportunity would have been accepting mediocrity . . . Was that why she'd gone back inside? Partly, she admitted now. Some of her wobbliness was stage fright. And besides, she had – who didn't? – the indestructible sense that things would work out; that her story wasn't going to be cut short. Hand in hand with the consciousness of mortality went the sense of invulnerability – sure, death would happen, but not today, not to her. How could it? She was only thirty-two . . . Did she really think all that? She thought she did. That was enough for now.

If people didn't feel invulnerable, bungee jumping would be science fiction. But then again, sometimes the rope snapped.

Miss Kennedy? Would you come to the fence? We have a phone for you.

She looked at her feet. *Do your stuff?* It was like wearing diver's boots, making that ten-yard trek to the locked gate – and like remembering pre-history, looking back to when she'd chucked the keys over the fence, having herded the last stragglers through it. There'd been civilians here then, scattering for the safety of their cars and their ordinary mornings. Being here now elevated Louise Kennedy above the ordinary. She wondered if her mother knew yet; if her former colleagues at DFM were picking this up on their constant newsfeeds. If Crispin knew, and what he was thinking.

Meanwhile, her feet were doing their stuff. Here was the fence that separated the annexe from the outer nursery grounds; and here, coming to meet her, was Peter Faulks, who turned out to have an unexceptional voice when it wasn't processed through hardware. His face, too, was unexceptional; round and ruddy-coloured and forgettable. When the movie was made he'd be a character part; ideal for somebody seen in *The Bill* once, but whose name was never going to wedge itself ahead of the title.

It was one of those Cold War moments; two people meeting with a fence between them. A little stretch of no-man's-land on either side.

'Are you okay?'

'I'm as well as can be expected, thanks.'

Amazingly, he laughed at that: a short quick bark reminding her, again, of the fox.

'How many of you are in there?'

She had to think for a moment. 'Five. No, six. You mean, including him?'

'Yes.'

'Six.'

'Names?'

'Pedlar. Eliot Pedlar and his boys, Timmy and . . .' Her mind went blank. 'The other twin. Gordon.'

'. . . That's three.'

'Me and Judy. Judy Ainsworth, she's the cleaner.' It wasn't just the men on the road watching; there'd be others, unseen, and she'd be in their sights. That's what happened in siege situations – marksmen collected unfolding events in the prisms of their crosshairs. She'd be their target now – just in case.

'And?'

'Him,' Louise said. 'The gunman.'

'Of course. Just wanted to be sure.'

'He's waiting.'

'Where are you?'

Where was she? She was at the focal point of the universe; where the crosshairs met.

'Inside. How are you grouped?'

'He's watching. I have to go back. He says he'll use the gun.'

He was handing her something through the railings: a very normal-looking Nokia. 'My number's the only one on this. How are you grouped?'

'Against the wall. He's in the middle of the room. Or was. The children—'

'The twins, right?'

'Twins,' she said stupidly. Then: 'I have to go back.'

'You're a brave woman. We'll get you out of there. All of you.'

Yes. Will we be walking or carried?

Because suddenly, thirty-two or not, she noticed that she was human – a collection of soft parts wrapped around bone, which could warp and damage if struck bluntly enough. A piano, dropped from a height; an unremarked streetlight, walked into. A bullet from a gun not far from here.

He said: 'He'll come out or we'll come in. We're good at this.'

'I hope so.'

'Be brave, Louise. Take that to him.'

She wrapped her hand round the mobile phone, as if it were a crucifix or a magic wand, and headed back into the annexe.

Eliot Pedlar had his sons wrapped round him close as moss, and when Louise Kennedy returned, he felt like light had just re-entered the room. It wasn't that he'd doubted she'd come back. She'd proved herself capable of that. But despite the nearness of his children, he'd felt alone until she walked through the door, holding the mobile phone out for the Gun as if this offering might defuse him – he carried a gun, but he amounted to a bomb. One that could go off any moment.

Louise. She was the reason he was here – he ought to hate her for that; and part of him was working on it.

She said, 'Here.' She was talking to the Gun. 'His number's pre-programmed. Call him and talk.'

But he admired, too, the steadiness of her voice, as if the gunman were no more than another recalcitrant child, who only needed to be shown where the boundaries lay.

Gordy shifted, trying to usurp part of Eliot that Timmy had already laid claim to. This was both familiar and unfamiliar; like those times he returned home after they were in their pyjamas. For a couple of minutes he'd be the centre of the universe, and they'd fight for his attention and his cuddles, and then remember they still had a mother on the property, and devolve to her orbit instead. But here there was only Eliot. While the Gun took the phone – his back to Eliot, so there was no telling his expression – Timmy growled. In ordinary life, this would be the start of something big; the boys were close as terraced houses, but there were no fights quite like those enjoyed by neighbours.

'Hush, boys . . .'

That was his role here. *Hush, boys. Everything is going to be all right.* If Eliot had a slot, you could put your penny in and that was the noise he'd make. But he wasn't fooling the boys, and he wasn't kidding himself. The whimpering Judy made every so often probably indicated she wasn't taken in either. But fuck her: his soothing sounds weren't for her benefit; truth to tell, they were mostly for his own.

Louise took her place against the wall. She didn't look his way or Judy's. She glanced at the boys, though, and he knew that if either had caught her eye, she'd have made a welcoming gesture, would have shared his burden by taking one or other into her arms, but both had their eyes locked shut, and remained clinging to Eliot as if he were all that kept them rooted to the surface of the planet.

The Gun faced them; weapon in one hand, mobile in the other. *Put it to your ear*, Eliot prayed . . . He meant the gun. *Put it to your ear and pull the trigger.* Didn't that happen? – this whole situation, all it meant was some confused kid was trying to make a splash, without ever having considered the stains that splash would make. He'd thought about his name in the papers; about hearing it spoken before Big Ben bonged. But this was the here and now, and there were policemen outside with bigger guns than his, and better versed in how to use them – shouldn't he have noticed by now there was no way out? He could use the phone, and say he was giving up. Or put the gun to his ear and blow his brains out. Either way, Eliot would be taking his boys outside in a minute or two. There were different levels of trauma involved, and he did not want his boys to see a man shoot himself – but they had their eyes shut. They had their eyes shut, and at least it would be over.

And at the back of his mind he was picturing Chris, who'd have arrived at her office by now, expecting no greater shocks than those of seeing her old colleagues and being reminded of the world of work, only to find greater disturbances elsewhere . . . There'd be a radio playing. No, there'd be an online news-cast, filtering on to her colleagues' monitors, and the catch-up chatter would falter as one of them would pick up on an Oxford nursery getting airplay . . . and that it was Chris's kids' nursery . . . Eliot could see, exactly as if he were there, the way the knowledge would settle on her; the same awful knowledge any mother would suffer at news affecting her children. If her boys weren't involved, Eliot would have called to say they were safe.

She would blame him. That went without question. The one time he took the boys to nursery (that would be how she'd phrase it: *the one time*, though that wasn't true; there'd been dozens of occasions, with no weaponry involved), the *one time*, and he'd led them into a battleground. If he couldn't do anything else, at least he could avoid actively putting her boys in mortal danger . . .

'Daddy?'

'Hush now.'

Because he didn't want to hear what Timmy had to say – whatever it was, he had no answers. *Hush now.*

The Gun said, 'He said call him, yes?'

'He said to call him,' Louise said. 'Yes.'

'And he give me whatever I want.'

'I don't know what he'll give you,' she said. 'But you have to call. It's our only chance of getting through this.'

Between the spoken words, odd snatches of outside noise broke through – discordant but purposive, as if a circus were striking ground nearby.

Judy said, 'I feel sick.'

Oh, fucking great, Eliot thought, in a sudden access of anger – *my boys are coping better than you, you stupid fucking bitch* . . .

Louise said, 'Judy. You've got to keep a grip. For all our sakes.'

She spoke more calmly than Eliot would have managed, but there was an undercurrent all the same.

The Gun said, 'I call him. Do not be sick yet.'

He put the phone to his ear, and kept the gun pointed in their direction.

And what would a hero do, Eliot wondered bitterly. A hero would have made his move by now – there'd been moments, like when Louise had pushed the man to the ground, when it could all have been laid to rest: Eliot could have stepped forward, stamped on the man's head, picked up the gun, and kept him for the cops. He'd have been reassuring Chris before she'd known anything was going on – *Nothing that happened was my fault, except the good bits*. And his excuse for not doing so was what? That he had his boys in his arms – that they were holding him back. It would have been dangerous and they might have been hurt, so instead here they were: in a dangerous situation, in which they might be hurt. Or worse. He'd known the alternatives even as he'd watched Louise sprinting for the door, and it was something worse than cowardice that had held him back – it was the simple inability to rise to the occasion. Every man's worst nightmare, whatever the context. That events will simply leave him at a loss: legs jellified; brain frozen. His boys were an excuse, not a reason. The reason was simply that he, Eliot Pedlar, wasn't up to it.

'Who do I speak to?'

Like sitting on a bus, listening to one half of a stranger's conversation.

'No, I tell you this. I have a gun, you know? And there are people here. Children also.'

As if that were a cue, Timmy and Gordy fastened their grips, and Eliot held both as tightly as he could. Whatever was happening, and however inadequate his responses to it, he would hold his children while he could, and put himself in the way of whatever came towards them. That much, he was capable of. It was hardwired, wasn't it? – it was what men did. He was sure it was what men did.

'Now I tell you this. I do not want to speak to you. There is a man, he works for your secret services, yes? His name is Whistler. He work in Soho.'

They were listening, but all they knew was that this had nothing to do with them.

'You fetch him here, I talk to him. Yes?'

This had happened almost an hour ago now.

'I am not listening any more. I have a gun, yes? You know this. I will shoot some people if you try to come in. Goodbye.'

The way he had looked at them after saying that – after telling the policeman that he'd shoot them – was like nothing Eliot could put a word to.

And then they had waited, and the policemen did not try to enter.

Eventually, they heard the helicopter.

5

WHAT DID IT FEEL like, stepping out of the helicopter? It should have felt like being a star – one rather obviously fallen to earth – but it hadn't been a great landing, to be honest. An uncomfortable bump that had Ben Whistler reaching for his religion, only to find he hadn't packed it. The field they'd touched down on was next to a suburban road littered with police cars, with blue-and-white emergency bunting strung at the nearby crossroads. Behind this tape a crowd was gathering, prominent among which would be press, Ben guessed. He hoped none of the cameras picked up his face. It was impossible, he discovered, to walk away from the chopper without crouching, though its blades were too high to touch a hair on his head. One of those precautions common sense demanded, even while logic chuckled.

The man approaching – tall, middle-aged, his uniform singing of authority – was extending a hand towards Ben; a courtesy that didn't reach as far as his unsmiling face. It turned out he was proffering a mobile phone.

'It seems we're running a secretarial service.' His voice wasn't smiling either.

'My phone,' Ben realised. 'I left it on my desk.'

'So it would seem.'

Ben took the device with an apologetic shrug, just as the

chopper lifted off, its racket making communication impossible – he sketched a wave at the departing pilot while the grass all around bowed down. The helicopter buzzed improbably away; its noise enormous, then medium-sized, then smaller. The phone in Ben's hand coughed, or perhaps had been coughing all this time, unheard. Already Ben knew who this would be. Bad Sam, everybody called him.

'Are you there, for Christ's sake?'

'I'm here.'

'Whistler?'

'Yes.'

'Don't fuck this up.'

'I thought you'd already managed that,' Ben didn't say. Instead, he said: 'What should I know about this guy?'

But Bad Sam Chapman had his own agenda. 'You're fourth floor, right?'

'That's hardly a secret.'

(Professional joke.)

'So you've never done fieldwork.'

Ben took a deep breath; hoped it didn't carry. 'I've had the training, I've done the Leipzig course. I scored in the top five per—'

'So you've never done fieldwork.'

'. . . What should I know about this guy?'

'You're the big blond, right? Cubicle by the emergency exit?'

As if Sam Chapman didn't have total recall.

'They made me fire warden. It's a huge responsibility.'

'That why they put you on a helicopter, Whistler? Fourth floor's Accounts.'

'I know.'

'So why you?'

'That, I don't know,' Ben said.

After a moment, Sam Chapman said, 'Jesus fucking Christ.'

'I don't even know who he is. But I'm the only one he'll talk to.'

'They say he's got hostages.'

'There's four of them. Two adults, two kids.'

'So send for the accountant.'

'Wasn't my idea. Perhaps if he didn't have a gun—'

'What?'

'Nothing.'

'And they didn't tell you who this joker is?'

'They said you'd fill me in.'

'You sure you're prepared for this? You didn't even bring a frigging mobile, for Christ's sake.'

Way over yonder, the helicopter was a dot in the sky, and then not even that. There were clouds too; the white fluffy kind – children in nurseries draw clouds like that, the same way they draw the sky as a thin blue line, under which a round yellow sun hangs. Probably the gap between childhood and life was the moment you noticed the real world didn't follow art's rules. There were two small boys in that nursery right now. Ben wondered whether they'd be bridging that gap today.

'You still there?'

'There's a lot of policemen about. Some of them seem testy. The one whose phone I've borrowed is particularly upset.' He hoped the cop in question couldn't hear this, and made him a reprise of the wave he'd offered the pilot – a piece of social semaphore; apology for events beyond his control. The glare he received in reply singed his eyebrows. 'Do you want to tell me anything important?'

It was distance allowed Ben to say this – distance and the heady rush of those events he couldn't control. The day was gathering pace; he was a hunk of driftwood on an incoming tide. The next few hours would determine whether he was cast up safely on to the beach, or splintered on untidy rocks.

'I'm heading your way. I'm ten minutes off.'

'I'm not sure any of us can wait that long.'

'You're an amateur, Whistler—'

'Nott sent me. I think he outranks you.'

Distance, yes, and the freedom that comes with falling . . . What was happening, Ben was helpless to stop. Pretty soon, he was going to be negotiating with a gunman. There had to be some perks attached. Dissing Sam Chapman was a good place to start.

'You sure you're not gay, Whistler?'

This wasn't the response Ben expected.

'This again?'

'Just a thought.'

'Maybe one we should discuss later. Sometime when there's not a hostage—'

'Whistler—'

'—situation I'm supposed to handle without even—'

'Weiss was gay. Miro Weiss?'

'—What about him?'

'That's his boyfriend in the nursery, Whistler. Miro Weiss's boyfriend. His name's Jaime Segura. Ever heard of him?'

'. . . No.'

'Neither had I before last night. But he's heard of you. Is there something you're not telling me, Whistler?'

Ben ended the call. The policeman came to meet him.

Eliot Pedlar wasn't much given to metaphor, but he had an apple tree in his garden, and he knew what anxiety felt like. Anxiety was clearing a lawn of fallen apples on a windy morning; the basket in his arms getting heavier every moment, while the constant *thud-thud* spoke of more fruit hitting the ground. It was both the weight and the knowledge that things weren't getting easier. Every *thud* tugged at something inside him, like a fish-hook in the heart.

His arms were full of his boys, not apples, but that hook tugged all the same.

Until the helicopter landed something approaching calm had settled on this strange grouping. Something like an intermission in an organised event, though without coffee and sandwiches. Not that he was hungry. The ordinary appetites belonged elsewhere now; was it less than three hours back he'd been in bed, right hand reaching for his member? That, too, felt like a weird joke, even though the body that had been in his mind back then was less than two feet away now. Some fantasies, it seemed, broached reality, though in kicking their way inside, they took down foundations you didn't want disturbed. So here he was, in another arguably intimate scenario with Louise Kennedy, and what he mostly wanted was to be far away: with his children, safe at home.

He remembered other daydreams. There'd been a recurring fantasy in adolescence of himself as an astronaut, kind of, though hardly the brave heroic astronaut most fantasies rely on. In Eliot's version, his spaceship was little more than a pod, and his role was to be placed in suspended animation within it; a painless, totally unfeeling state. Then the pod would be boosted into space, its sole purpose to hurtle through nothingness until it arrived – if it ever did – at another planet capable of sustaining life. This would take thousands of years – maybe hundreds of thousands. Who knew? And when he reached this other planet, if he ever did, everyone he'd ever known or heard of, along with their hundred-times great-grandchildren, would be dead and forgotten. He'd never see another human again.

It didn't take genius to understand that this was a variation on every teenaged boy's alienation issues. More disturbing was the fact that lately he'd been relying on it again, to cast himself into sleep at night.

And now, the nearest thing in the area to a space-bound

pod was that helicopter, which had landed nearby and taken off again, carrying some lucky beggar to a place of safety, but leaving Eliot here.

The boys shifted in his arms. He should be whispering comforts but couldn't bear to fracture the silence. He had sunk to the floor, and the boys were concentrated either side of him, trying to huddle into as contained a unit as possible – to crawl so far inside his embrace, they'd actually be inside him. Eliot was their space pod now, though unable to break gravity's spell. He was letting them down by not lifting them up. And they were stuck here as long as the Gun demanded.

Louise and Judy were both on the ground too; Louise with her legs tucked beside her yogically; Judy in a squalid heap. It was wrong, doubtless wrong, to be sharing this situation with another frightened victim and feel such dislike of her, but it was probably human too, if that were an excuse. Judy, he was sure, would see the rest of them in hell if it would set her free. Nor did she have the intelligence to hide this.

And as for the Gun, he was the only one upright. Well, he'd have to be, wouldn't he? There was vulnerability involved in wielding power; it demanded showing no weakness. Power fed on its own absolute nature. Any flaws would require immediate attention; any chink in the armour need balancing by swift brutality. The boy looked too soft to be playing this role – his cheeks fuzzy; his eyes a liquid brown – but children climbed onto Tube trains, their backpacks stuffed with dynamite; young women corseted themselves with Semtex, and headed off to market. There was no reading the mind's construction in the face, and never had been.

'. . . Daddy?'

'Hush, Gordon.' And immediately Eliot hated himself for that: what would the Gun do, shoot them for talking? If he was going to shoot them for talking, he was going to shoot them anyway. 'What is it? What do you need?'

As if there were any way he could meet his children's needs right now.

'Gordy needs a wee?'

'So do I, Daddy,' Timmy said. Then corrected himself: 'Timmy does too.'

'Gordy needs a wee *now*?'

Timmy whimpered at this, as if he'd been unjustly relegated to second place, despite being senior by seven minutes. Looking down on them, Eliot remembered a time when he'd only been sure which boy he was holding by checking the crowns of their heads – Timmy's was off centre. Now approaching four, they were more sharply individual; both fair, like their mother, and both blue-eyed, but Timmy's nose was slightly squashed; Gordy was thinner of face. And Gordy had the habit – born of coming second, he suspected – of making everything a question, even his statements. *'I want a drink?'* It sounded like his first language was valley-girl. And now he was slipping into the third person again, which wasn't a great sign.

Eliot said, 'Just hold on a minute.'

'We *can't* hold on, Daddy.'

He could have sworn they said that simultaneously.

'Please, you make them be quiet,' the boy said.

'They need to use the toilet,' Eliot said.

'Nobody is going anywhere. You stay where I can see you.'

'They're very small boys,' Eliot said. 'If you don't let them go, there'll be accidents.' Too much euphemism there. Too much ambiguity. 'If you don't let them use the toilet, they'll wet themselves.' All over me, he didn't add.

'No,' said the boy.

Louise said, 'I'll take them.'

'No.'

'It's just over there, through that door. There are no windows, no ways of escape. You can check if you like.'

'You should not be arguing with me like this.'

'I'm not arguing,' she said. 'You're in charge. But it's not going to be pleasant for any of us if you don't let them use the toilet.'

There was a crackle of energy from outside: an engine firing up, a car leaving – any other time, it would have meant nothing. Now, it reverberated. There were other forces acting; machinery grinding away in the background. There had been two phone calls since the Gun had demanded that somebody called Whistler be sent: the one side Eliot had heard had been negative, unco-operative. The Gun did not want food or drink sent in; was not prepared to let Peter Faulks speak to the hostages. Was not intending to surrender. All he wanted was the man Whistler. When was the man Whistler arriving? Probably Faulks had told him 'Soon'. . . . Eliot had an image of an avuncular type; someone morally grounded – Morgan Freeman sprung to mind. He would be reasonable and sympathetic, and his calm counsel would make short work of whatever ugly scenario the Gun entertained.

'They're children,' Louise said. 'Whatever you're after, they're not part of this. They have no part in this.'

Recognising a cue when he heard one, Gordon began crying again.

'Let me take them to the toilet. They'll calm down, and none of us will have to listen to this.'

And I won't get wet on, Eliot silently added.

The Gun thought about it. Judy seemed about to add something; incredibly, she thought better of it.

'I go check,' he said at last. 'If there is a window, I . . .' Apparently unsure of what he would be, he found the vocabulary at last. 'I am annoyed.'

'Wouldn't want that,' Louise said, sincerely.

'I am annoyed,' he repeated, though the tense was born of grammatical uncertainty. He wasn't annoyed yet. His gun remained silent.

Without taking his eyes from them, he walked across to the

toilet door and kicked it open. What he saw matched Louise's description: no windows; no ways of escape. Just two cubicles, and a sink in the corner. He returned to the centre of the room.

'Okay, take them. The door stays open.'

Gordy removed his head from his father's thigh, and blinked.

'Go now.'

It wasn't clear if it was the boys he was addressing.

Timmy too unwrapped himself. The pair looked so sleepy it was heartbreaking. Eliot struggled to his feet, feeling his joints creak in splintery protest, but the twins weren't waiting. For the first time since the Gun had appeared, both left his side at once, stumbling across to Louise, and taking a hand each.

She was already on her feet. 'It's okay,' she said to Eliot. 'I've got them.'

Yes, he might have said, or No – he didn't really notice. All this happened at a remove, and ordinary vocabulary was suddenly a foreign language.

'It's what they're used to,' Louise went on. Perhaps she had noticed his confusion, and felt compelled to explain. 'They're here, and I'm their teacher. It's not the first time I've given them a hand.'

This too was a series of statements slightly adrift from sense to Eliot's ears, but he knew she was trying to bolster his boys by asserting normalcy. Yes, they were here, and yes, she was their teacher. He was grateful to her as she led his boys into the toilet; grateful, too, for a few unencumbered moments in which he could try to take control of his own fears, most of which expressed themselves as a single question. Would he and his boys leave the annexe alive?

The Gun held the answer to this, but wasn't saying anything. Yet.

'I take it you've done this sort of thing before.'

'We get a lot of training,' Ben improvised.

The man he'd returned the phone to was Superintendent Malcolm Fredericks, who evidently wasn't happy about playing switchboard. Other events had contributed to this dissatisfaction. 'I already have a hostage negotiator.'

And if it was up to Ben, he could get on with it. 'Being here wasn't my idea. It's the man inside who asked for me.'

'You know him?'

'I didn't know he existed until an hour ago,' Ben said.

'So why you?'

'No idea.'

'Is there any chance I'll get a straight answer?'

'I've already given several,' Ben said truthfully. 'Shouldn't I be getting on with what I'm here to do?'

Fredericks looked at him, hard. Under other circumstances, Ben might have wilted, but freefall still held him in its grasp – either today would work out fine, in which case Fredericks wouldn't matter, or it wouldn't, in which case ditto. But Fredericks, reasonably enough, had his own perspective. 'I don't like spies descending on my patch.'

Ben assumed this wasn't a reference to his mode of arrival. 'I assure you, nobody wanted this.'

'So what's going on? This man's a terrorist, right? So have you tracked him down just in time? Or just too late?'

'Even if I knew, I'd not be at liberty to—'

'No, you lot never are, are you? And when you've finished playing your cloak and dagger games, you bugger off back to the South Bank for latte and croissants, and it's us poor sods left clearing up your mess. There are five innocent people in there, two of them children, and your lot armed the bastard holding them. But you're not going to be breaking it to their loved ones when this goes arse over tit, are you?'

'That's not going to happen.'

'Is that a guarantee?'

'What guarantees do you give? Didn't you have a hostage

situation two years back? I don't remember that ending happily.'

Fredericks flushed. 'There've been others since. We've done just fine. While your branch of the so-called security services has been sending us into war, when it's not been failing to prevent bombs on the Underground. If those people in there had a choice, you think they'd want you on their case?'

Politics was nowhere Ben was about to wander. Besides, something had struck bells. 'You said five. *Five* innocent people in there.'

It took the superintendent a moment to change gear. 'You didn't know?'

'You're on the ground. I've been . . .' He pointed skywards.

Fredericks stared a while longer. Wondering whether to tell him to fuck off, Ben thought – no policeman liked having to stump up info while being stonewalled in return. But there were lives at stake. Fredericks said, 'There's a teacher, Louise Kennedy. She had the chance to escape, but didn't.'

This was news. 'Do we know why?'

'Perhaps she has a sense of responsibility.'

Pretty to think so. 'Her, I knew about. There's a man called Pedlar, too. With his twins. Who's the fifth?'

'The cleaner. A woman called Judy Ainsworth. I suspect she's the kind of person easily falls through the gaps where you're concerned.'

Ben said nothing.

Fredericks said, 'I didn't mean you personally. But this is what pisses me off. We have local knowledge. We are, as you say, on the ground. But we have to put up with so-called experts being drafted in as if we're a bunch of amateurs.'

Ben said, 'I don't claim to be an expert. But I have been invited.' He looked around, and could see, crouched at intervals behind the hedge this side of the footpath, policemen in heavy-weather gear. 'Time's passing. Are you giving me permission to go in there?'

'Do you really need it?'

'That's not a conversation either of us wants right now. Sir.'

Fredericks breathed out heavily. This spook wasn't as bad as the first – seemed to grasp the roots of his anger – but both were playing the same game. And both knew Fredericks couldn't win. 'All right,' he said. 'Let's get started.'

Ben hid his relief. He was in no hurry to face a gun, but he'd rather be inside before Chapman turned up. One bad man at a time.

The pair headed for the nursery gates.

Inside the annexe, Judy was all alone, all alone.

Oh, there were *others* – the thug with the gun; the useless man slumped against the wall; and, in the toilet now, Louise Kennedy with those children – but Judy was all alone. Policemen outside would know she was present, but none would actually care. She'd be a name on a list, was all. But these others – they'd have people worrying about them; people in tears, wondering if they'd see their loved ones again. Even the thug with the gun looked the type to have a mother. And she, somewhere foreign, would soon know what her son was up to, and would weep, and hope he lived through it. But no one wept for Judy.

If Derek were alive . . .

But Derek wasn't, and even if he were, he'd be happy about her predicament. That was obvious. He'd left her, hadn't he? Found some trollop and spent every last penny they'd saved – and some they hadn't – on making a new life for himself. So even if Derek were alive, he'd be smiling to think of Judy in mortal danger; all it would take would be one squeeze of a trigger and *bang*, no more Judy. It had almost already happened. And then he could forget about her even more completely than he already had, and Judy's life would dwindle to an unregretted close. Unregretted by everyone but Judy. She wanted to live – it wasn't fair she had to die. Which you couldn't say about Derek.

Once or twice, she'd dreamed his death. It had taken place far away, and had been a hot death: a death in a car. Judy didn't watch the kind of films where that happened, but her dream had felt accurate enough. Derek had been at the wheel, his trollop beside him. The road they travelled was long, and there was no other traffic. There was nothing at all, in fact; just miles and miles of sand stretching every direction; mounds of it folding over and over; sinking from sight, then rising to greet the sky. The road was long and straight and bumpy. It was also mined. When the jeep hit a bump which wasn't a bump, it turned to a ball of fire, somersaulting once, twice, three times, before coming to a rest upside down, while the flames that enveloped it blossomed brightly – an orange and black rose – and smoke purled upwards in a never-ending stream. What happened to the bodies, Judy didn't know. She always woke before that part. But she suspected they'd be charcoal husks: faintly human shapes twisted to attitudes of pleading. Stripped of flesh and clothing, their teeth would be roasted corks; their organs a thick gravy, puddled beneath their heads.

It wasn't that Judy invited such images, but she was helpless to keep at bay the things that visited her at night.

And now a noise escaped her lips again; something between a whine and a prayer for mercy. She hoped they'd all come out of this alive, but if there could only be one survivor, she wanted it to be her.

Anyone would feel the same. Not anyone would admit it.

And neither of the men paid attention, because Judy was all alone.

The boys huddled into the same cubicle and weed either side of the bowl, their trousers and pants pooled round their respective ankles. Any other time, it would have been funny. Now,

Louise just wanted it to be over. Who'd have thought little boys had so much piss in them?

'Hurry,' she told them. But no, that was wrong. 'I mean, take your time. Don't worry.'

But hurry.

Neither looked up, both intent on the job in hand.

Their twin streams dwindled and finished at the same moment. Hoisting their trousers, they left the cubicle together – for full comic effect they should have jammed themselves in the doorway, but were little enough to exit side by side.

'Hands,' she said.

Obediently, they turned to the sink, and four small hands shared the same stream of water for a micro-second. Timmy had turned the hot tap on; Gordy turned it off. There was a natural, unrehearsed choreography to this that informed a lot of their actions.

'Good boys.'

For a moment, everything was normal. Nothing was happening here that couldn't be found every weekday in this building.

Then normality sucked away at the sight of the Gun.

The boys skittered to their father as fast their legs would take them. If things were still ordinary, Louise would have barked 'No running!' Instead she waited until they were safe in his arms, or as safe as the situation allowed, and then waited some more.

'You come out now.'

'I need to use the toilet.'

'You come out.'

'No,' she said. 'I need to use the toilet. I'll be two minutes.'

But rather than turn her back on him, she remained in the doorway, staring. He stared back, his face a confusion of strong emotions, of which anger was the clearest. But his gun remained by his side. He was not about to kill her; not yet. And with that realisation came another: that he was as much their prisoner as they were his. All he had was his gun. And as soon as he used it, policemen would burst in, and whatever demonstration he was intent on would be over, along with his life. Where terrorism was concerned, no prisoners were taken. That rule had been written in blood under the streets of London, and would hold true here.

He said, 'You must do as I say.'

'Yes. But first I need to use the toilet.'

'You are very stupid!'

She said, 'What I told you before, about what a mess there'd be if you didn't let them go?' She couldn't remember whether she'd told him that or just thought it. 'It's true of me too. Of all of us. There's no window, no way of escape. I'll be two minutes.'

Judy was staring at her now; had lifted her head from whatever well of misery she'd been drowning in, and was beaming pure hatred, as if Louise were endangering them all. And maybe she was. But this was part of *becoming human*; part of letting him know they were people. If he cut them, they'd bleed. And every so often, they needed to piss.

After the longest seconds in recorded history, he said, 'Leave door open.'

'Yes.'

She propped it open with the wastepaper bin, and stepped into the second cubicle.

Inside, she relieved herself, because this hadn't been just for show, and as she did so bent forward, fished in her jeans pocket, and freed her mobile phone.

I don't have one, she'd told him. *I mean, I've got one, but not with me . . . It's in the other office.*

It had been in her pocket. But it was a compact model, and didn't make a bulge – slim was good; slim was cool and sexy, though no advert she'd ever seen had made use of this scenario.

Mobile in hand, she felt she'd won a round. Had tricked

him; had earned a minute's space, and the freedom to communicate.

It was only as she pressed the button that brought her phone to life that it occurred to her that everyone who needed to know she was here already did.

At the gates to the nursery, Ben Whistler met Peter Faulks. He'd just emerged from the Major Incident Vehicle.

'So you're going in there?'

'That's right.'

'Done this before?'

'Your boss already asked me that.'

'We have five hostages. I'd like to think your joining them will do more good than harm.'

Faulks was a round man with ruddy-coloured cheeks; had a face just begging for a disguise – pin a big white beard on it, he'd be Santa Claus. No problem about forgetting what he really looked like, because that could happen while you were talking to him. But he was a copper, and he'd done this before, and Ben hadn't. And he was worried about what might happen to the hostages, which Ben was too, largely because he was going to be one of them soon.

He said, 'I've not done this before. I'd rather not be doing it now. But this man, whoever he is, asked for me by name. Going in there has got to do more good than harm, wouldn't you say?'

Whoever he is . . .

'Let's hope so. You're not armed?'

'Christ, no.'

'Wired?'

'Should I be?'

'It might annoy him. Besides, we've got a mobile inside. It's picking up everything in a five-yard range. Things are quiet now, and ideally they'll stay that way. If you can't talk him out – if it goes arse over tit – we'll be with you inside four seconds.'

'How long does it take to squeeze a trigger?'

'Think positive thoughts. He knows who you are, right?'

'Seems to.'

'That's good. The last thing a hostage wants to be is a stranger. You need to be a full person, with family, with feelings. He's got to understand you're not just a pawn in whatever game he's playing.'

'He's given no hint of what that is?'

'Your lot know more than we do. And none of you are saying anything.'

'Trust me, I'm in the dark.'

'We have to trust you, Mr Whistler. We have no choice in the matter. Got any electronics on you? Mobile, iPod?'

'BlackBerry.'

'Let's have it. It might throw off transmission from our mobile. Besides, if he's got any sense, first thing he'll do is stomp on it in case it's bugged.'

'But he didn't stomp the mobile?'

'He needed that. He doesn't need this.' Faulks took Ben's gadget and dropped it into his jacket pocket. Ben wondered if he'd ever see it again, and not because he thought Faulks might steal it. 'Once you're in, remember this. In intense situations, one person's mood infects others with lightning speed.'

'I've been in relationships like that before.'

'And try not to be funny. He might take it the wrong way. And he has a gun.'

'How many times have you done this?'

'Talked people out?'

'Gone inside.'

'Never. We don't do that. It's stupid and dangerous.'

But think positive thoughts, Ben remembered. 'Are you wearing a vest?' he asked.

142

'Of course. Standard practice. We can get you one if you want, but . . .'

'It might annoy him?'

'Odd as this sounds, you've got to establish some kind of normality in there. Don't forget the gun. But don't act like it's all there is. Would you wear Kevlar when you're out on a visit? Oh, I forgot. You've been in relationships like that before.'

And he grinned, which transformed his face. Maybe not so forgettable after all.

Ben looked around – it felt like one last look. He knew no more about how to handle the situation now than when he'd got up this morning. When he hadn't even known there was a situation. He checked his watch: 10:22. Any minute, Bad Sam Chapman would turn up and start throwing weight around. And Ben wasn't wearing Kevlar.

'Good luck,' Faulks offered.

'Thanks.'

Superintendent Fredericks was standing a little way off. He nodded at Ben, as if echoing Faulks's salutation, but the grin escaped him. Fair enough. This wasn't a social gathering.

On the other hand, Ben had been invited.

He said, 'See you later,' and tried to sound like he meant it.

'Yes. I'll call him. Say you're here.'

For no reason he could have articulated, Ben checked that his collar was straight. Faulks was holding his mobile to his ear as Ben walked into the nursery grounds, where he truly felt alone.

'. . . Mum?'

'Louise! Where are you? There's policemen up the road and—'

'Mum, I'm okay.'

'I can't hear you. You'll have to speak up.'

She might have known this would be a mistake.

'Mum . . . I'm in the nursery. There's a man with a gun, and—'

'That's what they're saying. God in heaven, you're not trapped with him, are you?'

'Yes. But—'

But what? But don't worry?

'—But it's going to be all right, Mum. It will work out fine.' She hoped.

'Oh Louise, you should never . . .'

But whatever it was Louise should never, to have avoided ending up where she was, Louise's mother couldn't get to grips with.

Louise was whispering – breathing the words, almost; it was a wonder they were finding their way through the ether. And as she opened her mouth, to see if anything resembling comfort would emerge, she heard, out in the annexe, the familiar sound of another mobile coming to life. The outside world was breaking in.

'Mum? I love you.'

'I can't hear you, dear. What are you doing? I think you should come home now.'

'I can't do that yet.' The other mobile's trill cut off: she heard the boy answer it. *Yes.* Not a question. She dared speak louder, now he was occupied. 'I have to go. Things will be all right.' The second time she'd asserted this. 'Mum? Can you hear me?'

'Oh, what have you *done*, Louise?'

'I haven't *done* anything,' she couldn't help snapping. 'Oh, Mum . . . I have to go. I love you, Mum.'

She didn't wait for a reply. Perhaps she was worried it wouldn't echo her own words. Instead, she stood, adjusted her clothing, and flushed the toilet. When she rejoined the others, the boy was putting the phone back in his pocket. 'He is here,' he said. It was as if they were complicit; as if they'd been waiting for the same thing.

'Whistler?' she said, just to maintain that pretence.

'He is here, yes.'

Louise went and stood against the wall again. Eliot looked at her, but she only glanced back.

Mostly, she was wondering who'd come through the door.

Fredericks joined Faulks at the gate, and the pair watched Ben Whistler as he made his way across the small car park, unlocked the gate in the dividing fence with the keys Louise had thrown over it, and headed for the annexe.

'What are the chances of a good result on this?'

Faulks said, 'He's never done this before.'

'Bloody spooks.'

'We have to assume he knows things we don't.'

'But mostly,' Fredericks said, 'we have to assume that his being here means this isn't some misplaced domestic. Why do you think the girl went back in?'

'You think she knows the gunman?'

'God knows. She was with a City bank. Why did she leave to come and teach kiddies?'

'And is there a connection?'

'He hasn't made any demands yet. When he does, I wonder if we'll get to find out what they are. Before the spooks clamp down.' He shook his head. 'We should have brought her out while we had the chance.'

'We didn't have the chance,' Faulks told him.

'She was there, in plain sight . . .'

'She was there on sufferance, sir. "If I don't go back, he'll use the gun." That's what she said.'

'And if he uses it now, he's got one more body to use it on.'

'She went back inside. She didn't have to. Before we got here, I mean. She brought a little girl out, raised the alarm, then went back inside. Because there are other children there.'

'I don't trust heroes,' Fredericks said.

'Me neither, sir,' said Faulks. 'But they're more use in there than out here. You know what we really need?'

'I'm sure you're about to tell me.'

'Thermal imaging. Show us exactly where everyone is, what they're doing. With the right equipment, we could take this guy out with no risk to the hostages. We have trained men, he's just a kid with a stolen gun. We don't even know he can use it.'

'So killing him might be an overreaction.'

'And might be saving five innocent lives. We don't have to do the maths ourselves. The press will do that afterwards.'

'Is that what recent history's taught us, Peter?'

'De Menezes wasn't who they thought he was. This guy's got a gun.'

'But we don't have the equipment, that's what you're saying.'

'We could have it within the hour. One call to the Met—'

'That's not going to happen.'

Faulks said, 'Between the Chief Constable and the security services, we're going to be lucky if today turns out right, Malc.'

Fredericks didn't respond. Instead, he surveyed the house next to the nursery grounds, twenty yards or so behind them: a large detached building which had gone up at the same time as the nursery. Nice-looking piece of property, with two substantial chimney stacks, one either end of the roof. A figure nestled against the nearest; strapped to it, Fredericks assumed. The rifle it held was trained on the annexe door.

On which Whistler knocked twice before pushing it open, and walking in.

Knocking – the wood harsh against his knuckles – returned Ben to reality. As he'd walked through the deserted nursery grounds, this quality had been suspended: he'd entered instead some post-apocalyptic environment, though the nature of the apocalypse remained obscure. But it was clear that there had been people here, who had left in a hurry: there was even a doll face down on the grass, a movie-version staple of catastrophe. Other clues abounded: footprints in the flower beds; an abandoned sweater. Mostly, though, there was an indefinable sense of recent evacuation. Ben could almost see the shapes hanging in the air: cutouts of children who'd been playing here, until fear dispersed them. The same fear was infecting Ben. Here in the quiet zone, the only living human was himself, though countless watchers studied his every footfall, their unrelenting gazes scoring hot marks on his back. Strange that he felt like a target to those behind him, when it was the man up ahead he really had to worry about.

That's his boyfriend in the nursery, Whistler. Miro Weiss's boyfriend. His name's Jaime Segura. You heard that name before?

No, Ben hadn't.

But Segura had heard of him.

There was a voice. 'That is Whistler?'

'This is Whistler, yes. Should I come in?'

His voice scraped, as if he'd not used it in a while. He swallowed.

There fell a pause. All this way: what were the odds Segura had sent for Ben just to put a bullet in him as he walked through the door? Numbers rattled through his mind, but none were any help. That was the thing about probabilities: they became irrelevant in the face of event. In the face of a gun.

'. . . Yes.'

Ben pushed open the door and walked in.

There were six people in the room, but he only saw one to start with. Jaime Segura was a lot younger than Miro Weiss – and Miro, troubling forty, had given the impression of being older. One of those people who'd been middle-aged the day he first picked up a razor. But Segura had olive skin, dark hair, brown eyes, and though he evidently hadn't used a razor himself

147

recently, this mostly showed on his chin and upper lip, the way it does in adolescence. His hair was a tangled mass of feathery curls. And his clothes were a generation removed from anything Miro might yet be found dead in: jeans and a brown fake-leather jacket over a zip-up top.

He wore boots that looked like they'd seen a mile or two.

He carried the gun Neil Ashton had dropped when the car uncluttered his brain.

Closing the door behind him, Ben said, 'So,' which even to his own ears sounded like make-weight conversation.

'You will stand against the wall?'

'If that would make you comfortable.'

Jaime didn't answer.

Ben crossed to the wall, keeping a careful distance between himself and the gun as he did so.

Though it wasn't like there was enough space in this room to confuse a bullet.

There were other eyes on him, of course, and now Ben counted them down: they belonged to two women, two boys, and a man about his own age. The eyes of the twins gazed out from a pair of heads half buried in their father's thighs, and even Ben – unused to children – could tell they didn't know if he represented threat or promise. Fair enough. He wasn't sure himself. Their father's look was less complicated, as if Ben's arrival bore the stamp of authority. And with that look, some-thing other than fear settled on Ben's shoulders – for the first time, it weighed on him that it wasn't only his own life he had to worry about here. Strange that it was the man's look rather than the children's that brought this home to him.

Strange, too, that it had taken this long for the message to get through.

As for the women, the older – she'd be the cleaner; the one he'd had no information on – looked down almost before she'd looked up. But hatchet-faced; that was the expression that fitted – though almost before it occurred, another replaced it: anvil-faced. Anvil-faced. Her round, bitter mask bore the marks of the blows life delivered. Or maybe he was reading too much into an extreme situation. The younger woman didn't look away. She'd be the teacher, the one who'd come back inside when she'd had the chance to flee. Which spoke of bravery, obviously, but again it might be foolish to jump to conclusions . . . And she was pretty; dark-haired, light-skinned, with eyes full of feeling – anxiety, but defiance too, and maybe hope. And here was another strange element in a moment full of them: that even with a stranger's gun pointing at him, and a wall to stand against, he could notice a woman's looks, and appreciate that he was the focus of her attention.

'My name's Ben Whistler,' he said to the room at large.

'Thank you,' Louise Kennedy whispered.

He wondered whether she always sounded like that, or whether her voice, like his, was coming out twisted and unnatural. He was not trained for situations like this. He was – as Bad Sam Chapman had mentioned – a backroom boy. An accountant. *I've had the training, I've done the Leipzig course. I scored in the top five per cent.* Which was true, except for the bit about the top five per cent. Like any good figures man, Ben knew when to fiddle the numbers.

'Okay,' he said. 'I'm here. Now what?'

The boy pointed the gun at the space precisely between Ben's eyes.

6

M EANWHILE, JONATHAN NOTT WAS south of the river.
South of the river was Vauxhall Cross, where Nott
had once spent a working life crammed full of meetings like
this, though on the other side of the desk. His role had been
to smile politely at out-of-house visitors while feeding them
through a mincer. The day he'd been told he was being relo-
cated was black-ribboned in his memory.

'Operations Director, Jonty. It's not a demotion.'

It's not a demotion carried a subtly different meaning to *It's
a promotion.*

'Directing the operations of a bunch of money shufflers.'

'Which is important. Keeping track of the pennies, that's
what it's about these days, yes?'

'I thought it was about defending the Commonwealth.
Foiling terrorists.'

'Well, that's important too. And it's felt that such an, ah,
delicate task is best left to those who show aptitude for it.'

In the aftermath of 7/7, a lot of careers received unwanted
attention. Jonathan Nott's desk was packed and boxed before
that chat was over.

And now he was back on-site for the weekly debriefing, an
increasingly uncomfortable session. These past weeks he'd
eschewed the official car; had taken to walking along the river.
A small enough economy – he'd have to maintain it for a

couple of millennia to cover his section's shortfall – but the river was more conducive to thought than the stream of honking traffic. Not that the relative calm had produced any brainwaves.

Other side of the desk was Roger Barrowby: aka the Barrowboy. The grammar school/redbrick background helped. Roger had thinning sandy hair, a prominent chin, and a habit of pressing the tip of a finger to its central dimple, as if trying to encourage it back into his jaw. His jacket was flaked with dandruff. Perhaps he worried too stringent a shampoo would lay waste to his suffering hair.

'Terribly pleasant morning, don't you think?'

'I hadn't noticed.'

'South Bank's lovely, weather like this. Sun glinting off the river sort of thing.'

Nott hadn't imagined his travel arrangements had passed without notice, and wasn't about to rise to the bait. 'If you say so.'

Small talk over. 'Anything to tell us, Jonty?'

'Apart from the fact that I'm only Jonty to friends and equals?'

Roger smiled, as if Nott had made an amusing observation. 'I'm assuming there's no news of Mr Weiss.'

'No.'

'Because if there had been, you'd have let us know soonest.'

'Soonest. Of course.'

'You're not being blamed for this, you know.'

'No? I rather had the impression I was.'

'Nobody expects anyone of your, ah, *seniority* to be up to speed with the digital world.'

'We wouldn't be bordering on age discrimination, would we, Roger?'

'Heaven forfend. I have trouble setting the video myself. No, I simply meant that with these keyboard whizz-kids, anything can happen. Turn your back for a moment, they've diverted the Service's PAYE funds into their Halifax supersavers.'

'I'm not sure "whizz-kid" applies to Weiss. The man's thirty-nine.'

A flash of annoyance crossed the Barrowboy's face. 'Not really the thrust of my point, Jonty. All I mean is, you're still one of us. Exile doesn't change that.'

'Exile? I was under the impression I'd been *not demoted*.'

'Of course.'

'Though I seem to remember you used to call me sir.'

'It's the new informality, Jonty. Makes the wheels turn faster.'

'This is before they run you down, yes?'

'Speaking of which, what happened this morning? Some, what would you call it, *incident* out Oxford way? Bit off your patch, isn't it?'

'I haven't been to Oxford since my last gaudy. Which, by the way, does make it my patch, rather.'

'Ah, the old college ties. One of your boys run over, am I right?' Fake concentration briefly furrowed his brow. 'Ashton?'

'Neil Ashton.' As you know.

'Bit of a turnaround, eh? When the Dogs get involved in hit and run, they're normally doing the driving.'

'The driver was an estate agent, for God's sake. He had two children in the car. Getting a jump on the school run.'

'Interesting wrinkle.'

'It was an accident,' Nott said.

'Good to know. So what was Ashton up to? With Sam Chapman riding shotgun?'

'Routine business.'

'Sure about that, are we? Nothing to do with Weiss?'

'Not as far as I'm aware,' Nott said.

Barrowby leaned back. His index finger strayed to his chin before he jerked it away – habits were something you broke in this business, whatever they happened to be. 'And now there's a hostage situation in a nursery school.'

'An unfortunate chain of events. Or possibly coincidence.'

Nott allowed his gaze to drift to the window, and a skyline that seemed to change by the week. Sometimes he wondered whether Six's remit went far enough. Terrorists were one thing; were architects another? Hauling himself back, he went on: 'Ashton's gun was lost in the accident. It may – *may* – have ended up in the wrong hands. But nothing's certain. The hostage taker might be a wild card. Nothing to do with us at all.'

'Making it, as you say, a coincidence. That would be a first. Why the helicopter?'

'Chapman's offering aid and assistance. He was *in situ*, after all. I sent back-up. End of story.'

'Rather stretching the definition of your function, wouldn't you say?'

'I've been running operations since you were failing your eleven-plus, Roger. Sam Chapman's an experienced field man. If there's anything for us in this nursery incident, he'll be the first to know.'

'Experienced, I'll give you. But experience doesn't always equate with reliability, does it?'

'You'll have to run that by me again.'

'It's been three weeks since Miro Weiss disappeared with enough money to start his own country, and Bad Sam's no nearer finding him. How hard is he looking?'

Nott said, 'Like you say, it's a digital world. And Weiss covered his tracks well.'

'I don't care if he's the last of the fucking Mohicans, if Chapman was trying, he'd have him by now.' Roger Barrowby paused – he didn't swear often, and knew Nott knew this. 'There have been rumblings,' he went on. 'You police your own, we know that. In principle, we stand by that.'

'You sound like New bloody Labour all over again,' Nott said. 'Identify the principle, then shoot it down in flames.'

'It's been three weeks. A quarter of a billion pounds. And you're getting nowhere. We need a fresh approach.'

'You want to call my Dogs off,' Nott said calmly. Frankly, he was surprised they'd held off this long. 'You're sending your own in.'

'Yes.'

'But it's my section. I have jurisdiction.'

'As I said, we stand by that principle.'

'When I hear you people say *principle*, I reach for my sick bag.'

'No need for *you people*, Jonty. We're all on the same side.'

'Easy to say.'

Roger Barrowby said, 'The money will get lost in the wash, Jonty. You know how much cash has gone missing in reconstruction so far? Of course not. Nobody does. The brothers across the water are throwing billions at friendly contractors, and those are the sums we know about. Every time Cheney blinks, his fraternity pals go *ker-ching*. You don't have to be a *Guardian* reader to know that.'

'So you're happy to forget all about it.'

'But what we really don't need,' Barrowby went on, 'is for anyone to point the finger at our own accounting systems. It's one thing being made to carry the can for a misguided war. It would be quite another if we're caught robbing the corpse afterwards. Careers have foundered on less.'

'I'm sure Sam Chapman knows what he's doing.'

'I'm afraid I agree with you. The question is, did Miro Weiss?'

Nott didn't reply.

'Sad little numbers man, I'd call him squeaky clean except there's something rather grubby about the type, don't you think? Staring at screens all day, then shuffling home to an evening's porn. I'm surprised he had the imagination for a coup like this.'

'What's your point, Roger?'

'We think he had help.'

'And you think Chapman's it?'

'Like you say, he's an experienced agent. But he never made the management grade, and isn't likely to now. Just the kind to spend the long winter nights working out his pension entitlement and feeding his disgruntlement.'

'I don't agree.'

'We're past the consensus stage, Jonty. Call him in.'

'He's not going to like that.'

'He'll be given every opportunity to make his feelings known.' Barrowby looked at his watch. 'I'll expect him at one. Tell him to bring the case file.'

Heading back the long way, Nott stopped for a smoke on the jetty below the Oxo Tower, where he watched the Tate boat plough its polka-dotted furrow through the Thames. A group of tourists took photos. Presumably tourists. But he wouldn't be surprised to find himself under surveillance: Barrowby said not, but that was the trouble with spies. You couldn't believe a word they said.

A cormorant skidded low over the water, heading wherever cormorants went. The tourists pointed, and aimed their cameras.

Nott brought his cigarette to eye level and examined the tip, which glowed brightly as the breeze caught it. He should call Sam Chapman now, and haul him home. Chapman would not be happy. Chapman would especially not be happy if what Barrowby had suggested was true, but if so, the order wouldn't be unexpected. Nott wondered if he'd be able to tell the difference, over a mobile connection? And answered himself: not if he had Bad Sam wired to a seismograph while it happened.

He also wondered if he'd still be Operations Director come the end of the week. And knew the answer to that, too.

When the boy pointed the gun at the space precisely between Ben's eyes, Ben stared straight back. This was the moment his life should have been flashing before him, but what he was mostly looking into was the future that wouldn't happen now – his trip to Brazil: margaritas, señoritas, *hasta la vista*s . . . A very long moment passed.

The boy lowered the gun.

Ben released the breath he hadn't realised he'd been holding.

The boy said, 'You are Ben Whistler.'

Ben nodded. He wasn't sure he could speak.

'Why you send men to kill me?' the boy asked.

The instructions on the packet read *Smokers die a slow and painful death*, but in Bad Sam's mood, frankly, that was a plus. He lit up while waiting for the woodentop on duty to locate someone who understood the game's rules: that a spook was a picture card, while a local plod was a two. The skies overhead rolled big and ordinary, but that was just one more piece of today's global mistake – there should be lightning bolts, seismic shifts. Whistler was inside the annexe, but Bad Sam was stuck out here, on the wrong side of the cordon.

Thou shalt not fuck things up. That was the lost frigging Commandment, as far as Bad Sam Chapman was concerned. As for Thou shalt not kill: it didn't take a genius to find a loophole in that one.

His mobile chirruped and he fished it out. *ooooooooooo* read the number ID: third time in ten minutes. But he wasn't interested in calls from the office right now. They'd be trying to pull him home. He dropped it in his pocket, muffling its drone.

The woodentop returned. 'Sorry, sir, I'm going to have to ask you to move away.' He didn't sound sorry.

He took a breath. 'You read my card?'

'Yes, sir.'

'I mean *read*. You can read, can't you? You didn't just look at the picture?'

'We have a situation in progress, sir. All civilians are to maintain a safe distance from the perimeter.'

Situation. They watched too much television, these idiots. *Perimeter.* 'I look like a civilian to you?'

'I couldn't say, sir. But if I have to ask again, we're approaching an arrestable offence.'

This kid was, what, twenty-five? Twenty-six? Shit: whatever experience he had, attempting to arrest Bad Sam Chapman didn't figure in it yet.

But he didn't need to look around to know there were five other cops in striking distance, this being the operative phrase in an armed *situation.*

'Is Fredericks here?'

He knew damn well Fredericks was here.

'Sir?'

'Your commanding officer. Superintendent Malcolm Fredericks.'

'He's who suggested you move away, sir.'

Chapman nodded, twice. Lightning flashed and earthquakes rumbled.

And here came another cartoon character: a round, red-cheeked man who probably showed borderline on the annual medical. He made a waving gesture for the woodentop. 'I've got this, Morse.' He couldn't possibly have said Morse. He turned to Bad Sam. 'You'd be Chapman.'

'And you?'

'Faulks. Detective Inspector. We're rather stretched. I've better things to do than play messenger.'

'So.' Chapman forced his shoulders back, an age-old method of easing tension. Didn't work. 'You've word from your Super, right? I'm *persona non.* Well, maybe he's forgotten the facts of life—'

But Faulks was shaking his head. 'The Supe wouldn't care if you fucked off and died. But this is your boss, not mine. Spook Central? They want you home. I got the impression they're not too happy with you.'

Chapman, cut off mid-stream, couldn't find his direction straight off. '. . . Spook Central?' Aiming for sarcasm, but missing.

'You're Six.' Not a question. 'And this is a domestic hostage taking. I've no idea why Whistler was invited, but you're not. Leave, or you're heading for the cells. Lives are at risk here.'

'You spoke to Whistler?'

'Like I say, he was invited. Sonny Jim wasn't talking to me. So I briefed your pal, I'm holding his hardware. And your bosses want you home.' He arrived at a nasty smile. 'Seems you're no more popular there than you are here.'

Chapman went white.

Faulks said, 'City policing's bad enough without your lot importing toerags then arming them. The boss says you're keeping a zip on who this menace is. That's helpful, thanks. Any deaths today, we'll know where to send the bill.'

Chapman put a hand to his chest . . .

And the angry cop who was also a decent man registered that the fucking spook might be sick.

'Oh Christ, that's all we need . . . You okay?'

Sam Chapman gasped for air, nodded; waved a hand about, as if ushering away whatever bad angel had kissed him. But he didn't look okay; looked like he needed to lie down.

Faulks said, 'There's a medic. I'll—'

'No.'

'Well, you look like—' Tact kept Faulks from finishing. He glanced around. Beyond them the fourth estate was gathering, along with the usual suspects: locals who hadn't seen this much excitement since a house had blown up a few years back. Faulks had better things to do than babysit a spy. But couldn't let the man die in the street: it wouldn't show up well on his Performance Development Review.

'You want to sit?'

'I'm okay.' But then he said, 'Maybe for a moment. Fuck. This never happened before.'

He looks scared, Faulks thought.

The nearest police car was empty, parked in front of the big house that was the only non-nursery building on the business side of the cordon. Faulks led Chapman to it, inwardly cursing; hoping this would be one of those swiftly resolved episodes whereby Chapman would sit down, perk up, then bugger off in quick succession. Colour was already returning to his cheeks, though he stumbled as they reached the car door and leant heavily against Faulks.

'Sorry,' he mumbled.

'I'm calling a medic,' Faulks said. 'Better safe than—'

'No.' Chapman eased himself onto the back seat, feet on the pavement, and fumbled a packet of cigarettes from his jacket. 'I'm okay. Just need to sit for a moment.'

'You sure that's wise?'

'Sitting never hurt.'

Faulks didn't pursue it. He eyed Chapman: the man was physically Faulks's opposite: thin, pale, dark – Faulks got stick for his weight and florid complexion, but he wasn't the one who'd just strayed onto heart-murmur territory. A cloud of smoke proved Chapman was still breathing.

Chapman looked up. 'See? Told you I was okay.'

'You want a check-up.'

'I want a lot of things. Mostly, I want to be on the other side of that fence.'

'Not going to happen. You're wanted back at the office.'

Chapman stood. 'Bloody pencil pushers. Bane of every profession.'

'Take it up with your bosses. You can walk, right?'

The spy nodded. Whatever had scared him – caused him to turn white – had receded; in its place was that cynical mask he'd worn on arrival. But Faulks believed in certain adult character-istics; that when you'd just showed compassion, for instance, it would be acknowledged. 'I nearly applied for Six once,' he said.

'Standards have dropped. You should try again.'

Faulks had preferred him when he was having a heart attack.

Chapman watched him go. Turning pale was an old trick: he used to practise in front of a mirror, armed with bad memories. Whistler's BlackBerry in his pocket, he left before Faulks noticed his own was empty.

Ben said, 'I didn't send anyone to kill you.'

'I arrange to meet, you send men to kill me.'

'Whoa. Slow down. When did we arrange to meet? I never heard of you before this morning.'

'I leave message.'

'You left me a message?'

'I ring your telephone. I leave you message.'

'You rang my mobile?'

'No. I ring your office.'

'. . . When?'

'Last night.'

Ben said, 'I think we'd better back up a bit. I didn't receive any message. All I know is what I've learned this morning, and what I see in front of me now. If anyone tried to kill you, it had nothing to do with me.'

The boy blinked slowly. Whether he believed him or not, Ben couldn't tell.

Louise Kennedy said, 'What's any of this got to do with us?'

Ben said, 'Let me handle this, okay?'

'No, it's not okay. You have no more idea of what's going on than we do. And we're the ones who've spent the past few hours at gunpoint.'

'This'll be a lot easier if—'

'Quiet!'

They both shut up.

The boy said, 'I have the gun. You talk to me only.'

Ben looked at Louise, and nodded slightly. What the nod meant – *do as he tells us; you have a point; fancy a drink after?* – neither could have said.

The boys increased their grip on Eliot's legs. Since their trip to the bathroom, they'd said little. Eliot wondered what the effect of stress on young minds was, and how long they could endure this without snapping. Maybe they would emerge physically intact; maybe Ben Whistler's arrival signalled the beginning of the end of their ordeal. But it wasn't happening soon enough, and the damage already done might linger, infecting the remainder of his sons' childhood.

It was tempting to slip away from the present. To slip back on to his mental spacecraft, and sail into darkness until all this went away . . .

The Gun said 'Quiet!' and a hush fell on the room.

Outside it was quiet too, though there had to be activity there. The kind Eliot had frequently seen on TV: drama, mostly, and the occasional slice of news coverage, which always seemed less urgent than fiction. In real life events stretched into hours, with no slow fade to indicate time's passage. Updates between regular programmes failed to convey the painful drag of the minutes crawling by inside the building. Perhaps those outside thought they felt the tension too – it can be stressful waiting for something bad to happen. But it was a lot more stressful when you were the one it might happen to.

Tear gas and SWAT teams – did the British police have SWAT teams? It was frightening how much of life was coloured by the American version: books, TV, films. You could be so clued into contemporary culture that you lost touch with the way things were . . . Which wasn't the issue right now: the issue was, why hadn't they used tear gas, or SWAT teams or whatever? And the answer was, because that was a last resort.

Introducing smoke and more guns increased the chances of hostages being hurt, and would not happen while there was a chance this boy could be talked out of the room.

The new guy, Ben Whistler, said, 'You're a friend of Miro Weiss.'

'Yes.'

'His boyfriend.'

'We were lovers, yes.'

What was this, a soap opera? Eliot looked at Louise, but Louise wasn't looking back. The Memory whimpered at the back of his mind, but it turned into a story that had happened to different people. His sons' bodies pulsed beneath his palms. They didn't know what he'd done to them. If not for the Memory, the three of them would have arrived at the nursery later. They'd have been home now; the twins playing in the back room, while he and Chris huddled on the sofa, watching the what-if unfold on TV, all of it happening to others. And it would have seemed slow and unreal; would have begged for a fade-out, or the merciful release of a commercial break.

'Being private is not the same as lonely,' Jaime was saying.

Ben said, 'That's true.'

'And you were his friend too, yes? He spoke of you.'

He was losing it – Eliot was losing it. He hugged his children closer, the effort of maintaining a gentle pressure beyond him. And he looked at Louise again, and this time their eyes met, and for Eliot that moment felt like sanctuary – carried him out of the here and now to a place without guns, and reminded him, as precisely as an anatomical drawing, of the first time they'd shared a glance, in a school up the north end of the city. It didn't seem likely right now that that could have happened. On the other hand, it hadn't seemed too realistic at the time, either.

Something in Louise's eyes clouded, then cleared. She was remembering too, he realised. And as she looked away he hugged his boys tighter, and allowed himself the release of stepping back in time five days.

He had been roped into it, was the funny thing – not that he couldn't do quizzes. His general knowledge, he guessed, probably ranked in the top ten per cent nationally; his particular strengths being those of any graduate his age: contemporary literature, seventies TV, late eighties pop and pre-Blair politics – well, contemporary lit minus the last four years. Having children was a learning curve all its own, but did tend to exclude you from other fields of knowledge. Anyway, perhaps he'd mentioned this once too often at the office, because suddenly he was on a team for a quiz event, raising funds for a local school.

'I won't know anyone there,' he'd told Christine. 'Just Lizzie.' His colleague, who'd pressganged him. 'And seven hours a day of her's more than enough.'

Chris said, 'Oh, go. At least you won't sit slumped in front of the box all night.'

While I do all the work was her unspoken corollary – by which she meant, of course, all the work he didn't do, which included washing up, laundry, playing with the boys while she spent an hour in the bath; not to mention actually going out and working all day long. A typically unfair accusation, then, and all the more so for remaining unspoken. He wasn't even allowed to defend himself. If he tried, she'd point out she hadn't said anything.

Slumped in front of the box, too: that wasn't him. He didn't do that. Using the remote, he'd switched it off, and reached for the paper. 'Okay, then,' he'd said. 'It's next Tuesday.' *So I won't be around to do the washing up* was what he meant, but that, too, remained unsaid.

So the following Tuesday, mid-evening, Eliot caught a bus up the other end of the city: this because Chris needed the car first thing in the morning, and it was outside the house right then, but they'd lose the space if he used it, and then she'd have to cart the boys round the block looking for it and . . . Nothing was ever simple any more. Even the simple stuff was complicated. Eliot couldn't fill the kettle without being told he was doing it wrong, and if the stated reason for whatever error he was committing always sounded reasonable at the time, it nevertheless felt like Chris was pursuing a hidden agenda, designed to underline how useless he was at everything.

At the school he made his way to the hall without seeing anyone he knew, and for a few moments stood watching people clustered round tables, laughing and talking. It occurred to him that he could slip quietly away now and do anything he wanted – go to the pub, go to the cinema – but before either of those things could happen, Lizzie hailed him. 'Eliot! You made it!' Everybody turned to look. Lizzie was not a quiet woman. 'We're on Table 4! They all have numbers! On a piece of card!' Soon she'd be describing what a number 4 looked like, and possibly explaining counting: to forestall this, he told her he'd see her there, and made his way across the hall indelibly marked as the loud woman's companion. Table 4 was occupied by an attractive brunette; familiar, though Eliot couldn't pinpoint why at first – she had grey eyes, was early thirties; wore jeans and a white collarless blouse, open at the neck to reveal a pendant on a thin silver chain. Lapis lazuli, he thought, irrelevantly. He had no idea what lapis lazuli looked like.

Louise had said, 'Oh, hello. Aren't you Gordon and Timmy's dad?' and as soon as she spoke, he realised who she was.

'And you're their teacher. How come you're at this table? Sorry, I didn't mean that as rudely as it sounded.'

'I do t'ai chi with Lizzie. I'm Louise. Louise Kennedy.'

'I remember. And I'm Eliot. Colleague of, er, Lizzie's.'

He sat. 'I didn't realise she did t'ai chi. That's a martial art, isn't it?'

Lizzie was still the other side of the room, chatting. Lizzie, he reflected, really was large and altogether too loud; *jolly*, obviously, was the adjective most often applied to her – well, apart from *fat* – but every few months she'd have an emotional meltdown, and lock herself in a toilet or leave work hurriedly mid-morning. One or other female member of staff would then spend the rest of the day on Lizzie duty, while the men studiedly refrained from noticing anything amiss. Chris knew all this, of course, which doubtless accounted for her equanimity about Eliot coming out for the evening. If she'd known Louise would be one of the party – or any other thirtyish attractive single woman – she might have been less encouraging. However little interest she had in Eliot these days, she didn't want anybody else taking up the slack.

Meanwhile Louise was smiling politely, but with a visible tightening round her mouth; far from being about to take up Chris's slack, she was evidently wondering what she'd let herself in for . . . *Stop living in your head*, he told himself. Talk to the woman. And for fuck's sake don't start thinking she fancies you just because you're sitting next to her and she hasn't yet called for help.

Eliot said, 'I suppose it's too much to hope they've got a bar here,' and the tightness left Louise's smile, which this time reached her eyes.

'You're a friend of Miro Weiss.'

'Yes.'

'His boyfriend.'

'We were lovers, yes.'

'I didn't know.'

'You did not know he is gay?'

'I'd got that far. I just didn't know he had a boyfriend, Jaime. I thought he was . . .'

Ben looked for the right word.

'I thought he was lonely.'

Jaime gave that some thought. 'He was private man,' he said at last.

'I know.'

'Being private is not the same as lonely.'

'That's true.'

'And you were his friend too, yes? He spoke of you.'

'Nothing but good, I hope.'

Jaime looked blank.

'I mean, I hope he didn't say anything bad about me.'

'He said you were his friend.'

'I'm glad he said that, Jaime. But it wasn't exactly true.'

'You were not his friend?'

'I didn't know him that well. We worked together, yes. But like you say, he was a private man. He didn't open up much.'

'Open up?'

'He had his secrets. He never told me about you, for instance.'

'He said it would be best if people did not know about us.'

'Because you're gay?'

'He said people would not understand.'

'It's not the 1950s, Jaime. I'm not sure anyone would care.'

'He said where you worked, they do not like such things. Being boyfriends. Being gay men.'

Ben said, 'Once upon a time. Things are different now.'

'You are gay?'

'That's the second time I've been asked that this morning. I might change my aftershave.'

'I do not understand.'

'I'm sorry. Trying to be funny. No, I'm not gay.'

'Then you do not know what it was like for Miro.'

'No, I suppose I don't.'

Was this going well? Ben couldn't say. *Let me handle this* he'd told Louise Kennedy, and she'd quietened down, either in direct response to instruction or because that's what she'd planned on doing anyway. And the boy, Jaime, was at least talking freely, and *you've got to establish normality* – that was what Ben had been told. Don't forget about the gun, but don't act like it's all there is. Not forgetting about the gun was going to be the easy part. But maybe the gun would fade into an unimportant accessory; something that might be dangerous if misused, but otherwise could be safely ignored, like a ballpoint pen, or a corkscrew.

Keep talking.

'Have you seen him lately, Jaime? Been in touch?'

'He is dead.'

'Why do you say that?'

'If he is not dead, he would contact me. He would not just disappear. He would not go without goodbye.'

'Well, that's the thing. When he disappeared, Jaime, he made a lot of people very unhappy. Not just you.'

'He did not disappear,' Jaime repeated. 'He is dead.'

'Dead people turn up sooner or later.' They float to the surface, thought Ben. Or the smell gives their location away. 'And when Miro disappeared, a lot of money disappeared with him. An awful lot. People jumped to the obvious conclusion.'

'You think he took this money?'

'That's what people say.'

'He is not a thief.'

'It surprised a lot of us.'

'So why you think he is a thief?'

'Well . . .'

'Because everybody say he is? Everybody where you work?'

'. . . Yes, Jaime. That's pretty much what everybody where I work said.'

'I do not think you are much of a friend. If people say bad things about my friend, I do not believe them. I believe my friend.'

'Except we weren't exactly friends. And Miro wasn't there

to put his side of the story, Jaime. He was gone just like the money was.'

'He rob your safe?'

'In a manner of speaking.'

'He steal hundreds of pounds?'

'A lot more than that, Jaime.'

'Thousands?'

'A quarter of a billion, Jaime. That's how much money went missing when Miro disappeared. A quarter of a billion pounds.'

This number registered in Louise's brain with something like familiarity: back at DeJohn Franklin Moers, such sums had been the common currency. Not that she'd grubbied her hands with actual lucre. Money had been a notional commodity; much discussed; glimpsed briefly as online transactions; and put to bed as the bottom line of a descending row of figures, a sum belonging to somebody else, and so huge as not to exist in any meaningful way. A billion dollars in hundred-dollar bills, she'd been told, weighed ten tons. How much space it occupied, she couldn't guess. A quarter billion sterling in, say, twenties . . . And was that an English or a US billion? Either way, it was more cash than you could steal without forethought, muscle and transport. But out there in the ether, money – in its pure, incorporeal state – was vulnerable; could be ripped off, raped or burned by anyone with digital flair and inside knowledge. The kind of knowledge she'd dealt in, day by day.

The joke was, they'd called it *real* money – telephone numbers; serious dosh. She'd earned real money too. But she'd never seen that, either; for several years, Louise had barely carried cash, beyond the odd fiver for emergencies. Life and shopping had been conducted with plastic. The realer money was, the less you had to confront it. It operated differently; you never fished it from a pocket and counted it out, but its presence lent weight to your daily existence, enabling you to see things others didn't, and ignore things that shouldn't be there. Real money's weight was a buffer against the unpleasant. Louise had eaten in restaurants where they didn't put prices on the menu, and hadn't even noticed at the time.

'There is lot of money involved.'

'Sometimes.'

'Miro was good at his job,' Jaime said.

Louise had been good at hers.

Good at it, but had found a way to screw it up all the same: sleeping with the boss, it turned out, was a terrible idea. Who'd have thought it? There was a man with a gun not ten feet away, and another man trying to talk him down from whatever ledge he was on, but although she was listening to these men talking—

'He could tell you square roots of big numbers, from his head. With no paper.'

'That's quite a talent.'

—part of her mind was on Crispin Tate, and the reason for that was stamped on the calendar. *Today, of all days, he was likely to weigh heavy on her mind.* Even before all this, he'd been rattling in her head, because she could remember exactly where she'd been two years ago.

But every day was an anniversary; something had always happened, good or bad. And sometimes whichever it was shaded from one to the other with the passage of time; last year, today had been a good anniversary; this year, it was bad . . . Last year Louise and Crispin had celebrated their first anniversary, returning to the restaurant they'd first visited (of course), where she'd even – a blush-making admission – chosen the same dish from the same, unpriced menu. And had assumed the evening would be ending in the same fashion, but *Darling, I'm so sorry – I have to be home, it's Charlie's birthday tomorrow.* So how come it hadn't been Charlie's birthday tomorrow last year? But she hadn't thought of asking until he'd left. And anyway, by then,

Louise had grown used to abrupt departures and curtailed conversations; to being placated instead of wooed.

In well-arranged marriages, brides learned to love their husbands one quality at a time: a particular habit of kindness, the curve of an elbow, the occasional display of tact. For other women, when their poorly arranged affairs ended badly, the problem was neatly reversed, with no shortage of qualities to learn to hate – the assumption that she'd be there when he wanted her; the cancellation of dates without warning. His particular habit of being married, with children. The name *Crispin* was hardly a bonus, either. Such matters began small, but grew and grew. She wasn't sure she hated Crispin yet, and knew she was leading a better life now – felt a fuller person. But also knew that he'd come out of it unscathed; that she'd been the one forced to make changes.

Changes which had left her here.

The spy and the gunman, Jaime, were still at it; the name *Miro* flashing back and forth, as if the two were on their own separate page. *Are you the lady?* Jaime had asked. She was the only lady here, since you couldn't count Judy. Maybe Eliot had had it right, and he'd meant Claire Christopher, who'd chosen today of all days to have a dental appointment – unless that had been deliberate . . . And as soon as the thought formed, Louise knew she was starting to lose it. Claire involved with gunmen? That was about as likely as . . . Louise herself being here, now.

She looked around. Judy was a heap on the floor, a bag ready for collection. The boys were wrapped round their father's legs; their father caught her eye before she could avoid it, and there it was again: the whipped-spaniel look, as if she were deliberately avoiding a serious discussion they needed to have. *More important stuff happening, Eliot.* Maybe that thought wave reached him, because the whipped expression intensified. Oh Jesus . . . It ought to be enough that there's a gunman in the classroom, but no: Eliot had to be here too, giving her *do you remember* glances . . . At least the gunman wasn't her fault. Whatever morbid psychology was greasing Jaime's pistons, Louise couldn't be blamed for it.

Are you the lady?

Louise closed her eyes. The men were still talking, but she was slipping back into last week.

She wasn't much interested in quizzes; wasn't, when you got down to it, much interested in Lizzie, but there was guilt attached to acknowledging that you didn't enjoy the company of the unattractive; and besides, about the same time it became clear that Lizzie wasn't taking no for an answer, it had occurred to Louise that this might be something her mother would like. And getting her mother to enjoy herself would be a pretty unequivocal indication of improved health, which would be a step on the road to . . . well, the road. More guilt came attached to that, of course. Tricking her mother into feeling better, so she'd go home: that couldn't be good daughterly behaviour. Louise couldn't be a good daughter.

All belief systems come with appropriate punishments built in. Even Louise had to acknowledge the humour of the situation when her mother started feeling unwell an hour before they were due to go out.

'I'll have an early night. You go.'

'But I can't leave you if—'

'No, I'm fine. Really. Just tired. I don't want to spoil your evening.'

Well, you're making a pretty good fist of it.

And it occurred to Louise as she collected her car keys – because this was a no-win scenario – that her mother had never had the slightest intention of attending the quiz; that all her words and actions, from the moment she'd expressed pleasure at the thought of an expedition to the first intimations of head pain an hour earlier, had been a calculated act of vengeance for whatever teenage gamesmanship Louise had employed twenty years earlier, when visits to friends of her parents had been in the offing.

'I won't be late.'

Her mother was already tuned into *The Bill*.

They were a team member down, then, but in the event it didn't matter. She'd recognised Eliot as the twins' father as soon as he entered her field of vision: wandering across the hall, unsure of his destination. Already, she knew it was her table he was heading for – events slotted into place like that. Some people remained strangers for good and sensible reasons. With others, the connections were hardwired from the moment you noticed you shared the planet with them. It had nothing to do with sexual attraction, or even liking. It was simply that you were plugged into the same network.

She'd said something like, 'Aren't you the twins' father?' and he'd replied, 'What are you doing here?' as if he'd thought teachers were packed away in cupboards with the rest of the equipment come four o'clock.

A couple of hours later, they were masters of the evening.

10:47.

'Where does this money come from?'

'It's complicated.'

'And I am stupid foreign person.'

'I didn't mean that, Jaime. All I meant was, I don't know all the details, and even if I did, I wouldn't be able to talk about them.'

What was the time? He could hardly check his watch. Bad manners, even when the recipient wasn't holding a gun.

And the only clock in sight was a teaching tool: its plastic hands aimed at an optimistic ten to four.

'Because you are spy.'

'I'm not a spy, Jaime. I'm an accountant.'

172

'You are spy accountant.'

'I'm a civil servant. As Miro was.'

'You work for secret services. Miro tell me this.'

'Well, he obviously wasn't all that good at keeping secrets.'

'He should not have said?' Jaime shrugged. 'But he tell me.'

'I don't think it matters much,' Ben said. 'We advertise these days. Yes, Miro and I work, worked, for a branch of the security services. But not as spies. We have desk jobs. Accountancy jobs. We work in the same department, on the same floor. So do a lot of other people.'

'And there is big money involved.'

'Sometimes.'

'Miro was good at his job,' Jaime said.

Ben said, 'He was better with numbers than anyone I've ever met.'

'He could do . . .' Jaime struggled for a word. 'He could do tricks, yes? Tricks with numbers. You know this?'

'I heard.'

'He could tell you little numbers that make up the big ones.'

'Square roots, we call them,' Ben said.

'Yes. He could tell you square roots of big numbers, from his head.'

'That's quite a talent,' Ben said. He didn't add that that level of numeracy often accompanied a degree of social inadequacy. And Miro Weiss had been something of a social inadequate. Those nights in the pub, the football struggling in the background: conversation hadn't exactly been free-flowing. It was a wonder he'd found a boyfriend at all, let alone one like Jaime.

'Where did you meet?' he asked.

'Why you want to know?'

'Just curious.' He was trying to have an ordinary conversation here, chatting with a boy who was nursing a gun. 'Where'd you meet?'

Jaime said, 'In club.'

'Right.'

'I like clubs.'

'I'm sure. I'm surprised Miro did, though.'

'You do not believe me?'

Ben raised his hands, palms spread. 'I just can't picture Miro clubbing, that's all. Not unless it was a chess club or something.'

'It was proper club.'

'Okay. I believe you.'

Trying to banish alternative visions of what a *proper* club might look like: leather armchairs, roaring fires, broadsheets on handy tables. *Pass the port, old man. Dammit, not that way. To the left.*

Jaime said, 'You are right. He was lonely.'

'Well, he had you.'

'Only because I talk to him.'

Ben wasn't sure what he meant.

'In club. I talk to him. Or he would not have spoken. I know this.'

'Yes,' Ben said. 'I think you're probably right. Why did you do that?'

Jaime said, 'You think it is because he is spy? You think I go speak to him because I know this?'

'I don't mean to upset you. But the people in my business, that's the sort of question they would ask, yes.'

'He calls them Dogs.'

'I beg your pardon?'

'The people you talk about. The ones who ask questions. He calls them the Dogs.'

Ben said, carefully, 'I see.'

'That is why he says we must be private, about being friends. These people, the Dogs, they would ask questions. They would say what you just say. That I am only his friend because he is spy.'

'But that's not the case,' Ben said.

'No,' said Jaime. 'I am his friend because he is lonely. And because he is nice, good man. You believe this?'

'If you say so, Jaime.'

'No, I not ask you what I say. I ask if you believe he was good man.'

'He never struck me as anything else,' Ben said.

'But you think he is thief.'

'Well, I didn't know him too well. As I keep saying.'

'He think you would believe him.'

'What makes you say that?'

'It is what he tell me. If there is trouble, you find Ben Whistler. Ben is my friend.'

'He said that, did he?'

'Yes.'

'Well,' Ben said after a while. 'If this doesn't count as trouble, it'll do until some comes along.'

Picture this: the car, the man, the trollop – the black and orange rose.

Slumped on the floor, head in her hands, Judy let images swallow her.

For weeks before it happened, there had been telephone silences: the short silences of Derek phoning but having nothing to say, followed by the longer ones of Derek not phoning. During those weeks, the telephone squatted on its table like an unexploded bomb; like the bomb, say, that was waiting for him – the one he drove over in the jeep, with his trollop. A mine, they said. This particular mine being his; it had his name on it.

And after that, the even longer silence of the phone not ringing at all.

This silence, though, was preferable to the random outbursts from the bigger world; the white noise that fills your head to bursting. Noise from banks, from the building society, from lawyers; noise that came roaring upon her, like something tumbling down her chimney.

'I don't understand.'

Take all that noise, turn it into a song, this would have been the chorus: *I don't understand.*

'Your husband—'

'He's dead.'

'Yes. But he remortgaged the house before he died.'

'He never *told* me—'

The bastard bastard bastard . . .

'I'm sorry.'

And he probably was, this banker, financial adviser, lawyer: probably was sorry, though once their meeting was over, he'd have sighed, shrugged and closed the book on Judy, then gone to do whatever he had to do next. Whereas Judy had to keep on being herself, in alien circumstances. At some point in this reordered life she had acquired new adjectives, each of which had had bite when applied to others, but felt second hand on her, like clothing picked up at a charity shop. *Abandoned, widowed, reduced.* And wearing this new outfit – her widow's words – she'd had to take, in this order, a room in someone's house and a cleaning job. Judy had never had a job while Derek was around. He'd sometimes suggested she might like to work; had broached the subject in a tone that sought to imply there might be fulfilment in it for her, but there'd never been what you might call a *discussion*, because there had never needed to be: she had no intention of taking a job, which was precisely where the matter concluded. But now – abandoned, widowed, reduced – she had taken up mop and duster, because what else could she hope to do, after years of unqualified housework?

'I'm sure we'll get on famously,' Claire Christopher had told her, offering her the job.

'You can use the kitchen between six and six thirty,' Deirdre Walker had said, ceding her the room.

If Derek was alive were more widow's words; banging away beneath that other chorus like a demented drum kit.

If Derek were alive, she'd have killed him. This is where he'd left her, after all those promises of instant riches.

And as for his trollop . . .

As for his trollop, when she summoned up pictures, the face she discovered was Louise Kennedy's.

Judy wasn't sure how this had come about. It hadn't been intentional. You did not conjure up your dead husband's dead lover's face and deliberately superimpose upon it the features of someone you worked with: whatever *Jenny Ross* had looked like, she wouldn't have looked like Louise Kennedy. Face facts: Derek had been pressing sixty, and hadn't been prized for his looks forty years ago; Jenny Ross, the newspaper reports said, had been just one year younger than Judy herself. But there were facts, and then there was underlying truth: this woman – this trollop – had stolen Judy's husband: what image was she supposed to come up with? Trollops were trollops, and however you painted the package, they came over-pleased with them-selves, like a cat that had sucked up the cream. Disgusting.

What had she seen this morning by the gate? You couldn't tell Judy there wasn't something going on: once a trollop, always the same. Paint didn't peel off easy.

She was hearing words bounce back and forth, but with eyes tight closed, slumped on the floor, all she could see was a rose in the desert – blooming orange and red.

'This club,' Ben said. 'Where you met Miro. What sort of club was it?'

'I tell you. A proper club. A place you go for music, for dance.'

'And you struck up conversation with him.'

'Yes, I tell you. He look like a nice man. He *is* nice man. So I talk to him.'

'Aren't clubs a bit noisy for casual chat?'

'Sometimes we need to shout.'

'And that was the first time you met him?'

'First time, yes.'

'The first time you saw him?'

'You think I am tricking?'

Ben thought so, yes. He thought Miro had been a pickup. Jaime had a rent-boy look: slightly girlish exterior wrapped round a rock-hard soul, though the gun might have exaggerated the rock-hard part. But mostly what he was thinking was, he couldn't picture Miro Weiss chatting up a boy this pretty. A man like Miro, middle-aged before his time, dressed like he'd fallen out of his grandfather's wardrobe – only desire, buried by daylight, owlish by night, could have taken him into a club where the music banged like a drunk with a dustbin, and the drinks were adolescent mixes, astronomically priced. He must have looked like a credit card on legs. There'd probably been a queue forming behind Jaime. The evening would have ended in compliments and banknotes, with Miro thinking the latter a loan or a taxi fare.

'I am not spy. I do not know *he* was spy. Not then.'

Tricking . . . Different kind.

Ben said, 'Did you go to that club often?'

'No.'

'Do you go to lots of clubs?'

'You think I am prostitute?'

'I don't think anything of the sort,' Ben lied.

'I like clubs. I like to meet people. Not to sleep with. Just people.'

'Okay.'

'He did not give me money.'

'Okay.'

'No, is not okay. Sometimes, yes, he give me money. Because we are friends. But he not pay me for being lover. He give me

178

presents, sometimes money, because he has more than me. He does not like me to be poor.'

'What do you do, Jaime?'

'For work?'

'For work, yes. How do you earn a living?'

'I work in kitchens.'

'You're a cook?'

'I wash up. Sometimes serve food.'

'You're a waiter?'

'Fast food. I work on counter.'

'And when did you meet Miro?'

'Before Christmas. December. Maybe November.'

'Do you still work at the same place?'

'I do not know,' said Jaime. 'I am not there yesterday. Maybe they sack me.'

'So you've been working all this time. While you and Miro were lovers.'

'You think he keep me? You think I live in his flat, lie on his couch all day? Or maybe you think he give me flat of my own?'

Ben didn't think that at all. If Miro had been keeping Jaime, the Dogs would have sniffed him out day one.

'He kept you very secret.'

'I already tell you this. He not want you people to know about me.'

'But he told you about me,' said Ben.

'Yes.'

'Why did he do that?'

'Because he is scared,' said Jaime.

ABIRD'S-EYE VIEW OF Grandpont, this time of a weekday, would reveal a largely deserted area, compared to the bustle half a mile north – there'd be life, but it would be moving slowly. A different clock would be calling the shots; a female clock, on the whole. The bird – most likely a pigeon, though gulls aren't uncommon, and the odd swan bisects the suburb's airspace, its heavy flapping loud as a heartbeat – would be looking down on mothers or nannies heading nurserywards, to put in an hour's help before collecting their charges for lunch; on the mothers or carers of smaller tots, wheeling prams along pavements, except where maliciously parked cars forced them onto the road. One or two retirees heading home from the shops, though most would have finished their chores long since. And there'd be little urgency about any of this; no rush, either, around the benches at the junction near the nursery, where the local homeless sometimes sit in conference; cans of Special Brew oiling the wheels of their discourse, more cans refitting those wheels each time they came off. Perhaps there'd be lorries making the rounds – supermarkets delivering wildly inaccurate stabs at the weekly shopping; friendly red vans leaving mail-ordered treats. Or removal trucks. Barely a week goes by without somebody moving out or in. This is the life that's lived when you're at work.

Today is different.

The mothers aren't in evidence so much, though there are one or two down there, among the crowd clustered on the safe side of the cordon. Theirs are the paler faces; they don't have the experience of such situations that some others in the crowd enjoy, but their understanding of its essential evil is probably greater. The combination of guns and children hurts them where they live. If everything turns out all right – if the children emerge unscathed – this will be due to the power of their prayers. It's both good and necessary that they're there. None of them feel either of those things, though. What they feel is dread, in its purest bitterest form. They feel as if something is crushing them from the inside out. It's the squeeze equivalent of microwave action. If it persists a moment too long, they will explode.

The rest are mostly journalists. There's been no formal press conference, though that never stopped a story yet. Film crews have staked patches of kerbside, and there's a lot of straight-to-camera going on, the absence of hard information lending itself to story-making – there's a classful of children held by bala-clavaed terrorists: there are fifteen children in there; there are nine; there are six. The phrase *Islamist extremist* is bandied around the way *IRA* once was, and means the same thing. With nobody knowing anything, even the winos' views are polled – and they are certainly available for comment. They have huge opinions. There was definitely a lorry rolled up earlier; a definite troop of authentic, camo-fatigued, unshaven suicide bombers disembarked. Where the lorry went isn't clear. What happened to the bombers is a mystery too.

If the police officers maintaining the boundary were a bit more forthcoming, this whole business of news gathering would be a lot simpler.

Meanwhile, truth emerges in fragments, initially indistinguishable from gossip. There was a woman here – she was inside with her child when the gunmen broke in. Except there was only one gunman, and he was already there. Nobody knows where this woman has gone; she's returned to a place of safety, or else been spirited into that van inside the cordon: the Major Incident Vehicle – they don't roll out the Major Incident equipment for petty events. It's all in the name. So perhaps she's in there, being debriefed, while inside the nursery, banged up with the gunman, with the gang, with the armed militia, is a teacher, though she was outside earlier – somebody spoke to someone who said she'd gone back inside of her own free will. Why would she do that? It's not just suspicious, it's downright sinister . . . Anybody who might know anything concrete is absent. But small tendrils of the truth snake out here and there, attempting to take root on the slippery ground of rumour.

Our bird, not hampered by cordons, moves in nearer.

The officers manning the boundary are in the familiar blue shirt/Day-Glo waistcoat combo, nothing about this suggesting that anything more than a traffic-related event is in progress. They're not here to enlighten the crowd. But nor are they bulky enough to prevent the press seeing over their shoulders: there are armed officers present too, more sinisterly garbed – nothing light-reflecting about their get-up: they wear black, bulky outfits, like Batman stand-ins, and hold themselves with a degree of macho assurance that Day-Glo waistcoats prohibit. It's possible that our bird – even without knowledge of weaponry, beyond the occasional loud bang and feathered explosion hardwired into its species memory – would recognise a difference between these two groups; the reinforced, heavy-vested contingent, and the public face of crowd control.

And then over the nursery itself the bird flies; and over the annexe, whose quiet roof gives no hint of the damage-waiting-to-happen within, and across the adventure playground, on whose apparatus, most of which resembles medieval siege devices, more black-clad officers perch. They don't matter to our bird – pigeon, gull or swan, it keeps on beating; crosses the playground, crosses the railway tracks and then more fields, then roads, then more fields, until it finds a body of water or clump of trees or electricity pylon, on which it comes to rest, and doesn't die.

There are other views too. You don't have to be a bird to be looking down on all this.

A marksman's rifle is trained on the doorway to the annexe. The rifle is DS Bain's, and DS Bain is perched on the roof of the large detached house which is the nearest building to the nursery grounds. A length of crime-scene bunting attached to one of its gateposts has come loose, and flaps like a kite's tail in a sudden breeze. The house has been evacuated, and its occupants are currently enjoying that mixture of aggrievement at the inconvenience and possessive thrill of being involved in events, if at a remove. In time to come the extent of that removal will diminish, and their roles, as recounted at dinner parties, will bloom, as if their expert opinions had been sought by the police, rather than their well-positioned chimney block. For the moment, though, they're out of the picture. For the moment, the picture, as seen from the chimney block, is this:

An unremarkable doorway into an unremarkable, prefabricated, one-storey building. The door opens inwards – that's hard fact, though there's no way of telling from this angle, at which the door's hinged edge is hidden by the jamb. There's no glass in the door; what there is is a rainbow-crayoned cardboard sign reading *The Palace*. This has been tacked in place at its corners but is starting to curl, and there's a rip in the upper left quadrant – a tear no more than half an inch long, but these things never heal themselves; torn cardboard only becomes more torn, the way a late train only gets later. DS Bain doesn't know, but isn't hard pushed to guess, that this sign needs remaking every term. The various designs employed – the rainbow motif, and also stars, rabbits, footballers, zoo animals and Harry Potter characters – are recycled on a regular basis, core elements of an unwritten curriculum. The hand-crayoned sign, in its recurring versions, is an affirmation that some stories keep happening. Though no one involved in any of its designs ever imagined it as DS Bain sees it now: through the crosshairs of a high-powered rifle.

And framing that cardboard sign is the door; framing the door is the building. The building is set in the nursery grounds, and the nursery grounds lie in this pleasant area . . . So the picture moves ever outwards, the way children pencil their addresses on their schoolbags: their name, number, street, neighbourhood, town; then England, Europe, the Northern Hemisphere, the World, the Galaxy, the Universe – an outward spiral gradually wrapping everything in its geography, with that child at the centre, held in place by gravity. Except that DS Bain is here to put all that in reverse. From where DS Bain crouches, harnessed to the chimney block of a large suburban house, the picture is always getting smaller; the area of focus always narrowing. The Universe, the Galaxy, the World, the Northern Hemisphere . . . all the way on down to this door, and whoever might come through it, and then even tighter: body, upper body, chest – *there* – a spot no more than an inch across which, pressed hard enough, can undo the work of gravity, and blow everything apart.

Target acquired.

Steady.

DS Bain waits.

The door refuses to open.

I'm not a spy, Jaime. I'm an accountant.

You are spy accountant.

I'm a civil servant. As Miro was.

You work for secret services. Miro tell me this.

'This is spook business.'

The mobile telephone was doing its work – the phone

Faulks gave Louise Kennedy before she went back into the annexe. On or off, it broadcast sound from the annexe into the Major Incident Vehicle, where Peter Faulks was listening attentively, as was Malcolm Fredericks. Except Fredericks was thinking out loud at the same time, which wasn't helping Faulks.

'Who the hell is Miro Weiss?'

'Sir, I need—'

Fredericks waved a hand and shut up. He knew what Faulks needed.

The van was smaller inside than it looked, because of all the equipment it contained: it was mobile crime lab as well as listening post. Faulks sat before a bank of monitors broadcasting four live feeds of the annexe exterior, with no action on any of them. Real Big Brother stuff. Next to Faulks was a uniformed tech in a headset, who every so often spoke in an undertone: confirming call-ins from officers on the perimeter. When guns were in play, you kept a check on who was still alive.

He could feel tension knotting in his stomach; actually feel it writhing around, as if he were about to spawn an alien bug. This was what the Job was about – being in charge of situations that resembled, Jesus, a simile failed him. That resembled the space shuttle: one of those enterprises with a million ways of going wrong, and only one of going right. When that happened, everyone forgot about it. When things went wrong, the fallout lasted forever; a constant scar on the skies above, in the shape of a dying swan.

'I'm going outside,' he said. 'Keep me informed.'

Outside was a movie set; somewhere where a particular reality was being created, but whose immediate effect was of artifice. A lot of urgency, with little to show for it. Fredericks walked round the van, off-camera, then lit a cigarette. All this activity: hurry-up-and-wait . . . He'd had two hostage situations in three years: in the first, what should have been a routine drugs raid ended with a dealer holed in a flat with two working girls, a Glock, and an industrial amount of crack cocaine. Which there'd been a lot less of when they'd carried three bodies out. The second had been a domestic: a father pushed to an edge that was waiting for everyone, though the lucky never get near it. A crumbling marriage; non-existent financial grounding; a tendency to keep drinking long after time should have been called. Once in a million goes, this happens with a grandfather's wartime souvenir on the premises. The gun wasn't even loaded. But you didn't take chances with children in the picture. DS Bain's shot from an attic room over the road had been Olympic standard.

The wife – the one they had on tape, screaming for her life – was currently chasing the Force through the courts. And what was the betting that would be rehashed over pages 2 to 7 tomorrow?

He crushed his cigarette underfoot; called to mind again the sketch of the annexe Claire Christopher, the nursery head, had drawn. One biggish room with a small office and a lavatory down the far side; windows facing into the complex, and metal shutters pulled over these. There was a skylight in the roof, and they could drop an officer through that, but placing somebody up there silently was another problem. *When it rains*, she'd told him, *it's like being inside a tin drum.* And all of these problems could be handled – they could take the annexe inside twenty seconds, Faulks assured him. But twenty seconds was a long time when the opposition was armed. In less than half of that, those two little boys could die: like the dealer and his unlucky prostitutes, or the melt-job with a World War II pistol.

Fredericks went back into the van, to find out what was being said.

Because he is scared . . .

'Why was Miro scared?' Ben asked.

Jaime took a while to answer.

The annexe's dimensions seemed to have altered since Ben's

arrival: the walls had shifted inwards, as if outside forces were squeezing them into an ever-smaller container. He could feel his shirt dampening, his thighs growing clammy. The nearby bodies were also reacting in predictably unhygienic ways to stress, and the annexe, face it, was never going to be the most fragrant of rooms – any other weekday, it would be a laboratory of infant accidents. The children, fastened to their father, were pumping out heat like twin immersion heaters, and the squat woman, Judy, was a heap on the floor, the stink of fear coming off her in waves. Only Louise Kennedy, closest to him, seemed under control. All he could smell of her was soap; an expensive blend of fruit and herb.

Jaime said, 'I do not know. He keeps secrets. He always know things he do not tell me.'

'Well, that's all very well, Jaime. But it doesn't help me a lot.'

'Were you watching him?'

'Me?'

'You are spy.'

'I've told you, Jaime. I work in an office. Like Miro. They clock us in, they clock us out. We don't drive fast cars and we don't spend our nights in casinos. If you're thinking James Bond, you're way off mark. I wasn't watching him. I don't even know where he lived.'

'Is there any chance you're going to tell us what this is about?'

And there was her voice again: less exotic than her soap, but every bit as controlled as her body.

But he said, 'Please. Let me deal with this.'

Louise said, 'You think we're not involved?'

'I know you're involved, it's—'

'We're here. We're stuck in here. You don't think we have a right to know what's going on?'

'I think you have a right to get out, and that means—'

The noise that interrupted them didn't at first sound organic.

Ben broke off, looking first at Jaime, then at Jaime's gun –
but no gun made that high-pitched noise; few things *shot* made
that high-pitched squealing noise, which rose swiftly from
unpleasant to ear-splitting, like a smoke alarm. Jaime's eyes lit
with shock; he turned, and the hand holding the gun dropped
– that was the moment to jump him, if Ben had been the right
kind of spy. It passed. Jaime stepped back, and raised the gun
again. One of the small boys screamed, but this was lost in
sudden movement as the heap that was Judy Ainsworth became
a mobile flurry on its way to the door, still wailing.

'Oh God,' said Louise.

'Stop!' said Jaime, aiming the gun.

Judy didn't stop.

'What's that?'

'The woman,' said Faulks. 'The older one. Shit.'

Stop!

'Send them in,' said Faulks. 'He's going to shoot.'

It wasn't the being there; it wasn't the talking – it was something
she couldn't put into words. No: it was the sense of becoming
less and less important, as if the forces that had squeezed Judy
out of her old life were intent on finishing the job. There she
was, trapped in a nursery by a crazed gunman, and still she didn't
matter; still she was peripheral . . . None of this was about her.
She shouldn't be here. She should be safe outside – the thought
didn't form so much as take over; expressing itself first as noise,
then pulling her off the floor and propelling her towards the exit.

'Stop!' said Jaime, aiming the gun at her.

She couldn't stop.

Though it was mad how the door got no nearer.

'Sir, there's no time to—'

'Yes. Go.'

Before Fredericks had finished, Faulks was echoing the word down his microphone.

Go.

There were fences here that to the children they penned might as well have been giants' fortresses; a grassed distance between gate and annexe door that stretched wide as a football pitch. To the black-clad officers who moved on *Go*, both were negligible: it would have taken too long to go through the gate, so they went over it, clearing the grass in less than two seconds. Impossible to say whether they registered a rainbow-crayoned sign reading *The Palace*. To the watchers in the van, they were a well-oiled team; to the press on the street, a blurred event – proof that something was happening frustratingly out of focus.

Go.

One either side of the door. A third kicking it open.

To the people inside the annexe, they were avenging angels, or devils, or both.

Some words:
you fuck, you bastard
stop shut up I shoot you now I shoot you
don't
boys
Mummy
ungh
everybody down!
everybody down!
Everybody down . . .

The door got no nearer because an arm had wrapped around Judy's waist, so her legs stopped propelling her forward – they wheeled crazily above the floor like a cartoon woman's, and

then she was tumbling backwards, not screaming but shouting – 'You fuck, you bastard' – and her fall was broken by
Jaime's body, though that was neither safe nor comfortable,
because his arm shifted, his hand was at her throat, his gun
pressed to her temple.

'Stop! Shut up! I shoot you now! I shoot you!'

'Don't!' Ben shouted. He'd raised his hands, stepped away
from the wall; the only one there who knew what was going
to happen next.

Eliot Pedlar said, 'Boys,' and hugged them closer . . .

And both boys, that same moment, said, 'Mummy' . . .

Only Louise had nothing to say. She opened her mouth, but
all that came out was *ungh*. It was the noise she'd have made
if punched in the stomach, and made as much sense as anything
else she might have come up with.

And then the door burst open, and sudden light framed a
black-clad man, and a second, and a third, each with ugly sticks
in their hands which made no sense because sticks weren't
allowed inside, except for nature-table purposes . . . They
weren't sticks. They became guns as Louise watched, and one
of them covered the hostages against the wall as the other two
trained on the motionless pile on the floor that was Judy and
Jaime.

'Everybody down!'

'Everybody down!'

Everybody down . . .

In the moment that followed there was silence in the annexe,
but for the squeaking of the wheel in Trixie's cage. Maybe
something about the sudden noise and movement had convinced
the hamster that life was back to normal; maybe this was more
the sort of thing she expected. Children were huge, and wielded
toys. Big men with guns weren't such a departure. It was a
matter of degree.

The wheel squeaked. Round and round she ran, getting nowhere.

'Everybody down!'

Ben dropped, followed by Louise. Eliot crouched, pulling his children with him until they began pulling him: attempting to squash themselves into the floor; to make themselves a puddle that could soak through the boards, reassemble in the earth beneath, then edge into the freedom of the outside air. They liquefied in his embrace. And he wanted to find words that would comfort them, but the only word in his head was the one they'd just banished him with: *Mummy.*

Everybody down . . .

'Target is on the ground, repeat, target is on the ground.'

'And has a hostage,' Ben said loudly. His hands were on the back of his head – he knew what you did; you made yourself a non-combatant. Guns plus excitement equals accidents. A friendly bullet ripped exactly the same size hole in you. And a hostile one would punch through Jaime's head, smearing whatever he knew, or thought he knew, across the boards of a nursery floor.

'Be quiet!'

'And has a hostage,' Ben repeated loudly. 'Call them out. He'll kill her.'

'Target is on the ground. He has the woman.'

A faint crackle from a headset; a question relayed from a hundred yards away.

'No.'

Do you have a clear shot? Ben translated.

'They can't shoot without hitting the woman,' he said clearly. More crackle.

'Be quiet!'

More crackle.

The hamster wheel squeaked, slowed, squeaked . . . stopped.

There'd be instructions flowing through those headsets, but things weren't going right. The annexe should have been crawling by now; the innocents dragged out to freedom; the gunman disarmed and either docile or dead. Instead there was a new stand-off, and unless someone made a decision soon, someone else was going to be dead.

More crackle . . .

'Pull them out.'

'They've just got in!'

'Pull them out. They've lost the moment. Whistler's saying they can't shoot without—'

'Whistler is not part of this operation!'

'He's the only one keeping his head. How old are those kids? Pull them out.'

But for another few seconds, Fredericks hesitated.

Peter Craven was twenty-seven, stood just over six foot; had recently asked Tasha to marry him, and was spending more free afternoons leafing through colour swatches than booting a football around South Parks – just reaching that point, in other words, when the difference between training and the real thing kicked in. So here he was, real weapon in hand, real sweat on his forehead, real villain in front of him, gun to the temple of the hostage on top.

Another hostage saying, *Call them out. He'll kill her.*

All very different from the practice runs.

'Target is on the ground. He has the woman.'

Do you have a clear shot?

Did he have a clear shot? On the training ground, there was only one answer, and it was always *yes*, even when it should have been *no*. *Can you hit the target from here?*, said target being the size of a peanut. But *yes* was the right answer, because you never let anyone know there were things beyond you, not if you wanted to earn your stripes, climb the ladder, make Tasha proud. So you said *yes* and took the shot and the worst that happened was the wrong dummy lost its head . . . Well, not quite. The worst that happened was the bawling out you got for being too stupid to know the difference between *yes* and *no*.

That's your plan, is it? the instructor had said. *Cross your fingers and hope for the best? If you can't manage the shot, you can't manage the shot. Life or death means precisely that. Life. Or. Death.*

'They can't shoot without hitting the woman,' the hostage said clearly.

Who's speaking?

'Be quiet!'

And Peter meant both of them, the headset and the hostage . . . Peter Craven, first through the door, was the only one with a prayer of a shot at the gunman, and he knew the difference between *yes* and *no*.

Do you have a clear shot?

It was a matter of life or death.

All AFOs with two-years' plus experience to attend the refresher in Yorkshire . . . As of this moment, Fredericks had only one authorized firearms officer on-site who'd actually worked a hostage situation.

This was what was meant by economies of scale.

'Pull them out,' he said.

Faulks relayed the order to the officers in the field.

Like one of those moments when the brain plays catch-up, Louise thought afterwards. When it files a recent event in the wrong folder; classes it as memory instead of ongoing event. Now, everything was happening backwards, as if her brain was respooling, undoing the noise and confusion of barely a minute:

everybody down!

ungh
Mummy
boys
don't
stop shut up I shoot you now I shoot you
you fuck, you bastard

And then they were gone, and it was just the seven of them again, with the door still open, and Trixie's wheel silent in the background ... Gordon whimpered. Timmy belched. Eliot looked at her, but with nothing in his eyes; he might have been trying to remember what everything looked like before she was there.

The outside world leaked in, carrying strange hints of upsets continuing elsewhere.

Ben Whistler rose, walked to the door, and closed it.

When Sam Chapman knocked on Louise Kennedy's door, it was opened by a cop, but that was okay. The woolly-suits at the nursery had more to worry about than letting the strength know he was ignorable. He flashed his card, and the cop said, 'MI6?'

'Don't tell everyone.'

'This is terrorism? I thought that was Five's—'

'It's a foreign national with a gun, son,' he said quietly. 'Is her mother in?'

Louise Ann Kennedy: b.1975 in Chester. Educated there and Sheffield University (PPE), then a PGCE (Oxford Brookes) before a stint in banking: DeJohn Franklin Moers. He'd collected this from Whistler's BlackBerry; had read, too, the follow-up, which had come after Whistler had surrendered the gadget to Faulks. *Current circumstances: single; mother on premises.* They delivered the goods, the Queens of the Database, though their manner of expression tended towards the robotic.

The front door opened on to the living room. And there

she was, the mother on the premises, in a straight-backed chair with her back to him; another cop opposite her, face carefully composed into an attitude of sympathetic concern. Unless that came naturally. You couldn't always tell. The officer got to her feet, and the mother turned to see what was happening. The cop behind Sam mouthed *spook*, and the officer sat back down.

'Is my daughter all right?'

'As far as I know, Mrs Kennedy.'

'Who are you?'

'I work for the government,' he said. 'Security services. I wonder if I could have a word.'

He looked at the female cop. Who looked at the cop behind him.

'We're supposed to stay here.'

'You can stay in the kitchen.'

'Our orders—'

'Just changed.'

It wasn't the card he carried – a lot of the time, it was anything but. It was the way he said it: years of experience plus attitude. It was okay if people ended up nursing a grudge; that was the basis of most of Bad Sam's relationships.

When they were alone, he sat.

'Your daughter's alive. The more we know, the more likely she is to stay that way.'

People made the mistake of thinking older people weak. But you only got old by surviving. Things wore out, but the core got harder. And Sam was in a hurry; he had no time to pussy around.

'What is that supposed to mean?'

'Exactly what I say.'

'This man broke in, he just chose a school. My daughter's unlucky, that's all.'

'More than likely. But we have to explore the possibility

that this isn't random, Mrs Kennedy. We have to look at the background.'

She glanced toward the television, which was off. 'They're showing pictures. But nothing's happening.'

'Lots is happening. We can't see it, that's all. Time is of the essence – tell me about your daughter.'

All these people – how come there were all these people, when the only one involved was her?

Christine Pedlar pushed through the crowd like a blind woman crashing through a wood.

There were journalists, and locals, and way up above a helicopter buzzed like a demented mosquito. This would be filming the event – which is what this was: an *event*. And from that high perspective, its rotor blades trimming the undersides of clouds, an event no different from any other mass gathering; animal rights or football mob. One in which there was no telling anyone from anyone else, though really she should show up as the single splash of colour – a bright red anguished figure clawing through a black and white uncaring mass.

Her boys were in there. Her beautiful twin sons. In that building, around which armed policemen waited.

This information was too big for her head. Any moment now her skull would crack, and the horrible fact it held come screaming out, to shatter the daylight.

How did it happen? What caused this slippage in normality? Today should have been ordinary – different, but *normal*; she was visiting her old office, to discuss a return to work. Did she want to return to work? Not especially, but it had to be discussed, if only to keep Eliot quiet. But shortly after her arrival, something unexpected had tugged inside Chris, and she realised that she had missed this: the business of being at work, performing tasks that did not revolve around the needs of children. Christine had been a legal secretary; a good one. The solicitors she worked for could do with her return. And somewhere between being offered coffee and receiving it, this notion had come to seem not altogether far-fetched: perhaps, after all, it was what she needed. And it came with options attached – flexible working plans were mentioned. By the time the coffee was drunk, her former boss was acting like her future boss. She'd have to discuss it with Eliot, she reminded him. But something in his friendly goodbye hinted that he thought she'd made her mind up.

Perhaps she had. And now was being punished for it.

So was that the way the world worked? Four years' full-time devotion, and the first time you thought of blinking – *bang!*

She was pushing to the front now; was pushed back by those who thought she was just another rubbernecker at someone else's car crash.

You don't understand – my children are in there.

Words rocketing round her brain without finding an opening they could use.

This is not an event. *This is my life exploding.*

Hers was the kind of nature, if someone honked their horn at her, it wrecked her for half an hour. This: this could kill her.

But don't use that word. Don't use that word. It might give the world ideas.

Something flashed in her mind like a bulb in a cellar, and her darling babies splashed around the nursery floor. And with the image something else broke, because her vision swam apart, and all the black and white figures around her fissured into blurry messes, their edges foamy and transparent.

Someone touched her elbow.

'Chris?'

She turned and tried to speak, but all she could do was burst into tears.

That was probably the most fucked-up hostage rescue attempt since Tehran. Even allowing for scaled-down consequences –

there was small chance Ronald Reagan would be re-elected – Fredericks could feel the backlash already: *you don't send a team in if they're not up to the job.*

'It's nobody's fault,' Faulks told him.

'Guess who just got to be nobody?'

'There's only one point of entry. What were the chances he'd be underneath a hostage? I mean, *underneath* . . .'

'You think the *Mail* will be that understanding? We put the team in, we pulled it back out. And nothing's changed.'

'Everyone's still alive,' Faulks said.

'Only because I haven't debriefed them yet,' said Fredericks, and then both men fell silent, because there was talk in the annexe again.

'Get up.'

She didn't move.

'Get *up*!'

Jaime shoved, and Judy rolled off him. And then he saw Ben by the door, fresh from closing it, and screamed: '*You. Against the wall!*' and aimed the gun, his hand shaking so much, Ben would have had to be fibrillating hard to be in its way. '*Now!*'

Ben stepped carefully, hands in the air. 'I was closing the door,' he said.

Jaime was breathing hard.

'They've gone, Jaime. But you saw how fast they moved.'

'I am still here.'

'Because you got lucky.'

Ben, back at the wall, was the only upright body in the room. But Louise was pushing herself up, and Eliot Pedlar coming out of the crash position. The two small boys were still dead lions: not a happy association. Beside Jaime, Judy – the cause of the recent eruptions – was a badly filled bin liner.

'It's just a matter of time, Jaime.'

'Shut up.'

'No. Keep talking. It's the only way.'

'They want to kill me.'

'They don't want to kill you. But that's what they'll do. Because you've got a gun, Jaime, and six hostages. Killing you is what happens next. Unless you keep talking.'

Jaime stepped away from Judy, and looked down on her. For a moment, Ben thought he was going to spit.

Instead he said, 'You. Go back over there.'

After a moment, she stirred into life. She crawled, didn't walk, back to the wall.

The squeaking from the hamster cage began again, slowed, then stopped.

Jaime looked behind him, at the door that could no longer be trusted. Then back at Ben.

Ben said, 'Talk about Miro.'

'Louise used to work for a City bank,' Bad Sam Chapman said.

'It was a good job. It paid well.'

'I'm sure.'

'But she worked long hours, weekends, everything. I never saw her.'

'What made her give it up?'

'Well, she trained as a teacher, you know.'

'So I gathered. But it doesn't pay as well, does it?'

'Money isn't everything,' Mrs Kennedy said.

'But it's unusual to give up such a well-paid career so young.'

'Louise has always done precisely what she wants to do.'

This with a tightening of the mouth, as if in memory of certain occasions when Louise would have done better to heed others' advice.

'So it was her own idea to quit?'

'Which part of the security services did you say you worked for?'

'I didn't. Was it her own idea to quit?'

'There was . . . trouble.'

'What kind of trouble?'

'She wouldn't say. But I could tell. A mother always can.'

'Did they catch her with her hand in the till?'

Further mouth-tightening, and enough frost in the eyes to blind a windscreen. 'Louise would no more steal than she would . . .' A comparison failed her. 'There was a man involved.'

'And *he* was caught with his—'

'She had an affair. With a senior partner. And it's always the woman who pays for that sort of indiscretion, isn't it?'

Bad Sam had operated enough honey traps to know otherwise, but had conducted enough interviews not to contradict. He said, 'She told you about this?'

'Not in so many words.'

He waited.

'But my daughter is an ambitious woman. She crossed teaching off her career list once she found she could earn ten times as much doing something she was better at.'

'And she wouldn't have walked away if it hadn't become necessary.'

'Quite.'

'There are other banks.'

'Yes. But whatever happened hurt her. She wanted out of that world. That's how I know a man was involved.'

And she gave him the name. *Crispin.*

He had led her up a cut into the estate opposite the rec ground. When they reached a row of garages he stopped, and held her while she sobbed out what was left of her heart, or that's what it felt like. When she was dry at last, she was emptied of more than tears; had had every last drop of emotion wrung out of her. This state persisted for twenty seconds, and felt literally a blessed relief. And then reality booted up and left her standing by a row of garages, her boys still locked inside the annexe.

Dave Osborne said, 'I'm so sorry, Chris.'

She released herself, shaking her head. She meant nothing by this, and might as easily have nodded.

'How did you find out?'

This strange question forced her to rearrange her thoughts. Perhaps that was its purpose. 'I—this morning, I was busy. Eliot brought the boys in.'

'I know.'

'I was visiting my old office on the Cornmarket. And I went into the shopping centre afterwards, and walked past that TV place . . .'

And had seen the *event* beamed out to shocked shoppers. Shocked, but not ungratified; there was a sense of importance attached to being a local when news was breaking. Chris Pedlar had been rooted to the spot: important was not how she felt. What she was feeling – what she was feeling was in her pocket for her mobile. And yes, it was on; and no: no texts, no voice-mail, no missed calls were registered. And however flaky Eliot could be, however detached from family life, no way he couldn't know what was happening in Grandpont right now; no way he wouldn't have called her the second he heard . . .

Unless he wasn't able to.

Dave handed her a tissue, and she blew her nose loudly. 'Things are going to be okay, Chris.'

'My boys are in there, aren't they?'

'Yes,' he said. 'I'm sorry, Chris. I think so. Yes.'

'Why? Why them and not—'

She couldn't finish the thought. Whose children would she substitute for her own, and place in mortal danger? Any-one's – that was the raw truth. She'd have her children change place with anyone's right now, but finding a name was thankfully beyond her. She realised Dave's hand was still on her shoulder, and he must have registered that too, because he removed it.

'Who else?' she asked.

'In there?'

'Who's with my babies?'

'Your husband,' he said. And then said, 'I'm so sorry' again.

'At least they have him.' God, that that could be a comfort.

'And Louise, Louise Kennedy. She didn't have to be, Chris. She went back inside. She could have escaped.'

She looked at him, not understanding.

'There'd have been others in there, but she got them out. Then went back.'

'But not my boys.'

'They must have been first. The rest of them, the ones who arrived when I did, she chased them away.'

'But why were they there first? Eliot was taking them to kick a football around.'

Dave shook his head. 'I don't know.'

'But that's what he told me they were doing.'

This little snippet of memory was worth holding on to. It could form the basis for a whole new reality; one in which Eliot and the twins were kicking a ball on the rec ground, oblivious to the passage of time and the massed police forces nearby.

He said, 'Maybe it got too cold for them.'

'But it isn't cold.'

'But maybe it was then. Chris, I'm sorry. I wish this wasn't happening, and I don't know why it is. All I know is . . .'

He lifted a helpless hand, then let it drop. *That it is* was what he couldn't say.

She blinked, then rubbed her eyes. It didn't help. She was still here, the world was still wrong; Dave was still looking at her, fear and compassion mixed in his eyes. He was good-looking, Dave Osborne, all the mothers agreed, and he'd figured in the occasional reverie, though recalling that was like looking through a window into make-believe. Had she really enjoyed moments when her mind wasn't screaming? The last time she'd kissed her boys – oh God don't say *the last time* – she'd been waving them off to play football, not sending them into the arms of a gun-wielding maniac. So she'd thought. Could the point of slippage really be that they'd felt cold, so went into the nursery early? How could something so mundane be life-altering? And how come they'd got in anyway, if Dave hadn't been there to open the gate?

Her black angel hovered overhead, masquerading as a helicopter.

Dave said, 'You'd better talk to the police.'

'Why? Will they do things differently if I do?'

'I don't know, Chris. It's just what you have to do, I think.'

She thought so too. But it would be another line crossed, indicating her acquiescence in this nightmare. If she couldn't turn the clock back she wanted it to stand still; wanted now to last forever, a now in which there was at least the possibility that things would turn out all right. Allowing things to continue was to open the door to all manner of grief. And again that image splashed across her mind: of her babies ruined on a nursery floor.

More tears fell. Nothing could dam them up.

'Chris? Chris?'

Dave shimmered before her, for an instant becoming twins. And then was blurrily solo again, holding something out.

'Don't tell anyone, okay? It's more than my job's worth.'

He smiled a conspirator's smile.

After a moment she took the cigarette, and he lit it for her, then one for himself.

Time wouldn't stand still, but at least she could lurk outside it for a while. These things took minutes off your life – the next few wouldn't be missed.

They stood close as lovers, by the garages, smoking. A short distance away, her children shook.

Time was back to doing somersaults: every moment crawled; every minute jumped. Outside, the sun would be edging through the sky, or that's what it would look like it was doing. Here in the annexe, electric light was all they had to go on.

Eliot thought: *Any other day, any other lifetime, I'd be at my desk, thinking about lunch.*

Lunch wouldn't figure on today's menu.

Judy was back on the floor, in a crouch. Head between her knees, arms around her legs. The only one among them to make a break for freedom. He ought to admire that, but instead felt disgust that she'd endangered their lives . . . Circumstances altered perspective. The one who'd put their lives in danger was the young man with the gun. But Eliot blamed Judy for attempting escape, and all the justification he needed for that was wrapped round his thighs.

Timmy and Gordon. Gordon and Timmy.

'Talk about Miro,' Ben Whistler had said.

Eliot didn't give a fuck about Miro, whoever fucking Miro was. This had nothing to do with him or his boys.

At my desk, thinking about lunch . . . This should have read: At my desk, thinking about Louise. If not for Louise, he and his boys would have been elsewhere.

Jaime said, 'You are one of them. You are on their side.'

'I just closed the door, Jaime. I could have walked right through it. The next time they come in, you're dead. So talk about Miro. Why was he so sure he was in danger?'

'Because of things he knew.'

'Not because of what he stole?'

'He was not a thief.'

Question answer, question answer . . .

If Eliot shut his eyes, he could be back at the school quiz.

But he couldn't remember the questions now; that was the funny thing. At the time, he'd never forgotten a detail in his life; no fact too trivial, no statistic too insignificant, to have escaped his attention – the Cato Street Conspirators' ringleader;

Hitchcock's first American movie; the third man on the moon. He'd recalled the depth of the Marianas Trench. On a multiple choice, true, but a breathtakingly unlikely answer to the less well informed. And then, of course, there'd been the downhill stuff – contemporary lit, seventies TV, late eighties pop and pre-Blair politics.

'You are the king of trivia,' Louise had whispered.

'Oh, I'm good at important stuff too,' he'd whispered back.

They'd formed a faction: the two of them v. Lizzie. Safety in numbers; plus, Lizzie knew remarkably little about anything – refusing to believe, for example, that Cliff Richard wasn't his real name. 'It's a trick question,' she'd said.

Louise was hot on botany, geography, and – surprisingly, though Eliot pretended otherwise – sport.

'You're good at this too.'

'Oh, it's not the only thing I'm good at.'

The other tables: they blew them away. It was the scene in the movie – give him a moment, Eliot would tell you its director – when everything goes right, the background's a soft buzz, and there's no doubt who's in focus.

It didn't even feel like a mistake that it wasn't Chris sharing it with him.

When Eliot tried, he could remember life as a sequence of tracts of time controlled by Christine; the early days, when her choices determined his mood. 'That's what we'll do for Christmas,' she'd say – or for her birthday, or his, or for the first Sunday after Whitsun: whatever – and something inside him would relax, and he'd think: okay, she intends us still to be together then. And it had quietly become established that their future was a series of shared events. When had that stopped? The king of trivia couldn't put his finger on it. Like everything else that had happened to him, the opening of that chasm had been a gradual process. You could pick the twins' birthday, of course, but that had been a sharing day; he honestly couldn't remember being happier. The slippage was buried somewhere since; the dim falling off from his centrality in all their lives to being the ghost who left for work every morning, and didn't come home till the fun was over. For all the boys' important steps – their first, for instance – he'd been elsewhere. Which he could have lived with if it weren't for the guilt he was made to feel: it was as if Chris resented his having a career, when it had been her choice to stay at home. Neither liked the idea of full-time childcare; he earned more than she did; she was their mother – it was a no-brainer. So why had it become another of those unspoken-of areas; part of their relationship's no-man's-land? And how did no-man's-land work, anyway, when one of them was a man? Well, it worked in the obvious way – he'd had more intimate moments with his dentist lately than he'd had with his wife. And he hadn't seen his dentist in a year.

You could blame him for what had happened with Louise – of course you could – but you couldn't *blame* him for it. This was a subtle shade of difference that he wouldn't have liked to justify before an audience, but nevertheless it was deeply felt. You could blame him. But you couldn't *blame* him.

. . . Even here, even now, he could look at Louise and know that in a single encounter, he'd established a greater connection with her than he'd known with Christine in years. And for all this turbulent danger that had jumped out of nowhere, there was a comfort in knowing that she'd found that too.

Even so, she was avoiding his gaze.

'It began when he went to Iraq,' Jaime said.

If he'd stop looking at her, this might be easier. It wasn't first on her list – if the boy with the gun hadn't turned up; if they weren't arranged against a wall; if there hadn't just been an armed incursion into the annexe – if none of that had happened either, this would definitely be easier; but still, right that moment, what Louise mostly wanted was for Eliot to stop looking at her.

Then again, if none of that had happened, she'd have to be talking to him.

Ben was saying, 'Iraq. Right,' as if a coin had dropped into his mental well.

Iraq had been one of the answers at that damn quiz.

None of it had been deliberate, not on her part. If she'd been given a map of the evening before starting out, she'd have vanished screaming. There was solid circumstantial back-up for this, and it was scribbled all over her recent history: Louise had already teetered on the edge of her life's Big Mistake – her version of 'teeter', admittedly, being another woman's 'plummet' – and no way was she approaching that cliff again. It wasn't as if the danger wasn't posted. There had been a significant increase, Claire had mentioned, in fathers delivering their young ones since Louise had started work, and while Claire hadn't neces-sarily meant it as such, Louise had taken it as a warning. 'Maintain distance' had become her mantra. It had worked until that evening.

You could avoid wine and moonlight, steer clear of roses and poetry, and still come undone over something as simple as shared victory.

Iraq had been the final answer, and even as their sheets were collected in, Louise was saying, 'I think we've won.'

'Put it this way,' Eliot said. 'We haven't lost.'

'Put it this way' was already a familiar Eliotism; frequently attached to statements so straightforward, it was hard to know what more obvious formulation he'd rejected. But knowing they'd just managed something special together had a warming effect. So Louise simply smiled. 'Yes. We haven't lost.'

For the next ten minutes they listened to Lizzie explaining that it didn't matter who won, that she'd read in a book that

Cliff was his real name, and wasn't this nice, and it was a pity Chrissie couldn't be there, though obviously that wasn't possible, what with the little ones. Then she broke off to accost some passing acquaintances, while Eliot explained that 'Chrissie' was Christine – Chris – and that nobody called her Chrissie except Lizzie, who'd never met her.

'I like Chris,' Louise had said. In fact, she wasn't entirely sure she had the right woman. The twins were a clue, being the only pair in the nursery, but sometimes the mothers melded into an abstraction of exasperation and busyness.

Their prize was a bottle of champagne.

'Well, isn't that *lovely*,' breathed Lizzie. Then: 'I don't drink, of course.'

That *of course* was an insight into a whole other mindset.

'So I think it would be nice if Eliot took it home for Chrissie to share.'

Louise didn't mind one way or the other, but cared a lot less about Lizzie making the offer for her.

'That's kind,' Eliot said. 'If it's okay with Louise.'

A ghost of a wink accompanied his words.

They left not long after. Lizzie was on her bike – another *of course* – and Eliot was heading for the bus stop. They were out of the building before Louise said, 'I can drop you. I'm in the car.'

'Well, I live over East Oxford. It's out of your way.'

The bottle was in a bag he was holding carefully; not letting it swing.

'That's all right.'

They'd driven maybe two hundred yards when he said, 'You should have this.'

'Have what?'

'The bottle. Lizzie doesn't drink, did you notice that? So she doesn't think it's much of a sacrifice you shouldn't either. But you won it really. Besides, I'd just glug it.'

'We both won it. And I'm sure Chrissie would enjoy a treat.'

He smiled.

'Or doesn't she drink either?'

'Well, with kids, you know how it is. She's so exhausted by the time they're packed off to bed.'

'So glug it yourself. Once she's gone to bed.'

'Can't drink champagne on your own.'

That hung between them for a while. They came to a halt at pedestrian lights, though no one was using the crossing.

'Well, we could share it,' she said.

And there it was – *of course* – unplanned, but definitely stated. The point at which the evening's map sheered into uncharted places. Beyond here lie monsters, they used to say. The fact that the monsters were instantly recognisable didn't make them any less scaly.

'Um,' said Eliot. 'I think drinking in cars is a bit of a no-no. Put it this way. It's definitely frowned on.'

The little green man gave way to the red, and she drove on, passing the junction which would have taken them east. 'Well,' she said. 'You can always say we went to the pub after.'

'I'd probably better say we were part of a crowd.'

And then, a minute or so later, he added, 'Actually, it'd probably be best if I didn't mention you at all.'

The downstairs light was on when they got back, and Eliot had asked whether that was for burglars, and she'd told him, lightly, oh, her mother was staying. Every sentence was conspiracy. This particular construction nearly unravelled everything, but mischief was rearing in her soul: 'It's okay. She'll have gone to bed.'

Which she had.

So what happened next? The inevitable happened next. They whispered on the sofa and drank the bottle, and then stopped whispering and started kissing instead, and before either of them got much older her knickers were round one ankle, and maybe three minutes after that she was pulling them up again; the whispering a little more formal, the bottle definitely empty.

'I'm not sure I should drive you home.'

'It's okay. I can walk.'

'It's just, I'm over the limit . . .'

'Don't worry.' He insisted on kissing her again. 'When can I see you?'

'Eliot, you know what we just did was stupid, don't you?'

But his face wore a moon-fogged expression, which he might have thought tender, but only spelled trouble. Already, he was cherishing a Memory. Already, she was regretting an Incident. One of those irresistible force–immovable object scenarios, which could be postponed but never avoided.

Though dumping it in a hostage situation might throw it into perspective.

And now Louise thought: what had it all been about? Really? And understood that it was mostly payback for her mother shirking the evening quiz. *You want me to have fun? Okay. This is how grown-up girls have fun.* With half a bottle of bubbly inside her, she hadn't even cared if her mother had heard them, though it was amazing how quickly that had turned into a damp sticky fear that her mother had heard them. Not the only thing that had been amazingly quick. At least there'd been no cries of passion to stifle.

'When was that?' Ben asked. And then said: 'No, I remember. It was last year, wasn't it?'

Other people's memories now.

She tried to shut her mind down.

But found herself asking anyway: 'What was he doing there?'

Fredericks was smoking again. Chances were, he'd have been smoking even without a cigarette in hand: it would be coming out of his ears; comically erupting from sleeves and trouser cuffs.

Not just fucking up: he'd been there before.

But fucking up with the world's press a typewriter's throw away.

Faulks had said: 'There'll be time for post-mortems later.'

'Good choice of words.'

'We don't need this, Malc. Sir. The important thing is—'

'That they're still inside. I know.'

And okay: *world's press* was an exaggeration. But the whole damn story would be on the Web before he'd finished his cigarette, which he shouldn't be smoking in the Incident Vehicle anyway. He dropped it into the dregs of a cup of tea.

It began when he went to Iraq.

Fucking great. His career fizzing out like that butt, and all over spook stuff – they should keep their cloak and dagger games where they belonged, not drag them into a nursery practically outside his office window.

What was he doing there?

Faulks said, 'That's the woman. Kennedy.'

'Do they even *know* we just tried to get them out? It's like they're—'

'Sir . . .'

They listened.

'Talk about Miro.'

'You are one of them. You are on their side.'

'I just closed the door, Jaime. I could have walked right through it. The next time they come in, you're dead. So talk about Miro. Why was he so sure he was in danger?'

'Because of things he knew.'

'Not because of what he stole?'

'He was not a thief.'

'You'll have to do better than that. Are you keeping up, Jaime? You have one chance of getting out of here alive, and that's telling me what you know.' Ben paused. 'Please. For all our sakes.'

Jaime said nothing.

'And don't think the gun will help. Those weren't toys those guys had. Pull that trigger, they'll spray you over the walls. You might as well put it in your own mouth. If you want to live, tell me about Miro.'

Just look at him, Ben thought – his hair sticking up in improbable tufts; eyes wild, sweat glistening on his forehead. The gun in his fist was an anomaly. You wouldn't put money on him having strength to pull the trigger. For half a second, Ben thought about striding across and taking it away – it could be done. And then Jaime would be tied up in knots and delivered to Bad Sam Chapman. And that would be the end of him.

'It began when he went to Iraq,' Jaime said.

'When was that?' Ben asked. And then said: 'No, I remember. It was last year, wasn't it?'

'What was he doing there?' Louise asked.

They both looked at her. It was as if they'd forgotten there were others present.

Ben said, 'That's really not important.'

'You think?'

'The reason I'm here—'

'The reason you're here is to get us out alive. That's what you're going to say. But there's more to it, isn't there? The reason you're here is because this man knows something, and you're trying to find out what.'

'This would be a lot easier if you kept quiet.'

Eliot said, 'This would be a lot easier if we weren't here.'

Now everyone turned to Eliot.

Who said: 'None of this is happening by accident. This man called you last night.' He was looking at Ben. 'He just said so. And people tried to kill him because of that. That's why he's here. That, and because of . . . the "lady".'

He looked at Louise.

She said: 'I've got no idea what makes me important.' Though wasn't sure she believed that herself.

Ben said, 'You really don't want to be part of any of this.'

'It's a little late for that,' Louise pointed out.

Jaime was following this, or not following it, with growing confusion. And like any boy, he grabbed the first thing that made sense and shook it. 'Yes,' he said. The others turned to him. 'I call you. Miro give me the number. Where you work.'

Ben chewed that for a moment. Then asked, 'What time did you call?'

It had happened subtly, this shift, but it had happened. Jaime still held the gun, but was no longer calling the shots. 'Late. I do not remember. Ten o'clock?'

'I'd long left by then, Jaime. Who answered the phone?'

'You did.'

'Ten o'clock, I was in the Three Whistles. And I don't have call forwarding.' This left Jaime a good way behind. He tried again: 'It wasn't me who answered, Jaime.'

'The person say it was you.'

'You got through to the switchboard, right?'

'. . . Yes.'

'And asked for me.'

'I ask to speak to Ben Whistler.'

'And the woman said?'

'She put me through.'

Ben was nodding before Jaime had finished. 'She put you through all right, Jaime. But not to me.'

'The man say he was you.'

'Well, like I said, Miro and I weren't exactly spies. But we work for the security services. A lot of lies get told. What did you tell this man?'

'I tell him who I am.'

'That you're Miro's boyfriend.'

'Yes.'

'And what else?'

'That I am frightened. That I want a place to hide.'

'Where were you, Jaime? Where were you calling from?'

'From a phone box.'

'Not your mobile?'

'I have no money on my mobile. No pay-up.'

'No prepay, okay. So a call box. Where?'

'Near Marble Arch.'

'Why there?'

'It is near where I work.'

'Okay. And you wanted to talk to someone. Someone who might know where Miro is. Did you tell him – this guy you thought was me – did you tell him where you were calling from?'

'Yes. He tell me to wait there. That he come to collect me.'

'But you didn't.'

'How do you know?'

'Because you're here, Jaime. What happened at Marble Arch?'

'I wait near corner. Near Underground. Not in main road. By a turning.'

'Okay.'

'I am not the only person waiting near there.'

'I can imagine. What happened?'

'A car arrive.'

'Just one car?'

'Lots of people come and go. People getting into cars. I think some are prostitutes.'

'I wouldn't be surprised. And a car came for you, right?'

'Yes. But it have two men in it. I tell you – tell him, the man who answer phone – I tell him to come alone. I trust no one else.'

'How did you know they were looking for you?'

'I can tell. They are serious people. They look at faces. They see me straight away.'

'Tell me what they looked like.'

'First is big man. He have close haircut.' Jaime ran his free hand through his own locks. 'And big grey coat.'

'Right.'

'Other man is short and dark. But scarier.'

'Right . . .'

Ben looked around. Nothing much had changed. The daylight had shifted slightly, perhaps. He glanced up at the skylight; wondered if anyone was on the roof. But that was corrugated iron: only a pixie could get up there with nobody inside knowing. On the other hand, there were any number of policemen mere yards away, and sharpshooters well within killing distance. But all of that, right this moment, was irrelevant. There was an ear inside the annexe, and it was picking up everything. And pretty soon, Ben thought, the conversation was going to take directions nobody out there should know about. One nobody in particular.

He left the wall, and walked to a table in the corner.

'Where you go? You come back.'

Ben put a finger to his lips: the universal sign for silence.

'You come back now!'

Jaime raised the gun.

Ben put his hands in the air. 'It's okay,' he said softly. 'Everything's okay.'

'You go back against wall. You go back now!'

'There's something I need to do.' Again, he spoke softly; his words only just carrying. 'It's all right. Don't panic. Stay calm.'

He turned, and made for the table once more.

Jaime pointed the gun at his back.

'No!' Louise said.

The twins tried to melt into Eliot's legs.

Ben heard the bullet pass through him just as he reached the table; felt the clean round hole it cut in his body before passing through the outer wall of the annexe – on and on it flew, leaving clean round holes through everything in its path, before tiring of flight and burying itself in the earth miles away. Strangely, this was painless. He put a hand to his chest and found no hole; there had been no shot – only Louise's cry. Almost immediately the mobile in Jaime's pocket rang; that dreadful, irritating Nokia tune, more ubiquitous than the Beatles.

He picked up the sheet of paper he'd come for, and a thick black marker pen, and turned round.

Jaime was still pointing the gun at him.

'Better answer that,' Ben said. 'Don't want to alarm them.'

He walked back to the wall, and joined the others.

8

I<small>T WAS SO MUCH</small> a cliché it had passed through to the other side, re-emerging as irony. Three ducks on the wall went with everything else in this little house – the bookshelves loaded with knick-knacks and videotapes; the sofa sheathed in protective covering; the Toby jugs on the mantelpiece. What bothered Sam Chapman was that there were only two of them. Ducks, he meant. One of those details he'd find hard to forget.

'So you're not with the police,' Deirdre Walker was saying.

She was upper fiftyish, and not giving ground gracefully; her hair not so much permed as soldered into place, and enough make-up to keep a clown troop on the road. Whatever perfume she was wearing had a cloying, insect-repellent quality, and only just made its presence felt above the mustiness of stale cigarette smoke. A situation whose parameters Deirdre Walker altered now by adding fresh cigarette smoke, belatedly waving the pack at him.

'Thank you.'

'So you're not with the police.'

He had already shown her as much identification as he was prepared to, and wasn't about to let her see it again.

It was 11:59.

Not a long walk from Louise Kennedy's place, but a different world all the same. After leaving Kennedy's mother, Bad Sam had walked back up the road; had had to make his way round the crowd at the junction waiting for events to percolate. This was the reality beaming into Kennedy's living room, and bore little more clarity than the onscreen version. The crowd was press plus slack-jawed accident-watchers, one of whom had stepped back without looking. Bad Sam – a Tube wars veteran – had brought his heel down on the man's instep without breaking stride. Then he'd walked as far as the river; over an iron bridge beneath which fuzzy lumps of froth floated, clinging to polystyrene flotillas and soggy cardboard rafts. Oxford or not, this wasn't quite punting in boaters.

He'd lit a cigarette while waiting for Whistler's BlackBerry to buzz.

One day, the next inevitable step would be taken, and hand-held gizmos like this would come with video link-up. Until that happened Chapman had Whistler's BlackBerry, and as far as the Queens of the Database were concerned, that meant it was Whistler asking, and they'd provide the required information. Whistler was an agent in the field for the moment, and joes always took priority.

Which was a joke. Bad Sam had served in the field. There'd been boys and girls at Vauxhall Cross who'd waited anxiously for his every transmission, true, but further up the ladder all you had was suits measuring budget shortfalls. These days, Bad Sam's own suit was a budget shortfall all its own. He was staring down the barrel of forced retirement – he'd last no longer than Nott, and Nott was on the skids – and the rewards of his service were pennies in a tin compared to what he'd be worth if he'd taken the corporate shilling. How surprising was it when an old hand went freelance? In his years as a Service Dog – since his cover had grown too tattered for *foreign holidays*, as every joe called them – Bad Sam had collared former colleagues whose treacheries would have been stillborn if their pensions had matched their valour. These people had heard the call, and replied, you point me, I'll march. In return they got a handshake and a pat on the back: now piss off. It wasn't that Chapman was sentimental – those same former colleagues would testify to that. But he understood the nature of loyalty, if only because he'd learned the hard way about betrayal.

Betrayal began with the small stuff; the lapses that didn't seem to matter.

I didn't mean to spy on her. You'll think that's funny, I suppose, a man in your profession. But I really didn't. It's just . . .

It was just that Louise's mother was on the scene, and how could she help knowing what she knew?

'This man Crispin was married, of course. I expect he gave Louise the usual story – that he'd leave his wife, set up home with her. Promises are cheap, aren't they?'

'Does she keep a diary?'

'You think I'd read my daughter's diary?'

Bad Sam hadn't answered.

She'd said, 'Sometimes, when I was visiting – this was when she had the London flat – there'd be a phone call she didn't want me to overhear.'

He waited.

'She'd pretend it was work. But there are tones of voice, aren't there? The kind you use when you're talking about work, and . . . the other kind.'

Crispin was another query Chapman had fed into Whistler's BlackBerry.

He'd been about to leave when she'd said, 'There was a night last week . . .'

'He rang?'

'No. We were supposed to go out to this school quiz, not Louise's school, a different one. A fundraiser. And I . . . well, I told her I wasn't feeling well. I thought it would do her good, to get out on her own. Meet new people.'

He waited.

'She brought a man back with her. Probably she thought I

couldn't hear them, but . . .' Her eyes strayed back to that TV set. 'Do you have children?'

'No.'

'It's hard to know what to wish for them. You want them to be happy, but the things that make them happy aren't always . . .'

Maybe, back in her daughter's sitting room, she was still finding her way to the end of that sentence.

On the bridge, a cigarette later, some answers had come streaming through the ether: Crispin was Crispin Tate, and came attached to one of those job titles that had been strung together from executive fridge magnets: Vice-Control, European Investments. Rearrange these words in any order. It was possible Bad Sam would have to call on Crispin Tate. It depended on how the dominoes fell. Also, he now had Judy Ainsworth's address: she lodged with a woman called Deirdre Walker. He put the BlackBerry away. Sooner or later it would start asking questions of its own, but until then he'd hang on to it.

Chance had brought Sam in the right direction; Ainsworth lived the other side of the estate the bridge led to. Some while ago a tin of paint had been dropped on the concrete apron near the bridge's stairwell, and its contents had hardened to a mustard-brown tattoo. A stained mattress germinated against a wall. He caught a whiff as he passed, on his way to the house with two ducks on the wall.

She was waving her cigarette packet at him, a beat behind what would have been polite.

'Thank you.'

'So you're not with the police.'

He leaned forward to take the light she offered, and said, 'Tell me about Mrs Ainsworth.'

'I thought there'd have been someone here by now. I rang the police earlier, of course.'

'Why was that?'

She shrugged. The movement came with exhaled smoke,

like a well-rehearsed piece of stage business. 'That's where she works. The nursery where those gunmen are.'

The TV had told her this. It stuttered away in the background: the same unvarying pictures of a building under siege. A reporter in a corduroy jacket was repeating a well-aired slice of speculation, and soon they'd cut to the studio, where an expert would attempt to speak for a whole minute without saying *Stockholm syndrome*. Any useful information was under wraps. The locals had a bug inside those walls – in the mobile the fat cop had given Louise Kennedy – and Bad Sam would have given anyone else's left nut to be listening in on it. He was trying to cover his arse, and all he could manage was background information.

'They said her name a while ago.'

'You must be worried about her.'

'Well, of course. She pays her rent on time, not like some of them.'

'How long has she been here?'

'I'd have to check.' She had the pinched look of a woman who gave nothing for free. 'But around a year.'

'And did you know her before?'

'Most of my circle live in North Oxford. I prefer it here. It's handy for the city centre.'

Spies have to learn foreign languages. Deirdre Walker's circle didn't take rooms.

'And do you get on? What's she like?'

She lifted an eyebrow. Surprisingly, she did this without using her fingers; her facial hydraulics evidently accustomed to the cosmetic weight they bore. 'Well . . .'

He waited.

'She's not exactly . . . a *people* person, our Judy.'

Not exactly a people person himself, Sam Chapman nodded understandingly.

'Bitter isn't the word.'

Which meant it was.

'I think when her husband left her – well . . . You can see why he did, actually.'

'She's divorced?'

'She's a widow. Like me.'

He waited.

'But would have been divorced.'

He waited some more.

She took a last drag on her cigarette, then crushed it in an ashtray embossed with Princess Diana's portrait, though which event in that short, hysterical life it commemorated wasn't clear. 'He went off with another woman. Then they were killed in a car crash.'

'I see.'

She looked at the TV screen, which had just flipped pictures and was now showing an airport scene: hostile crowds waiting while security measures eked themselves out. Chapman recognised stock footage when he saw it. Somebody was making connections: hostages equals terrorism. Terrorism causes death and panic and outrageous queues at airports.

'It's one of those Arabs, isn't it? At the nursery school.'

'Is that what they've said?'

'More or less. Don't get me wrong, I'm not prejudice.' The *d* had dropped off the end: strange how often that happens with this particular assertion. 'But I once had a tenant from that part of the world. Saudi or wherever.' She waved an airy hand. Don't bog her down with geographical precision. 'She barely *bathed*, I can tell you. The atmosphere became quite oppressive.'

'I can imagine.'

'Not as bad as darkies, though,' she dared.

'I know what you mean.'

'Talk about filthy habits.'

'My place is full of them,' Bad Sam Chapman told her.

'The government makes you, I suppose. I watched that spy

thing on telly. There was a blackie in that.' She exhaled smoke. 'Course, they shot him in the head in the end.'

'Does she talk much about him?'

'Keeps herself to herself, mostly. Only told me that much when she'd . . .' Walker made a tippling motion. 'Shame. But she's not got much else in her life.' She glanced at her watch. 'Would you like one, by the way? It's after twelve.'

'That would be kind.'

'Well, maybe I'll just have a small one.' He was twisting her arm, judging by her tone. She moved into the kitchen where he heard her opening a cupboard, then a bottle, then two, then the fridge, with such unclumsy swiftness it was difficult to believe she didn't do this regularly. When she returned she had a fizzing G&T in each hand. As soon as he'd relieved her of one, she reached for her cigarettes.

'Here. Have one of mine.'

'Don't mind if I do.'

She steadied his rock-steady hand with her own as he offered his lighter.

Chapman said, 'So where did it happen?'

'This is like an interrogation, isn't it?'

'Except without the rubber truncheon.'

She wagged a finger. 'Now now. I may be a single woman, but that doesn't mean you can take advantage.'

'I wouldn't dream of it, Mrs Walker.'

'Deirdre.'

She looked at him over the top of her G&T and sniggered. 'You ever do proper spying? Or just go round talking to people?'

'You'd be surprised how much spying gets done, just talking to people.'

'Have you ever killed anyone?'

'I could answer that,' he said. 'But then I'd have to kill you.'

She sniggered more, then stopped.

Something in Chapman's eyes made his joke a lot less funny.

Jaime put the mobile back into his pocket.

Ben wrote on the sheet of paper he'd collected.

'I tell them everything is okay.'

'I heard you.'

'What now?'

Ben shook his head.

'I am in charge here!'

Jaime's voice rose at the end of that. Jaime's voice nearly broke.

Ben held the paper up.

SAY NOTHING

'What the hell's going on in there?'

'Sounds like our spook is taking control.'

'Trying something on, you mean.'

Faulks said: 'Whatever just happened, Jaime didn't pull the trigger. And you heard him just now, he says everything's all right.'

'But it isn't,' Fredericks reminded him.

Because they were still out here, and the kid with the gun was still in there. Jaime. He didn't like it that Faulks was calling him 'Jaime'; he'd preferred it when they'd all agreed that the kid with the gun was the bastard.

'What's Whistler playing at?'

'I don't know.'

'He's supposed to be calming things down. Finding out what the bastard wants.'

'He's the one with the gun pointed at him,' Faulks said.

'Meaning?'

'I doubt he's deliberately trying to wind Jaime up. Where would that leave him?'

It is not on.

'What's not on?' Fredericks immediately asked.

Doesn't matter.

'Hush a mo,' Faulks said quietly.

In the Major Incident Vehicle, time ticked on at the same speed as everywhere else. But as the voices coming through the speakers thinned, it seemed to Fredericks that it slowed to a crawl; that he'd be here forever, head tilted slightly upwards to catch whatever might come next: a random word, a shriek, a gunshot. Or a sudden unexpected splash, followed by nothing at all.

SAY NOTHING

Jaime looked at the paper.

THE PHONE IS BUGGED

His face creased.

Ben was starting to feel like Rolf Harris. Or someone, anyway. He wasn't positive it was Rolf Harris.

THEY'RE LISTENING TO EVERY WORD WE SAY

Jaime looked at the phone in his hand, then back at Ben. 'It is not on.'

'Doesn't matter,' Ben whispered.

Eliot said, 'Look, exactly what the—'

'Shush.'

'It's not up to you to—'

Ben looked at him.

Eliot shut up.

Ben scribbled again, the black marker pen squeaking as he wrote: THE MAN WHO TRIED TO KILL YOU IS OUTSIDE

'Are you crazy?' Louise said, in a harsh whisper.

'Make him angry, and he might kill all of us,' Eliot said, same volume. 'I have children here. Or had you forgotten?'

Ben looked at Judy. 'Anything to add?'

'Don't fucking talk to me.'

'Fair enough. Now shut up, all of you.' He turned to Jaime, holding the paper at arms' length: here is the news. The word KILL arrested him, Ben could tell.

For a wonder, they'd all done what he'd said. The only noise leaked through from outside: no discernible voices, but an overlapping murmur, and the occasional electronic squawk. They might have been trapped in a zombie movie: just the odd shuffling sound breaking in, as if there were a brain-dead army hovering out there, waiting for a clue as to their presence.

At last Jaime said, 'What we do, then?'

We.

He was holding the mobile phone in his gun-free hand, staring at it as if he'd wound up holding a live grenade, with no idea how.

Ben turned the sheet over and started scrawling again, then thought better of it. Dropping both pen and paper, he held a hand out to Jaime, who didn't notice.

'Jaime?'

The boy looked up.

He didn't want to say it out loud. Just nodded his head in the direction of the phone, and wiggled his hand.

Even the little boys were quiet. Perhaps they'd stopped breathing.

Jaime put the phone on the floor, and took two steps back. The gun in his hand was still pointing at Ben.

It wasn't far to where the phone lay. And it wasn't as if having his back to the wall made Ben safer: he could be shot just as dead standing there as anywhere else. He forced himself to keep his eyes on Jaime as he collected the phone and straightened up: this, his body language said, was the essence of honesty. *We.* You just said *we.* This is what *we* do next.

He put a finger to his lips.

The phone was just a phone: how many times had he held a mobile phone? There was a great long chunk of his life during which he never had, him or anyone else; then bang – it happened every day. How many things could you say that of? It probably wasn't the moment to make a list. This one was no different to any of the others: whatever the makers wanted you to think, every mobile was basically the same lump of plastic. This one, though . . . This one felt heavier than it should. And while Ben knew that was his mind playing tricks – taking the knowledge that this phone was bugged, and transmitting that knowledge to the palm of his hand – that feeling wouldn't leave him as he carried the phone through the door to the toilets, and dumped it down the pan in the first cubicle.

'What was that?'

Faulks ignored Fredericks for a moment. Lowered his face to his hands instead, and rubbed it, as if he were washing himself.

'Did he just . . .'

'He just dumped it down the toilet. Yes.'

'Jesus fucking Christ.'

The van was growing smaller – all those banks of listening equipment seemed to swell in direct proportion to their new-found uselessness.

Fredericks said, 'I should never have let him in there.'

'I don't remember you having much choice.'

'He's endangering every hostage. What are we supposed to do now?'

Faulks said, 'He's a spook, Malc. He's got his own agenda. But I doubt that includes getting innocents killed. He's in the firing line too, don't forget.'

'But whatever he's up to, we're not allowed to hear it.'

'We've got directional mikes. They'll pick up something.'

'Everything?'

'Depends how loud they are.'

Fredericks shook his head. 'He's cutting us out of the loop.'

'Or somebody.'

'What?'

'Us or somebody.' Faulks reached for a set of headphones. 'It might not be us he's keeping secrets from.'

He was back from his mission. He'd drowned the phone. Everything was exactly as it had been, except that the digital spy had been removed from the scenario.

There were other ways of eavesdropping, of course – directional microphones; possibly other bugs clamped to the outside walls during that aborted incursion. If Bad Sam Chapman was outside, he'd be glued to the speakers now; wondering why the hell the main attraction had just dissolved into watery silence. And possibly switching to one of those back-up devices: bug on the wall, directional mike.

On a table beneath one of the shuttered windows sat a tape recorder; a children's model in big chunky plastic, with primary-coloured buttons. A slew of prerecorded tapes surrounded it, and Ben chose one at random; slotted it in. It burst into life at a frightening volume:

EELS ON THE BUS GO ROUND AND ROU

He fumbled with the dial.

nd round and round round and round

Better.

The others were staring as if he'd gone mad. Even the little boys – nursery music? They raised their heads from their father's thighs, and gazed like woodland creatures who've just heard a piper in the trees.

He said, 'Okay. Now we can talk.'

Words just loud enough to be heard above the music.

'You're at Marble Arch,' he said. 'Waiting for me. And two men arrive in a car looking for you.'

'Yes.'

'The same men who tried to pick you up this morning.'

'Yes. That is right.'

'But you must have got away from them last night. What did you do?'

'I run down into Underground.' Jaime's whisper was hoarse: this wasn't easy for him. Whispering in a foreign language – two things to concentrate on at once. 'But I don't get on train. I come up other side. Other side of road.'

'Got you.'

Jaime looked puzzled.

'I understand. Never mind. Carry on.'

'They follow me, but I think I lose them. I am good at disappearing in crowd. They think they trap me, but I lose them.'

'What time was this?'

Jaime said, 'It is late. Many people, though. There are many people coming from pubs and shows. Enough to disappear in.'

'And you're sure they followed you down?'

'Tall man did. I not see other one.'

From what Ben had heard, it was when you couldn't see Bad Sam that you had to worry.

'I hide behind ticket machine. The tall man—'

'His name was Ashton.'

'Ashton, he go through barrier, and stand at top of moving escalator. There are lot of people going down, young people, all with rucksacks and making noise. He think I am one of them.'

'But you were hiding by the ticket machine.'

There was a rhythm to this. The occasional prod was all it took. Jaime's story was up and running.

'Yes. And while his back is to me, I go out other entrance. I come out other side of road.'

Ben flashed on Marble Arch. That side of the road was where the bus stops were – the intercity buses, on their way out of London from Victoria.

'And you got on a bus.'

the wheels on the bus go—

'I did not plan to. I plan to run, to keep running. I do not plan to leave London.'

'So why did you?'

'Because there is bus there, as I reach the bus stop. It say Oxford on the front. And I remember something Miro tell me.'

From below, DS Bain must have resembled a gargoyle on a college battlement, but nobody was looking up right now. After a while, you don't see the gargoyles; they're just another kind of brickwork.

Though the occasional crackle in an earpiece confirmed a connection to the earthly scene.

Target acquired.

Steady . . .

But no: that was last time.

This time, things were quiet below – quiet, anyway, inside the crucial circle. This was the area mapped out by the rifle's crosshairs; a tiny, intimate region only Bain currently understood. To step inside that area was to surrender to the possibility of death.

The man in the dirty vest appears once more, and the thing in his hand acquires definition as he turns to the window, looks directly through it, and brings the object level with his chest, pointing it outwards, into the night . . .

Who could have known that his gun wasn't loaded?

The wind gusted without warning, and made its usual re-arrangements: rustled grass; plucked at sleeve and hair; attempted to dislodge a weapons specialist. But Bain wasn't moving. Movement was the marksman's enemy; every limb adjustment demanding a recalibration of the required shot . . . Bullets couldn't be recalled once the trigger had been squeezed. Nobody needed to tell Bain that.

But the inquiry had determined that the shot had been justified – the man had been holding a gun, after all. An unloaded antique, but still a gun. A hurled bedside lamp – a bang and a flash – had completed the picture.

shots fired shots fired

'And you're comfortable with returning to duty?'

'Of course, sir.'

'In your firearms role, I mean.'

'Of course, sir.'

That conversation also figured in dreams; an endless recurring dream, it felt like, and thus an accurate reflection of an endless recurring reality. Loaded conversations in airless offices. Conversations that always had the same subtext:

You killed a man.

I know. I was there.

Could you do it again?

The role was not about shooting people, so the wisdom went. The role was about containment.

Containment, though, covered a broad spectrum, and occasionally involved shooting people.

Below, the crowd milled about with the apparently pointless but somehow graceful motion of dust motes in sunlight. Everything moved. The wind tickled the trees and bushes lining the rec ground; a train within hailing distance buffeted its way along the tracks. A car Bain couldn't see roared into life. The only motionless object was the door framed by the crosshairs of the rifle's scope.

Target acquired . . .

Steady.

'Anyone could turn up at the door, say they were with Special Branch, or whatever you said.'

'You'd do well to bear that in mind. Tell me about Judy's husband. Did she talk about his business interests at all?'

'I'd like you to go now.'

'And I'd like you to answer my questions. Did she talk about his business interests at all?'

'She—he—she only talked about him once. Really talked. Other than that it was Derek used to this or used to that. Like he was still alive, except they were divorced.' She was forgetting to smoke; forgetting to drink. Sam Chapman was no longer partner in scandal. He was more like the big bad wolf this foolish piggy had invited in.

On the TV screen, the nursery view had again given way to the larger picture: a pixellated version of join the dots – Dunblane/Hungerford/Columbine. A little lacking in narrative cohesion, but the names pushed buttons that would guarantee viewing figures. On another channel, they'd be flogging the numbers game: 9/11; 7/7. A sequence of diminishing returns – so far – whose consequences rattled round the world.

She was flapping, but he'd stick around a while longer. To find out how much she knew, in case this turned out to be another loose end in need of tying off.

'Your glass is empty,' he said.

'I—I don't want another.'

'Of course you do. One last one. I'll fetch it.'

Stepping into the kitchen, he looked back, but she hadn't turned. In the mirror, he watched her fiddling with the top button of her blouse; twisting it nervously, as if it were constricting her breath. And then she shook another cigarette from her pack, and lit it with a trembling hand.

When she leaned forward to meet the flame, the back of her neck exposed itself whitely, as if it were laid on a block.

The wheels on the bus, having gone round and round, were fading into silence.

It was 12:22, and Eliot's legs had turned to stone. His children's grip had murdered his circulation, and if he ever walked out of this building again, he doubted he'd manage it on his own two feet – which would be all he needed: footage of him being stretchered out of the annexe. Undying proof of his utter wimpishness.

Jesus, Eliot. Is that the worst that could happen?

The music, having stopped, began again. *The farmer's in his den . . .*

At least this one, he hadn't been listening to while lying in bed this morning, five and a half hours and one hundred years ago.

Gordy looked up at him. 'Why is the music playing?' he asked.

He was trying so hard to whisper, it almost came out as a shout.

'Yes, Daddy. Why is the music playing?'

You never heard from one twin without hearing from the other. They lived in stereo.

Gently prising them from his thighs, he sank to a level where he could put an arm round each.

Eee eye addy-oh, the farmer's in his den

'They don't want anyone to hear what they're saying.'

He surprised himself with this. *Hush* was what he'd been intending; truth just slipped out, the way truth sometimes does.

'Why?'

'Why, Daddy?'

'I don't know.'

This truth business could be addictive.

'Gordy doesn't know either, Daddy?'

'And Timmy doesn't know either.'

Well, at least they were all on level pegging. As he looked across at Louise, he could tell something furious was raging inside her; a storm about to break. And with that a stray thought sank a hook into half a memory, dragging it up to the light, and he remembered words exchanged on a sofa while champagne worked its mischief.

I used to work in a bank.

I'm glad you brought that up. I ordered a new chequebook weeks ago.

She had laughed, but with a slight edge to it.

Not high-street banking. This was more your good old, leather-bound merchant variety.

Gordy's lips were working again, but only the faintest sound was coming out. 'What's the matter? Are you okay, Gordy?'

'Eee eye addy-oh,' his youngest son whispered.

'The farmer's in his den,' Timmy finished.

He held them tighter, tears pricking his eyes; tears he didn't want them to see. How was that for wimpishness – he'd stared down a gun this morning, but his sons' attempts to sing through this unmanned him entirely.

And still a memory continued unreeling; of voices – one of them his – thickened by alcohol, and rehearsing the small talk that was prelude to the main event. Something to get them through this interlude where their glasses remained full.

This was more your good old, leather-bound merchant variety.

(Which wasn't, Louise reflected even as the words left her lips, quite right. There was precious little leather bondage round DFM, where the prevailing culture was hi-tech, stainless, broad-band – cutting-edge acronym, not polished courtesy; cocaine jag, not brandy snifter. But she wasn't so drunk she needed to clarify every detail. Which meant she had a better head than Eliot, who was already saying things twice, to be sure she'd got it.)

'Shuffling currencies in the big money markets.'

'That sort of thing.'

'Trading the yen against the dollar.'

Yada yada yada.

She liked him, though. He wasn't without charm, and outside the nursery whirl – freed from the twin restraints of children and the encroaching working day – seemed younger, happier, and enthusiastic about her company, which was nice. Plus, something devilish had taken hold of her; something partly sex, and partly an urge to kick over the traces; to remind herself that life hadn't always revolved around the needs of infants. And hadn't always been lived with a mother on the premises.

Besides, she didn't want to hear him talk about banking, because he knew nothing about it.

'I didn't have much to do with money,' she said.

'That's a disappointment.'

'I worked—'

'I don't have much to do with money either.' He gazed at his glass; at the bubbles vanishing upward from a seemingly ever-replenishing source. 'Not as much as I'd like, anyway.'

She waited, but he'd finished.

'I worked in acquisitions,' she told him.

'I'm guessing you don't mean things like buying stationery or office furniture.'

'You'd guess right.'

'Paperclips. Post-its. You know how they invented Post-its?'

'I'm not even sure who they are.'

'Me neither, but they were trying to invent a kind of glue, and what they came up with didn't work too well. Stuck things down, but they peeled off again. So some bright spark . . .' He lost his thread. 'Came up with Post-its,' he concluded lamely. 'Brilliant, really. Put it this way, out of the jaws of a failed glue-making experiment, he snatched a world-conquering item of desk equipment.'

Well, at least he wasn't talking about banking any more.

Head for the bubbles or not, she couldn't now reconstruct more of that night's conversation. And these weren't the best circumstances for trying to glue memories together, except that moments were being knocked loose in her mind – memory was a web, with any plucked thread *here* reverberating *there* . . .

'It began when he went to Iraq,' Jaime had said.

Are you the lady?

Well, how many ladies present had had daily contact with unreal sums of money?

That string plucked, a memory came back unbidden. Difficult to nail down in time, but the place was intact: her London flat, which had been a big clean space full of light, with a marina view. Crispin had always been at ease there; it was somewhere, he once told her, where his suits wouldn't crease however relaxed he got. Which she'd been idiot enough to feel gratified by. Towards the end, Crispin had talked less and less on work-related subjects; had worn, it seemed to her now, a furrowed look whenever the subject of their common employment came up. And at other times had seemed lost in contemplation of unspecified difficulties, though not without a sometime glint in his eye, as if there were light at the end of whatever tunnel his train of thought had entered.

But the particular memory nudging her now belonged to happier days, when Crispin had been open and expansive, and more than likely post-coital.

'There was a case a couple of years ago,' he'd told her, 'in the States. Classic example of fat-finger error. Some clerk was keying the taxable values of properties in some Midwest town or other, and took his eye off the ball long enough to rate a property at four billion dollars instead of forty thousand or whatever it was. By the time anyone caught the error, the notional taxes raised on the property had been allocated in the town's annual budget.'

'Did he get fired?'

'Don't know. But the point is, money can be conjured out of nothing. Once it's on the books, it exists. That was real money on their records, there was just no way of collecting it, that was all. And real money had to come off the budgets. Services were cut, probably people laid off. The money only existed for a little while, but its disappearance affected the lives of the local people.'

Louise conceded the story was sort of funny, but only if you weren't one of the local people.

'Imagine,' he'd said. 'If that could happen by accident, it could happen on purpose too.'

'How would that help anyone?'

'I don't mean in that specific way. I mean money, you could make it. Out of nothing. All you'd need is the right circumstances.'

Which might include, say, setting up a merger with a DFM subsidiary and a Swiss-based but American-owned bank, which . . .

'Well,' she'd said, 'if you ever do. Conjure up a billion out of the ether, I mean. I hope you won't forget about me.'

. . . was bankrolling a consortium of US building contractors, which . . .

'Course not, sweetheart. I'll credit you with the inspiration.'

'Shame that's not all it takes,' she'd said.

. . . was tendering for one of the contracts filtering down from the White House Santa-sack for . . .

'How do you mean?'

. . . the reconstruction of Iraq.

'Well,' she'd said. 'I don't doubt you could figure out the scheme. But you'd need some pretty impressive technical support to pull it off, wouldn't you?'

Because Crispin, wired as he was into any number of global big-buck networks, had difficulty changing a plug.

'Oh,' he'd said. 'I'd need some supergeek onside. But they're plentiful, cheap, and you can throw them away afterwards.'

'Like female staff members?'

'Exactly like female staff members,' he said. 'Except you don't necessarily use those only once.'

She remembered him shifting against her as he'd said this, or something very like it.

Talking about money often had that effect on Crispin.

This might have been the last time they had such a conversation.

There are a hundred ways accounts can be fiddled . . .

'I used to be in banking,' she said.

'There is bus there, as I reach the bus stop. It say Oxford on the front. And I remember something Miro tell me.'

'What did Miro tell you? Something about Oxford?'

'He get very drunk one night. He talk about . . . I do not understand what he is saying. He say that things that happen, they have consequences. He talk about the war.'

'Iraq.'

'Yes. And about things that happen there afterwards. I don't like the war, I am against the war. But I do not know much about what happens since. Miro, he knows. Because of being there. You know why he go?'

The farmer, now, was in his den. Ben could hear the little boys murmuring as much to each other, even as the tape recorder broadcast the information. He said, 'Yes, I know. He was doing an audit.'

'I am not sure what this means.'

'He had a very specific task, Jaime. There was a sum of money – well, there were lots of sums of money, still are – and his job was to follow this particular sum, and find out what happened to it. It was sort of a test case.'

'Test case?'

This was going to take a while.

'It was an example, Jaime. This one particular sum of money, among the very many sums of money pouring into, and out of, Iraq – Miro's job was to discover precisely what happened to it. Whether it was spent the way it was supposed to be spent, or got diverted along the way. And if it was diverted, to find out where and when that happened.'

238

'And he had to be there to do that?'

This was the woman, of course – Louise Kennedy. Who seemed to think she had a duty to be heard, just because she was in charge here on ordinary days.

'Yes,' he said bluntly.

'Because I thought a forensic accountant followed paper trails, not—'

'Which is well and good when the paper can be trusted. Or when the figures are hidden in different columns, or someone's keeping two sets of books, or any of the hundred other ways accounts can be fiddled.'

'I used to be in banking,' she said, a tightness in her voice.

'I know. And the level you were working at, you're presumably familiar with the way money laundering works.'

Jaime was looking first at him, then at her, like this had descended into a TV show. The thing in his hand was a remote. He could shut them down any time he pleased.

Louise Kennedy said, 'You've checked up on me.'

'I work for the security services, Ms Kennedy. As has been established already. So yes, you've been checked up on. And like I say, you know how money laundering works.'

Listen to him speak, he thought . . . Okay, it was opening up now. The outside world was deaf, or as deaf as he could make it. It was just this little crew in here: Bad Sam Chapman was out of the circle.

She said, 'I'm not an expert. But yes, I've attended seminars.'

Eliot looked at her as if she'd just admitted a taste for Morris dancing.

Ben Whistler said, 'The really serious stuff, the organised crime money, comes in from overseas. Even if it started here in the first place, it rides the carousel through about fifteen different jurisdictions, and by the time it comes home it looks no grubbier than any other truck-load of venture capital. So it's invested in one of a hundred going concerns, legit businesses established for exactly that purpose, and a shopping mall sprouts in Manchester or a multistorey in Glasgow. Cash that started life as a drug deal in Marseilles, a bank job in Palermo, or a child prostitute ring in, I don't know, Bolton, is now bricks and mortar. It's there. It's real. It's a taxable institution.'

'Your point being?'

'Somebody invoices you for a water pipe they've laid in Amara, and the paperwork's in order, and it's three sheets among three thousand, and you're in an office in London, what do you do?'

'Okay,' she said after a while.

'It's not like you're about to drop into downtown Amara and turn on a tap. That's why Miro wasn't sitting behind a desk, Ms Kennedy. He was out there turning on taps.'

The spangly guitars were spiralling down into silence.

'And what happened?' she asked. 'Did water come out?'

Ben said, 'You're asking if Miro found corruption? Of course he fucking did. It was everywhere he looked.'

9

T HEY HAD ART.

The first had been faxed, a passport shot: it showed one Miro Weiss, who either took an unflattering photo or was an unflattered man. Everyone looks washed out in those damn booths, but still. Weiss's hair was thinning, and his face pudgy; his eyes looked like black marbles, and the left-side collar of his shirt poked up. Though no, come to think of it: it was the right side. It was a photo; you had to reverse the details.

This was the man responsible for a missing quarter billion pounds?

And there was, Malcolm Fredericks knew, no point asking for information from Six, not unless he wanted to know what a *Big Issue* vendor felt like. Nor was anything sensible coming out of the annexe, unless you were interested in soft-rock versions of nursery rhymes. He turned to the other picture: a police artist's impression drawn from Carrie Mannion's memory – a local mother who'd seen the mad bastard wreaking this mayhem on the morning. Who was young, dark-skinned; hair a black and curly mess; eyes brown. His cheeks were stubbled in the way kids thought sexy, and grown-ups a nuisance. And he was wearing either a dark green or brown jacket – like most eyewitnesses, Carrie Mannion was weak on detail: all she'd really wanted to do was grab her kid and get out—

Well Jesus of course she did . . .

He shook his head wearily. Of course she did.

The gun, at least, was beyond dispute. It was a Heckler &
Koch – ten-round version – which, before fetching up in South
Oxford Nursery School, had belonged to Neil Ashton of Her
Majesty's Spooky Service – currently resident in the John
Radcliffe, wired to a lot of interesting machinery. A phone call
had established that the machinery was still functioning, though
whether Ashton himself would ever breathe, speak or fart again
without its assistance remained in doubt. As for his erstwhile
partner, there were people you didn't need to know well to
know you didn't want to know better. Chapman fitted that
profile. Hell, he fitted the full frontal.

Artist's impression in hand, Fredericks glanced up at the
chimney stack of the house overlooking the nursery. No way
of letting Bain see the sketch; on the other hand, what difference would that make? Bain knew the difference between the
good guys and the bad. Only one person would come out of
that building with a Heckler & Koch in hand: and if and when
that happened, Bain would know what to do.

Target acquired.

Steady.

No target yet.

Steady anyway.

A bird flaps overhead, but Bain's eyes don't follow it; DS
Bain's eyes remain glued to the space in front of the annexe
door; to the rainbow-crayoned cardboard sign reading *The
Palace*. And Bain is still, very still. Bain could be a statue, though
it's an improbable place to fix a statue: next to a chimney block,
where pigeons roost and aerials listen. Bain's there, though. Is
part of the skyline's furniture. A motionless thoughtless figure,
an observer might suppose, but 'thoughtless' would be wrong;
'thoughtless' would be way off target. In the back of Bain's

mind, like in the back of anyone's, history repeats itself. Conversations are rehashed. Dialogue reconstructed.

There's someone we think you ought to talk to.

How are you sleeping?

Fine, thank you.

No dreams?

Everybody dreams.

And yours, are they bad dreams? Nightmares?

Do I wake up screaming? No.

How about crying. Do you wake up crying?

No.

Anxious? Raised heartbeat?

This is starting to sound like a warning label on a cold cure. No, none of that. I sleep fine. I dream normal dreams. I wake when the alarm goes off.

What are normal dreams like?

Are you kidding me?

You said you dream normal dreams. I was wondering what you meant by that.

Jesus . . .

[Pause.]

I'm here to help, you know.

Maybe I don't need help.

You shot a man.

I remember.

He died.

I remember that too.

And you're telling me you have no feelings about this.

Of course I'm not. Of course I have feelings about it.

And what are they? Precisely?

What they are, *precisely*, is that I wish it hadn't happened. I—look, do you mind if I call you doc?

'Doc'?

Yes. This is so like being in a movie, it doesn't feel right, me not calling you doc.

[Pause.]

Call me that if you feel the need.

It's not a need. I'm just entering into the spirit of the thing.

Then go right ahead.

Thank you. What my feelings are precisely, *doc*, is that I wish it hadn't happened. But what I also feel is, I was doing my job. Now, we both know how things turned out. The gun that man had was useless. He could have battered someone to death with it, but pulling the trigger wasn't going to hurt anyone. But I didn't know that at the time, doc. At the time he was an enraged man with a gun, who was holding his own family hostage and looked like he was about to commit murder by gunshot. Doc. So I did what I was trained to do, and followed the order I was given. If he hadn't picked up that gun, I wouldn't have had to put him down.

I see.

I'm glad. I'm glad you see. I'm glad the official inquiry saw too, because you know what they found, don't you, doc? They found that it was a justifiable killing. And that guy knew that. He knew the risks he was playing. There's an American expression, suicide by cop. Did you ever come across that?

You think he committed suicide?

I think if it hadn't been me, it would have been the next officer on duty. That's where my responsibility ends.

And you're happy with that?

Happy's not the word, doc.

But you'd do it again.

I hope never to have to do it again.

But if you had to?

To protect innocent lives? Yes, doc, I would.

Yes, doc.

I would.

★

Here and now, Bain's not sure that conversation ever took place in quite that way, but this much is true: conversations like it have happened, and Bain has taken part in some of them.

Besides, here and now, all that's irrelevant. All that matters is the space crosshatched by the rifle's scope; and the certain knowledge that, if called upon to do so, DS Bain will do what's necessary.

Target acquired.

Steady.

Ben Whistler to Jonathan Nott, about three hours ago:

If he ever made a pass, it was too subtle for me. When a man asks if I'd like a drink after work, I generally assume he wants a drink after work.

And did you?

Occasionally. Never just the two of us.

Ben to Jaime, more recently:

I didn't know him that well. He was a private man. He didn't open up much.

He had done once, though. Ben remembered it well.

There was a pub on the corner – name a junction in Soho there wasn't – with a widescreen TV in the front permanently tuned to sports channels and a row of booths in the back affording private conversation. Either was a good reason for it becoming a department favourite; the fact that it was nearest clinched the deal. One evening last summer, World Cup in full swing, half the building had been there. Ben wasn't an enthusiast, but he had a sense of occasion. He also had a keen memory for which colleagues owed him a drink, and the prospect of catching them all in the same venue was too enticing to miss.

It was coming back from the Gents that he'd encountered Miro. He was edging past the row of booths when:

'Ben.'

He'd looked round. Miro Weiss was slouched untidily against the wall, having claimed a whole booth to himself. There was a half-drained Guinness in front of him, and a badly stubbed cigarette smouldering in his ashtray. Ben wouldn't have pegged Miro for a Guinness man. If pressed he'd have suggested dry sherry; possibly port and lemon.

'Miro. Didn't realise you'd come.'

'I slunk away once the outcome was obvious.'

It took Ben a moment to understand he was talking about the football.

'You okay there?'

'Yes. Yes, I'm fine, Ben.'

He didn't look it, but this wasn't worth calling the news desk. Miro, Reggie had once said in Ben's hearing, 'Looks like somewhere hair loss is slugging it out with astigmatism. Basically, it's battle for the planet of the Miro.' If you had to cast him, you'd go for Peter Lorre. It helped that his voice bore a trace of Eastern Europe; a gift from his immigrant parents. Still: Ben had never seen him getting legless before. He doubted any of the others had either. 'You should come and join us.'

'Oh, you think they miss me?'

'Well, I, ah—'

'It's okay, you don't need to answer. Is Reggie there?'

'Probably.'

'Reggie amuses me. He's one of those people whose sense of humour is absurdly reliant on use of the word *basically*. Did you ever notice that?'

Ben hadn't. 'Now you come to mention it.'

'But I wouldn't in his hearing. The Reggies of this world don't compute criticism. It would be like addressing him in Swahili. Would you like a drink?'

'I think I left one on the bar.'

'You think so? I won't keep you then.'

'No. No, it's probably gone by now. The staff here, they whip your glass away if you take your hand off it.' This wasn't true. 'Can I get you one?'

'I offered first, Ben.'

There was great precision in the way Miro excavated his wallet from his jacket pocket.

Ben settled in the booth, wondering what he was missing in the front bar, then deciding he didn't care. The evening was on its last legs, and Miro in his cups was a new experience. Miro the Mirror Man – where'd he get a nickname like that? Miro the house mouse, more like. Sequestered in his cubicle all day, traipsing through the money maze. Barely poking his snout out long enough to grab a foul coffee from the machine. Yes, this was new. And that *basically* comment was good. Ben'd be a fool not to hang about long enough to see what else Miro came up with.

Plus, Miro was not long back from Iraq, where he'd been chasing a money trail through bomb blasts and gutted buildings. Miro the house mouse, back from the war. Now dipping his whiskers in Guinness.

He returned from the bar, Guinness in one hand, lager in the other.

'Cheers, my friend.'

'And to you, Ben.'

Some of the most ravening drunks Ben had ever known became politer and politer before collapsing into formal oblivion.

He took a belt of lager. 'So how are things, Miro?'

'Things? Oh, peachy-keen, Ben. How are they with you?'

'Same old same old. You know how it is.'

'Not really, Ben. Sometimes I think, the older I get, the less I know of anything.'

'Yeah, well. The trick is not to let it get you down, I suppose.'

'And that's the trick old dogs find hardest of all, eh? The new one. The new one of not letting it get you down.'

Okay, thought Ben. This might have been a mistake after all.

'How did you find Iraq?'

'The way we left it, Ben. In ruins.'

'Not a fun-filled jaunt, then.'

'Not, as you say, a fun-filled jaunt.'

He lifted his glass, and Ben saw an amazing thing: he saw Miro the house mouse drain half a pint of Guinness in a single swallow. He might have been pouring water down a plughole.

'It's left you thirsty.'

'It's left me a lot of things, Ben. Tell me, among whatever it is you don't allow to get you down, have you given much thought to what's happening in Iraq?'

Definitely a bad idea.

He said, 'Well, I was never in favour of the war. But what can you do?'

'Precisely. We are not doctors, so there's nothing we can do. The bombs still go off and the power's not yet on. Children die for lack of the facilities we robbed them of with shock and awe. Families live in holes in the ground. But we are not doctors so there is nothing we can do.'

'We can send money.'

Miro threw back his head and laughed – it was a night for firsts.

'I only meant—'

'I know what you meant. I am sorry, Ben.' Miro switched his laughter off as abruptly as he'd switched it on. 'I was not laughing at you. And it is not especially funny anyway. You are not drinking your lager.'

Ben drank his lager.

Miro said, 'They do not need our money. They need their own money. Iraq is a major oil producer, we don't have to be rattling tins in pubs at closing time. Sending them our spare change. We simply need to hand back what is being taken from them.'

Someone passed on the way to the Gents, but Ben didn't catch who it was.

He said, 'You found a lot of corruption out there.'

'Oh yes.'

'Millions going missing.'

'Yes, Ben. True story. When the CPA was closing down – you know what I'm talking about? The Coalition Provisional Authority?'

'They ran Iraq after the war. Before the elections.'

'For a year, yes. During which time more than eight point eight billion dollars' worth of oil revenue vanished, Ben. Money that belonged to the nation, that should have been used to get the place on its feet again. Anyway, this incident I'm talking about, there was one point four billion dollars transferred from Baghdad to the Kurdish Regional Government. In cash. You know how much that weighs?'

Of course he didn't. He'd only ever seen that amount in pixels.

'Fourteen tons. Think about it. Fourteen tons of cash. In vacuum-packed bricks. Transported by helicopters through what was, to all intents and purposes, a war zone. The war was over, Ben – it still is, technically – but helicopters were being shot down on a daily basis, so it was not exactly peace in our time.'

'And is that what happened? They were shot down?'

'No, they got there safely. Great relief all round, I imagine. And they took the money to the Central Bank of whichever town they were in. I am too drunk to remember which.'

'And that's it?'

'Not quite. What they forgot to do was ask for a deposit slip.'

Miro picked up what was left of his Guinness, and sent it the way of the rest.

Ben said, 'You're kidding.'

'If only.'

'So what happened?'

'Nobody knows. The money's not been seen since. Apparently attempts were made to transfer it to a Swiss bank. But this much is clear – fourteen tons of money evaporated, in one afternoon. And this mess has been going on for years.'

'Jesus.'

'There are contractors routinely overcharging by one thousand per cent. There are security firms guarding those contractors who are hiring mercenaries, ex-cons, and anyone else who is prepared to pick up a gun in exchange for money. And all this time the country's oil is still pumping out, except there is no metering in place, so nobody knows how much is being produced, or what revenue it should be making. The only sure fact is that that revenue is not going into Iraq's development fund, which, by the way, is in violation of UN resolutions. What it comes down to is, anyone who successfully tendered for any of the reconstruction projects – which essentially means those with contacts in the White House – won a licence to print money. Hallelujah, and God bless Dubya.' He paused. 'If they ever design a million dollar bill, whose image do you suppose they'll use? Except they'll have to do a full body version, so it can show Dick Cheney emerging from his arse.'

'Whose arse we talking about, Miro?'

And this was the somebody on his way back from the Gents: Neil Ashton. Department Dog.

Miro said, 'It was a long joke. I don't think I can repeat it.'

'Ben doesn't seem to be laughing.'

'It wasn't that kind of joke,' Ben said.

Neil Ashton, who was a large man with an attitude to match, said, 'So Miro gets round to telling a funny, and it's not the funny kind. Why doesn't that surprise me?'

'The crew still out front?' Ben asked.

'They're thinking of moving on. How long have you been skulking here?'

'You're keeping tabs on us off duty now?'

'That's practically the job description.' Ashton stood by the booth, looking down on them; seemed as if he might, at any moment, slam his fists on their table. 'Discussing our little field trip, Miro?'

'Our?' Ben asked.

'I was accompanied by Mr Ashton,' Miro told him.

'Oh yeah,' Ashton said. 'I was there to hold Miro's hand. Make sure he didn't wander into any minefields, or get himself picked up and chained to a radiator. Or would that have been your idea of a good time, Miro?'

'My idea of a good time would not involve being in Iraq. If you will excuse me a moment, gentlemen.' Miro freed himself from the booth, and made his way to the toilets.

Ashton said, 'Interesting conversation, Ben?'

'He has quite a riff on the role of the metatarsal in England's World Cup ambitions.'

Ashton lit a cigarette. 'He didn't mention the Iraq trip, then.'

'No,' Ben said.

'Until I brought it up.'

'No.'

'That's good.' He exhaled smoke Ben hadn't noticed him drawing in. 'Talking out of turn in pubs, that's the kind of thing I'm supposed to take notice of.'

'Right,' Ben said.

He didn't mention the Iraq trip, then.

Later, Bad Sam Chapman asked Ben much the same question. And Ben gave much the same answer.

Now, he said: 'Jaime, did Miro mention the Dogs, at all? By name?'

Jaime blinked, surprised to be addressed.

'Jaime?'

'Once,' said Jaime. 'He talk about a man he call Bad Sam.'

'Yes,' Ben said gently. 'That's the man you were running from at Marble Arch.'

'How did he know where to find me?'

'Because you told him, Jaime. He was what they call a duty officer last night. Chapman's Top Dog. And ever since Miro disappeared, the Dogs have been monitoring unusual calls to the department. Hell, for all I know, they've been monitoring the usual ones too.'

'So he is listening when I call you?'

'The call would have been put through to him, Jaime. Out of hours, from a foreign national? Ordinary circumstances, it would have been logged and your number taken. I'd have an email in the morning, telling me you'd called. But since Miro . . . Things have been uptight.'

'You think he is dead.'

'Yes, Jaime. I think he's dead.'

Jaime nodded, but a cloud passed across his eyes. He'd already known this, but knowledge shared grew harder and rougher. Grew true.

Ben said, 'So you got on the bus. But they saw you, didn't they?'

Jaime blinked himself back to the moment. 'I think I am safe, on bus. I think they are still looking for me at Marble Arch, where everything is busy.'

'But they saw you.'

'The smaller man—'

'That's Bad Sam.'

'I pay the busman. I take my ticket. The bus starts to move. And then I see him, through the window, running over road. He is nearly hit by car.'

Ben thought, shame.

'He does not catch the bus. But he sees me. I know this.'

They had reached another of those plateaus: everyone had shut up, and Jaime was allowed to move on with his story. There wasn't silence, of course – the farmer had found a wife, and retreated to his den; *Ring-a-ring-a-roses* was circling the annexe now – but for the moment, it was just himself and Jaime.

'And it wouldn't have taken him long to work out where the bus was heading.'

'That is what I think too,' Jaime said.

Jesus, the boy must have been frightened. His boyfriend vanishes without trace, and the first hand he reaches out for help, he's got the heavy squad after him. 'Did you see what he did?'

'He stand by the road until he is out of sight. The bus goes round the roundabout. He just watches.'

'Did the bus stop again? Before leaving London?'

'The bus is full now, so it does not stop, no. Not until it gets near Oxford.'

It must have been full dark by then. Ben remembered looking down on the Oxford road from the helicopter: a buzzing mass of angry cars, but that was rush hour. The bus would have made good time. But Bad Sam and Neil Ashton would have made better: once they were on the motorway, they could easily have caught up . . .

He said to Louise Kennedy: 'What are the buses like, between here and London?'

She blinked. 'Like?'

'How frequent?'

'Very. There are two services. Every ten minutes or so.'

'All through the night?'

'As good as. Probably not quite so often. But at eleven, twelve o'clock, there'd be plenty of them, I'd have thought.'

'Do they all run through Marble Arch?'

'I don't think so. But they all use the M40, obviously.'

They must have tagged the wrong bus, Ben decided. Or they'd have picked Jaime up the moment he stepped off.

'So what did you do?' he said to Jaime.

'I know they have a car. I think they will follow, try to catch me at the other end.'

'So you got off before then.'

He said, 'They know the bus is coming to Oxford. Maybe they get there first. Maybe they wait there for me. So I get off first place I can. They call it parker-ride?'

'Park and ride.'

'I do not know what that means.'

And Ben didn't feel like explaining. 'It's not important. This was before you reached Oxford, yes?'

'Yes. In a big car park. Other people get off too, but they get into cars.'

'So you're on your own.'

'Soon, there is nobody there. It is cold and tired. Very dark and very late. And I am frightened.'

For a moment, he wasn't a man with a gun any more, but a cold tired frightened boy in a car park.

attishhoo attishhoo

'I wait in the shelter, but a car comes. I think it is them, but I cannot run or move – I am too frightened. I think I just wait and let them take me. There is nothing I can do any more.'

we all fall down

The music stopped, as if we'd all done just that.

After a moment he went on, 'But it isn't them. It is just people. They look at map, and drive away again.'

Ben said, 'And then what?'

'I look for somewhere to hide. The bus shelter is not good place. So I walk back along road, but I worry that they drive past and see me. I think they probably have gone into Oxford, and will drive back, looking for me. So I climb into field, and find place to lie down.' Without thinking, he let the gun wander from them; wrapped his arms around himself, miming the actions of the cold boy he'd been last night. 'I lie under bush. Every time a car passes, I think they have found me.'

He must have been freezing, Ben thought.

'And I think about what Miro tells me. About place in Oxford.'

'Which place?'

'This place. I remember name, Grandpont. It means big bridge.'

'In Spanish?'

'In French. I speak good French. Better than English.'

I am not stupid foreign person, Ben remembered. 'And why did he mention Grandpont?'

A faraway look came into Jaime's eyes. 'He is quite drunk when he say this. Normally he does not drink very much.'

But when he felt like it, he knew how to tie one on, thought Ben.

'He tell me the world is a strange place. That some people get rich, and others die, and others fall in love. That big business grows fat while children suffer, and a lady ends up working in a nursery in Grandpont in Oxford, and all because of a war that shouldn't have happened.' He paused. 'He say lots more things. But I remember the Grandpont lady, because it is strange thing to say.'

Ben said—

But before he said it, the voice of the Daleks broke in again.

We need to know everything's all right in there.

'Ask him—'

Can you hear me, Jaime?

Yes, thought Fredericks. Ask him if he can hear you.

He'd have given his left lung for another cigarette, but committing social crimes on prime time wasn't going to help.

They knew each other well, Malcolm Fredericks and Peter Faulks, and Fredericks was glad he had Peter onside, but face facts: things had fucked up. They'd lost the inside track once Whistler had dumped the mobile; now they were back to the megaphone, keeping fingers crossed that Jaime would decide it was worth his while to answer.

You need to give us some signal that everything's okay. Otherwise we're going to have to take a closer look, Jaime.

And why had Whistler dumped the mobile anyway? Spook business: give him an honest axe murderer any day.

Faulks said, not through the handset, 'This isn't happening.'

'Tell me about it.'

'We've got a negotiator in there. So-called. That should be opening channels up, not closing them down.' He wiped something from his lip, never taking his eyes from the annexe. 'Chapman disappeared, I suppose.'

'You spoke to him last.'

'He took Whistler's BlackBerry with him. It was in my pocket.'

Fredericks said, 'We're supposed to be on the same side. Who'll be crucified in the dailies if we have to bring bodies out, do you suppose?'

'He came on like he was having an episode. Heart attack or something. Didn't realise what that was about until five minutes ago.'

'They're covering their backs.'

'This isn't a random invasion, Malc. That kid with the gun, I don't even think he's a terrorist.'

'It was his choice to pick the gun up.'

'Wasn't his choice they came after him with it.' Peter Faulks raised the handset again.

We need an answer, Jaime. What's happening in there?

A gust of wind hit his words and threw them at the annexe. Fredericks imagined them smashing against the woodwork; shattering into disjointed syllables and fractured letters, to lie like dropped Scrabble tiles outside the door.

But maybe they scraped their way inside, unbroken.

'They're getting restless.'

The megaphoned words had the kiddy-cassette to contend

with, but had snaked in anyway, providing a robotic counter-point to the jangly rhythms skipping about. You'd have to go some distance to find a less appropriate soundtrack, Ben thought.

'Jaime?' he added.

Jaime said nothing.

'And they know your name.'

'They hear it before,' Jaime said. 'On the bugged phone.'

That was true. That was more likely than that Bad Sam Chapman had shared info with them: still, it was impossible to know who knew what out there. 'We need to reach some decisions, Jaime.'

You need to give us some signal that everything's okay. Otherwise we're going to have to take a closer look.

'They don't like not hearing us. Sooner or later they're going to do something about that.'

'I don't know what to do.'

'I guessed. People who know what they're doing don't do things like this.' That was too fast for Jaime. 'Things have got confused,' Ben went on. 'Everyone's over-excited.'

There are an awful lot of guns outside.

Jaime said, 'I do not think Miro was thief.'

'Okay.'

'I think other people take this money. The men who chase me last night.'

'Why do you think that?'

'Well, they try to kill me,' Jaime said.

'And, that's a problem too, Jaime. Because Ashton might be out of the picture, but Chapman's still in it. And the thing about Bad Sam is, he doesn't like loose ends.'

Louise Kennedy said, 'What does that mean?'

'It's probably best you don't—'

'What does that mean?'

He said, 'Chapman's kind of a policeman, only not as

257

answerable, if you get my drift. And if he's as deep in this as he appears to be, then loose ends are a danger to him.'

'But if he took the money, why's he still around?'

'Well, disappearing immediately when the money did might have been a giveaway, don't you think?'

'Like Miro did . . .'

'Bad Sam, if he did it at all, couldn't have done it by himself.' Then he said, 'Jesus. I can't believe I'm telling you this.'

He had the sense of time running out. Of Bad Sam Chapman circling ever closer; prepared to go the usual lengths to find out what they'd been discussing. He had to get out of here soon. They all did.

'You're telling us because we're involved,' Louise said. 'Go on.'

He said, 'Okay, fine. You're involved. But that stops here.' He looked at Jaime. 'You should let them go now, Jaime.'

Jaime blinked. 'Let them go?'

'Yes. You've got what you wanted. I'm here now. Let them go.'

'And you will make it all right?'

'I can help you with that. They can't.'

Louise said, 'Wait a minute—'

'Shut up.'

'If I let them go, the police arrest me.'

'And if you don't, they'll kill you. Do it, Jaime. The two of us, we'll work out what happens next.'

'I let them go, I'll be—'

We need an answer, Jaime. What's happening in there?

'I will be alone,' Jaime said.

'No you won't,' Ben told him. 'I'll be here.'

They were talking about letting her go. That much broke through Judy's wall, the wall she'd been building since she'd crawled from the earlier ruck-up: Judy lying like a duvet on top of gun-boy, exactly this far from death: the space between your thumbnail and your thumb. Armed policemen had come and gone, and she'd had her eyes jammed shut throughout, but she knew without being told that they'd just itched to open fire on lovely boy, and spray his terrorist arse all over the walls. And she'd have been gone too. Didn't matter who shot her: she'd have been as dead either way. And she knew something else: that the secret service man who'd come poncing in like he was God's gift hadn't given a tinker's cuss for Judy Ainsworth – he'd sent the policemen packing because he didn't want gun-boy hurt. That was what things had come to. Judy Ainsworth, innocent victim, was worth less than the animal who'd trapped them here in the first place. Every day you got up, you struggled, you did your best. And in the end, life sucked you down the plughole and spat you into a drain.

What happens next?

What happened next didn't matter, so long as it didn't involve Judy. Everyone left in the annexe could die in a blaze of hot metal and collapsing scenery. Just so long as she was watching from the sidelines.

And then something else struck her – if she could walk away from all this, she wouldn't reach home empty-handed. She wasn't a fool, for all these people thought her an idiot; she knew that none of this was unregarded. The eyes of the world must have been focused on the nursery for hours. There'd be TV crews slavering for footage; newspapers foraging; cheque-books opening. Her story would be sought out and fought over – it would be bought and paid for.

And it would be her story.

For the first time in what felt like hours, Judy Ainsworth opened her eyes.

'Let the children go, Jaime.'

'If I open the door . . .'

'If you open the door, nothing. The boys can go, their father can take them. I'll shut the door again. That's it.'

'I have fewer hostages.'

'You're not going to hurt them. So what's the point of keeping them here?'

'Those men tried to kill me. This morning, Bad Sam, this Ashton. If I give myself up, they kill me again.'

'Ashton's not killing anyone soon, Jaime. And I can help you with Bad Sam. But not in here, not as long as you're armed. Not as long as you're keeping hostages.'

'How do I know I can trust you?'

'That's the reason I'm here, Jaime. You asked for me, remember? Because Miro said you could trust me.'

Jaime looked down at the bundle on the floor that was Judy. The woman had opened her eyes, Ben noticed, and he hoped to God she wasn't about to try another run for it. 'Once they walk out, everyone will relax a little. Things will get easier.'

'And what happens to me?'

'I'll make sure you're safe. When we leave, it'll be with people you can trust.'

'Where is Chapman now?'

'I've no idea. I'm in here, remember?'

Judy said, 'Let me go.'

It was the first time she'd used her voice in a while, and it scratched her throat coming out.

Louise's eyes flashed. 'Are you not finished yet?'

'I shouldn't even be here. I—'

'There are children here. Do you really think you're more important—'

'Yes.'

Eliot said, 'You stupid—'

'—children, for God's—'

'—bitch, if he doesn't—'

'Shut up.'

'—I will!'

'Shut up,' Ben repeated. 'All of you.'

And thought: if I was him right now, I'd put a bullet through the ceiling.

Against her wall, safe in her cage, Trixie was going through the motions again; *squeak squeak squeak squeak*.You had to wonder what kind of mileage the average hamster achieved in a lifetime.

He said, 'Judy. We're all getting out of here, alive. You have to wait your turn, that's all.'

'And what if things go wrong?'

'They're not going to go wrong.'

Louise said, 'Jesus Christ!'; such contempt in her delivery, he could only hope it was aimed at Judy, not him.

'He's not going to kill those children,' Judy said. 'If he kills anyone it'll be me. Can't you see that?'

'He's not going to kill anyone,' Louise said.

'That's easy for you to say you stupid—'

'Shut up, Judy. You nearly got us killed already, so just fucking shut up. Now.'

oranges and lemons

say the bells of St Clement's

Ben, looking at Louise, saw her teeth: they looked wicked. Sharp, and flecked with white. And then she clamped her mouth shut, as if heeding her own instructions, and her glance flicked to the boys at Eliot's side.

squeak squeak squeak squeak

He said, 'All of you. He'll let all of you go. He only needs me.'

Jaime said, 'No.'

Judy said, very quickly, 'If you don't let me go I'll tell them what you've been saying you want that? You want them to know what you've been saying with this fucking racket filling their ears up? I'll tell this Chapman what you've been saying about him.'

Louise just shook her head.

Ben said, 'Judy. Judy? You want to be very careful what you say to anyone. Especially him.'

'Then let me *go*!'

In Ben's dreams, Jaime raised the gun, put a bullet through the ceiling.

here comes the chopper
to chop off your head

He felt like he needed a bath, or a scouring with a wire brush, but neither would get him really clean; besides, neither was available, so he made do with a cigarette. He'd turned left on exiting Deirdre Walker's, then left again at the river: he was following this back towards Grandpont now. A helicopter buzzed overhead, and a swarm of midges at face level. In the river, a lost swan drifted regally. After a while the path wound round to a bridge, at the far end of which lay the nature park. If he approached this way he'd end up on the recreation ground, surrounded by trigger-happy policemen.

Sam Chapman had no gun. Ashton had been armed – for obvious reasons – but Bad Sam didn't routinely carry, so far without fatal consequences. Ashton had once referred to Sam's habit as 'going commando', which was not without wit, but where had his gun got Ashton? Bad Sam, meanwhile, had grass underfoot and no artillery weighing him down. The Deirdre Walkers of this world didn't warrant a bullet. He could still have done with a shower, though.

The woman had been Catty. That was the lost frigging dwarf, as far as Bad Sam Chapman was concerned. As for Happy, Sam would have drowned him in the sink.

His collar rasped against his neck. The dead weight of his switched-off mobile slapped against his thigh.

Up ahead, but out of sight, something new was happening.

'Door's opening.'

Faulks knew this. He'd seen doors open before.

'Someone's—'

'Yes. Move back.'

The crowd behind the cordon caught the event a second later, and reacted as crowds do: as if the same strange idea had struck each particle of it at once. This manifested, briefly, as a hush. And then new noises intruded, mostly variations on the same digital buzz, as God alone knew how many recording devices thrummed into life.

Faulks's hand clasped more tightly round his handset, and as soon as he realised this, a worry sparked into life: what other hands were tightening now? Some of them clutching weaponry? While the door opened, and someone stepped out . . .

Specifically, he was thinking of DS Bain.

Who might also have tensed at that moment, but you wouldn't have known it from watching. There was no tremor in the barrel of the rifle; no twitch in the muscles of the mouth. From a Bain's-eye view, too, the world remained steady: the crosshairs fixed in place, though the target had not yet been acquired.

Whoever came through that door belonged to Bain.

Nobody else on ground level mattered.

Peter Craven was among them. He was crouched between stacks of outdoor play equipment on the terrace bordering the nursery; had retreated here after leaving the annexe with no prisoner in tow; no hostage rescued. His focus since had been the door. His outstretched arms rested on a plastic-wrapped bale of hay, part of a set used as outdoor building blocks which lent the air of a sanitised western to proceedings; the more so since he held a gun. And what he was finding, despite this gun, was that it remained possible to wander, mentally; to let concentration slip, and, instead of living the moment, imagine its triumphant conclusion – recounting it later to Tasha or the Supe; supplying their responses: thoughtful approbation from the Supe; enthusiastic adulation from Tasha, involving certain other elements it was best not to be distracted by right now – that was what Peter Craven was discovering: how very very hard it was to remain fixed in the moment. He could have learned a lot from Bain. He blinked, and the door started opening, and yes: his fingers tensed on his itchy weapon.

No door had ever opened as slowly as this.

Christine Pedlar broke apart from Dave Osborne without realising there was anything to break apart from: only gentle touching, arm against arm. They had been standing close was all. And Dave was forgotten, might have shattered into atoms the moment the door moved . . . Christine was behind the cordon, cattled with the rest of the onlookers, some of whom were professional; the rest simply duped by reality TV into thinking observation involvement. *You'd better talk to the police*, Dave had said. And she'd agreed, but her objection still ran – *Why? Will they do things differently then?* – and after smoking the cigarette and making her way back to the street, had snaked her way to the front of the crowd, which was as close as she could come to her children. And now the door was opening, and Dave Osborne had ceased to exist . . .

Let it be my boys let it be my boys. There was no end to this sentence. It looped eternally, because eternity could be neatly encompassed within a finite amount of time. Eternity was what it took a door to open, when your boys might be on the other side: safe and well and leaping for her arms; or bound and bloodied and dead, leaping nowhere. Or neither. Or both – there were two of them, and one could be dead and the other living, and if so which would she choose, which would she choose? That thought struck her like a madman with a cricket bat – *answer, quickly, now* – there was no way she would ever forget that thought. No way she would forget answering it. And then the door was open and blinking into the light, like a mole emerging from spring cleaning, came Judy Ainsworth: exactly the same Judy who'd turned up for work four hours previously, but piss-stained and dumpier and confirmed in her world view: that things existed to make her life worse, that everything would always be this way. She hadn't intentionally opened the door slowly; the handle had weaselled in her grasp. Behind her, the Gun was taking aim – she wouldn't even hear the bang – and still the door wouldn't open, still those children were watching, but the Gun wasn't going to open fire on those children; it wasn't like she was reaching safety at their expense – she was the victim here, just like always. The handle worked at last, and she stepped out into what should have been an ordinary day.

. . . Later, she would be asked what she felt on her ordeal ending, and so attuned was she to this from *Big Brother* evictions that part of her mind was recording her thoughts and feelings as they happened, but they arrived so swiftly, so wrapped around each other, that an honest articulation was a jumbly list: *the gun the man the noise the songs the shot the screams who screamed?*

None of it my fault he let me go he kept the children he had the gun

And underneath, beating like an unacknowledged drum, an image that refused to go away: of a one-inch plastic bear in leather jacket and sunglasses; that a child had given her; that she kept on a shelf in her room.

10

BACK IN HIS OFFICE, the first thing he did was open a window, or pretend to open a window: an old-fashioned sash arrangement lifted if you tugged hard enough, but fitted into the external brickwork was a sheet of reinforced glass strong enough to stop a bullet, apparently. This didn't open. But you could stand by it anyway, and gaze at the rooftops and their electronic furniture – aerial masts and miniature pylons – and what looked like privies or garden sheds, but were presumably access wells. The hooded carapaces of CCTV cameras hung at innumerable junctions; some static; others twisting on pivots to a preordained pattern, or at the whim of a distant watcher. Perhaps one was pointed his way now. But the glass was treated. No one could see in. That was the theory, and, like the glass's protective qualities, Jonathan Nott presumed its effectiveness in this area was tested regularly.

Must make a note of that.

He turned to his desk, pressed Tina's number on a keypad: 'Anything from Chapman?'

'He's not answering his mobile, sir.'

'Do we have a fix?'

'It was in Oxford an hour ago.'

Tina was Queen of the Database. She knew Bad Sam's phone wasn't Bad Sam.

'What about Ashton?'

'He's off the table.'

For a moment, he wondered if this was euphemism, then it clicked: operating table. 'Anyone with him?'

'I sent a car for his wife. She'll be by his bed.'

Not what Nott had meant.

'Duffy's there too.'

One of the Dogs.

'But he's not expected to gain consciousness any time soon.'

'Right. What's happening at the nursery?'

'Live on News 24, sir.'

'If I want to know what the media choose to reveal, I'll pay my TV licence. Has Whistler checked in?'

'He's been asking for background.'

'On?'

'Hostage contacts. The teacher, Kennedy, used to be in banking. A City job with an international outfit. Whistler wanted to know more.'

'When was this?'

'11:15.'

'While he was inside.'

'Yes, sir.'

'And he didn't give a sit rep? What are we teaching these kids?'

'He presumably had a gun on him.'

'Which is why we have codewords. You spoke to him?'

'An email. He has a Black—'

'I don't care what they're called, we're sure it was him asking?'

'It was his device. In or near the nursery.'

'So for all we know it was the gunman.'

Her pause answered that.

'What are the rest of Chapman's team doing?'

Chapman headed a team of six.

'Moody's in the building, sir. The others are off-shift.'

'Well, get them on-shift and get them to Oxford. Tell them

I want their boss back here, sooner than now. And if Barrowby calls from over the water, tell him Chapman's on his way.'

He killed the call.

Mobiles, as long as they're on, send out a regular pulse to the nearest transmitter: if you have one in your pocket, we can find out where you are. Chapman would have switched his off as soon as it started saying things he didn't like, such as *Return to base*. If it ever switched on again, they'd have the double fun of trying to second-guess Bad Sam: was the phone still on him, or on a jolly of its own? Nott had a vision of Bad Sam on a railway bridge, dropping his mobile onto a northbound container.

It's been three weeks since Miro Weiss disappeared with enough money to start his own country, and Bad Sam's no nearer finding him. How hard is he looking?

Maybe the Barrowboy was right, and Chapman was up to his neck in missing money.

Nott returned to the window to glare down at the pavement opposite: the 'private bookshop'; the tourists idling past; the girls like a mobile strip show. Two men stood smoking by a drainpipe, evidently sharing a hilarious conversation, not one speck of which reached Nott's ears. It was important to remember that such people were the public – his sole professional purpose being to keep them intact and unslaughtered – but face it: they were small souls mired in banality, and would literally shit if they had his problems. Literally.

His department had a number of functions, one of which, until recently, had been the funnelling of various astronomical sums of money – astronomical being a precise term: the figures resembling lunar distances – through different channels, each of which put a baffle between the money's origin and its current whereabouts. These sums spent so much time offshore, they probably developed fins. Which was fine: disguise was good. Though in retrospect, not all that good, given how impeccably invisible a recent sum of money had become; an amount so huge, there was no way of making it real. An amount that weighed more than the average house.

The first thing you did when you lost this much money was shut all the doors and hope no one had noticed. The second thing, you did a headcount, and found Miro Weiss missing too.

Once the doors were all shut, the headcount done, Sam Chapman was the obvious one to loose: former field agent and current Top Dog, with years of experience at keeping the kennels in order. Put his track record against that of Miro Weiss – seven years a desk man – and the story wrote itself: twenty-four hours tops, and Sam would have Weiss's head on a stick. But it hadn't worked out like that. Weiss had disappeared so comprehensively, he might not have known where he was himself, and Bad Sam's investigation had generated more heat than light.

I don't care if Weiss is the last of the fucking Mohicans, if Chapman was trying, he'd have him by now.

But that was another desk man talking, wasn't it?

Nott sat down.

Bad Sam wasn't following orders: anyone else, you might take that as an admission of guilt. But guilt didn't figure on Bad Sam's list of attributes, and he'd never been a Dog you called to heel. Loose ends were his specialty – he chased them down and annihilated them. Maybe the Barrowboy was right and Sam hadn't found his man because he hadn't been looking, but that meant one of two things: he and Weiss had been in it together, or he had some other associate, and Weiss had been his fall guy. Either way Miro Weiss wouldn't be turning up any time soon, and Bad Sam would either never be seen again or appear with tracks swept so clean there'd be no chance of working out what he'd been up to.

A desk man himself, Jonathan Nott swept his hand across its

clean surface almost fondly. The money had been first to go – the desk would be next, along with the visions Nott had nursed of graceful retirement: a K and the occasional discreet consultation. Best he'd get would be a warm glass of white and a few lacklustre speeches; consider himself lucky, too. Back when the Crane brothers were Service hellhounds, a particularly uncompromising attitude towards failure had been the norm. Retirement notices had been known to arrive marked *Send No Flowers*.

Hard to tell how long he sat there, making no visible progress in his life or career. When the phone rang, the noise scraped against his consciousness like fingers on a blackboard.

'Sir?'

'What is it?'

'Maybe you should turn the TV on after all.'

'You should have let my boys go,' Eliot said.

'I do not like her. She is gone now.'

This with blank finality, as if to leave the annexe was to step out of any known realm.

Truth to tell, Eliot was starting to feel the same way. They'd been here so long, it was hard to believe the world outside remained familiar. And the Grand Old Duke of York, he remembered, had ten thousand men. He was so adrift, it was a moment before he understood that the thought was triggered by another damn nursery rhyme.

and when they were up they were up

and when they were down they were down

Though they were moving slowly, sluggishly; as if the hill was too steep for their battle-weary limbs; or the batteries powering their pointless manoeuvres dwindling out of life.

Louise said, 'Tell us about the money.'

'It wasn't exactly real money.'

You can make money, Crispin had said. *Out of nothing. All you'd need is the right circumstances.*

'I'm familiar with the notion. I told you, I've worked in banking. And you work in accounting for the secret services, and so did this Miro guy. What got stolen, some kind of slush fund?'

Eliot said, 'It was a war dividend, wasn't it?'

He had a twin wrapped round each leg, and both looked up; Gordy murmuring along to the tortured nursery rhyme. He said, 'We heard a lot about the peace dividend back when the Cold War ended, but cutbacks in military spending didn't make the taxpayer better off, and if it did the NHS or schools any good, it was well hidden. It was ploughed back into government, wasn't it? It's what they've been fighting the war on terror with.'

He couldn't remember the last time he'd strung so many words together. It felt like a speech.

Louise said, 'He's right, isn't he?'

'The money came from untraceable sources,' Ben said.

'What does that mean?'

'He means it was stolen in the first place,' Eliot said. 'That's the easiest kind to steal. The kind you can't report missing.'

The children gripped him tighter. Though terrified, they'd grown used to what was happening; had accustomed themselves to a reality in which each clutched a leg and muttered rhymes while their father held them tight. And now he was talking to the other grown-ups as if this had become normal to him, too. And both had the same thought at the same moment: both wished their mother were here instead of their father. Their mother would never break her focus on their well-being.

Eliot went on: 'You said this Miro was out in Iraq looking at all the ways money was going missing. But that wasn't so you could stop it happening, was it? It was so you could join in the looting.'

Louise looked at him. For a moment, something passed

between them, or Eliot thought it did. He hugged his boys tighter, having registered a shift in their postures, then looked to Ben Whistler for an answer.

Who was shaking his head. 'This isn't wise. You're going to be asked what we talked about in here. Chapman – this guy, Bad Sam, he's going to want to know what was said.'

'It's not like he can interrogate us.'

'Don't be too sure about that.'

'You didn't put that tape on to protect us,' Louise said. 'You didn't ditch the phone for us. You did it so he wouldn't hear what you say to Jaime and what Jaime says to you.'

Jaime said, 'I ask for you because Miro trust you. This Bad Sam try to kill me.'

Jaime?

They all paused.

Thank you, Jaime. That was the right thing to do.

For a moment, it was as if the annexe had reverted to its stated purpose, and Jaime was an infant, praised for a sensible act.

Are you going to send the others out now, Jaime? How about the children?

Ben said, 'Exactly what I was about to say.'

'And I do this, I release them, what happens then? What happens to me?'

'I can get you out of here. But not while you're keeping hostages. Those guys out there—'

Jaime? Can you hear me? Maybe you should think about turning the music down.

'—they're not about to let you go anywhere.'

Jaime stared at them, one by one. The gun hung by his side as if its weight had grown too much: he looked tireder by the minute, Eliot thought. It was wearying being a hostage – despite the noise and constant fear, the worry of the children, the never knowing what would happen next, more than once Eliot had caught himself wandering onto the edge of sleep; that barely rational state where the real takes a sharp left turn. If he hadn't been holding the children, he might have followed its lead. But it hadn't occurred to him how exhausting it must be, holding the gun instead – no spare moment to close an eye. No lapse in concentration allowed. Being the focal point of so much hatred, it could probably power a car. And all this without a grip on the language, after a night on the run. It made Eliot want to say something, but Ben Whistler spoke first.

'Besides, you only need me, Jaime. Because I came in of my own accord.'

Are you sending the children out now?

The cop had found extra volume on his gizmo, so he could be heard over the nursery rhyme racket.

Jaime?

'Let's let them go, Jaime.'

Putting himself on Jaime's side, as if they were in this together. Probably something he'd been taught at spy school, though Whistler still didn't look like Eliot's idea of a spy: resembled, rather, the boys who'd been the bane of his life at school – the ones who were good at sports, and wore their ties and blazers as if uniform were their own idea.

'Let's let them go,' Ben repeated.

For hours, this was what Eliot had been focused on; the only outcome he'd allowed himself to visualise. So why did he feel a sense of exclusion, as if he were being denied the chance to know how things turned out?

'Wait,' he said.

Ben said, 'Excuse me?'

'There's something I need to hear.'

'Are you—'

'Shut up.' Eliot felt good saying that; felt he had a grip on the situation, instead of the other way around. 'What happened this morning, Jaime?' he asked. 'Tell me that. What happened this morning? They caught you, yes? But how did you get the gun?'

Jaime looked at Ben.

'Jesus, don't ask his permission, you're the one with—'

'Eliot.' Louise spoke as softly as she could, and still be heard above the tape recorder. 'Don't lose it. Not now.'

He said, 'I just want to know, that's all.'

Ben Whistler was shaking his head, but said, 'Why don't you tell us, Jaime?'

'Tell you what happen this morning?'

'Yes. After you walked away from the road.'

Eliot said, 'You found somewhere to lie down, but you didn't sleep.'

'You were cold,' Louise said.

Jaime looked from one to the other, baffled by their recitation. 'It gets light,' he said after a while. 'Perhaps I do sleep. Because it gets light very quickly.'

'Where were you?'

'Not far from road. There are cars, many cars, but all heading the other way. Away from Oxford.'

The early draft of rush hour, with traffic anxious to reach the outskirts of London before the system's arteries hardened.

'I see a building not far away, behind trees. By side of road.'

'In a lay-by?' Ben asked.

'Lay-by?'

'A place to stop your car.'

'By the side of the road, yes. A brick building, I think it is a toilet. I need to go to toilet,' Jaime said.

'Okay.'

'I not want to go in bushes. I have no paper.'

They all knew they'd never forget that detail.

'So I go towards it. There are lorries parked in this lay-by, and maybe people, but nobody is watching. Perhaps they are sleeping.'

There was an electric squawk from outside; the megaphone calling Jaime's name again. But no one was listening.

'I stay in toilet a long time. I feel safer there. I do not have money to buy bus ticket back to London. All I know in Oxford is what Miro say about the lady in the nursery. But I have nowhere else to go. I think perhaps I come here, borrow money for ticket. So that is what I decide to do. But when I leave the toilet, they are waiting for me. They are waiting in a car.'

He shook his head, as if he still couldn't believe this had happened.

Ben said, 'They must have overtaken you at some point, without realising it. If there was more than one Oxford bus on the road, it might have confused them. Anyway, I guess they ended up here in the city.'

'Gloucester Green,' Eliot said. 'The bus station.'

'They'd have questioned the drivers, found out who picked you up at Marble Arch, and asked them where you got off.'

'They were probably driving up and down that stretch of road looking for you,' Louise said.

'If you'd hitched a lift back to London, you'd have been home free by now,' said Eliot.

All of them filling in gaps for Jaime; pointing out where he'd gone wrong.

He said, 'To hitch lift, you stand by road in plain sight.'

'Good point,' Ben said. 'For all Jaime knew, they were right behind him. He'd have been making it easy.'

'So they kept looking all night?' Eliot asked. 'For four, five hours, whatever it was?'

'They're professionals,' said Ben. 'Miro's been missing for weeks, and they've found no trace of him. Suddenly a young man calls, saying he's Miro's . . . friend. They're not about to lose him twice in one night.'

'They got lucky.'

'After a while, you just play the odds,' Ben said. 'If he was on the road back to London, they'd not find him. So they weren't looking there. They were looking in places he might conceivably be.'

'So what happened?' Eliot asked.

They turned back to Jaime, who blinked.

'I come out of toilet,' he said. 'And there they are.'

'In the car,' Ben said.

'I am frightened,' Jaime said. 'I do not expect to see them. I do not know how they catch me.'

'. . . Plain dumb luck,' Eliot muttered.

'Say?'

'Say, Daddy?'

'Hush,' he told them. 'Not now. We're going soon.'

'The tall man, he gets out,' Jaime said. 'He come towards me.'

'Did you speak?'

'I ask him, are you Ben Whistler? And he say, Ben cannot make it.'

'I didn't know about any of this,' Ben said.

'You say.' Jaime glanced at the gun in his hand. 'As he come towards me, his coat . . . flaps open. Flaps open?'

'Yes,' Louise said.

'And I see his gun. This gun.'

He showed it to them, as if they'd not seen enough of it yet.

'And I think, so . . . They have come to kill me.'

'Why did you think that?' Louise asked.

He looked at her.

'If you'd done nothing wrong, why did you think they meant you harm?'

'Because he has gun,' Jaime said slowly.

'But . . .'

'Because my friend is spy, and he has gone missing. Because someone search his house. Because these men follow me from London. And because he has gun.'

276

'Okay.'

Jaime turned to Ben, as if he'd best understand what came next. 'He say something else, but I do not remember what. I know he want to catch me, to pull me into car, and I do not want to get into car. I think . . .'

'You thought what?'

'If I get in car, I will not get out again. That is what I am afraid of. That they drive me somewhere, and nobody see me again.'

'Like Miro,' Louise said.

'I have rucksack on my shoulder, and I . . .' The word failed him. He mimed it instead; a shrug that allowed an imaginary bag to drop down his arm, into a waiting hand. He gripped its strap. 'I swing it into his face.'

(Neil Ashton had stumbled but not quite fallen; he'd recovered before he hit the ground, propelling himself onward with one hand on the tarmac. Behind him the car door opened, and the second man emerged.)

'And then I run, out on to road. The same way the traffic is moving. A car goes past me very fast.'

(Belted past, in fact, hitting its horn as it did so, and Jaime hurled himself on to the verge, as if the shock had stolen his grasp on gravity.)

'When I look back, he is running after me. He is holding the gun, and I think he is about to shoot me. and then . . .'

(And then more cars were on them; the first a great grey swoosh that buffeted Neil Ashton off his feet – Jaime was watching: he saw this happen. Instead of falling inwards, Ashton fell into the road where the next car hit sucked him under its front wheel . . . There followed a squeal, a slam, and a point at which organic noise stopped, and mechanical screeching took over. The gun went flying high and wide into the air. It fell to earth at Jaime's feet. He took it, and ran.)

'I think the other man will chase me still. But I do not see him again.'

If they'd been asked what their day felt like, anyone there might have likened it to a car smash. But this glimpse of splintered bone and punctured organs somehow robbed them of a justified sense of drama.

'Daddy?'

'Daddy, what did he say?'

'What happened, Daddy?'

'. . . Nothing, boys. Don't worry. Nothing happened.'

Ben said, 'Where did you run?'

'Away from road. I crossed another field, wasted land. Then I find myself on streets again. I find a map for tourists pinned on a wall. It has Grandpont on it. That is when I remember Miro saying this.'

Big bridge.

It was the slickest kind of vanishing act; the kind where you don't even know you're disappearing. Nobody ever traced his route. Jaime couldn't have traced it himself.

Ben looked at Eliot. 'There. That what you wanted to hear?'

A flash of anger lit Eliot. 'I don't know what makes you so—'

'Eliot.'

Which was Louise's way of saying *hush*.

Ben said, 'Time to let them go, Jaime.'

The way he said it, you'd have thought he was the one holding the gun.

Jaime looked at Eliot, and then, perhaps for the first time, at the twins, who peeped back at him from between folds of their father's trousers.

'Tell them I did not hurt you.'

Eliot nodded.

'And tell your boys I am sorry.'

He said, 'I still don't understand any of this. But I don't think it was all your fault.'

Then fell the awkward sort of pause that happens at a party, where you're desperate to leave, and don't want to make it look that way.

'I—'

'Eliot.' Which was probably the first time Whistler had addressed him by name. 'Take your boys. Go.'

'Louise too,' Eliot said.

But Ben Whistler shook his head.

'But—'

'Eliot? You're in charge of those boys' safety. I'm in charge of this one's. Now take them out of here.'

He looked at Louise, who looked directly back.

'It's okay,' she said. 'I'll be fine. Take your children out.'

Eliot would have liked to remember this later as a *Casablanca* moment, one in which his Memory met her Incident, and fused into something both could look back on with tender regret. But it was more like someone refusing a lift. He was stung once more by how easy it was to keep on having the same stupid responses. An event like this should be life-altering: he'd already worried it would change his boys forever. Now he worried it wouldn't change him. With an arm round the shoulders of each of his children, he headed for the door.

'Is Miss Kennedy coming?'

'Why isn't Miss Kennedy coming?'

'Hush now,' he said. 'Everything's going to be all right.'

And now look at this.

The door opens again, with less hesitation: the rainbow-crayoned cardboard sign reading *The Palace* disappears as the door swings backwards, and vanishes inside the dark recess of the annexe. Dark from where DS Bain sits. When you're up on a roof, perspective matters. And when you're focused on one square centimetre of space, whatever wanders into that space is yours.

Last time this happened, a woman had emerged, stumbling through the door as if she were an extraterrestrial delivery, returned to earth after a spacenapping. Her head was oddly round, with sad flat hair painted on, and in her eyes was a look of utter strangeness – and for a tiny, unmeasurable fraction of time it felt to Bain that it would be a kindness to squeeze the trigger, and put an end to everything written on that face: fear pain anxiety hatred fear sadness fear . . . But what's drummed into the brain comes out in the fingers, which wouldn't allow this to happen. Bain's fingers awaited their proper moment.

This time it's a man, with a boy under each arm. And here, too, is complicated emotion, which shines fluorescently through the rifle's crosshairs. Here, in place of fear or pain or anxiety, Bain sees disgust, and it is inwardly directed. That's how it reads – inwardly directed disgust. Which makes sense. Bain, way above the herd's responses, can understand how self-disgust might have a part to play. You're thrown into a situation not of your choosing, one calling on deep reserves of various capitalised virtues: Honour, Strength, Courage, Loyalty – if you're ever going to be a hero, now's the time. And it turns out you aren't. There are different gradations of heroism, true – it's one of those garlands the tabloids bestow at random, like celebrity – but there's a level at which there's no fooling yourself. So Bain believes. That there's a part of everyone's mind where it's always 4 a.m., and whatever face you put on for the world, that's where you truly see yourself.

And that's what this man is seeing, as he emerges. The photographs, the footage, the blurry little images on mobile phones: all will show a father bringing his children home intact, and that will be the story most observers carry away. But long after this official version's been archived, the truth will be worming away inside the man, a truth nobody will ever have a hint of. Because it's a truth calibrated against an ideal yardstick. Chances are, he behaved impeccably – protected his boys, did not squawl or shriek; refrained from begging for his life – but none of that counts when set against everything he didn't manage; the cool swagger with which he disarmed the gunman; the wry grin as he rubbed his knuckles afterwards.

The sad truth, in the book of Bain, is that we secretly believe we're heroes. Ideally, this man would be leaving with a boy under each arm and the woman at his side, and anything less amounts to slinking away. Everything that happens to him in the next few days will undermine that feeling: he'll be feted as a hero, his opinion sought on a range of tangentially related issues (gun crime, the death penalty, the anti-terrorist act), and the longer this goes on, the more important he'll start to feel. But underneath, it will remain 4 a.m., and he'll always know he failed himself when he walked out into the limelight.

And again, Bain's fingers suggest a different ending. It would be so easy to prevent any of this happening. But the fingers are simply responding to Bain's own 4 a.m. slot, and that's not in charge right now. It's the upper brain – the uniformed brain – giving the orders. So Bain's fingers relax into standby, and another possible future remains untriggered.

All of which happens within half a second. Next, a swirling, emotional movement erupts on the periphery of vision, and without twitching an eye, Bain knows that the man's wife, the children's mother, is on the scene, and that for her, rightly, notions of heroism matter less than a broken match. All that counts is the number of breathing figures emerging from the annexe: her son, her son, her husband. One part of the story is about to reach its close, and it's a part Bain has nothing to do with, and wants to be over quickly. So it goes. The man moves, hurrying towards the waiting woman, exiting Bain's target area. And Bain continues to wait, because the rest of the story has yet to unfold.

Target acquired.

Steady.

It's only a matter of time.

Fredericks said, 'It's the children. Thank God.'

'Yes.'

Someone yipped behind them, and Fredericks jumped, turned – a woman had ducked beneath the crime-scene ribbon, and was being closed in on by a pair of officers, who were perhaps under the impression she was a crazed vigilante or copy-hungry journalist. He looked back, saw the children in their father's arms and called 'Leave her,' though he stepped in her way as she rushed forward. 'Easy now. Just one minute.' His brain supplied her name. 'Mrs Pedlar? It's okay. They'll be here any moment.' He wasn't a person. He was an object in her path. 'I can't let you go closer.' *My children my children* she crooned as she struggled. The image sprang into Fredericks' mind of an injured bird he'd once found: the memory stored in his palms that of a heart beating in a cage of bones; beating so fast, it almost smashed free.

My children my children

And then she was past him, and the released hostages were there, and it was impossible to tell who was crying hardest, mother or sons – 'Get them out of here,' somebody shouted, which should have been Fredericks, though was in fact Faulks. Parents and children disappeared; were shuffled into the Incident Van, free from the attentions of the Press Pack. He should go with them, but couldn't drag himself away: something had happened, so something else might happen soon. The domino effect. If all went smoothly from here on in, earlier mistakes might be forgotten.

He said, 'We're nearly there,' and it was a request for confirmation.

'Nearly's not enough,' Faulks said.

Fredericks looked back down the road. The crowd was mushed up hard against the cordon, though if it had really wanted to move forwards, a length of tape wasn't going to stop it. There was a young, good-looking man at the front of the crowd: one of the nursery staff, staring at the vehicle inside which the family had been packed. What was that look on his face? Something wistful, approaching regret. Not what you'd expect from someone witnessing joyful reunion. The man turned, and pushed back through the throng, and Fredericks forgot him.

Louise said, 'And then there were three.'

She looked around. The room ought to have been familiar. This was her working environment, whose order she was responsible for – it was Louise who had placed the nature table just there; it was on Louise's instruction that Dave had moved Trixie's cage against the far wall, and a week later moved it back. 'Feng shui, right?' The art on the walls, Louise had drawing-pinned in place; its rotation her responsibility, dictated by a secret, colour-coded chart whose intricate workings ensured that every child saw his or her masterpiece hung in pride of place at least once. None of this happened by itself. She knew what every shelf, every surface, held: pens pencils paper paints; soft toys, wheeled toys; books and puppets. And object after object, naturally, designed and created by the Darlings themselves: papier mâché friends and relatives; cardboard zoos; patchwork flying carpets. Now it was all taking on the attributes of dream-scenery, and it struck her how often nursery images appeared in horror films – spooky plinking music accompanying shots of scary toys. But it was nearly over, wasn't it? Soon she'd be leaving too. There were things to learn first, though. What was the point of being a teacher if you never learned anything?

'So,' she said. 'It wasn't Miro at all. That's what you're thinking, isn't it?'

It was Ben she addressed. 'I didn't say that,' he replied.

'But you're thinking it.'

Jaime said, 'You have a plan?'

'Yes, Jaime. I have a plan.'

'And soon we leave, yes?'

'You and me, yes, soon. We're leaving in a car.'

'Which car?'

'The car Louise is going to arrange for us.' He hadn't taken his eyes off her, which she didn't especially mind. He was good-looking, if you went for the public school rugger type, and she had a certain amount of form there. More accountant than spy, he'd said. On the other hand, he'd arrived in a helicopter.

'That is why she is still here?'

'We get them used to the idea you're cooperating, Jaime. Once you let Louise go, they'll relax. It's her they're worried about. They're not concerned about me.'

'Because you are professional.'

'Well, I don't do this for a living. But the cops know who I work for. They'll play ball, up to a point.'

'So you're just going to drive away?' Louise said.

'A car and a phone. That's what you ask them for. I'll arrange the rest.'

Jaime said, 'They will follow us.'

'That won't matter. Not once I've phoned my bosses. They'll call the cops off.'

'But your Bad Sam, he is one of the bosses, yes?'

'Not quite. It's his boss I'll be calling.'

'And you'll tell them he's the one stole the money,' Louise said.

Ben said, 'You really don't need to know any more.'

'But you need me to make your demands.'

'All this, everything that's happened, you're an innocent victim. A few minutes more, then you can get on with your life.'

'I'm the lady, remember? I'm why Jaime's here in the first

place. You think Miro was a dupe, that Chapman set him up. But Chapman couldn't have stolen that money on his own. It needed someone who knew what they were doing, knew how to cover their tracks. The money itself was just numbers. Your Bad Sam's not a numbers man.'

Jaime said, 'What are you saying?'

Louise said, 'That if Bad Sam did this, he didn't do it alone. Either he was in it with Miro, or he was in it with someone else, and made it look like it was Miro. And either way, Miro ended up . . . whatever.'

'Miro is not a thief.'

Ben said, 'Maybe Bad Sam forced him to do it.'

'He torture him?'

'I wouldn't put it past him,' said Ben. 'But this wasn't an overnight job. Miro was around up until the day it turned out the money wasn't, and he didn't have visible bruises. If Chapman used brute force, Miro would have had time to cry for help.'

'Or perhaps he have nothing to do with it at all. And he disappear because Bad Sam make him disappear.'

'To make him look guilty,' Louise said.

'Either way,' Ben said, 'Chapman would have needed information, and Miro's the one who had it.'

'Only Miro?'

Ben said, 'Pretty much. The accounts we're talking about, the looted accounts, they were set up after Miro's Iraq trip. They were his portfolio.'

'What were they for?'

'I've told you, you don't need to know.'

'And you've told me you need a car.'

Ben said, 'Okay, you really want to hear this? What Miro was doing, what he did, was build a file on companies making a killing out of reconstruction. Firms that banked cheques for work that was never done. Water pipes that never got laid, electricity grids that remained unlit.'

He'd stepped away from the wall. Jaime's gun seemed irrelevant now.

'A lot of these companies were too big to take on. The Service is a branch of government, but some multinationals are bigger than governments, you don't go near them unless you're ready for all-out war. But there were smaller targets, and more importantly, there were individuals – guys pocketing cash their companies never got to hear about. Those guys were Miro's favourites. He'd turn their finances inside out.'

Old Mother Hubbard died away. Louise must have heard this tape twice a week for the last six months, but she couldn't for her life call to mind what came next. Ben waited out the scratchy pause between tunes. He wasn't about to speak without background interference.

My grandfather's clock was too tall for its shelf

'Then he'd wrap their file in a ribbon and deliver it to Operations, who'd confront the target with it. We called it a looter's tax. Miro worked out how much they'd skimmed, and the Service took it all. If the targets didn't like the offer, they could take their chances.'

'You're not talking about prison, are you?'

ti—ick tock

ti—ick tock

Ben shook his head. 'No need. These people ripped off the companies they worked for, and we're talking about the construction industry. The best the targets could expect was broken bones, maybe a lot worse. It's a rough business.'

'So the Service took the money.'

'Eliot wasn't wrong. The war on terror's expensive. It helps to have a treasure chest.'

'And that's the money that went missing.'

'The principle was there from the start. Stolen money's the easiest kind to steal. Who do you tell?'

'But a quarter of a billion pounds?'

'There's been a lot of looting.'

'And there's been no sign of Miro since it went missing,' Louise said.

'So maybe he's holed up in the Swiss Alps, recovering from plastic surgery,' said Ben.

'Or in a different kind of hole altogether.'

'Which brings us back to Chapman. Even if he is behind all this, he didn't know about Jaime until yesterday. He's got to be tearing his hair out, wondering how much Jaime knows and how much he's told. That's why I've got to get Jaime away from here.'

but it stopped
short
never to go again

Ben said, 'We'll go to London, find a safe house, until all this gets sorted. You won't need to worry about Chapman any more.'

'I don't know about this money.'

'I believe you, Jaime. It's all going to be okay.' He turned to Louise. 'You can do this? You ask them for a car, for a mobile.'

She said, 'I can do that. But Ben – if Chapman did have someone helping him, someone who knew how to shift money around – I think I know who it was.'

'Because you're the lady in the nursery.'

'He was my boss. Back when I worked in banking.'

'So how would he know Chapman?'

'It might have been the other way around. Chapman might have gone looking for someone exactly like him.'

Ben said, 'Either way, Miro was still involved. Otherwise how would he have known about you?'

'I don't know.'

He said, 'Chances are, Chapman knows about you too. And may think you know more than you do.'

'Does that make me a loose end?'

'I hope not. Once I get Jaime out of here, he'll have too much else to worry about anyway.'

ti—ick tock

ti—ick tock

'You'd better go,' he said.

'Yes.'

Jaime said, 'I am sorry.'

'Well, this isn't the day I was expecting when I got up this morning.' Jaime bowed his head at this, and she almost laughed. Some of the kids were the same way: express your disappointment, and they wanted to go and hide. Of course, some others were proto-thugs. 'It's okay, Jaime. I hope this works out.'

'Get us the car,' Ben said. 'And it will.'

So this was what it was like in an Incident Van. So this was what it was like in an Incident Van. So this was what it was like in an Incident Van. Eliot's responses had become trapped in a loop, as if a safety valve had triggered to prevent his heart bursting – it was working all too well. He should have been overjoyed; emotion should have been leaking through his pores. 'Oh my sweet girl,' he murmured. He hadn't called her his sweet anything in years. And Chris wasn't listening anyway; was wrapped up in her children; literally *wrapped up* in them; they were clamped to her like parasites: *Jesus, don't call them parasites.* But he could have said it out loud and not been heard; could have nipped off for a pint without anyone noticing. A synaesthetic would go blind, witnessing this reunion. And how many people, *normal* people, would have reached for a word like 'synaesthetic' right now? He was an actor delivering an unconvincing performance: all he could really feel was that he was somewhere new. And that this was what it was like in an Incident Van.

'Mummy?'

'Mummy Mummy.'

'We were scared but we hardly cried at all.'

'We hardly cried ever.'

He was waiting to be asked for confirmation of their bravery, but they were caught in their own loops, each one's words circling the other's.

'Mummy.'

'Mummy Mummy?'

And Chris was talking and crying at once, issuing fragments of their names between sobs and hiccups—*tih*—*megor*—*dytim*—*egord*—

'They were very brave,' he said.

'Mummy.'

'Mummy Mummy.'

'They hardly cried at all.'

He should be crying now, though – there was something wrong with a husband, a father, who did not cry at such a moment. It wouldn't be difficult. Here was the trick; you summoned up a scene of enormous sorrow, or long-spent happiness, and embraced it; wrapped yourself round it the way the boys were wrapped round their mother, then let it pour out. Simple. But Eliot couldn't latch on to the right scene.

They were bundled in front of him: Chris on her knees; the children all over her; his hands on Chris's shoulders, and all this was happening in the Incident Van. Which was large, but smaller inside than out because of all the equipment it held, and the number of people crammed into it suddenly struck him as oppressive: two officers were close by and there were two others up the far end; a woman perched on a stool, with another officer, also female, hovering awkwardly by – the seated woman was Judy Ainsworth.

Who would have sacrificed his children to save her own skin.

And this too looped. Sacrificed his children to save her own skin. Sacrificed his children to save her own skin. She looked like a frog, squatting on that stool – she'd have sacrificed his children? What made her skin valuable? It was lousy skin, sagged and wattled, and that was just those parts he could see. And she thought herself worth more than his smooth unsullied children, whose lives lay all ahead of them? His hands tensed involuntarily, and Chris jerked free from his sudden grasp.

'God sorry—'

But she was away again. The children were her world.

Eliot felt himself being judged, though he wasn't sure who by. None of the cops were looking his way. His own eyes remained on Judy. A sudden flashback bit him: that inhuman noise she'd issued just before propelling herself for the door – Jaime had jumped on her, and men with guns had burst in. He could still feel the grip the boys had taken on his thighs. Before his own hands could tighten again, he jammed them into his pockets, and moved along to where she sat.

She didn't look up.

'Judy?'

'Sir, I think she's still a little upset—'

'We're all a little upset.'

'Perhaps you should be with your family, sir.' The officer read him, his stance, his expression, and softly said, 'It's been a dreadful morning. You can't blame her if she feels threatened by—'

'I'm not threatening her. Judy?'

Sacrificed his children to save her own skin. This time she did look up, and in the time it took her to do so, everything changed. There were tears in her eyes. Same Judy, but it was like looking at her through a different doorway; a doorway he'd walked through himself.

Whatever he'd been going to say came out as, 'You're okay?'

She nodded.

'That's—good . . .'

'Your boys,' she said.

'They're fine. They're with their mother.'

'He didn't kill any of us,' she said.

'No. No, he didn't.'

'Is she—?'

'She's still in there. But he's not going to hurt her.' He hunkered down to her level. Her face was the same, and there was a very specific unloveliness to it, as if her body had played a practical joke on her. But he'd never looked her in the eyes before. What reason would he have had to do so? Here in the Incident Van, where artificial light imposed a forensic bleakness on everything, Judy's eyes were vague and colourless. Out of danger, she remained frightened. He wondered if that were always the case.

He said, 'It's over.'

She nodded.

'What happened in there – it doesn't matter, you know.' He meant her snarling outbursts; her attempt to run; the way she'd have sacrificed his children to save her own skin. 'People react in different ways.'

She looked at him blankly.

'I mean . . .'

And he realised he couldn't say what he meant, because he meant too many things at once: that everyone was weak, everyone was guilty; that only having his boys there had kept him from melting down too . . . And that he might have done or said things this morning that would keep him awake in nights to come, but nobody else would remember them, not with Judy's outbursts to recall instead. But Judy wouldn't have wanted to hear this; and besides, the words would have choked off as Judy's face dissolved into tears, along with everything else – just washed away in front of him as if a plug had been pulled; simply swirled round going nowhere, until it struck him that Judy wasn't crying, he was – Eliot Pedlar. Just when he'd been about to offer comfort, a terrifying reversal took place, because she was reaching her arms out for him instead, and if anything should have stopped his sobbing it was the prospect of this squat witch comforting *him*, with his wife and kids not feet away. So why was he leaning into her embrace? He didn't know, but he did it anyway.

It's okay.

Don't worry.

You just cry.

So Eliot Pedlar, who'd just found out what it was like in an Incident Van, closed his eyes and sobbed his heart out. And before it was halfway gone, his family had come across and joined him.

Down by the river, smoking wasn't enough: the pinprick afterslap told Bad Sam Chapman those bastard midges had bitten him. It was otherwise lifeless; the locals having more to occupy them today than early afternoon strolls through an urban approximation of nature. And even if he hadn't known anything was happening, he'd have known something was happening. The day was pent like a tightly laced boxing glove. Where Bad Sam lived, alarms erupted with monstrous regularity, but most were triggered by nothing substantial – some areas had a hair-trigger atmosphere, that was all. Grandpont wasn't like that, he guessed, but today wasn't normal, and out of sight, though not far away, whatever freakish charge had gripped the neighbourhood was fizzing and sparking, desperate to ground itself.

He slipped Ben Whistler's BlackBerry back into his pocket. He was thinking, as he walked, of Louise Kennedy.

Kennedy had gone back into the nursery, and Sam Chapman didn't know why. Maybe it didn't matter: the same circumstances produced different reactions in different people. Most of us are average – it's what the word means – but there's always variation. We all hit the ground at the same painful speed, but some of us get up and walk away. Louise Kennedy was one of the lucky ones, and either brave or arrogant enough to think she could survive the same fall twice. That had been his first impression, but then he'd learned about her connection to Crispin Tate. With that in mind, you had to throw the same circumstances back in the cup, give it another shake: maybe Ms Kennedy was not what she seemed. If it looks like a duck, walks like a duck and sounds like a duck, it probably wants you to think it's a duck. A thought which brought him to Whistler . . . What was Whistler's game, anyway? And how much did he know?

Thinking all this, Bad Sam had taken the wrong track on the far side of the bridge, and had wound up next to the railway line. So that's where he was when the birds took off; a sudden spume of them lifting out of the trees lining the tracks, their wings thrashing and clattering as they mowed the air. It was less than a second before the significance of their flight struck him.

He started to run.

'What did he say about me, Jaime?'

'He call you his friend.'

'Anything else?'

'That if something happen to him, I should call you.'

'So – what made you wait so long?'

Jaime tried looking puzzled.

Just the two of them now. Louise was back in the world, either arranging a car or not – Ben thought she would. When she'd left, it was with the look of a woman who'd registered that what had happened this morning was just a small part of something that had happened elsewhere; that Jaime had no more wanted any of this than she had. Which didn't mean Jaime had been entirely open with them.

'It's been three weeks. He gave you instructions what to do

if anything happened to him. Did you not think vanishing counted?'

'. . . I think he might come back.'

'How long did you keep thinking that?'

'I not understand you.'

'For the first couple of days, I'd have thought the same thing. That he'd come back. That he'd gone on a bender or whatever. A drinking spree,' he added. 'But after a week, I'd be worried. I'd assume something had happened. Just like he said it might.'

'I ring you,' Jaime said defensively.

'After another fortnight.'

'He is very private man. You know that.'

'And that might have kept me quiet another couple of days. But not for three weeks, Jaime. Three weeks is well past worried.'

Jaime said nothing.

'You weren't there, were you, Jaime? You didn't know he'd gone.'

Jaime looked at the gun in his hand. After all these hours, it was starting to look normal: the way an umbrella or a clipboard might. 'I—he—no. We were not speaking.'

'You'd had an argument.'

'He is nice man. I like him. But I also like . . .'

He fell quiet; a parade of other things he liked marching through his mind.

Ben said, gently, 'You like clubs and dancing. Parties and young people.'

Jaime said, 'It does not mean I do not like Miro.'

'No.'

'But he never want to go out. He says there is no need. He says we can have a nice life together, without noisy clubs and . . .'

'And parties.'

'Now he has met me, he does not need to go to clubs any more. That is what he tell me.'

'But you did. Didn't you?'

Jaime said nothing.

'Jaime. I'm not blaming you. I'm just trying to work out where you were for three weeks. Why you didn't know Miro was missing.'

And why the Dogs didn't know Jaime existed.

Jaime said, 'Miro is a good man. He is kind. But . . .'

'But not terribly exciting.'

'So I go to club without him, yes. And I meet a man.'

'These things happen.'

'This man like the same things I like. And he tell me has money, and that we can do nice things, go on holiday, and . . .'

And eat in nice restaurants and drink nice wine and take nice drugs and fuck each other stupid, thought Ben.

'But it didn't work out.'

'He is a bastard.'

'Men mostly are,' Ben admitted. 'So you went home to Miro.'

'I ring him up,' Jaime said. 'On the telephone,' he explained.

'But you didn't get an answer.'

'This is not like Miro. Not many people call him. And he always answer telephone.'

That figured, thought Ben. On any list of assumptions he'd make about Miro, the ability to ignore a ringing phone wouldn't appear.

'I thought . . .'

'You thought what?'

Jaime looked at the gun again and then at Ben. 'I thought maybe he hurt himself.'

'Okay.'

The nursery rhyme tape was faltering. The batteries, thought Ben – its batteries were dying. Jack and Jill were struggling up that hill. The summit receded the further they got, and perhaps they were having doubts as to the wisdom of heading uphill to fetch water.

He said, 'He was a lonely man.'

'So I worry. Yes.'

Ben suffered a sudden flash of empathy with Miro Weiss, but this wasn't the time or the place. 'I'm sure he was sorry to lose you, Jaime. But that wasn't the reason for anything that happened to him.'

Jaime's eyes were wet. 'He was nice man. I'm sorry I treat him like that.'

'So what did you do? When he didn't answer the phone?'

'I go to see him.'

'But he wasn't there.'

'I still have keys.' He looked away from Ben, then back. 'I have copy made. Just in case.'

'We call that a contingency plan. What was his place like?'

'Like?'

'Was it the same as when you left?'

'No. Messy. Very messy. Not like Miro would leave it.'

And that would be the Dogs. Protocol demanded they left a place the way they found it, but frustration had a way of nudging protocol aside. The more time passed – the more Miro stayed disappeared – the less they'd have cared about keeping things neat.

'You were lucky,' he said. 'If you'd gone back sooner, they'd have picked you up. After the first couple of weeks, they didn't have his flat under surveillance. They'd have known he wasn't coming back, because they knew he was too careful for that.'

'Or because he is dead,' Jaime said flatly.

'If they'd thought he was dead, they'd have thought he was innocent,' Ben said.

Jaime furrowed again, as he worked his way through that one.

'So maybe they wanted everyone else to think he was still alive,' Ben said. 'Because they already knew he wasn't.'

Whistler.

'I think that's our ride.'

We've got your car. Just like you wanted.

Jaime said, 'It might be trap.'

But Ben didn't think, at this late stage, they'd go for anything tricky. The hostages were safe; Ben himself didn't count – he was a spook. He said, 'Give me the gun a moment.'

'Why?'

'Give me a break, Jaime. You're not going to shoot me.'

'Where do we go? When we get in the car?'

'London. They'll follow us, sure. And the car will be bugged anyway. But once we're clear, I'll call my bosses. You're not going into police custody, Jaime. You're coming with me, and you'll get to tell your story again. About Bad Sam and Ashton coming after you. Now give me the gun.'

Jaime opened his mouth. Closed it. He'd run out of options, Ben didn't need to remind him. He did what Ben said.

The gun felt heavy in Ben's hand. He'd done weapons training, but there was something quintessentially different about holding a gun outside a practice ground, where you wouldn't just get up and walk away afterwards.

He said, 'You know, if you hadn't made that call – if you'd closed Miro's door and walked away – no one would have been looking.'

Jaime's eyes flashed. 'I know that. Of course I do.'

'I mean it. As far as anyone was concerned, Miro had no close ties. They'd gone through his life with razor blades, slicing everything they found just to see what it hid, but they didn't come up with you, Jaime.'

Even as he was speaking, he was having a vision of what Miro's life must have been like: paranoia raised to an art form. He must have logged every item Jaime ever brought into his flat, and logged each one out again after he'd left. Burned the bed linen, replaced the crockery; vacuumed the ceilings in Jaime's wake, so there'd be nothing to remind him he'd ever been there. Which was a kind of self-protection; one that erased happiness as soon as it departed, so its souvenirs didn't lacerate the present. The one time Ben had seen the flat, he wouldn't have guessed Miro ever had a boyfriend. Everything he laid eyes on had Miro printed all over it: the boxed sets of operas; the Everyman hardbacks; the Klimt reproduction in the hall. It was true: if Jaime had kept his head down, his existence would have stayed secret.

'I guess you're just really unlucky,' Ben said. He removed the clip from the Heckler & Koch; handed the gun back to the boy. 'Here. You're going to have to hold this to my head. And I don't want you accidentally pulling the trigger if you step on a tennis ball.'

'Tennis ball?'

'Or something.' The nursery rhyme tape was really painful now; sounded like an infantile version of grunge. Jack and Jill with fuzzbox. But there seemed little point in turning it off. It could play itself out while this chapter ended.

Whistler? The car's at the gate.

'Okay,' he said. 'Let's see if they mean it.'

There was a rule about these situations: when you emerged, you were given a cup of tea and had a blanket draped around your shoulders – Louise had shaken her head at the tea; shrugged her shoulders so the blanket hit the ground. 'They want a car,' she'd said. After a while, they let her say it to someone who mattered.

Peter Faulks had asked, 'Which one of them wants it?'

Did that matter? She supposed, to the cops, it might. 'And a phone. They want a phone, too.'

Faulks had muttered off; minutes passed. The blanket re-appeared on Louise's shoulders; a cup of tea in her hand. Somewhere, someone was boiling water: lots of it.

She'd lost track of time. It was broad daylight, which felt

wrong: they should have been standing under stars – there should have been snow on the ground. Eliot and his boys were nowhere in sight; Judy had vanished too. Perhaps they were in the Incident Van; a large rock-band-on-tour vehicle by the junction, one of the elements converting the familiar to the surreal. Louise recognised a few faces in the crowd down the road, but all seemed weirdly out of context, like family members spotted in a dream. Which brought to mind her mother – she should call her mother; let her know she was safe. Should go to her. But she couldn't move. Whatever happened next, she would be here to see it. The cops were unlikely to use force to shift her. Not with all the cameras about.

Whistler?

Faulks was back at his loudhailer.

The car's at the gate.

A bland blue four-door, parked where he said. Ben and Jaime would have to leave the annexe and cross both playgrounds to reach it, under armed scrutiny every step of the way: there were policemen round the side of the nursery, and perched on the adventure playground equipment, and up on the roof too – the one with the rifle trained on the annexe door. All would be watching Ben and Jaime.

And now the time she'd lost track of speeded up, as if it had forgotten its major function: to prevent everything from happening at once. The immediate area tightened its belt. Sound wavered; when it started again, it was mostly background noise – the crowd by the junction; distant traffic. An electric squawk, which was probably a radio. Then the annexe door opened and Ben and Jaime emerged, as close as newly-weds. It was a moment before Louise could unravel the picture: Jaime's arm was round Ben's waist; Jaime's gun to Ben's temple – Ben was Jaime's shield.

For a moment they remained immobile; every eye trained on them – this image was being beamed into houses across the country. How weird that the world could focus like this, on somewhere only ever meant to be ordinary. And then they were moving. It was a shuffle, no more; four legs trying to move like two. This whole huge stage waiting, and the best they could manage as they edged into its spotlight was a graceless, uncoordinated amble; Ben's face defensively blank; Jaime's patently terrified. As if they'd had their roles reversed, and Ben was the nerveless hostage taker, Jaime his jelly-limbed victim. His gun was shaking, Louise could see. Which spelled what to the body-language experts? That he was armed and nervous; and might break at any moment. That there was little chance of him missing Ben Whistler's head if his trembling fingers squeezed that trigger.

They stepped on to the path leading to the gate in the inner fence.

It might have been – the thought occurred later, on the bus into London – the same spot on which the fox had sat; the fox she'd chanced upon one morning, which had graced her with a look so superior, it evidently knew everything she didn't. All the secrets she'd once supposed would reveal themselves with age, but never had. After briefly pitying her ignorance, it trotted off into its own version of her neighbourhood. It didn't take much to turn everything you thought you knew upside down. It didn't take much to make you lose your foot, or your head. Ben slipped as they reached the path; ever afterwards, recalling the moment, Louise constructed the comical image of the blank expression on his face giving way to absolute puzzlement as he surrendered to gravity's pull, and dropped free of Jaime's embrace. Who was left standing for a fraction of a second, probably aware that a fraction of a second was all that it would be. Because something bloomed at last in the barren morning, and Jaime lost his head, its contents spraying across the rainbow-crayoned cardboard sign on the annexe door, splashing it red and grey and red and grey, while pigeons lifted in a spume from the trees lining the railway at the end of the lane, their wings thrashing and clattering as they mowed the air.

Up on the roof, job done, Bain lowered the rifle and removed the black cap that had held her hair in place these hours past.

Target acquired.

She was steady.

PART TWO

P.M.

II

ONCE UPON A TIME, City banks were large, solid construc-
tions; their entrances supported by unmissable pillars;
their plate glass windows reminiscent of churches. The scroll-
work over their doors assumed a working knowledge of Latin,
their floors were tiled, and their partners' names were gilt-
etched on to large wooden boards in the lobby, possibly facing
a Landseer, or something equally permanent. Ceilings were
high, voices low. Tickertape chattered behind cashiers' desks.
The necessary vulgarity of the telephone was mitigated by
the instrument's being fashioned of black Bakelite, with a cup
you held to one ear while rattling the handset for the switchboard's attention. All of which Louise knew to be true, because
she had a weakness for old movies. These were the banks
where characters from *Brief Encounter* cashed a cheque when
the butcher's bill arrived. And everything about them was
intended to reassure; their very presence a valet's murmur
confirming the rightness of your choices. They were the
repository of their clients' futures, and did not take this trust
lightly.

Which was long before Louise came in, because sometime
in the nineties, an architectural shift had matched the social
revolution of the eighties, and the dominant style was now the
big fuck-off. Huge glass and chrome buildings vied to dominate
the skyline, and when they weren't telling each other to fuck

off, they were reminding passers-by that they could fuck off too. Because these banks weren't safeguarding petty cash, they were bankrolling governments, multinationals, insurance companies, arms firms, big pharma, record companies, fast-food franchises, media conglomerates, supermarket chains, and every other organisation whose fundamental if usually secret purpose was to remind the little folk that they were powerless and, if they didn't like it, could fuck off.

She stood on the pavement opposite, looking at fourteen storeys from a previous life. The time was 4:34.

Because the mind records everything – because we all carry a black box in our brains, ceaselessly taping our every move – it probably wasn't true that she had no idea how she'd ended up here: which route she'd taken, or at what point she'd known what she was doing. But access to the black box wasn't readily available, so the ninety minutes she'd spent on a bus looking out at the unwinding landscape, the disappearing slip roads, and finally the factory walls and rotating billboards that lined the road into the capital currently existed in a fog. It was earlier events that stained her eyelids every time she blinked, like a snuff movie showing in her head. It happened again now. She blinked, and for a fraction of a second saw it all in lurid slow motion. Ben slipped; gravity pulled. Then something bloomed in the barren morning, and Jaime lost his head, its contents splashing across the rainbow-crayoned sign red and grey, red and grey, while pigeons lifted from the local trees, their wings mowing the air.

The fox was nowhere to be seen.

Look both ways before crossing the road. This was a sign of how out of touch with the City she'd become: regulars never looked both ways; they looked the relevant way first, and got as far as they could. Worried about the second half later. Above her head a walkway angled into a maze of concrete and brick-work. Ahead of her, the bank: DFM. DeJohn Franklin Moers. And just to one side – curious how often this happened in the City – hid a quiet little mews; a lane she'd wandered down, sandwich in hand, more lunchtimes than she could put a number to. That had probably happened in dull weather as often as not, but the way she recalled it now, those lunches had always been sunny.

She hadn't eaten today. It didn't matter. She reached the other side, and walked into the lobby of the bank.

When Jaime's head exploded, it had done so in slow motion. Maybe Louise's responses had become cinematised. There'd been, it felt now, a swelling in the atmosphere; a wave sucking back on a pebbly beach. All the sound dragged out of the air, as if she were hearing everything through the wrong end of an ear trumpet. And she'd remembered what he'd said earlier: that he'd use the gun. He'd spoken truly. But she'd been looking into his eyes as he'd spoken, and was sure that what he'd meant was, he'd use it on himself.

As for the aftermath, there'd been that same atmospheric swelling. All the noise rushed back into the air at once: the noise of horror, fear and disgust, with an undercurrent of satis-fied cruelty, that withered to nothing as the coppery smell of blood filtered past the cordon.

Louise had never watched anybody die before.

Stepping into DFM was like what? Going back to school? If she'd been asked this morning for her worst moment, Louise would have said: her last day at the bank. Everyone had known the details; no one spoke them aloud. Multimillion harassment suits weren't uncommon in the Square Mile, and battle lines were sharply drawn. It wasn't that her colleagues favoured Crispin over her; it was just that they had mortgages and coke habits to feed. Louise had never had the slightest intention of heading down the litigation corridor – the idea of reprising her love life in open court filled her with disgust – but at the time it hadn't occurred to her that this was on anyone's mind. Later it explained the attitudes she met. Women she'd thought friends ducked out of her way or looked right through her; the men displayed open contempt or else hit on her, hoping for a rebound shag. There'd been a short career's worth of desk junk to stuff in a box; there'd been a security gauntlet to run – the desk junk itemised before she was allowed to remove it from the building. Yes: before this morning, that day would have made her top worst, no problem.

Not much had changed. Big lobby, full of wasted space, with a water feature in one corner: seventeen shades of grey gravel and a fountain. Four lifts behind the security guard: one for senior execs exclusively; men too important to stop on floors not their own. 'Men' used advisedly. Lots of glass, lots of light – where banks of old had relied on Latin and stone to inspire confidence, the new ones flung glass and light about to demonstrate the transparency of their dealings. This, too, was part of the big fuck-off.

Louise approached Reception, from whose desk a young blonde woman smiled at her: black jacket, white shirt; ever so slightly over-made up. HR, she used to think, didn't so much hire these people as download them.

'Can I help you?'

'I'd like to see Crispin Tate.'

(Why would she have thought that – that Jaime had been ready to use the gun on himself?

Because he'd been scared. Two men had tried to kill him: he'd been chased round Marble Arch and wound up in a lay-by with a thug and a gun. Next thing he was the villain of the piece, a hundred armed coppers aching for his scalp. And all because he'd been involved with, been the lover of, the wrong man.

Why did that sound familiar?)

'Do you have an appointment?'

'No. But he'll see me.'

Of course he will, the girl's smile lied. 'And you are?'

Louise told her.

From over by the lifts, the security guard was watching. But that was what security guards were for.

The girl hit some keys, then looked up from her monitor. 'I'm sorry, Ms Kennedy. Mr Tate isn't in the building this afternoon.'

'Are you sure?'

'I can leave a note on his calendar that you called.'

She had a sudden vision of how that would work: *Louise Kennedy called, and just look at the date.* Would he even remember it was their anniversary? If that's what you still had, after you were over.

'That's all right. No. Wait.' This could all just fade away; she could head back home, resolve broken. By tomorrow all her suspect certainties would have dissipated the way dreams do, even the good ones. Jaime would still be dead, though. And there'd be blood etched into the annexe door, no matter how hard it was scrubbed.

And she did not want Crispin thinking she'd dropped by because of the date.

'Okay. Tell him I was here.'

Behind the guard, the lift door opened, and a woman stepped out.

'Tell him I wanted to ask about the money. Oh, and to find out what happened to Miro.'

'Miro?'

'M-I-R-O. It's not complicated.'

'Louise?'

She knew that voice, but didn't turn. 'Did you get all that?'

'I think so.' The girl's tone would have cut glass if set side-ways.

'I'm so relieved.' Now she turned. 'Charlie,' she said.

'It is you.'

'Yes. But do you mind if we don't do the air-kiss thing?' This to forestall Charlie Stubbs, who was leaning in. A hurt, puzzled look swept across an expensively made-up if horsey face. 'It's just, I remember last time I was here. It's not so much that you didn't say goodbye. It's more that you hid in the toilet till I'd gone.'

This small triumph carried her out to the street, where whatever she'd thought she might achieve by coming here floated up before her eyes and popped like a bubble. If it was true, what could she have done about it anyway? If Crispin had realised his dream, and created actual money out of nothing – out of a digital stream of stolen pixels – what would have been gained by standing in front of him, and telling him she knew? Nothing, except – well, except the obvious. That it would have been her, standing in front of him, telling him she knew. Telling him she'd won.

Better that he hadn't been there. Ben Whistler had the story, anyway. Jaime was dead, but his story wouldn't die with him.

And here she was, standing on the pavement, wondering what she did now, when she saw she was being watched – that a man on the pavement opposite had been leaning against the wall, but was upright now. Upright, but not very tall.

The smaller man—

That's Bad Sam.

Traffic passed, strobing her view. He was short, dark, suited, smoking, though he tossed his cigarette into the gutter as she watched, then looked right, waiting for a gap to cross the road.

Miro is not a thief.

Maybe Bad Sam forced him to do it.

He torture him?

I wouldn't put it past him.

There were God alone knew how many short dark men in the world, and a racing certainty that the City had its share. But she knew this was him, and he was heading towards her. And she knew why, too.

She was a loose end.

A few hours earlier, the nursery annexe had been sealed off as if it were the birthplace of a brand new virus. Peter Faulks was in charge; Fredericks was back at the station. The boss wanted Ben Whistler in a locked room, with a tape recorder running.

'You won't have him long,' Faulks had said.

'I'll have him long enough.'

'He's Six. The heavy mob'll be at the door before you've got his name out of him.'

'I already know his name.'

You think? Faulks had wondered. 'Sir,' he'd said.

The Pedlars and Judy Ainsworth had been taken off in cars; one period of enforced incarceration giving way to another. They'd be fed, watered, and have every last memory of the morning squeezed out of them.

As for Louise Kennedy . . .

'You what?'

'She asked for another cup of tea. I went to get her one.'

Jesus Mary and Joseph.

'And when you got back she was gone.'

The officer bit a lip. A man had been shot dead twenty yards from where he'd been standing, and all he'd done was fetch a cup of tea for a victim. 'I didn't think she was under arrest, sir.'

'You didn't think, full stop.'

'Sir.'

'Find her.'

'Sir.'

Joseph Mary and Jesus. That had been 1:20, and the clown had returned within fifteen minutes: 'She's not here.'

'She lives down the road. Get her.'

Press was everywhere, squeezing past the cordons. One bullet had declared open season. This clown was in the right place. Today was a circus.

And then the spook appeared out of nowhere, right in front of him. 'I thought you'd been called back to heel.'

'Somebody got their wires crossed. I've been sitting tight. Observing.'

'Having fun yet?'

'Who popped him?' Chapman asked.

'The boy was holding a gun to your colleague's temple. A highly trained marksperson did what they were trained to do.'

Chapman raised an eyebrow. 'A woman?'

'Whistler's been taken to St Aldate's. I doubt he'll be there long. A big curtain's about to be dropped over everything, and guess what? It's us neds will be told we fucked up. So why don't you piss off somewhere else, and let us get on with our jobs.'

'Did you fuck up?' Chapman offered Faulks a cigarette. 'The hostages got out.'

'We've got a body on the doorstep of a nursery school. How do you think the leader writers will play it?'

'I assume you've got tapes.'

Faulks was shaking his head already: 'In your dreams. They're our property until you get a warrant says otherwise. Speaking of which, you picked my pocket. That was an expensive gadget.'

'I thought I'd be seeing Whistler before you did. Sorry about that.'

'Like hell.' He changed his mind and took the cigarette. 'So what did this kid do, anyway? Why did you want him in the first place?'

'Listen to your tapes.'

'Whistler junked the mobile. Then played nursery rhymes to drown the directionals. Whatever they were talking about, they didn't want anyone to hear.' Faulks raised an eyebrow. 'Doesn't look like any of us are on the same side, does it?'

'Did the name Weiss crop up?'

'What if I don't know? Will you fake another heart attack?' The spook offered his lighter so suddenly, Faulks flinched.

'Sir?'

The officer was back, the one who'd misplaced Louise Kennedy. Nothing about his expression suggested he'd found her since.

'She's not at her mother's.'

'For God's sake.' Faulks dropped the cigarette he'd barely singed. 'Crowd control,' he said. 'Now.' He watched while the relieved officer jogged off to join his colleagues. 'That's just great.'

'Oh, don't blame yourself,' Chapman said.

Faulks said, 'Your colleague, the one who was hit by the car. How's he doing?'

'Last I heard, he was still alive.'

'Pretty impressive. Three of you turn up in our patch this morning. It's barely lunchtime, and one of you's dead, one's in intensive care, and the third's a fucking twat. And it's us who'll be told we did things wrong.'

'You want to watch that temper. Next heart attack round here might not be faked.'

'The boy over there,' Faulks said. 'The one under the sheet.'

The body was still *in situ*; forensics were dotting i's, crossing t's.

'What about him?'

'There was no reason for him to die.'

'It was one of your lot pulled the trigger.'

'You can hide behind that as much as you want. But it's you who's responsible. We both know that.'

Chapman scanned the nursery grounds: a lot of activity, none of it amounting to much. It was the kind of mess you got when something's over, and no one's quite sure what the something was. For most of those here, even the cops, the body by the annexe was the first they'd seen. Factor in violent death, and the number dropped. Factor in gunshot, and it dropped still more. But there was a learning curve in every profession, and Chapman wasn't here to offer counselling.

'I didn't put the gun in his hand,' he said.

He dropped the cigarette, and walked away.

But not to the police station. He'd been there already this morning, and hadn't enjoyed it. Besides, it was easy to bluff someone who wasn't checking. Faulks had swallowed his lie because, right now, he didn't care. But if Sam Chapman turned up at St Aldate's waving ID, they'd check with Vauxhall Cross before letting him through the front door. And Vauxhall Cross wanted him home.

He had to know what had gone on in that nursery this morning. What had been said. Why Whistler had kept it quiet. And as Whistler was out of bounds, along with Pedlar and the cleaner and the two little kids, that left just one option.

He'd have to find Louise Kennedy instead.

A taxi pulled up in front of her. How often did that happen? But before she could reach for the door handle, a voice behind her said, 'This one's mine.'

Charlie Stubbs, immaculate if horsey, nodded 'Stubbs' to the driver through his window, and pulled the door open.

There was still no gap in the traffic, and the man across the road hadn't taken his eyes off her.

Louise said, 'You couldn't give me a lift, could you?'

'A lift?'

'It's important.'

'You were rude to me.'

'Yes. But now I need a lift.'

Charlie shook her head, but she wasn't saying *No*. She was saying, *Get the nerve on this*. 'You were here to see him, weren't you?'

Louise didn't have to ask who *he* was. 'Yes.'

'But they wouldn't let you in.'

'Can we discuss this in the taxi, Charlie?'

London: you couldn't count on the traffic keeping moving. Any moment now, he'd be over the road . . .

'Charlie?'

'Get in.'

The driver didn't wait for instructions: Charlie had booked him; he knew where he was going. They were inside the car, and the car was moving. It didn't move far – were yards from the junction – but it moved, and there were doors involved now; there was a metal shell around her. For the moment, this passed for safety.

'I didn't hide in the toilet.'

'What?'

'Could you do your belt up, lady?'

They both looked at the driver.

'You have to do your belt up.'

Louise pulled the seatbelt across her chest just as the car in front moved. She fumbled with the catch, and then they were mobile again, turning the corner; joining the stream of traffic on the main drag.

She turned and looked through the rear window. She couldn't see the man. Had he really been watching? There were lots of dark men in the City.

Charlie Stubbs said again, 'I didn't hide in the toilet.'

'What does that mean?'

'It's what you said. You said I hid in the toilet. The day you were fired. But I didn't.'

'If you say so.'

'I do say so.'

How many times in the last six months had she stepped into a conversation like this? *Yes you did/No I didn't/Yes you did* . . . The discourse of infants. 'I don't blame you, Charlie. Anyway, it was ages ago. A year. Forget about it.'

'You obviously haven't.'

'I don't brood on it. Where's this taxi going, exactly?'

'It's a taxi. Where do you want it to go?'

'Your taxi.'

'For God's sake, Louise, where do you want to be dropped?'

'Are you heading west?'

'Well, of course.'

'Anywhere west will do.'

She restrained herself from looking through the back window again; then she didn't – it was the usual welter of heavy metal and busy pedestrians: Louise couldn't get a fix on any individual. If Bad Sam was running after them, she'd probably notice. But if he'd flagged down his own taxi, the old follow-that-cab routine, he could be yards away, and she wouldn't know.

'I worried about you, you know.'

'Sure you did.'

'Why are you being so unpleasant?'

Louise turned to face her. 'Are you joking me?' A construction straight out of the Darlings' phrase book. She tried again: 'Are you kidding?'

'You had a bad time, we all knew that. Do you think we didn't care? You should have taken them to tribunal, Louise. You could've hung them out to dry. It happens.'

'You didn't care. If you cared, you'd have called.'

'I did call,' Charlie said.

'That's not the way I remember it.'

'I called twice. Left messages you never replied to. So if you want to get technical, you're the one who didn't call me.'

316

The taxi had come to another halt: this time at lights, with enough traffic in front of them that it could take several changes to get through. The outside world had an artificial orange glow. They were under the bulk of the Barbican. Engine noises, echoing round the tunnelled road, made it sound as if they were in a starting line-up, but London traffic often felt like that.

'I did call,' Charlie repeated.

Well, that was okay. She had her version. Louise knew which was true.

'Somebody said you're teaching now.'

'Somebody was right.'

'Are you enjoying it?'

Louise said, 'Yes. Yes, I am.'

Charlie looked a little wistful. 'I used to think I'd teach.'

'So why didn't you?'

'It seemed too hard.'

'It is hard,' Louise said. 'But at least the pay's crap.'

The taxi jolted. She looked out the side window. Across the road she saw a hurrying man, and her breath caught. But he was fair, and carrying a briefcase; and round here, if you weren't in a hurry, you weren't going anywhere.

'Are you still in touch with him?'

And now Louise had to look her full in the face, because there was no other way she could express her total amazement. 'Am I *what*?'

'Do you talk to him ever?'

'Well, of course I bloody—no. No, I haven't spoken to him in a year.'

'He's getting divorced, you know.'

The taxi came to a halt again, still on the bad side of the lights. And maybe that was the reason her heart thumped, but probably wasn't: he was getting divorced . . . Crispin was getting a divorce. For as long as it took the words to vanish, this whole vista opened up in Louise's heart: Crispin had realised he couldn't live without her; was sorting out his domestic mess before he came to weep his apologies, explain his new freedom. Christ, she'd feel his throat beneath her heel. The notion died even before Charlie said what Charlie said next, which was:

'It's this new associate, Karla she's called. Was she at DFM when you were still there? I can't remember.'

Louise said, 'You're a beautiful woman, Charlie. Never believe them when they tell you otherwise.'

'I'm only—'

'Thanks for the lift.'

She nearly caught a cyclist with the door. Charlie was speaking, and the taxi driver had an opinion, but Louise was on the pavement before either mattered; was across the junction before the lights changed again. At the entrance to the Tube someone tried to give her a newspaper, but she pushed past; was in the lobby seconds later. Another couple of minutes passed in fumbling for change and coaxing a ticket from a machine. She'd sort out destinations once she was sitting on a train

Already, the station was busy. When she'd worked round here, it was a big day if she was out of the building before six. Here it was, barely past five, and the platform was seizing up. She walked to the far end, and waited in weak daylight until the sledgehammer-echo of the track announced a train's approach, spending those minutes not thinking about Crispin, who, towards the end of their relationship, had talked less and less on work-related subjects; had worn a furrowed look when the subject of their common employment came up, and had often seemed lost in contemplation of unspecified difficulties. Though not without a sometime glint in his eye. The bastard. *Karla, she's called. A new associate.* Not that new, because Louise remembered her: young, of course, and with the kind of pale skin–dark hair combination that brought to mind fairy tales.

The bastard. And she herself had been just a sub-plot; a link in the chain connecting Crispin to his future. *He's getting divorced, you know.* She knew now.

She was on the train without having noticed getting on. The seat configuration indicated it was a Metropolitan Line, which meant she should change at King's Cross: such considerations ticked away at the back of her mind without conscious input. She should change at King's Cross, catch one of the westbound lines; get a bus back to Oxford. Assure her mother she was fine. Talk to the police, because the police would want to talk to her, right? Tell them everything that had happened, except those bits that had to do with Crispin, because Crispin was getting a divorce; Crispin was marrying somebody else. Which meant Crispin hadn't had anything to do with what had happened this morning, yes? Her suspicions had partly been based on his odd behaviour, but that behaviour had a different cause; his guilt was born elsewhere. Except, except, it was possible for more than one thing to happen at once, and if Louise was the lady – *you are the lady, yes* – it could only be Crispin who had made her so. She should have stayed in the taxi. Should have wrung every last scrap of fact out of Charlie Stubbs. Though at least she'd shaken her follower off, if he'd ever been that in the first place.

Farringdon was behind her already; people were clustering at the doors, ready for a quick getaway. The woman who'd been next to her stood, and a man slipped into the freed-up space. Louise glanced at the overhead map, wondering which line to change on to, and felt a hand take her by the arm.

'Let's not make a fuss,' he said. 'There's a card in my pocket says I'm MI6. And in today's climate, who's going to believe a suspected terrorist on a Tube train?'

Just another day at the office.

Ben stepped out of a helicopter for the second time in his

life, and felt a Soho rooftop beneath his feet, a moment before feeling a hand on his elbow. Moody, the hand belonged to. Service Dog. Who had turned up to rescue him from the Blue Brigade back in Oxford, but wasn't the kind of rescuer you wanted to fling your arms around.

He'd shown Fredericks – the cop in charge – ID, then offered him his mobile phone. 'You don't have to take my word for it,' he'd said. 'Sir.'

Ben hadn't known who was down the line, but could guess.

Fredericks had said into Moody's phone, 'There was a shooting. He was involved. I need to know exactly what—'

This was back at the local station. Ben hadn't been arrested, but hadn't been treated like an innocent party either.

'That's all very well, but—'

Maybe twenty-five officers had been crowding the lobby, and there'd been a low-level hubbub. Ben had been standing where he'd been told to, near a set of security doors, prior to being taken through them and escorted to Superintendent Malcolm Fredericks' office, when he'd felt himself the subject of a piercing stare. He'd turned, seen a blonde woman in what was probably firearms gear – several shades of black, tightly cuffed at wrist and ankle – and had felt himself a target. As if her gaze staked out an area all her own, and by being in its ambit, he was in trouble.

She'd looked away. Ben had felt a draught kiss his cheek, but that was just the door opening.

Fredericks was saying, 'I don't care who you are, I'll be making an official complaint about this.'

Moody had raised an eyebrow. A helicopter passed low over the building.

Fredericks slapped the mobile into Moody's palm. To Ben, he'd said, 'You'll be back. Twenty-four hours.'

'Of course.'

'I want to know everything that happened in there. You're going to tell me.'

There'd been something fizzing in his eyes, and his teeth shone wet when his lips drew back.

Moody, leading him out of the station, had said, 'They can throw all the toys out the pram they want, but if they think they're screwing with a Service op, they're out of their tinies.'

'It wasn't exactly an op.'

'Was now.'

'Where's Bad Sam?'

'That's Mr Chapman to you.'

On the flight back, they'd barely spoken. Moody chewed gum mostly, probably for effect. Ben noticed he avoided looking out of the window. But once they'd touched down on the Department rooftop, he had his hand on Ben's elbow. 'Downstairs.'

Ben shook his arm free. 'As opposed to?'

Moody's expression said, what?

'Never mind.' Ben dragged a hand through his shaggy hair, then examined it, his face blank. 'I was right next to him,' he said. 'I've got his blood on me.'

'Jesus, Whistler.'

'Maybe brain, too.' Ben wasn't kidding; his fingers felt slick. Jaime's memories, thoughts and desires had been sprayed into the open air; some of them were smeared on Ben Whistler's fingers now. The boy had been, what, twenty years old? Never get older now.

'I slipped,' he said.

'You what?'

Ben hadn't realised he'd spoken aloud. 'I need to clean up. That's all.'

Moody was giving him more space since learning he was carrying Jaime's blood. He flinched as the 'copter took off. 'I'm right behind you.'

Ben reached the door to the stairwell just as Reggie came through it. 'You're back.'

'That'll be those powers of observation I've heard about.' He felt light-headed, but what could he expect, fragments of someone else's history all over him?

'Nott wants to see you.'

'Why am I not surprised?'

'Basically, he wants to see you now.'

'Did anyone ever tell you you overuse that word?'

Reggie looked at Moody. 'Has he been drinking?'

'Where's Bad Sam?' Ben asked.

'Not here.'

'He's not here?'

'I mean,' said Reggie, 'we don't talk about that here.'

Moody said, 'He says he needs to clean up.'

'It's not a fucking audition, Whistler. You're about to be debriefed.'

They were on the stairs, clattering down: Reggie, Ben, Moody.

'There's probably blood,' Ben said. 'Soft matter. The boy looked healthy, till someone shot him. But he didn't have a careful lifestyle. If you get my drift.'

Reggie paused on the first landing: Nott's floor. 'This boy was Weiss's pop-tart, is that true?'

'You need to brush up your slang, Reggie.'

'Rinse off. Then Nott's office. Five minutes.' He looked at Moody. 'Watch him. I think our Ben's a little spaced out.' He visibly swallowed the word *basically* before disappearing through the swing door.

Ben said, 'I keep a clean shirt in my desk drawer.'

'Why am I not surprised?' Moody asked.

King's Cross had changed since last time she'd been here, when large parts of it had felt like a public urinal. It was cleaner now;

brightly lit. Had more flights of stairs. Bad Sam Chapman took her by the arm: as they'd stepped off the Tube, he'd applied the faintest pressure, and pain had scampered up her shoulder and into her skull, like a squirrel in a tree.

'You'll stay quiet.'

She couldn't speak.

'You won't run, won't make a fuss.'

He shifted grip, and pain vanished the way toothache can: seventy to zero in 0.1.

'You'll stick with me.'

Bastard . . .

It was alarming how easy this was: a man assaulted a woman on a rush-hour platform, and nobody noticed.

All these people, weaving past; each and every one in a private bubble.

He led her up the same stairs everyone else was taking. At the top, various directions offered themselves: St Pancras, more Underground lines, the main line station itself. Chapman seemed to be heading that way, along with a healthy fraction of the crowd – this new wide walkway with its gleaming tiles made King's Cross feel like an airport. They passed a transport policeman, but that painful squirrel reminded her *You'll stay quiet*, so she made no sound. Just before they reached the stairs to the concourse Chapman pulled her aside, towards a lift. He jabbed a finger, stabbed a button. Its doors opened.

'I'm not getting—'

And there was the pain again, squirrelling into her head. It robbed her of any ability to make a noise, and she was in the lift before she knew it: not a big lift – not meant for shuttling heavy cargo floor to floor. His body was close to hers. The door hummed shut, and Chapman pressed a button: she didn't see what. The lift began to move up. And shuddered to a halt two seconds later as he prised the inner doors open, and jammed his foot between them.

A tiny room, unmoving, between floors.

She said, 'What do you want?' Her voice was a scratchy recording on an old machine.

'I didn't want to hurt you. But I didn't want you making a scene.'

'So why—'

'How much does Whistler know?' he asked.

'About what?'

'What did the boy tell him?'

'What makes you think he told him anything?'

Bad Sam Chapman made a regretful noise which could have been read in a number of ways, but mostly meant *don't piss me off*. 'He produced a backing track, and not because he likes nursery rhymes. He didn't want the conversation to be overheard. So what were they talking about?'

'You're a spy, right?'

Spy, bully, civil servant, whatever: he loomed close to her, and seemed much taller in this enclosed space.

'More questions. I work for the security services. You either start supplying answers, or find yourself in trouble.'

'So take me in.'

'I'm not a policeman. I take you in, you won't be offered a nice cup of tea while we wait for your lawyer. You'll tell us everything we want to hear. It won't be pleasant. For you or me both.'

'But it's not going to happen, is it?'

'And why's that?'

'Because there's just you and me here. You're all on your own.'

'Don't you get it? I've arrested you.'

'That's not what this is.'

'It's what it'll look like.' He was standing awkwardly, facing her, but with his foot jammed into the door at a right angle. He had dark, lank hair. His skin was pale, and his suit smelled of cigarettes. This both repelled her and triggered her nicotine centre, and she had to bite down hard on that sudden desire, and on fear, and on panic.

'You tried to kill him,' she said. Her voice was coming back: was bordering on normal. Or as normal as anything the day had offered so far.

'I tried to kill who?'

'Jaime. Jaime . . .' Jaime's surname escaped her. 'Segunda. Segora. You know who I'm talking about.'

'I thought a cop killed him.'

'You're disgusting.'

'Because I didn't kill Jaime Segura?'

'You chased him, last night. At Marble Arch. Then tried to shoot him in a lay-by.'

'Obviously I missed. What else did he say?'

'That you don't like loose ends.'

'Huh.' He'd produced a cigarette from somewhere, though she hadn't seen his hand move. He looked down at it, unlit between his fingers. 'That doesn't sound like anything Segura would say. We only met once, and he was in a hurry. No, it was Ben Whistler told you that. What else did he say?'

She'd let him bring her here, into a room the shape of an upright coffin: she should have screamed her head off out there in the station. Perhaps the thought wrote itself on her face, because he was shaking his head at her:

'This isn't a game. What else did he tell you?'

'He said . . . He said you were duty officer last night. That that's how you intercepted Jaime's phone call.'

'He said that, did he?'

'That's how you found Jaime.'

'Well, almost. Actually, I wasn't duty officer. Neil Ashton was.'

'Who's he?'

325

'A soon to be former colleague.' He tucked his cigarette in his breast pocket. 'Loose ends,' he said. 'I think—'

'*Hello in the lift?*'

There was the usual hum on the floor, which broke when Ben entered. Moody hung by the door while Ben rooted around his cubicle, gathering the emergency kit he kept for unexpected dates or games of squash: washbag, clean shirt.

Rob Burke leaned across from the next workstation. 'What's happening, Ben?'

'Doing something for Nott,' he said, without looking up.

'They've found Miro?'

Ben shrugged. Finding his mobile nestled among desk junk, he slipped it into his pocket. 'Not that they've told me.'

He was expecting Chapman to show any moment. *He doesn't like loose ends*, he'd told Louise Kennedy.

It hadn't happened yet, but that didn't mean it wasn't about to.

There was a shower room on the first floor. On the way, Moody said, 'Three minutes and counting.'

'That joke's going to stale pretty fast.'

'What did the kid tell you about Weiss?'

'I'm about to be, Reggie called it *debriefed*. I'm sure he'll keep you in the loop.'

'Two minutes,' Moody said.

'Is Chapman up there now?'

'One fifty-eight.'

Ben slammed the door behind him, leaving Moody in the hall.

He removed his shirt, stuffed it in the bin, then pushed his head under a shower jet for fifteen seconds. Did anything of Jaime rinse away down the plughole? He shook his head like a dog; ran his fingers through his hair. The clean shirt clung to his shoulders. Turning a tap on to cover his voice, he rang the Queen of the Database.

326

'Benedict. You're back.'

'Tina, I've lost Moody. We're supposed to be in Nott's office any moment.'

'And you can't remember the way?'

'He just got me out of a jam. I don't want to drop him in it. Could you beep him?'

'Seeing it's you asking.'

Ben had messages waiting, but didn't have time to read them. 'Forty-five seconds,' he said, as he emerged from the washroom. 'That may be a record.'

Moody opened his mouth, but his phone trilled before any noise came out. He turned aside to answer it.

If your situation calls for violence, an unforgotten course had instructed Ben, *first distract the target.*

'Moody,' Moody said into his mobile.

Ben hooked his foot between Moody's legs and threw his weight against the man's back.

The corridor wasn't wide. Moody's head hit the wall, met Ben's forearm on the rebound, and his eyes googled. His phone kissed the air and fell for the floor. Ben hit him again en route. In truth, this wasn't so much unforgotten training as well-remembered rugby days, but you go with what works. Moody's eyes flickered *Page unavailable*, and he logged out.

The nearest door opened. An unfamiliar face leaned out. 'Who—?'

'I think he's choking,' Ben said. 'Do you know the recovery position?'

'What?'

'He's having a fit, for Christ's sake. Can't you help?'

'Oh—I—Yes. Of course.'

She swept out, began rearranging Moody in an approved fashion.

'He takes pills,' he said. 'Heart or something. I'll fetch them. One minute.'

Which was how long it took to conquer one flight of stairs, tap out the door code, reach the street. The man from the adult bookshop was smoking in his doorway as Ben Whistler emerged, and issued a half-hearted invitation with the slightest inclination of his head: Ben waved a regretful *forget it* without breaking stride. He picked up a cab on the corner and ditched it at the Circus, where he vanished underground. There was CCTV, there were eyes on each corner; there were, let's fucking face it, spies everywhere. But he hadn't done badly.

Bad Sam couldn't have exited much more cleanly. And it was Bad Sam Ben was thinking about as he changed lines at the first possible junction.

He doesn't like loose ends.

'Hello?'

Again, she barely saw him move, but he'd clamped a hand to her mouth before she could speak.

'Press the button on the panel, and talk into the intercom.'

Chapman used his free hand. 'What just happened?' he asked.

'The lift's stuck.' The voice came through the speaker on the panel, crackling like an ill-tuned radio. 'I'm fetching the engineer. How many of you in there?'

'Just the two.'

'We'll have you out in a jiffy.'

Bad Sam Chapman removed one hand from the button; the other from Louise's mouth.

'They'll be back,' she said.

'And you'll be good.'

'We're in the middle of a city—'

'Grow up. Besides—'

'You've got ID.'

'Which makes me the good guy. We're post-7/7, remember?'

She could faintly taste tobacco: his hand upon her mouth. 'He'll be back at your headquarters by now. Ben Whistler. It's all coming apart, don't you realise that? You might as well start running. Why did you come after me anyway?'

'Like he told you. I don't like loose ends.'

'And how did you know where to find me anyway?'

'I guessed.'

'You *guessed*?'

He said, 'All I know about you is where you live, where you work and where you used to work. You weren't at either of the first two places. So . . .'

'I could have been anywhere.'

'But you weren't. You were coming to talk to Crispin Tate, that right?'

'. . . Yes.'

'Because you figured he must have had something to do with the money Miro Weiss stole.'

'*If* Miro Weiss stole—'

'Oh, he stole it. But you think he had help from your ex-lover. And that's why Jaime Segura turned up at your nursery school.'

'Jaime said so himself. Something Miro told him. About a lady at the nursery school.'

Chapman nodded, more to himself than to her. 'Are you an only child?'

'Am I a what?'

'Do you have brothers or sisters?'

'What's that got to do with—no. No, I don't. Do you?'

'Second of four. All boys.'

'Well, that explains your ease with women.'

'Probably accounts for my competitive nature, too. I've never liked coming second.'

'Is there a point to this?'

'Something I've noticed about only children. They have a tendency to think events revolve around them. You weren't the *lady*, Ms Kennedy. You never were.'

12

I T WAS HARD NOT to wonder if anyone was watching; not to see in every stranger's stance a professional posture in disguise. Ben Whistler was upright in a full-to-bursting carriage, hurtling under the streets of London, while fragments of Service lore drifted into mind: people checking for tails tend to look beyond their immediate orbit, so a good tail hangs in close . . . Ben checked close. Hard by were an old man in a yellow cagoule; a woman with a child, five or six. An Asian kid who gave him a hard stare in return. But they couldn't be on to him yet. And if they were, they wouldn't be hiding it; they'd collect him mob-handed. They'd want to know everything that had been said between those four walls . . . They'd want to know why Jaime Segura had asked for him in the first place.

Sam Chapman, in particular, would have questions.

The tube slowed, stopped; the doors eased open. People got off, people got on. The doors shut. The train shunted forward. Ben looked round at those who'd remained, then at the new arrivals. Paranoia could be useful, and he'd need his for the foreseeable future. He couldn't ride the Underground forever.

He remembered that one time he'd been in Miro's flat. 'I don't have many friends,' Miro had said. With a lot of people, the cue would have been obvious. *Come on, man. All the guys think you're cool.* But Miro had no interest in hearing that, any more than Ben was tempted to say it. What he was thinking now was, there'd been no sign of Jaime in Miro's flat – not just of the boy himself, but of any boy: Miro's flat had been pure Miro, as if the place had been decorated to match him: boxed sets of operas; Everyman hardbacks; Klimt reproduction in the hall. But Ben had visited the bathroom, and while washing his hands had opened the cabinet over the sink. Not because he was a spy: just because it was what he did right then. He found an electric razor; a bar of soap still in its wrapper. Aspirin. Spare toothpaste. And a used toothbrush, lying on its side. He'd closed the cabinet, dried his hands, went back through to the living room, where Miro was pouring another drink.

'I've been thinking about those numbers,' Miro said as he entered, as if continuing a conversation long since started.

'Which numbers?' Ben had said. He didn't even know what he was doing here, except Miro had asked if he were free that evening, and he hadn't been quick enough to say no.

'The ones that pass across our desks,' Miro had said. 'On their way out of Iraq.'

Ben remembered an evening in the pub, months previously. 'We're not supposed to discuss this outside work,' he'd said.

'I know we're not,' Miro had said. 'But I had an idea.'

The tube came to another halt, and Ben stepped off. He stood for a moment in front of a poster advertising one of those Brit-flicks that vanish from cinemas before the hoardings are changed. Rush hour: people thronging the platform, making connections. Nobody looked at him twice.

'You've been thinking about the numbers,' he'd repeated.

'It's numbers when we see it. Somewhere, it's money.'

'And what have you been thinking?'

'I've been thinking we should take it,' Miro had said.

'Judy?'

'That's who he meant.'

'Judy *Ainsworth*?'

331

'Her husband died in Iraq. You must have known that.'

She must have. But did she? Louise thought back on what she knew and what she'd assumed, and wondered: had she even known Judy's husband was dead? She'd thought he'd left her. The information had come as no surprise. If she'd been married to Judy, she'd have left her too. 'He was a soldier?'

'Christ, no. His age?'

'So what was he doing there? And how did he die?'

Bad Sam Chapman said, 'He was an engineer.'

Contract work, Deirdre Walker had told him. *Rebuilding stuff. All that damage, it's not like they could fix it themselves.*

'He was working on a power station south-west of Baghdad.' This had come from the Queens of the Database. Deirdre Walker hadn't been big on specifics. 'A big project, obviously. It's not finished yet.'

'But it's proved expensive so far,' Louise guessed.

He said, 'This part isn't news to you, is it?'

She moved a quarter step away, and felt the wall at her back. Soon, the intercom would squawk back into life; soon he'd have to shift his foot from the door, and they'd be on the move once more. She'd be back in the world.

'What do you know about the money?' he went on.

'The missing money?' she said. 'That's where it came from. Iraq.'

'Jaime told you that?'

'Whistler did. Jaime didn't know anything, except that his boyfriend had gone missing. And that you tried to kill him.'

Chapman said, 'But Whistler knew. That's interesting. Did he know about Derek Ainsworth?'

'He wasn't mentioned.'

'Miro met him. In Iraq. Derek must have had a pretty good idea of how much money could be made over there, because he bought his way into a subcontract.'

'Bought his way in?'

'It was an American company. They were contracted to build four power stations, which must have made for a multi-billion dollar contract, but as they hadn't actually been involved in building power stations before, they had to subcontract the work.'

'But . . .'

Chapman waited.

'If they'd never done it before, how come they won the contract?'

He raised his eyes to where heaven might have been, if they hadn't been in a lift. Then said: 'Derek tendered for a piece of the sub, and no doubt threw in a bribe. He took out a big loan the same time he won the work. Cashed in his pension. Put up his house as security.' He was fiddling with his unlit cigarette again. 'The work was probably geared to take years. He must have assumed the outlay was worth it, that in the long run he'd be raking it in. But something happened which I don't suppose he was expecting.'

'What was that?' she asked.

'Our Derek fell in love,' he said.

Light was fading, and there was a hint of rain in the air, which had the effect of hurrying people up. If anyone was following him, Ben thought he'd notice.

It was less than thirty minutes since he'd clobbered Moody: more than enough time for a full alert to have been sounded. Ben didn't do operations, but knew the theory. There was enough CCTV coverage around to track a pigeon through the capital – but they had to pinpoint him first.

He crossed the main road. Loitered by a shop window: anyone following would have to break stride; or walk on, then look back. But Ben saw no one. He'd just left the Edgware Road. Now he turned down a side street, and let himself into the back door of an apartment block by tapping a code on a keypad. When the door, hydraulically sprung, closed in his wake, he felt as if a safety net had dropped over him. An illusion but a comforting one, which was all you could ask of illusions.

The flat was third floor. He took the lift, and wondered as he rose if the entire block was made up of boltholes: adulterers' pads and smugglers' roosts, only ever visited by the furtive. The lift was mirrored, and it was clear Ben would pass for furtive. It was as if another Ben Whistler hid inside his familiar skin; had been hiding there for weeks, but was only now letting himself show.

Had Miro seen that other Ben, even before Ben knew it was there? Was that why he'd made his overture?

Miro had said, 'You don't think I can do it?'

'I hadn't pictured you as a thief.'

'Disappointed?'

Ben shrugged. 'This is playtime, right? We can talk about whatever we want.'

'Or are you worried that it is a test? That I wait for you to agree to help steal a million pounds, and then I report it to Ashton. And you are out of a job in the morning.'

It was interesting that he'd specified Neil Ashton, rather than Bad Sam.

Ben had said, 'I can picture you as a thief more easily than I can picture you working with Ashton.'

Miro laughed. 'That is what I like about you, Ben. You are very honest in your responses.'

'Nice to know. But you're not being entirely straight, are you?'

'I have just asked if you want to help me steal a fortune. How straight do you want me to be?'

Ben had said, 'A million pounds? That would be like robbing a safe and just taking the spare change. Or do you think no one will notice a measly million?'

334

'A figure of speech, Ben. I wasn't asking if you wanted to be rich. I was asking if you wanted to steal some money.'

'And do what with it?' Ben had asked.

Miro had said: 'Return it to its rightful owners.'

'What's love got to do with it?'

Jesus: as soon as the words were out of her mouth . . .

Sam Chapman didn't pick it up. 'Man of his age, having spent a couple of decades outliving his welcome at home? Nothing more dangerous. Trust me.'

A faint draught wafted through the lift's wedged-open door. Noises off, too: footsteps, voices; whether from above or below, she couldn't tell.

'So he was feeling guilty. And spilled his guts to Miro Weiss.'

Chapman made a short noise that was probably a laugh. 'No, he was feeling happy. Far more dangerous. And this woman was working for Médecins Sans Frontières, so that must have pushed him further along. Poor sod was ripe for confession. I'm not certain how he bumped into Weiss, but the company he'd subcontracted to was one Weiss was, ah, looking at.'

'So Derek told him what was happening.'

Chapman said, 'It wouldn't have come as news. It wasn't like Weiss was checking on who was nicking office supplies. Derek Ainsworth would have told him the same old story, about payments made for work never done, kickbacks from companies supposed to be supplying equipment. About everyone jumping on the money-go-round instead of getting the power back on.'

'To make something happen when you turned on the tap,' Louise remembered.

'Whatever. Anyway, he spills what he knows to Miro Weiss. Probably nothing new, but it must have fattened Miro's files. And then something else happened.'

'He died,' Louise said.

'Jeep went over a landmine, or that's the official story.'

(*Some kind of landmine thing. Place is full of them, isn't it?* Deirdre Walker had said. Raising her eyebrows: what could you do? The places foreigners chose to live . . .)

'The woman died too. I wonder if that helped Miro decide to do what he did?'

Their conversation had slipped a track . . . This bastard had hurt her – not hard to guess where his nickname came from – but maybe Ben Whistler was wrong. Whatever else was happening, this man certainly believed Miro had taken the money.

She said, 'There were already people dying. Thousands of them. Children, babies . . . Why should one middle-aged man make a difference? He was only there to make money in the first place.'

'Depends how you look at it. Derek spilled his guts to Weiss, because he wanted to make a clean breast or saw a chance to make a difference. Then he died. That might have tipped a balance for Miro. There's a difference between scavenging the bodies on the battlefield, and murdering the stragglers.'

'You think Derek was murdered?'

Chapman shrugged. 'Maybe Miro did. The company Derek was subcontracted to took a big hit when the money went missing. Might have been coincidence.'

'You're guessing about a lot of this, aren't you?'

He said, 'If I wasn't, you think I'd be here?'

On the third floor, Ben Whistler let himself into a one-bedroom misery pit with a view of the neighbouring block. He drew the blinds and flipped the lights on, bringing the room into stark focus: sofa, table, empty shelves; the doorway into a kitchen barely wide enough to swing a Manx cat. *Adulterers' pads* needed revision. If the other flats resembled this, they were nowhere you'd look for romance.

'It's not supposed to be *pretty*. It's supposed to be anonymous.'
Neil Ashton had said this, giving Ben the key.

He went into the kitchen and opened the fridge, which held a bottle of vodka and nothing else. An upside-down glass rested on the draining board. He rinsed it, half filled it with vodka. He'd had nothing to eat since the Middle Ages, and needed a clear head, but needed alcohol more; needed the jolt as it scorched its way clear to his stomach. He wasn't a big vodka drinker, but it had been a long day.

'Every joe needs a safe house,' Ashton had said.

'That's what I am now? A joe?'

'It's an operation. You might need a bolthole.'

Ben had said: 'If things go wrong, you mean.'

'Nothing's going to go wrong.'

Words uttered more than a month ago, but would do for famous last ones: spoken by a man now tethered to a hospital bed.

Things could change in a month, sure, and also in less than a second. Ashton had been himself one moment, and smeared across tarmac the next. And Jaime Segura had been as good as bolted to Ben just a few short hours ago; close enough for Ben to feel Jaime's heat through his clothing as well as Jaime's empty gun at his head. And then the world had changed: Ben had hit the ground. A bullet space later, Jaime had joined him.

And then, of course, there was Miro . . .

I wasn't asking if you wanted to be rich. I was asking if you wanted to steal some money.

'And do what with it?' Ben had asked.

Return it to its rightful owners . . .

The vodka had completed its burning journey; he was waiting for its soothing effects to begin. They were slow in coming. *Return it to its rightful owners . . .* Who would have thought it: Miro the Mouse had come back from Iraq blazing with righteous

337

fury. Fury he hid because he intended acting on it. But in the end had to share, because he couldn't do it all on his own.

'It is not just theft they are committing. It's murder. People are dying, children are dying, because of what they're doing.'

'I understand that, Miro.'

'I met a man – he went out there to make money. No, let us face facts. He went there to get rich. And even he couldn't stomach it. He went to make as much money as he could, and he did not like what he saw.'

'Enough to give the money back?'

'He did not get the chance. He died.'

Another of those split-second moments that change everything.

But there were things it was best not to dwell on right now. Not if he was to put together the last shattered remnants of what had once been a plan.

Margaritas, señoritas, *hasta la vista*s . . .

Ben re-rinsed the vodka glass, and replaced it on the draining board. Then went into the similarly grim bedroom, with its stripped-to-the-mattress single bed, and opened the fitted cupboard against one wall, where a strongbox was built into the ground-level shelf of the fitted cupboard.

Sinking to one knee, Ben keyed its combination.

'Ben would have known about this, wouldn't he?'

'About Derek Ainsworth?'

'Yes.'

Bad Sam shrugged. 'I'd assume Miro told him.'

'So he'd have known Judy was the reason Jaime was there. That that was the connection he was making.'

Ben, she'd said. *If Chapman did have someone helping him, someone who knew how to shift money around – I think I know who it was.*

Ben had said: Because you're the lady in the nursery . . .

338

'But he pretended he thought it was me. Why would he do that?'

Chapman looked like he had a place to go to where he thought things through – his brow pulled tighter and his eyes became stones. The squawking intercom dragged him back: 'Hello in the lift?'

He put a hand to the button. 'We're still here.'

'Is there anything obstructing the door?'

He looked down at his foot doing just that. 'No.'

'Damn . . . Look, we'll have you out in a jiffy, okay?'

Louise said, 'Tell me again how you found me.'

Chapman released the button. 'Like I said. You weren't at any of the other places I knew about.'

'Because I'd gone to DFM, to confront Crispin.'

'What is this, a state the obvious contest?'

'He encouraged me,' Louise said. 'Ben. He wanted me to come after Crispin.'

Chapman was still partly in his thinking place. His voice might have been coming through a pipe. 'You went back in when you didn't have to.'

'What's that got to do with it?'

'He knew he could trust you to do the right thing. Or what you thought was the right thing. Which in this case meant coming to DFM. Confronting Crispin.'

'So you'd follow me,' she said, reconnecting with her train of thought.

'Instead of him. Sowing confusion. You'd think he was a field agent.'

'But you don't, do you?'

'No,' Chapman said. 'I think he's a thief.'

Ben keyed the number and, as the strongbox door swung open, rocked back on his heels. Paused. Through the windows came the usual squabble: traffic, weather, London. He reached inside.

Yes. That was what he'd said to Miro. *Yes. I'll help you. We'll take the money back.*

Another of those life-changing moments. Often you only recognise them in retrospect. That one, he'd given thought to in advance.

There'd been the possibility, of course, that it was indeed a set-up; that Miro was trailing a coat in the dust, to see if Ben would jump on it. Miro had even suggested as much: but then, he would, wouldn't he? Hints within clues within stories. The kind of game the bosses played, when they were working out whether you were destined for greatness or heading for the door. But Miro the Mirror Man wasn't the bosses' tool. He'd been strictly a number-juggler.

And Ben hadn't been in the frame for greatness.

So it was an honest approach: what next? Miro was smart enough to work out how to fool the numbers: Ben didn't doubt that. All he'd need from Ben was one brief moment of corroboration . . . Of course, they could wind up behind bars, or worse. Not everything finished in court. And supposing they got away with it: what was the upside? A ripped-off country got some of its money back? Ben doubted it would set up many roadside chapels in his honour.

Miro Weiss, there was no denying, was a good man, with ideals chiselled on his heart in stone. Ben Whistler, on the other hand, had a future to consider.

He reached into the safe. First thing his hand touched was a gun.

It was strange how the light in the room seemed to flicker.

'Miro must have trusted him.' Louise was thinking out loud. 'And said as much to Jaime – something like, anything happens to me, go to Ben Whistler for help. And he mentioned Judy, too. The lady in the nursery. Why would he have done that?'

'Guilt,' Bad Sam said. 'He reported what Ainsworth told him, and Ainsworth died. You don't have to be a genius to spot the connection. See it Miro's way. If Ainsworth hadn't gone to Iraq, he'd not have met his new woman. Wouldn't have abandoned his wife, who wouldn't have gone to work in the nursery . . .'

'I wonder what made him become a thief.'

'It wouldn't surprise me,' he said, 'if he planned to give the money back.' He put the cigarette he was holding in his mouth. 'I need to smoke this.'

'Not in here.'

He didn't light it. 'He made you think it was me, didn't he? Whistler.'

'You hurt my arm.'

'It's not the worst thing I've done today.'

'You were there this morning. You tried to kill Jaime.'

'Ashton did. Neil Ashton. He didn't want me there. Not a lot he could do about it though, me being his boss.' He leaned back against the lift wall. 'Miro was a clever sod, but we're supposed to be able to find clever sods. It's our job. Made me wonder if we were trying hard enough. And I knew I was. So maybe Ashton wasn't.'

'How long had you suspected him?'

'Not long enough.' He inhaled on his unlit cigarette. 'The three of them were in it together, but there wasn't much trust there. Ashton was monitoring Ben's calls.'

'And you were monitoring Ashton.'

'He was duty officer last night. Any unusual calls, he should have alerted me about. He didn't.'

'But you knew anyway.'

'I checked the call-log.' He paused. 'I think the first he knew about Jaime Segura was last night. He must have been crapping himself, wondering how much the kid knew.' He tucked his cigarette in his shirt pocket. 'Miro was a fall guy. He'll turn up sooner or later, in a car boot or a pothole. Maybe the same pothole Jaime was hiding in. Where he should have stayed.'

'But if they stole this money, Whistler and Ashton, they did it weeks ago. Why're they still here?'

'Same reason Miro isn't.' She was aware again of his mixed aroma: tobacco and sweat. 'You disappear the same time as a quarter of a billion pounds, you might as well write *I did it* in lipstick on the bathroom mirror. I'll tell you something else about Whistler. He's got leave coming up. He's going abroad.'

'A foreign holiday,' she said.

'Two weeks. It would turn into forever. But he'd have two clear weeks to disappear in. No one would even think about looking until the day he didn't come back.'

The sly bugger. That was what Neil Ashton had said, when Ben had told him of Miro's plans. *The dirty sly bugger . . .* He took the gun from the safe. It had a silencer attached, giving it a clunky elongated look. The lights had stopped flickering, if they'd ever started. Ben put the gun on the floor, reached back into the safe, and drew out the false passports and matching credit cards. Ashton wouldn't be using his, of course. It would be a while before Neil Ashton used anything as complicated as a toothbrush. But the gun — that had been there for one reason only. Ashton hadn't intended Ben to be using his false passport either. He'd intended Ben to be behind him while he knelt, opened the safe, turned, and put a silenced bullet through his head. The same end that had befallen Miro. The end Ashton must have had in mind from the start.

Tell him you'll do it, Ashton had said. *You up for this, Ben? You tell him you'll do it.*

All except the part about giving the money back.

It was no shock to Louise that men could lie. So Ben Whistler had been acting all that time: okay. What she had trouble with

342

was that she wasn't the lady, and never had been. Today had started with her, of course it had. *This is where it begins.* But she'd been peripheral: no more essential than Claire Christopher, absent because of a dental appointment, or Crispin, who was simply the hook she'd grown used to reaching for, whenever something happened. None of this was about her. She'd been discarded, jilted, dumped.

And now was stuck in a lift.

The intercom squawked, and Chapman slapped a hand on it, reducing its output to static: *crrrckzz lift crrrckzzsshhh moving soonsshhh*

He said, 'Okay, anything else?'

'How can anyone steal that much money?'

'I meant information, not questions. What else did Whistler say?'

'You want me to walk out of this lift without fuss, just answer.'

She held his stare for as long as he offered it.

Chapman said, 'Christ. Okay. Look. Mostly, you can't clean someone else's account out. I mean, you can with the citizenry, but not corporations, because they're firewalled to the eyeballs, and keep close tabs on their funds. But they frequently move money around, which people mostly don't. Their money has to keep working, has to be in different places at different times, often to make the business look richer than it is. And money's vulnerable on the move. If you know how much is moving when, and have the access codes of the accounts involved, which you get with what they call Trojan software, which our guys invented – trust me, you can steal it. If you're smart enough.'

'By yourself?'

'Theoretically. But use of the access codes needs co-clearance. You'd have to switch between two computers for validation. Miro didn't need to do that. He had Whistler to help him.'

'Didn't all this leave a trail?'

'Not once Miro burned his tracks. He wasn't an idiot.'

Louise nodded. 'So, what happens now?' she asked.

'You come with me. Whistler should be back in London. The local woodentops won't have kept hold of him long.'

'And now you've heard what he was saying, you're not worried about others hearing it too.'

'Well, I wasn't about to let them hear it first.' He moved his foot and the doors hummed shut. 'You won't care, but that hurt.' The lift moved to the next floor, and the doors opened. A couple of men stood outside, one of them dismantling the control panel. Both looked in dismay at the emerging couple.

'Six–foot–high club,' Chapman said. 'Sorry to be a nuisance.'

He lit his cigarette at last as they headed for the open air.

Jonathan Nott said, 'He *what*?'

'He decked Moody. He's gone. Legged it, basically.'

'Why, for fuck's sake?'

'Moody's not clear. Except that Whistler was keen on knowing where Sam Chapman was, and not in a good way. Whistler didn't want to run into him.'

Nott stared at his desk. *I don't care if he's the last of the fucking Mohicans. If Chapman was trying, he'd have found Weiss by now.* He said, 'I've had Barrowby on the phone every ten minutes. He wanted Sam Chapman over the river.' He looked up. 'Not a euphemism, Reggie. There's a real river between here and there.'

'I remember, actually.'

'He never showed.'

'Chapman's—'

'Sam's a loose cannon, but only because he misses being a joe. He'd get more of a kick out of stealing money than spending it. And he'd have needed technical help.'

'You think he and Whistler . . .?'

'I never think anything. I wait for the facts to arrange themselves. Find them. Find them both.'

Reggie said, 'It's being done.'

On the pavement, Chapman took out his mobile. 'It's me. Yes, I know he does. Tell him I'll be back when I'm fucking ready. Is Whistler there yet?'

Louise was looking out at the mad traffic weaving in and out of itself. If you stood way high and stared down on this, it would look impossible.

'He's *what*?'

Or resemble, perhaps, a mad act of terrorism; its sole purpose to frighten the living wits out of anyone foolish enough to participate.

'Tina . . . I know he's looking and I don't fucking care. When did Whistler go AWOL?'

The city was settling into mid-evening mode; its pavement hustle equal parts workers struggling to get home, and workers struggling not to. And none of it anything to do with her; all of it happening regardless.

'Okay, Neil Ashton . . . I know he is. I was there, remember? Has he authorised use of any safe houses lately? . . . I'll hold.'

'He's gone, hasn't he?'

'On the fucking wind.' He returned to his call: 'Tina? Damn. Okay.' He killed the call, and switched off his phone. 'About an hour ago. *Damn*.'

'He's on the run.'

'Did he say anything – anything at all – about where he might go?'

'Nothing. I can't think of anything.'

'*Fuck*ing hell.'

'He's a desk man, you said so yourself. How far can he get?'

'He's not done badly so far.'

345

She said, 'He said it too.' Something vague, unimportant. 'About not being a real spy. Not jetting off everywhere like James Bond.'

He waited. 'That's it?'

'I wasn't aware I should be memorising—'

'Okay, okay.' He bit his lip. 'Christ. That means he'd head for an airport or not head for an airport, you think?'

'I doubt it's a clue.'

'Everything's a clue. In the absence of hard evidence.' He produced cigarettes again already, and she reached out: she'd had a hard day. He tapped the base of the packet, and popped one into her hand. 'A pro wouldn't go for a plane, he'd lie low as long as possible. But he's not a pro.'

She leaned forward for a light. Her first drag, like always, felt as if everything else had been prelude. 'You're over-complicating.' The word dizzied her. 'He'll either get a plane or he won't. It's fifty-fifty.'

'That's what he'll do.'

'Unless he doesn't.'

'Fuck it.' He raised a hand; drew a taxi shape in the air. 'Change of plan. Go home. We'll be in touch.'

'And that's it?'

'Whistler's broken ranks. That'll do as an admission of guilt. We'll want your statement about what happened this morning, but right now, getting him back takes priority.'

A taxi pulled up.

She said, 'Oh, what does it matter anyway? It's *money*. He stole some money. Who cares if he gets away?'

'You want him to walk away rich, that's your privilege. But you really think Whistler tripped over his feet? That it was an accident that kid got shot? Dream on.'

He climbed into the taxi, and slammed the door behind him. As the car moved away, he didn't look back.

★

Ben put Ashton's fake passport back in the safe, and pocketed his own. The pair of them were currently richer than almost anyone on the planet, but if Ashton had planned to kill Ben, it wasn't for the money. It was because he'd wanted Ben's silence, the way he'd guaranteed Miro's.

'One half of one quarter of a billion pounds,' he'd said. 'You think you get that rich without blood on your hands?'

'We can skip once it's done. Vanish.'

'With a target on our backs. No, Miro goes. We disappear once they've worn themselves out looking for him.'

'They'll still come after us.'

'But I'll have had a head start. Traffic accident in Sicily, diving tragedy in the Seychelles . . . Bye-bye Neil Ashton, hello . . . whoever.' And he'd looked directly at Ben. 'And you'll do the same. I don't want you cocking the rest of my life up.'

Outside, a car accelerated. Ben closed the safe and stood, knees cracking loudly. Last time he'd seen Miro had been the day they'd done the deed – twenty minutes in cyberspace in the broad bright afternoon: the department hadn't even been empty. 'You think we should sneak in after dark?' Miro had asked. 'That would be less suspicious?' Miro had been less Miro-like since Ben had agreed to help him. Or since Ben had indicated his price for helping:

'Twenty-four hours,' he'd said.

'Twenty-four hours?'

'That's what I cost.'

'I see.'

'Nobody gets hurt, Miro. The money just has a little rest, a chance to catch its breath. Before you send it wherever you want it to go.'

'Leaving you,' Miro had said, 'with twenty-four hours' interest on a quarter of a billion pounds.' He'd paused. 'Have you worked out how much that will come to? At, say, four point two per cent?'

Ben said, 'Don't tell me you're disappointed.'

'Why should I be? As you say, no one gets hurt. There's not a bank on the planet won't jump at the chance to babysit that much, even for a day. Twenty-four hours. Okay.'

Which had been Ashton's plan, of course. To keep Miro from making the money disappear at a keystroke.

The accelerating car moved out of earshot. Ben put the gun in his pocket.

The lift going down was as empty as it had been coming up. In its mirror he was an ordinary man, on an ordinary evening: gun in one pocket, mobile in the other. He remembered his last sight of Miro Weiss. That same afternoon they'd left the building together and parted on the pavement, and Ben had watched Miro Weiss head down the road and into the heart of Soho; just another rusty man in the big city. Before he'd turned the corner, Neil Ashton had peeled from a doorway to follow him.

Ben left by the back entrance. Walked to the main road. As he hailed a taxi, he fished his mobile out and turned it on for the first time today. It buzzed once, twice, three times, as the taxi rolled to a halt.

'Paddington,' he said, getting in.

'What time's your train, mate?'

'Heathrow shuttle. They're regular.'

When Tina, Queen of the Database, spoke, you jumped: that was what the children said. When the grown-ups were around, she struck a less strident note. 'Okay,' she said now. 'That's him.'

'His phone's on,' Reggie said.

She didn't like Reggie, and did like Benedict Whistler, but yes, that was Whistler's phone. 'It'll pulse every six minutes. Or constantly if he makes a call.'

'Where is he?'

On her monitor, a red spot glowed on the Edgware Road.

★

Not the worst thing I've done today.

That was what Bad Sam said when Kennedy complained he'd hurt her, but it wasn't true. He'd been thinking about Deirdre Walker, and his casual connivance in her racist attitudes: that crap always left him needing a shower. But no: hurting Louise Kennedy was worse. She was a bystander, and a brave one – had gone into her nursery to face down a gunman – and he'd hurt her to keep her quiet until he'd discovered all she had to tell him. Which hadn't been a lot. He'd ended up telling her more: an apology, he supposed.

'Can this thing go faster?'

The driver grunted. 'No faster than the traffic, mate.'

Innit, Bad Sam mentally added.

Unlit cigarette in mouth, he stared out at the dwindling crowds, wondering if he still had time to get lucky: not a familiar feeling. Lucky was the missing frigging Marx Brother where Bad Sam Chapman was concerned. But right now, he'd take all the help he could get. If Whistler vanished, he'd take Bad Sam's career with him. It was one thing not having found Miro Weiss, but not finding Neil Ashton or Whistler – the pair of them there in plain sight – fuck, it was no comfort Jonathan Nott would be heading down the same set of tubes.

. . . Everything came down to one of two outcomes: you were either right or wrong. Whistler was heading for an airport or wasn't. The airport was Heathrow or wasn't. Bad Sam would catch him or not.

Besides, right or wrong, reaching Heathrow was the simplest option. Taxi to Paddington; shuttle to the airport.

If only the damn taxi would go faster.

'Where's Bad Sam now?'

Tina's fingers moved: a box unfolded on her monitor, and she fed it Chapman's call-sign. The machine digested the information, and the onscreen map shrank, then shrank again; the streets of London becoming lines scratched on a slate; its only recognisable landmarks parks and river, as the search program widened its parameters then widened them further, searching for the telltale pulse of Bad Sam's mobile. Which didn't come.

She said, 'He's off the mesh.' Her fingers danced once more, and the map reconfigured; a steady glow its heartbeat. 'But Whistler's online.'

'Amateur,' said Reggie.

'Heading for Paddington,' Tina said, broadcasting the lowdown to the waiting crews.

Waterloo was thronged and massive. Louise had forgotten what London stations were like: seas into which rivers poured without cease, until at last they did, whereupon the stations became empty and massive instead, like cathedrals.

You really think Whistler tripped over himself?

Mainline trains and the Underground and the Europe-bound express. Hundreds of people heading every which way. Shops and coffee bars, pubs and fast-food stalls – what chance of finding Ben Whistler, if he ever reached here in the first place?

There was a departures board overhead. The next Eurostar left at 19:43, from the concourse below – where Whistler would show, if he showed up at all. Needle in a haystack.

You really think it was an accident that kid was shot?

Even now, with rush hour fading, people piled past like lemmings. Which, she'd lately read, weren't the suicidal types legend painted; the abrupt declines in their population less to do with mass clifftop dives than with hungry predators – Arctic foxes, owls and the like. Which was more realistic, but disappointing too. Suicide had been the one thing everyone knew about lemmings. Now it turned out they didn't even have that going for them. If they weren't depressed before, that should do it.

You really think . . .

She didn't know what she really thought. Except that she wasn't going home yet. Ben Whistler hadn't just stolen a fortune; he'd engineered – possibly – Jaime Segura's death, and had hoodwinked – definitely – Louise herself. Had allowed her to think she was central to events.

A comfortable place, which had turned out a lie.

In the taxi Ben checked messages, the first being Neil Ashton's from the previous night. *Who the fuck is Jaime Segura? He called your office number, says he's a friend of Miro's. Are you up to something?*

Traffic edged past: everyone in London heading everywhere else. People left pavements without looking, and blaring horns emphasised the error of their ways.

Message two: *Fucking Sam Chapman's on my case, insists on coming with me. Whoever this kid is, he'd better not know anything. Where are you – fuck, here's Sam. Later.*

So Chapman had suspected Neil. How long before he'd have worked down to Ben himself? But Jaime had come out of the woodwork, skewing events.

And Jaime lost his head, its contents spraying the annexe door, while pigeons lifted in a spume from the trees lining the lane.

He could still feel it in his knees, the drop-and-push he'd effected coming through that same door, Jaime's empty gun at his temple. All around, marksmen's rifles waiting for an inch of leeway; the inch Ben's stumble gave them. But while he could reconstruct the moment, he could no longer recall exactly when he'd known what he was going to do. Was it when he'd told Jaime to empty the gun? Or only when they emerged into daylight, and he'd realised there was no way they'd be allowed to drive away?

It doesn't matter. You no longer have a past. You won't even be Ben Whistler much longer.

One last message on his mobile. Probably the one he'd turned his phone off for this morning; something bitter from last night's stand-up, or something tender from the girl he'd slipped away with.

Ben Whistler? Ben, you're a bastard and I hate you. I never want to see you again.

Which was fine by him, because he sincerely hoped nobody would ever see Ben Whistler again.

He dropped the phone in his pocket.

'He's finished his call.'

'Switched off?'

'Can't tell. If not, we'll get a pulse.'

'When, basically?'

Tina, Queen of the Database, bridled, and didn't care who noticed. 'Within the next six minutes.'

Over their heads, a digital clock sliced seconds from their lives.

She said, 'We know where he is. We know he's in a cab.'

There were three cars heading for the area, one holding Moody, nursing a grudge and a sore head.

'Who'd have thought our Ben had it in him, eh?' Reggie mused.

'He's had a long day,' Tina found herself saying. 'It's possible he's having some kind of . . .'

'He'd better fucking hope so.'

The clock didn't so much tick as make a chopping sound.

A footfall told her Nott was there too. 'Give me some good news,' he suggested.

And a glow pulsed on the map, as if the machine bowed to his will.

'He's in Paddington station. Paddington station.'

Over the wires, three different cars received it.

Reggie said, 'Heathrow shuttle. They leave every – quarter of an hour?'

Tina was already pulling on her web. 'Next one in three minutes.'

'How near are they?' Nott asked.

'They'll get him.'

An escalator removed Louise to the Eurostar hall. Descending, she could see the booking office on her right; to her left, the barriers leading to the platforms, with another huge timetable above them. Ahead, another set of doors: he could walk in from the street. He could pause by those machines, and collect an e-bought ticket. Or come down this same staircase from the concourse; or ascend from the Tube by another escalator behind her, which reached this level near a café area, about half of whose tables were in use. On reaching the ground, she stood for a moment.

What am I doing here?

You're either right or you're wrong. He's either running or not. He'll go for a plane or he won't . . . It didn't matter. She could only be in one place. If Whistler came for the Eurostar, she'd see him. Once he got on a train, he was captive. And she'd thus stake her place at the heart of events, where she'd been upon waking that morning.

Are you an only child?

She shook that memory away.

They have a tendency to think events revolve around them.

Whistler would come this way or not.

She bought coffee and sat near where the Tube escalator reached the concourse; where she could see every point of entry, though some were more distant than others.

'Jesus,' Chapman said.

'Traffic. What am I supposed to—'

Innit.

He threw money; threw open the door. Missed a stupid fucking cyclist by inches. Got out, and started to run.

★

Moody's voice over the speaker: 'I'm there.'

'Platform six.'

They could hear his ragged breathing as he raced across the concourse.

'Seventy seconds,' Reggie said.

'That's our clock, not theirs,' Nott said irritably. 'And it's a *train*, for God's sake. It's not like Mussolini's—'

The thought was lost in an eruption from the speaker:

'Security, let me through let me through let me *through*—'

Tina said, 'Cops.'

'Get back get *back*—'

He'd vaulted a barrier; had no time to go round . . .

'Show him your *card*, man,' Nott shouted at the speaker.

'Sir? *Sir!* Step away—'

Words swallowed in a thump and a scuffle, while in the background, a woman screamed. A sudden plastic clatter was followed by a skittling rush, as if Moody's phone had undergone brief flight and hard landing. They heard running, then more running, which merged into the sound of two bodies in motion hitting a third on a railway platform. And under that, or all around it, the loud and somehow hollow noise of big engines starting up, and heavy carriages beginning to move.

Ben, heart beating fast, thought: okay, I'm safe.

Then thought: no, not yet. What would a joe think? He'd think: *you're not safe until you're somewhere you can take your shoes off* . . . What you are is committed to a course of action. No changing your mind now.

So he closed his eyes and rested his head on the seat, and listened to the murmur of passengers around him.

Tina said, 'Whistler's phone is moving.'

'He's on the train?'

'Looks like it. Yes. Yes, he is.'

354

Reggie said, 'Fuck. *Fuck!*'

Nott said, 'Call Heathrow.'

Who knew smoking had this effect? Some fucker should have said something . . .

Sam Chapman reached Paddington with a sledgehammer heart and a coppery taste in his throat, just in time to see Jed bloody Moody covered in transport uniforms, with an absence in the background where a train used to be. He stopped, leaned against a pillar, and enjoyed a brief moment in which his vision clouded. When it cleared, nothing material had changed, though there were more characters converging on Moody, some of them Service Dogs. Whistler, doubtless, was on the departed shuttle. He'd be collected at Heathrow, but Bad Sam wouldn't be there, which was the same as failure where the powers were concerned . . . Not a great day at the office. If he'd collected Whistler he'd have cleaned the slate, but that wasn't going to happen. He didn't even know what they'd done with Miro Weiss. Though they'd get that from Whistler in the end.

He'd be picked up at Heathrow. Of course he would.

Chapman fidgeted another cigarette to his lips, thought about going to Moody's aid, and decided against. He walked back out the way he'd come in, to a sky that was darkening fast, and streets choked with traffic.

She sat with a clear view of the escalator, working her way through a latte she could barely taste.

What am I doing here?

The escalator fed travellers into the hall as fast as it took them away. Busy folk weaved in and out of each other but almost never bumped, as if a giant choreographer loomed overhead.

Do I really think he'll turn up?

And as the thought occurred, here he came, cresting the

artificial horizon; in profile, but definitely Ben Whistler, the day's fake hero; the day's real thief. He'd found time to change his clothing, and now wore a charcoal grey suit and open-necked white shirt; had even adjusted his hair colour, which was darker than earlier. And shorter too. In fact, to a less expert eye, he wasn't Ben Whistler at all.

Louise watched as a stranger headed across the hall.

This is where it will end, she thought. With me sitting here, imagining I'm the centre of events, while everything real happens elsewhere.

After what felt like forever, they heard: 'Shuttle's coming in.'

Tina had patched them in to Heathrow CCTV, and had a fish-eye view of their informant: Sergeant Ali Mills, airport security, leading a crew of eight. She said, 'Hearing you.' Nott was at her shoulder. She minded this less than having Reggie there: Reggie being close had a kind of universal unfamiliarity to it, as if Reggie being close to anyone were an anomaly. On the other monitor, a steady pulse thrummed: Ben Whistler's mobile, merrily whistling to the ether as the shuttle reached Heathrow. She wondered who he was talking to. A joe – a *proper* joe – would have maintained cellular silence from the start. Like Bad Sam Chapman, who'd fallen off the map.

'Coming to a halt now.'

They could see it doing just that; its straight-arrow approach curved into wormy motion by the lens. The waiting policemen were combat-geared just this side of fetishism, and didn't look like they'd brook disdain, much less resistance.

'We'll stop everyone at the gate,' Mills said. 'But peel off likelies first. Is he armed?'

Reggie muttered, 'He's a bean-counter, of course he's not ar—'

Nott cut him off: 'Assume he is.'

Mills kept talking while doors opened, and the screen filled with passengers: 'Thirty-five, forty. Most of them couples. Three lone men, one Asian, all with luggage – we've got 'em.'

'We need cleaner visuals,' Nott murmured.

Tina said. 'Do any of the couples look recent? He might have picked up—'

'I know how to do this – hey hey hey, guy with crutches. Your man into *Day of the Jackal*?'

'Collect him,' Nott said.

Tina tapped an instruction and the screen changed view, then again, then again; a quick tour of the platform until a man on crutches materialised, descended on by a pair of armed cops – 'Not him,' she said, flipping away to a thinning platform, to innocent passengers, empty walls.

'Let's see the departure hall.'

'Yes, but . . .'

'What?'

Tina, Queen of the Database, indicated the lower monitor's steady pulse. 'He's not moving.' She spoke to Mills again. 'He's still on the train.'

'Train's empty,' came the reply.

'You sure?'

It took a minute to check toilets and luggage racks. Tina's eyes remained glued to her screens.

Reggie said, 'He's with the crowd. They'll get him in the departure lounge.'

Nott said nothing.

The speaker crackled and Mills was back. 'He's not here.'

On Tina's monitor, the red glow pulsed.

'But there's a mobile phone. On a luggage rack.'

'He was never on the train at all,' Nott said.

Ben Whistler stepped off the Tube at Waterloo, checked the platform for cops and Service Dogs, and felt his heartbeat level off at the absence of either. But he wasn't safe yet. A pro would run to earth about now, and after the trick with the phone, they might be treating him like a pro. So acting like an amateur, grabbing the first transport out of the country, might be the clever move . . . He'd know when it happened: when he stepped through customs in Paris; his new identity passed on the nod, unlimited wealth in his future.

Her coffee cup was to her lips when he appeared on the escalator again, only this time it was Ben Whistler for real: height, suit, everything; carrying a rucksack now. And he looked at her and then looked away, and she knew it was true, that context was everything. You don't recognise people when they're not supposed to be there. Besides, she was peripheral. She'd never been the lady.

At the top of the stairs he turned left, and headed into the concourse.

Louise put her cup down, and reached for her mobile phone.

Ben had broken his journey to Waterloo; had stopped at an Internet café and booked a ticket using the fake credit card, then picked up a rucksack he'd stuffed with a swiftly bought change of clothing. Travelling without luggage might attract attention.

Looking round too much might do that too.

There were cops: two by the barriers leading to the trains; another lurking in the booking office lobby. There might be others, plain-clothed. Plus, there was CCTV: the moment anyone thought this was where he might be, the Queens of the Database would be chewing the live feed. So don't look up, don't look round; just head for the machines; the ones which dispensed prebooked tickets.

Eleven minutes until his train. Ben headed for the machines, an unaccustomed weight banging on his thigh as he did so.

★

No signal. *I mean*, Louise meant, *what the fuck? How fucking useless is a mobile phone if it won't fucking work in an emergency?* Though who she'd been going to call wasn't clear: the police? Her mum? Maybe MI6 were on Directory Enquiries. *I'd like to speak to anyone who'll know what I'm talking about.*

He'd walked straight past, looking neither left nor right; maybe too focused on the ticket machines to be entirely natural.

And then he stopped

and thought: *Christ . . .*

The weight on his thigh was the gun from the safe. He'd been about to go through customs armed.

He looked around. No one looked back. Coming to a halt hadn't set alarms ringing: people in railway stations made unexpected decisions, as they realised what they'd forgotten to bring. Pretend it's just that, he thought, moving to the nearest wall and resting his rucksack on a thigh-high clay pot holding a large dusty plant rooted in grey and pink gravel. He unzipped his rucksack and pretended to rustle around, shielding what he was up to with his body. *I could give everyone in sight a million pounds to turn their back right now. I wouldn't miss it, and they'd all say yes. It's not like I'm a terrorist. It's not like walking away will cause anyone grief.*

When he rezipped his pack and moved off, the gun was shallowly buried under grey and pink gravel, and he had nine minutes before his train left.

Louise put her phone away. Ben Whistler was across the wide hall, feeding information into the booking machine: as she watched, he bent and scooped a ticket from its trough. She left her table, and crossed to the plant pot where he'd paused to search his bag for wallet or passport. Except he'd been doing something more complicated than that. Overhead, a platform announcement boomed: *For security reasons, please make sure*

★

you keep your luggage with you at all times. And here came another life-changing moment; one in which Ben Whistler's luggage became somebody else's, and his identity morphed to match his passport. Only a short walk to freedom now; to margaritas, señoritas, *hasta la vista*s . . . Ticket, then passport control. Train, and another country.

The guard at the barrier was reaching for his ticket when Ben Whistler's name echoed loudly round the hall.

She stood ten yards away, wielding a gun. For an unmeasurable amount of time the hall became still, and what noise there was happened at a remove – drifted down from above, or crept through those big glass doors. And then havoc arrived, and everyone in sight was moving except Louise Kennedy and Ben Whistler; was screaming and diving for cover, or else producing weapons of their own and shouting instructions – *Drop the gun armed police drop the gun.* Someone pushed Whistler aside, but he didn't fall. He rocked on his feet, never taking his eyes from Louise.

Armed police. Drop the gun.

Viewed from above – from, say, a CCTV camera – Louise Kennedy was the centre of events; events that quickly tightened focus as the three armed cops surrounding her reacted precisely as they'd been trained to do. Though the aim she'd taken at Ben Whistler didn't waver throughout.

Later, the Queens of the Database reduced the available footage to a sequence of stills. In most, you could read Ben Whistler's expression as resigned, even rueful.

But in the last one, it looked to Sam Chapman like Whistler was laughing.

Custard Tarts
and Broken Hearts

MARY GIBSON

HEAD
of ZEUS

First published in the UK in 2014 by Head of Zeus Ltd.
This paperback edition published in 2014.

9 7 5 3 2 4 6 8

A CIP catalogue record for this book is available from the British Library.

Paperback ISBN: 9781781855768
Ebook ISBN: 9781781855751

Typeset by Lindsay Nash

Printed and bound by CPI Group (UK) Ltd., Croydon, CR0 4YY.

Head of Zeus Ltd.
Clerkenwell House
45-47 Clerkenwell Green
London EC1R 0HT

WWW.HEADOFZEUS.COM